"I suppose you're on the lookout for a new husband," said McCaffrey, the storekeeper

He turned his head to the sugar barrel, but not so quickly that Lindy failed to see his curling lips.

"I don't need a husband," she said. "I can run the farm myself."

"A number of men hereabouts might be interested," McCaffrey said smoothly, lifting two conical loaves of sugar onto a scale. "Let me know, and I'll tell them you're receiving suitors."

"If I marry again," Lindy said, "it'll be to a man who stays out of saloons and doesn't speculate in wildcat mines."

"You've set pretty high standards for Nevada Territory," Mr. McCaffrey said. "I can't, right offhand, think of a man in Washoe City or Carson...."

"And doesn't frequent the ladies on D Street up in Virginia City," Lindy added as an afterthought.

Mr. McCaffrey guffawed. "That's no man, Lindy. That's a saint, and I can't think what a saint would be doing in Nevada."

Dear Reader,

Rae Muir's first book, *The Pearl Stallion*, won her 5★s from both *Affaire de Coeur* and *Heartland Critiques* and made it onto *Affaire de Coeur*'s Top Ten List for 1996. This month, the author is back with *All But the Queen of Hearts*, a lively Western set in Nevada Territory, with an unsinkable heroine whose determination and skill in the kitchen finally win the heart of her reluctant hero.

And we are very pleased this month to be able to bring you Silhouette Yours Truly and Special Edition author Beth Henderson's first historical for Harlequin, *Reckless*, in which a young woman accused of being a jewel thief is rescued by a mysterious baron intent on clearing her name.

For those of you who enjoy the Regency era, Taylor Ryan's *The Essential Wife* is the delightful story of a dashing nobleman who suddenly finds himself in love with the penniless heiress whom he has arranged to marry out of pity. And keep an eye out for Laurie Grant's new Western, *Lawman*, the fast-paced sequel to her 1996 release, *Devil's Dare*, about a lonely lawman who rediscovers love in the arms of his childhood sweetheart.

Whatever your taste in reading, we hope you'll find just what you're looking for with Harlequin Historicals.

Sincerely,

Tracy Farrell
Senior Editor

Please address questions and book requests to:
Harlequin Reader Service
U.S.: 3010 Walden Ave., P.O. Box 1325, Buffalo, NY 14269
Canadian: P.O. Box 609, Fort Erie, Ont. L2A 5X3

All But The Queen of Hearts

Rae Muir

Harlequin Books

TORONTO • NEW YORK • LONDON
AMSTERDAM • PARIS • SYDNEY • HAMBURG
STOCKHOLM • ATHENS • TOKYO • MILAN
MADRID • WARSAW • BUDAPEST • AUCKLAND

ISBN 0-373-28969-3

ALL BUT THE QUEEN OF HEARTS

RAE MUIR

lives in a cabin in California's High Sierra, a mile from an abandoned gold mine. She is, by training, an historian, but finds it difficult to fit into the academic mold, since her imagination inevitably inserts fictional characters into actual events. She's been a newspaper reporter, written and edited educational materials, researched eighteenth-century Scottish history, run a fossil business and raised three children in her spare time.

She loves the Sierra Nevada, Hawaii, Oxford and San Francisco. Her favorite mode of travel is by car, and she stops at every historical marker.

To the Calico Quilters
Especially Peggy, Pat, Virginia, Nela and Dusty

Prologue

"You're on your way to the Comstock, Captain?" The ragged man stepped from the thicket of trees at the edge of the meadow. Lon, one foot already out of his stirrup, wavered in the saddle as Buckskin shied from the apparition. The horse calmed only when the stranger retreated into the shelter of the pines.

Lon dismounted. His eyes adjusted to the long morning shadows, and he noticed half a dozen men lounging under the trees amid their scattered bedrolls. Buckskin snorted and tossed his head in a new direction. The ragged stranger was circling the margin of the meadow, and emerged foolishly close to Buckskin's heels.

"Or perhaps Reese River?" the man cried anxiously.

Lon tugged on the reins and ran toward the sound of tumbling water. In a grove of aspens he discovered a shallow pool below a small cascade. He remounted, guided Buckskin through the water and turned him out to graze in a tiny meadow. He looked back across the stream, expecting to find his pesky inquisitor frustrated. Instead, the fellow resolutely waded toward him, water above his knees. Lon sighed in exasperation. Hucksters gave up only when threatened. He curled his hands into fists.

The man's rags had once been a suit of some distinction,

complete with a long frock coat. Now one sleeve hung tattered below the elbow, and a torn pocket dangled. As the man stepped out of the water, Lon saw he wore only gray woolen socks, out at both heel and toe. No boots! Poor bounder! Probably hadn't had a meal in days.

The decrepit gentleman paused for a moment to catch his breath and shake the water from his trousers. He drew a packet of greasy paper through a long rip in his vest.

"I have a few shares in promising mines, Major, which might be of interest to you. You're from San Francisco, I imagine, Major."

"No," Lon said flatly, eyeing Buckskin, considering the possibility of escape. Insistent speculators had offered bogus mining stocks at every stopping place on the trail, and he had found no polite way to avoid them. Offer them the time of day, and they clung for an hour.

"Sacramento?" Lon said nothing. The peddler lifted his sagging leather hat, exposing his thicket of gray whiskers and hair to the morning sun. "You're bound for Virginia City, I presume?"

"Where I'm bound's of no business to you," Lon said gruffly, hating the circumstances that forced him to be unpleasant to a fellow human being.

"Well, Colonel, I have shares in a few claims of great interest, both on the Comstock Ledge and in the Reese River. I'll give you first choice, although the gentlemen who camped here last night—" he swept his arm toward the men on the other side of the creek "—they've begged to be allowed to purchase fifty shares in the Green Gage."

Lon laughed out loud. He could imagine that the "gentlemen"—without even a burro to carry their gear—had money to invest in the Green Gage. The laugh improved his disposition. Let the fellow babble on; perhaps he'd come up with more amusing comments.

"I've no interest in the Green Gage," Lon said. "I'll let them have it."

"The Smiling Jane, on the Reese," continued the ped-dler. "The indications are identical, *identical,* mind you, to those of the Comstock in the early years. You ask, 'How do I know this man isn't a swindler?' Well, sir, I stood by, with Mr. Comstock, when his mules passed over the ground and kicked up the clod that exposed the richest place on earth. Moseley's the name, sir." He extended his right hand; Lon ignored it. He pressed his forearm against his belt, reassuring himself that the coins remained tucked in the fold of leather. Thirty-three dollars. Enough to live on until he established himself in Virginia City.

He turned his back on Moseley, walked upstream to where the water spurted through a rocky notch. He leaned to drink, and caught sight of a man on the opposite bank pulling off split boots, gingerly splashing water on feet blotched red and purple.

You are one lucky man, Lon Anderson. A good horse, money in your pocket and the health to land a job the moment you set foot in Virginia City.

He shook the water from his hands, turned, jumped when his extended fingers brushed Moseley, who hung behind him like a shadow.

"The Reese, that's where the great opportunities are." Looking down on the fellow's head, Lon saw a great chunk missing from the brim of his leather hat, as if a mule had taken a bite.

"But if you're bound for the Comstock, the Shirt Tail Mine—" The man babbled on, shoving a dirty piece of paper into Lon's hands. "Once the new drift strikes the main lead, and seeing that I'm in difficult straits, I'll let you have it for only—"

"Get out of here," Lon said, flattening the paper with some force against Moseley's vest. "I'm sick of hearing about mines that don't exist, except in some fool's imagi-nation! Who in hell would name a mine Shirt Tail?" The man tumbled backward. Sprawled on the grass, he stared at Lon with wistful, hungry eyes, then crawled to his feet and sloshed back across the stream, his shoulders bent.

Lon turned away, fighting a guilty conscience. He was not accustomed to treating people in this fashion. But the speculators tried his patience. He whistled for Buckskin.

The trail dropped into a canyon; rounding a final bend, Lon caught a glimpse of the gray and green Carson Valley. Sunlight on an open glade glowed between the trees; he dismounted and released Buckskin only when he was sure no one else had claimed the spot. He leaned against a spindly aspen, shrugged his shoulders into its riven bark, against his itchy spine. He sank lower and lower, until his rear end touched the ground; his eyes closed as he contemplated the pleasure of an itch well scratched.

He shook the last of the crackers and cheese from his saddlebags while he studied a sloping expanse of tall grass across the river. The pasture extended for perhaps a half mile, interspersed here and there with low bushes. He imagined it filled with cattle. His cattle. The mines in Nevada Territory paid four dollars a day. If he lived simply and carefully, in one year he could save enough money to claim land of his own.

One hundred and sixty acres free for the taking, said the Homestead Act. One year of frugal living would provide money to buy cattle. Work like hell for another year to get the ranch going and build a house. Then a wife!

Night after sleepless night, through all of last winter, he'd planned the ranch. The house, the wife and family. In saloons, while other men praised a carefree, bachelor existence, his heart had cried out for someone to care for. In Nevada Territory lived an unknown woman destined to be his wife. A little slip of a girl he could toss about and sling over his shoulder. He carried her in his arms as he jumped from boulder to boulder, across the river. They walked through the grass of the virgin meadow. Her arms wrapped about his neck, and he picked her up, away from the threat of rattlesnakes. A sweet-smelling, dainty woman he could lift with one arm.

He jerked awake. The trees leaned in a stiff breeze. He scrambled to his feet, whistled to Buckskin. No time now to nap and dream. He'd reached Nevada Territory, only a few miles from the mines that paid four dollars a day.

The strength of the wind had increased. Buckskin's mane streamed forward; the horse lowered his head to escape the worst of the blast. Grains of sand stung Lon through his coat. He pulled his hat lower, hunched his shoulders and surveyed Carson City, the capital of Nevada Territory. Nothing more than a village, a double row of frame buildings along the main street. He needed a retreat from the wind and dust, a drink to slake his thirst. Not a restaurant, for he must be careful of money; not a saloon, for a free lunch didn't make up for the nauseous taste of whiskey or beer. He saw no horse tank or town pump in the square.

McCaffrey's Mercantile Emporium, advertised a sign on a squat shanty. He'd start there. Maybe Mr. McCaffrey could furnish him with a drink of water.

Chapter One

"Well, Lindy," Mr. McCaffrey said slyly, "you're getting to be an old hand at tossing men off your place. First you tell Harvey to clear out, and now I hear you threw Deputy Clugg down your front steps." He scooped dry beans into Lindy's sack. Lindy studied the storekeeper closely. He leaned over the barrel, so she saw only his profile and couldn't tell if he smirked.

"Right on both," she said. She lifted her head and spoke boldly. "How'd you hear about Clugg?"

"It's all over town. Your neighbors say they rode by just as he rolled in the dust, and they're snagging free drinks in every saloon for telling the story. I suppose it gets better every evening."

"I suppose. Embarrassing for Clugg, but it serves him right. Just because a woman lives alone, it doesn't mean she's available."

McCaffrey heaved the sack of beans onto the counter. "So I suppose, seeing you don't call yourself Mrs. Harvey Saxton anymore, I shouldn't give him credit on your account?"

"He's asked for credit?" No way to hide her shock. Would she never be free of the man? "But he's up in Virginia City!"

"Today he's here in Carson. No, he hasn't asked for credit. Don't fret yourself." Lindy snatched her hands to her sides, aware she'd been wringing them like a weak woman.

"Last night he sprawled all over the bar of the Carson Club," continued McCaffrey.

"And he cried to everyone that I'm an unnatural wife, who chased him out of the house and off the farm."

"How'd you know he cried?" asked McCaffrey.

"Harvey always cries when he's truly drunk. He recites all the wrongs ever done him, and never considers that his friends or his wife might have a complaint."

McCaffrey twisted a bit of twine about the top of the sack of beans.

"Sugar," said Lindy, ticking off her list from memory on her fingers. "Ten pounds of sugar."

"I suppose you're on the lookout for a new husband," said Mr. McCaffrey. He turned his head to the sugar barrel, but not so quickly that Lindy failed to see his curling lips.

"I don't need a husband," she said. "I'll run the farm myself. Harvey turned out to be about as useful as a mustang hitched to an ore car."

"A number of men hereabouts might be interested," McCaffrey said smoothly, lifting two conical loaves of sugar onto a scale. "Men with better manners than Deputy Clugg. Let me know, and I'll tell them you're receiving suitors."

"If I marry again, it'll be to a man who stays out of saloons, with no gambling habit. And no speculating in wildcat mines."

"You've set pretty high standards for Nevada Territory," Mr. McCaffrey said. "I can't, right offhand, think of a man in Washoe City or Carson..."

"And doesn't frequent the ladies on D Street up in Virginia City," Lindy added as an afterthought.

Mr. McCaffrey guffawed. "That's no man, Lindy. That's

a saint, and I can't think what a saint would be doing in Nevada. Mining attracts a different breed of men.''

''Breed!'' Lindy exclaimed. ''Flimflam men aren't bred. They're accidents, freaks of nature. Not one of them would be interested in my farm, for in their business they dare not settle down. Once folks learn their faces, they've got to head for another settlement. Right now Nevada attracts all the humbugs in the world, but they'll drift away as soon as the rawness wears off.''

''Once they're gone, you'll find your saint?'' Mr. McCaffrey asked mischievously.

''Not a saint. A real man. An honest man, not afraid of hard work.''

''You left out the major feature you need in a husband.''

''What would that be?'' Lindy asked, trying to sound innocent even as she gulped, for she knew what Mr. McCaffrey would say next. What people always said next.

''He's got to be a big man to handle you. In all my life I've not met any saints well over six feet tall. Big men tend to be brawlers.''

Lindy leaned over the counter to take an inch or so off her height, but pulled herself erect when she remembered her grandmother's advice. Her head brushed a preserving kettle hanging from the ceiling, and it swung into a mackintosh, which slipped from its hook and slithered to the floor. Lindy picked up the coat and flung it over the jars of candy that crowded the counter.

''I need a whetstone,'' she said. McCaffrey pawed through a pile of merchandise on the shelf behind him.

''Got one about here somewheres.''

She would not apologize for being over six feet tall. On her seventeenth birthday, when her grandfather had backed her against the wall of the barn and measured her with his carpenter's rule, her grandmother hadn't shaken her head in distress, or cried out at fate. ''Whatever you do, Melinda, don't slump. Just stand tall and take whatever comes at you.

The good Lord made you more than six feet tall for some reason, and your job's to try to understand the Lord's thinking.''

McCaffrey plunked the whetstone down on the counter with unnecessary force. "I'll let you know if a tall saint turns up in town," he quipped.

The door opened behind her, a gust of wind, the patter of sand on the floor reminding her she must be on the road before the wind became a gale. The man ducked his head under the door frame. Half a head taller than she. He dodged the merchandise hanging from the ceiling, but as he leaned to avoid a length of chain, his head banged into a string of washbasins, which swung into the preserving kettle. The store echoed with a clamor of ill-tuned bells.

"Sorry," he mumbled, reaching up to still the swaying kettle. He pulled his hat off, and a lock of dark brown hair dropped across his forehead.

"May I help you?" inquired McCaffrey, his eyes swiveling from the stranger to Lindy, back again. Lindy knew exactly what McCaffrey was thinking, and resented it. All her life, friends and relatives had thought only of height when they set about matchmaking for her.

"I know this isn't a restaurant, but would it be possible to get something to drink?"

"Pryor's Saloon's right next door," said McCaffrey.

"I'm thirsty. I don't want liquor."

McCaffrey tilted his head to one side. "The wife churned this morning. Buttermilk do you?"

The corners of the stranger's mouth turned up in a suggestion of a smile, but they turned down when he asked, "How much?" And Lindy knew he was another broke man heading for Virginia City, counting on a job in the mines.

"Two bits."

"Do great!" He truly smiled now, little creased fans radiating from the corners of his eyes, and the dimple in his chin deeper. McCaffrey lifted the flour-sack curtain behind the counter and vanished into the back room that served as his home. Lindy turned her back on the stranger. The murmur of the wind seemed louder in the silence.

"New in town?" Lindy finally asked, feeling a bit awkward and confused, for when the stranger had smiled, little chills, like an ant with cold feet, had crawled up her backbone. She turned around, caught the man staring at her, but he in turn shifted his eyes and became terribly interested in a string of sausages over his head.

"Just rode in. Is there a camping place nearby?" Cultured manner of speaking. His eyes looked everywhere but at her.

"Over the ridge to the north lies Washoe Lake. You're thinking of staying the night?" The stranger nodded. "You'd best look for a place to stay in Carson. A zephyr's coming, and sleeping outside won't be pleasant."

"A zephyr?"

"The wind that blows off the mountains. The Washoe Zephyr. In an hour or two, anything not nailed down will take off for the next county. And some things nailed down will go, too."

He frowned. Maybe he didn't have the money for a room and a meal.

"Rich's Bit Café, down the street. He serves dinner ch— Priced reasonably."

McCaffrey returned with a pitcher and a tin cup. The stranger fished about in his pocket, pulled out a twenty-five-cent piece and laid it on the counter. He gulped the first cupful, the corded sinews of his neck working convulsively as he swallowed. The muscles rising from his shoulders showed the strength hidden beneath his shirt. Lindy spun about to face McCaffrey the moment she realized she was staring.

"That's everything for today," she said, too loudly.

"I'll carry these to your wagon," said McCaffrey.

She escaped out the back door into the alley, untied the

mules and headed out of town, into the teeth of the wind.
She seldom met men noticeably bigger than she was, and
when she did, they scared her. A man like that stranger,
tall and broad, could force her to do exactly what he
wanted.

"I'm too fond of having my own way," she muttered,
and was instantly sorry she'd opened her mouth, as the sand
blasted against her teeth and dust coated her tongue.

Lon stared after the wagon and mules. *This* was what
happened to a woman in Nevada! Not just that the top of
her head came to his eyes...but she wore trousers! Men's
trousers on the bottom, a sunbonnet on top! Never, in his
entire twenty-four years, had he seen a woman in pants,
except for the radical bloomer ladies. He had tried not to
stare, tried to act as if every day of his life he met women
six feet tall and dressed in men's clothes.

The storekeeper had waited on her without a second
glance. Did all Nevada women dress like this, so the men
accepted female legs and hips as a normal...? What did the
silver mines do to people?

The mines had corrupted respectable Mr. Moseley into a
huckster of worthless stocks. Perhaps the silver camps destroyed feminine instincts, until women heedlessly paraded
on the streets of the capital in pants and boots.

He didn't want to think of the gingham shirt, which
pulled tightly across her full bosom.... The ache in his loins
stabbed with sudden violence, but the rumble of his stomach saved him. He'd spent too many days eating cheese
and crackers and jerky.

A narrow passage separated Rich's Bit Café from a saloon, and offered some protection for his horse and bedroll.
Three dogs, two horses and a skinny, half-grown calf had
already taken refuge there. Lon tied Buckskin's reins to a
nail protruding from the wall of the saloon, then waited
with his back to the wall for a lull in the storm. The street

lifted with a roar; dust, leaves, brush, papers, branches, hats and gloves whirled in a devilish dance. Lon took a deep breath, dashed around the corner, took two strides down the boardwalk, shoved open the door just wide enough to sidle through. A cloud of debris slipped through with him. He leaned against the door frame to fill his lungs with air relatively free of sand.

The narrow room was dim, lit only by a single small window and a lantern hanging over a table at the very back. Three men sat at the table, and the positions of cards and chips told Lon he'd interrupted a poker game. A man wearing a long, dirty apron stood up.

"You looking for dinner?" he asked.

"Yes."

"Ham, potatoes, beans and coffee, four bits. No coffee, three bits. If you want beer, go next door. The barkeep'll let you bring the mug over here. Whiskey, one bit for two swallows from the jug, a dollar for the evening."

"I'll take coffee," said Lon.

"I'm Rich," said the man in the dirty apron. "Come join us, so I don't have to light another lantern. The dust's rising, it'll soon be as dark as the inside of a cow." He turned his attention to the cookstove in the corner.

The table had been assembled from packing crates, and nail kegs served as stools. A blue-and-gray earthenware jug stood in the center of the table.

"Have you come from California, stranger?" asked the man seated on the right. He had long, dark, untidy hair and a scraggly beard. He took a swallow from the jug.

"Yes."

"What of Vicksburg?" asked the man on the left, who wore a floppy hat.

"Vicksburg?" exclaimed Lon, astonished. Someone actually wanted to talk about the war, rather than the prospects of the silver mines.

"Has Grant been driven back?" the dark-bearded man asked.

"No, at least not when I left Placerville three days ago," said Lon. "I believe Grant defeated some general named Pemberton." The bearded man cursed fluently. Obviously a supporter of the Southern states.

"I'm Price," said Floppy Hat, holding out his hand. "This here's Saxton." He pointed to his companion.

"Anderson," said Lon, shaking the hand.

"Come, have a drink and tell us the bad news," Saxton said sadly. He eyed the jug for an instant, grabbed it, tilted it up for two long swallows, then held it at arm's length, staring with bleary eyes. Not his first drink of the day, Lon judged.

Price rolled another nail keg across the floor to serve as a fourth seat. "Now, tell us what you can of Vicksburg."

Lon stammered out all he could remember of General Grant's Mississippi campaign, uncomfortable at being the center of attention. With every mention of Union victory, Saxton eased his sorrow by sampling the jug.

"I'm sorry to bear bad tidings," Lon finally said to Saxton. "You're from the Southern states?"

"No. But I gambled on them, bought their worthless bonds, and they drop like lead with every Union success."

"Sorry," Lon said again.

"Care to join us in a game?" asked Rich, abandoning the skillet long enough to grab the jug before it reached Saxton. He drank, then wiped the mouth of the jug with the corner of his dirty apron before he replaced it on the table. "We'd decided the afternoon didn't bode well for outside work."

Lon nodded in agreement. The wind screamed around the corners of the shanty like a demented witch. The desert heat had dried the planks of the walls, leaving gaps through which the wind whistled. The lamp hanging over the table swung in the breeze.

Rich wordlessly plopped a cup of coffee on the table and returned to his cooking. Lon took the opportunity to study the cards and players over the rim of the cup, analyzing the situation. All three men had sampled the jug. If he accepted Rich's invitation, he had the advantage of being a teetotaler playing against drinkers.

Price gathered up the cards from the interrupted deal and ruffled the deck. He shuffled skillfully, but shook his head as if to clear away cobwebs. Rich staggered the slightest bit when he reached for a plate on a high shelf, but he might have caught his toe on the irregular planks of the floor. Only Saxton showed signs of being so far into his cups that he couldn't play a sensible hand.

You can't afford to lose a single dollar! You should leave as soon as you've eaten.

Gravel slammed against the south wall, the tattoo of an erratic drummer. Lon felt for the ten-dollar gold piece he'd transferred to the pocket of his vest. He shouldn't. Even one dollar bought a lot of groceries. He dropped the coin back into the pocket. The building leaned under a great howl of wind, and the pots and pans hanging behind the stove clanged together. The timbers creaked, and the arc of the swinging lamp widened.

Lon pulled out the gold piece. Rich laid out ten chips. Lon shoved one to the center. He held his breath as the cards fell from Price's hand.

The wind fell a tone, the pots and pans clinked together gently, reminding Lon of the jangle of harness. The wind of the prairie, a lonely sixteen-year-old sitting on a blanket, facing a man grown gray on a Mississippi steamboat.

"Don't move your cards about, boy! You know what's in your hand with one glance. Keep the cards down. Some men can read the pictures in your eyes. Don't fidget, boy! You've got promise in this game. You don't talk too much. Your face don't show what's in your mind. Before we reach California, you'll be a gambler to reckon with."

He spread the cards just enough to see the corners. Two jacks; he relaxed. Rich dumped a plate at his elbow. From the corner of his eye he regarded the gray ham, a heap of greasy potatoes, a dipperful of pale beans. Nothing that growing cold would hurt, he decided. Lon concentrated on how the three men moved their cards.

Fifteen chips lay before Lon as he dealt the third hand. The door opened, Rich stood to greet his potential customer and held back on the next card.

"Oh," Rich said, disappointed, sinking down on his nail keg. "It's you, Clugg. Come back and join the game." The man, slender and short, wore a long frock coat and tight gloves, neither of which showed evidence of work or wear.

"Deal you in?" asked Rich.

Clugg shook his head. No, not slender. Skinny. The skinniness of youth.

"Judge Otis wouldn't like his nephew being caught in a game?" Price asked sarcastically.

"What I do ain't up to Uncle Otis," snapped Clugg. "I'm my own man." Man, except, so far as Lon could see, no razor had ever touched the smooth cheeks. Seventeen, perhaps eighteen years old.

"This here's Deputy Clugg, who takes care of the jail for Sheriff Tipson," said Rich. "You've no guest who needs guarding? So you can wander about the town?"

"Not to speak of," Clugg said evasively.

"You in?" asked Lon, the next card still poised.

"No, can't stay long. Don't it blow, though!" he exclaimed, eyeing the swaying lantern.

"Just a Washoe Zephyr," said Rich. "Be over in a few hours."

"A few days ago Sheriff Tipson had an old Paiute in jail," said Clugg, his eyes shifting momentarily away from the lantern to examine the men.

"Sheriff Tipson's fond of putting Paiutes in jail," Price

said idly, sorting his cards busily, suggesting he had nothing, or then again he might have a full house.

"This fellow, he knew a lot," whispered Clugg, leaning forward to see Price's hand. Lon eased his own cards open briefly while Clugg distracted the other players. Trash and the eight and nine of spades.

"The old man, he's a medicine man, and he says the zephyr carries the angry souls of the dead Paiutes, who come rushing out of their graves to put the hex on the white man who's took their land."

Price snorted. Rich chortled and dropped a ten of spades. That cut his chances of drawing to a straight by fifty percent. Lon snuck a quick look at Clugg. The kid's pale face and haunted eyes begged for sympathy.

"Could be true, I suppose," Lon said as a way of bolstering Clugg's spirits, then regretted his inattention because he missed seeing what Rich had done with the ten.

"Don't you believe in ghosts?" asked Clugg, addressing no one in particular.

"Ghosts! That's different," said Price. "I once lived in house with a ghost—"

"Clugg, you in here?" came a yell at the same instant he door hinges squealed and the wind exploded inward. Clugg spun around on his heels, the skirts of his coat flaring out and taking Saxton's remaining chips off the table.

"Yes, Sheriff," Clugg squeaked in a sudden soprano.

"Well, get back to the jail. I came in and found no one with Sal Green, and his mates brag they're going to bust him out. Staying in the jail's your job."

"Yes, sir," quavered Clugg. He plunged toward the door.

"Why'd the sheriff ever take him on?" asked Price after the door slammed. "Fool kid. Afraid to be alone in the jail because of Paiute ghosts!"

"He got the job because his uncle's territorial judge," said Rich. "That's what's wrong with this place. Got to be someone's nephew or cousin to be hired into a soft job with good pay.'' Rich refilled the jug from a cask in the corner. Price nodded sleepily. Saxton threw in a hand without noticing he held a pair of eights. Lon tried to sit still on the uncomfortable seat. He disliked the inactivity of cards, but if Saxton's cash held out, by morning he might have an extra twenty or thirty dollars to carry to Virginia City. A nest egg to get his own place two or three months sooner than he'd thought possible.

Lindy sat in the open back door of her cabin, her night-dress pulled up to her thighs, her knees grasping the smooth sides of the wooden bowl. She pressed the clump of butter to the sides of the bowl with a wooden paddle, working out the milk. The moon, just a day from full, gave enough light for the job, and she was thankful for the moon, since lamp oil cost money, and only two candles remained in the box on the shelf.

She must finish the butter tonight because, come morning, she had to turn water from the spring into the garden, to make up for the drying zephyr. And she was overdue with plantings of turnips and beets and radishes, and the regular chores took so much time!

Soft, restless snorts came from the pigpen. Lindy stood and walked to the edge of the porch, straining her eyes to find a threat lurking in the shadows. A coyote reconnoitering the chicken coop? A snake slithering onto the damp ground around the tank? She'd rather not go out tonight, for she'd already bathed in the trough, washed her feet in the basin, brushed her hair and braided it. The pigs quieted down and she returned to the butter.

The wind carried the soft clomp of horses' hooves, quick on the slope heading toward the river. She lifted her head for a moment. Two horses. The brothers who lived a mile upstream, a bit late returning from town, with their chores still to do. She smiled to herself, thinking how they'd reveled in Carson for the second night in a row, getting free drinks by describing how she'd thrown Deputy Clugg down the front stairs. Bad luck for Clugg that the men had ridden past just as she tossed him out, but that was his lookout. Ridiculous child, thinking because a woman lived alone she'd let him fiddle with the buttons on her shirt and put a hand on her hip.

The hoofbeats turned sharp and hard on the packed ground between the road and the house. She shoved the bowl against the back wall, ran to the bedroom and grabbed her shawl. She stood between the front door and the window, bent her head to peek through an upper pane while she raised her left arm toward the rifle hanging over the door. Harvey's lopsided way of sitting a horse showed even in the moonlight. She stood, lifted the rifle from the wooden brackets and opened the door.

"I told you you're not wanted around here, Harvey Saxton," she shouted. Harvey reined in his horse several feet short of the hitching rail.

"Now, Lindy, I'm not planning to stay. I got something important to tell you. This here's Anderson."

He jerked his thumb over his shoulder. She could see little of the second man in the moonlight, just that he wore a broad-brimmed hat. Harvey she could take care of single-handed, but if he brought a friend... A woman couldn't be too careful. She raised the rifle.

"What's your first name, Anderson?" Harvey asked.

"Harlon."

"Well, Harlon," Lindy yelled, "you can just get out of here along with Harvey. Whatever possessed your ma to give you a name like that?"

"Wasn't my ma. Was my pa. It's his name."

"Too bad for him," she yelled. "Both of you get off my property!"

"Listen just a minute, Lindy," begged Harvey. "I feel

responsible, like it's my fault, and I should tell you before this gentleman breaks the news, and you faint.''

"I'm not likely to faint at anything you pull," she retorted, but she lowered the rifle slightly when she heard the sob in his voice. Harvey had drunk to his weepy stage.

"Anderson, you got a gun on you?" she asked.

"In my saddlebag."

"Leave it there. The two of you can come in for five minutes and have your say, but that's it. I've got to get to bed. Some of us have a full day's work tomorrow."

The men rode closer to the house, slid off their mounts and flipped the reins around the splintery rail. Lindy stepped back to the bedroom door, keeping the rifle in her hands, but pointed now at the floor. She could not hold both the rifle and the shawl, so she let the wrap slip off her shoulders. She hated to appear in front of a stranger in nothing but her muslin nightdress, but she felt better hanging on to the rifle.

Harvey staggered on the stairs and grabbed at the door frame, but he did not crawl through the door. Not as drunk as she had supposed. She raised the rifle a bit. Anderson followed, stepping firmly. Not drunk at all. She edged toward the back door. He stooped to enter! The stranger from McCaffrey's store, six feet five or six inches tall! The perfect companion for Harvey, if he meant to force her to take him back. Anderson pulled off his hat, and a lock of dark hair fell over his forehead.

"Can we have a light?" asked Harvey.

"I can't afford a light," she snapped.

"Just one candle, for a bit?" he begged.

She gestured with the rifle to a shelf on the back wall. Harvey walked across the room, stumbling where nothing existed to stumble over. He pulled down the candle box.

"Use the stub before lighting a new one." He held a match against the wick, put the wavering light on a saucer without first dripping a little melted wax to secure it. The candle slid to the saucer's edge, and Lindy gasped. Harvey replaced the candle in the middle of the saucer, then put the saucer on the table with exaggerated care.

Once Lindy was sure Harvey had managed the light without setting the house afire, she turned back to Anderson. He stood just inside the door, his head even with the top of the frame and his shoulders almost filling the opening. He stared at her, frowning, radiating anger, or maybe just unhappiness.

"I need to get into the chest in the corner, Lindy."

"Nothing in there that's any concern of yours."

"Yes, there is. I want to show this man that I'm married to you, legally."

"The key's in the lock. Go ahead."

He turned the key, opened the lid and raised the candle to light the interior. He shuffled the contents, picked out two folded papers, then leaned toward the wall. He stepped back, stumbling again, nearly dropping the candle. Lindy took one hand from the rifle, snatched the candle and returned it to the table. Harvey stood rooted, staring at the wall, transfixed.

"Why, Lindy! You've nailed my shtock…stock certificates to the wall. They'll get all du…dirty, and tattered!"

"Stock certificates!" she snorted. "And every one of them worthless. You have a talent for picking mines that produce nothing but hot air. I can't afford wallpaper. I'll use what I've got."

"Well, you never know when one of the minesh might hit a bu…bonanza." He pouted. "The Lilybelle…"

"Is just a spur off the Yellow Jacket. Not worth a dime on the dollar. The court settled the case last month."

"It did?" he asked, his astonishment genuine. He rocked back on his heels.

"Don't you hear the news in Virginia City? You've got an empty space between your ears, Harvey Saxton."

Harvey sighed, too drunk to object to the insult. He managed to lay the two papers on the table before he had to grab a chair for support. He hung on with his right hand, and clumsily unfolded one of the documents with his left.

"Here 'tis, Anderson. See—'United in holy matrimony, Harvey Sh...Saxton and Melinda Merryman.'"

"Why is our marriage of interest to Mr. Anderson?"

"Well, I got in a card game tonight, and I din' win."

"You're in a card game any night you scrape together a dollar, and all of Washoe, Carson and Virginia City would hear if you won. What'd you lose now?"

"Well, all my money to begin with, then I st...staked the ranch, and I lost that...."

"To Mr. Anderson, here?" she asked. She stared at the big man, swallowing her laughter. Poor fool!

"Yeah. Anderson won it fair and shqu...shqu...fair, even though he did it with a bluff and not an honest hand. Then the next deal..." He paused.

"And what next?"

"Well, Lindy, I was mighty anxious about what you'd say, about the ranch, that is, so I put it to Anderson, he might like to play for you to be *his* wife. Take the package."

Wagered her? The way a man wagered a horse, or a sow, or a stock certificate! Even Harvey had not been that crass before! Lindy took a deep breath before she asked, "And he won?"

"He won."

Chapter Two

Lindy looked from one man to the other, Harvey struggling to stay on his feet, Anderson struggling to keep his face under control but letting the glare of disapproval slip through. She glared back.

Twice he turned, as if running away. He swung back resolutely. *He thinks he's duty-bound to take me if he takes the farm,* she thought, and started giggling. Anderson frowned. Poor stupid man, to think he could move in and live with her, without asking for her opinion or permission.

"Mr. Anderson can be my husband on the same terms you are," she said to Harvey. "Get out and stay out."

"You filed that div...div...orshe paper yet, Lindy?"

"No."

"Then we're married. Where's the pen and ink?"

"Dried up in this heat."

"Well, pencil will do. Just scratch out Harvey Saxton—" the dull pencil traced a thick line through his name "—and put in Harlon—*h-a-r-l-o-n*—Anderson. Neat as pie." He tossed the pencil onto the table and paid no heed when it rolled off the edge. "Well, I guess I'll be going, Lindy. I'll hang around Carson City for a spell. Maybe my luck will change being out of Virginia, a hard-luck town for sure."

"Luck from a bottle never changes," she snorted, "for whiskey's the same everywhere."

Harvey nodded toward Anderson. "Now, you two just get acquainted. He's a good-sh...sized man, Lindy. Maybe he can control you. Lord knows, I never could." Anderson stepped aside to let Harvey out the front door. Harvey studied the steps, turned around and crawled down backward.

Lindy turned her attention to her unwanted guest. She'd explain things to him, nicely, and he could ride back to town and drown his sorrow in a bottle. She hung up the rifle and retrieved her shawl from the floor. Anderson was now sitting down, leaning back with the air of a man at home, looking about his house with satisfaction.

"Now, Mr. Anderson, you know no man can gamble away his wife."

"Why not? Marriage is a contract, just like a business deal. A man can gamble away his share of a business."

"Nevada's a free territory. We can't sell a slave here, so it stands to reason you can't sell a wife, either. A marriage license isn't a negotiable security, like those mine certificates over on the wall."

He smiled, a slow smile, as he'd smiled in the store in anticipation of buttermilk. Except flickering shadows accented the lines about his mouth and eyes.

"When I saw the rifle I sort of suspected you wouldn't cotton to switching husbands. But I've still got the ranch, fair and square."

"Look at the deed."

She shoved the folded document across the table. The stiff paper crackled as Anderson opened it; he slanted it toward the smoking candle.

"'William Merryman, in trust for Melinda Merryman.'" He sat bolt upright. "Who the hell is William Merryman?"

"My brother. He never did trust Harvey, so he kept the land in his name, although it was our wedding present. He figured we'd want a winter home, when the snow got too deep in Virginia. Will figured out Harvey a lot sooner than I did. Whiskey, cards and investing in wildcat mines for an instant fortune. That's about the limit of Harvey's comprehension.''

Did a newcomer understand about wildcat mines? To explain she pointed to the wall, and the engraved certificates that reflected the candlelight. ''They look fancy, but looks don't mean a thing! Each one, nothing but some prospector's dream! Not worth a penny!''

''So he wagered something he didn't own?'' Anderson asked, incredulous. ''I put my money on the table and he put up nothing?'' A crinkle of anger in the final words.

''Yes. He played you for a fool. You wouldn't wager with a man who claimed to have twenty dollars in his pocket but didn't lay it on the table, would you?''

''No.''

''Then why did you take his word that he really did own the farm?''

''It didn't seem the sort of thing a man would lie about,'' he said lamely. ''And the other fellows didn't tip to the fraud, either,'' he added in bold justification. ''The cook, Rich, he said you had a place here on the river.''

''Harvey's not known in Carson. He played the trick in Virginia City two or three times, until the word got around that his name wasn't on the deed. One night, when he proposed to continue in a game staking the farm, the men laughed at him, then threw him out the front door right into C Street. Don't feel bad. You're not the first one to be taken in.''

''How often has he wagered you?'' She balled her fists in the skirt of the nightdress, surprised at how much the insult hurt, how shamed she was to have a stranger know the kind of man she married. The affair betrayed her desperation, that she should accept Harvey Saxton.

''This is the first time,'' she said lightly. ''Why didn't you ask him to show you the deed to the farm?''

"He said the deed was clear out here at the house, so I trusted him."

"Big mistake, trusting Harvey. Not that he's really bad, but whiskey distorts his judgment."

He looked so crestfallen her heart softened. The lock of tumbled hair made him look like a gigantic boy.

"You rode into Carson today, didn't you, Anderson?"

"Yes. My friends call me Lon."

"Where from?"

"California. The pay wasn't so good where I worked, so I thought I'd come to the Comstock."

"Have you ever worked underground?"

"No, but I'm sure I can do it. I can do anything for four dollars a day." New in town, no place to stay, cheated by Harvey Saxton, she might as well be nice to him.

"You got a bedroll?"

"Yes. Out on the horse."

"Well, bring it in and you can sleep on the floor tonight. I usually put guests on the porch, but the wind kicked up a terrible amount of dust, and I didn't have time to sweep off the drift. Tomorrow you can ride on up to Virginia City."

"Thanks. Thanks a lot, Mrs. Saxton."

"I don't exactly like that name. Just call me Lindy."

She replaced the papers in the chest, blew out the guttering candle, stood in the back doorway until her eyes readjusted to the moonlight, then returned to her abandoned bowl of butter. Anderson's footsteps thudded on the front steps and stopped. She turned around, saw him bent over, removing his spurs. He jammed his saddlebags under the table in the corner, out of the way, and pushed his bedroll against it. Polite, even if he was stupid.

"You had any supper?" she asked.

"No."

"Sit down, I'll fix you something." Lindy took bread and a can of sardines from her tin-lined cupboard, flipped a bit of the butter onto a saucer. Not much of a meal for a man, but better than going hungry.

"I don't have anything but water to drink. For myself, I don't keep beer or whiskey about the place."

"That's fine. I don't really care for drink."

He did not sit down until she ordered him to. His huge hands obscured the plate before him. The cup of water disappeared in his massive grasp. A man the size of Anderson, the world should count itself lucky that he didn't drink. Drunk, he could tear a saloon apart. Not to speak of what he might do to a man who riled his temper.

She hauled the churn into the house and dumped the buttermilk into a crock. Too late now to take it out to the pigs.

"Could you spare a cup of that?" he asked diffidently.

"You want buttermilk?" His grin answered her, so she placed the crock on the table within his reach. She sat down opposite him to finish working the butter.

"Where're you from?"

"California. Southern California. I worked on a ranch."

"Before that?"

"Indiana. Raised on a farm outside Fort Wayne."

"Have you got a wife back there?"

"Great Scott, no! You think I'd wager for you if I had a wife back home?"

"That doesn't seem to make a whole lot of difference to most men in Nevada Territory. A woman has to be careful. If it's not a wife or sweetheart back East, it's an attachment to cards and a bottle, or long months out in the desert, running after the silver will-o'-the-wisp."

"You weren't careful when you married Harvey?"

"No. I took him at face value. He had the assay office in Gold Hill. A year ago Harvey flung money about like seed corn. Thousands of prospectors crawled over every hill in the territory, and they brought samples of ore to him, and paid him to write a report saying they'd struck it rich."

"There's not so much prospecting now, I guess."

"No. Every inch of this country has a claim on it. Late last winter the rumor went around Virginia City that Harvey's assays didn't always stick to the truth. One of the reporters for the *Territorial Enterprise* broke a chunk off a grinding wheel, but he told Harvey the rock came from a Reese River claim. Harvey reported it assayed at two hundred dollars a ton in gold, three thousand dollars a ton in silver. That hurt his business, when they printed the report in the paper."

"I imagine it did."

"Harvey always liked his drink, but after that he spent most of his time in the saloons, trying to explain away the mistake. I begged him to move down here and work the farm. I mean, it's not a fancy living, but its better than running up debts, and hearing yourself ridiculed. But he won't leave Virginia City. He says he's got to hear about the latest discoveries. Although not much good it does when he's drunk, and can't remember his name for sure from noon to night. Anyway, I gave up on him, the same as a miner does on a worthless prospect, and moved here in March."

Lon licked the sardine oil off his fingers, and ate another slice of bread.

"If you want to wash up, clean water flows out of the pipe at the springhouse. Out back, just up hill."

The back porch creaked beneath his weight. The pigs snorted at his unfamiliar scent. Poor fellow! Harvey would spread it about Carson City how he'd wagered his wife, because the tale would gain him free drinks. In a day or two, a teamster would repeat the story in Virginia, and Anderson would find himself the butt of jokes.

The moonlight glinted on his wet hair. He shook his head like a dog and shining drops scattered about him. He combed his hair back with his fingers, but the one disobedient lock fell forward. He stood at the bottom of the steps when she discovered her arm lifting. She stared at her fingers, unbelieving, for they curved in preparation for a gentle touch. She gasped, jerked down the offending arm, turned back inside. Brush back his hair. That's what she had intended to do. As one would do for a child. As a woman might do for a lover.

He was not her lover. Never would be. But Harvey spread the gossip right now through Carson. Letting Anderson stay the night added fuel to the fire. He stared at the brilliant moon. The cold-footed ants made a racetrack of her backbone.

She'd already invited him. A low voice in the back of her mind said, "It's too late."

Lon woke in the dark, but he sensed he had slept through the night and that morning hung right behind the hills. He pulled his legs from his bedroll, changed his mind and stuck them back in. If he walked across the floor he would disturb Lindy. Last night a single step on the warped boards had raised creaks loud enough to wake the dead. Plenty of time to crawl out of his blankets when he heard her stirring in the other room.

Best not leave for Virginia City before daylight, anyway, since he didn't know the road. Might she fix him coffee? He longed for coffee, cups and cups of real coffee, not the adulterated stuff Rich brewed. A whole pot of coffee. Last night she'd given him butter, so she milked at least one cow. Coffee with thick cream. With bread off the loaf she had sliced last night...

Too bad the whole crazy scheme had fallen apart. When he turned up three queens on the final deal—clubs, spades, diamonds, all but the queen of hearts—a flock of birds had invaded his chest, their wings brushing his heart. Land and a wife! No need to wait a year or two!

Of course, a few doubts surfaced when he read the engraving on the little gold heart Saxton had pulled off his watch. August 13, 1862. They'd been married less than a year. What kind of woman would marry a sot? But the euphoria had bubbled and stewed, his heart had fluttered between his stomach and his throat, until he saw the moon-light shiver up the barrel of her rifle. At that instant the doubts swelled faster than toadstools in spring woods. And when he'd stepped into the house, and saw who she was, the birds flew away like geese at the first hint of winter.

She didn't want him, but that didn't matter a pin, because he didn't want her. Big, rawboned and just short of ugly. She skinned her hair back into a braid, giving her broad face an undressed look. Her brows went straight across her face, as if they'd been drawn with a spirit level laid above her eyes, and the sun had darkened both her face and hands. Neither fashionable nor feminine. He recalled the slender fingers that sliced the bread. Pretty hands, but probably rough as a cob from outdoor work. And so big! Easily six feet. Not at all like the dream wife he could carry in the crook of one arm.

But if Lindy had been willing to take him, if Saxton really owned the ranch, if he'd won both land and wife, he would have made every effort to be a good husband to Lindy. Maybe if she had a decent husband, one who took care of her, she'd give up wearing men's clothes. But she'd still be six feet tall, and skinny.

He should be satisfied. As the three poker players had fallen under the spell of the jug, bets had risen to five dollars. In the secret pocket of his saddlebags lay five twenty-dollar gold pieces, and an extra twenty-five dollars jingled in his pockets. Of course, he should have even more than that. How many times had Saxton anted and raised on the strength of the worthless IOU that promised the ranch? After a few minutes of figuring, Lon decided Saxton had cheated him out of thirty-five dollars. No sense riding back and trying to get the money. Saxton didn't have a dime.

Chalk it up to experience. At least his winnings cut his time in the mines to six, perhaps seven months.

He turned in his blankets to face the window, now a rectangle of light. Outside, gray morning spread across the land that had been his, for an hour or two. Riding out after cattle—your own cattle, not cattle that belonged to the ranchero. Beefsteak every night of the week. Nothing like the poor, rocky farm in Indiana, where he had slopped pigs and milked cows and followed the plow, all for a living so scant he'd worn moccasins until he started school.

The light brightened, the shapes of the table and chairs became distinct. If Lindy kept chickens she must have a rooster. The rooster would let him know when to roll out of his blankets. He closed his eyes and returned to his dream of a ranchero, with eggs fried in butter, and steak in its own gravy.

The rattle of metal against metal. Stove lids! He pulled his legs from under the blankets. Footsteps on the porch! He scrambled onto his hands and knees. A head topped with a broad-brimmed straw hat poked in the door.

"If you're ready, breakfast is."

He snatched his blankets into an untidy bundle and pulled on his boots. How had she got up and out without him hearing? He gazed stupidly at his bare legs. He'd taken his trousers off to sleep, and they would not go over the boots. Boots off, trousers on, boots back on.

The morning light illuminated the engraved certificates on the wall. As he buttoned his trousers he leaned closer, curious about the papers the speculators flourished on the trail. Harvey Saxton owned two hundred shares in the Pine Nut Mine. Fifty shares in the Lady Bryant. One hundred shares in the Shirt Tail.

Shirttail. He hastily tucked in the ragged ends of his dirty, rumpled shirt. After all, Lindy was a lady, even if she did wear men's clothes.

One more glance at the wall. Shirt Tail? He'd accused

the huckster on the trail of making it up. Some prospector had really named a mine Shirt Tail!

He dashed to the back porch. Golden light crowned the mountain peaks to the west, and the eastern sky shone so brightly he had to squint. Just a few feet from the door the shutters of a window hung open, and through the opening he glimpsed the disorganized coverlets of a bed. She had simply stepped out the window, onto the porch, leaving him to sleep and dream.

Lindy stood under a brush ramada, dressed in the clothes she'd had on in town yesterday—men's trousers, heavy boots and a gingham shirt. The horrible example of what the frontier had produced—a mannish woman who chased her husband away with a rifle. A woman who spoke of divorce!

He'd heard whispers of people getting divorces, but had never known a divorced woman. His mother? No, she might flee her brutish husband, but she would never fall so far as to ask the law for a legal decree.

By the time he'd stuck his head under the pipe running from the springhouse and swallowed a pint of cold water, Lindy had scooped fried potatoes and bacon and eggs onto plates.

"You took me by surprise," he said, to deflect an accusation of laziness. "I expected to get up at cock crow, but you don't have a rooster."

"Yes. That's him over there."

Silhouetted against the morning sky, on the ridge of a shed, sat a large feathered blob. Every speckled hen wandered about the farmyard, searching for unwary bugs who had blundered in on the wind. Half-grown chicks came running at their mothers' clucks. Somewhere a cackle celebrated the laying of an egg. The rooster's head did not stir from under his wing.

"He's the laziest rooster in the territory," Lindy said. "Never gets up before midmorning at the earliest. Then he crows like the whole world needs waking up. I'd eat him, except he's good for laughs.''

Lon studied the labyrinth of sheds and pens. A cookstove crouched in the shadow of the brush ramada a few feet from the porch. The stovepipe poked a few inches above the dry leaves of the sketchy roof. Pans and skillets hung on the posts, advertising this hovel as Lindy's summer kitchen.

Beyond, pigpens and a chicken coop, another ramada, this one rather large, and a corral of peeled poles. Beyond the corral, a pasture with cows, mules and two goats; in the distance clustered ten or twelve sheep with a few half-grown lambs. No evidence of the herd, so she must pasture the cattle on the surrounding hills, or down the canyon.

"Here." She thrust a platter into his hands. "Take it into the house so we can eat at the table like civilized folk." Fried ham, with three eggs just the way he liked them, the yolks pale pink, soft and quivering. A heap of fried potatoes. He resisted lowering his head and snatching at the food like a dog. She placed a small glass pitcher on the table. It held knives and forks.

"Set the table," she said, "while I fetch the coffee." She returned with the coffeepot, took two painted china cups and saucers from a shelf, and put one at each place. This effort at elegance caused a strange ache in his throat. Some feminine delicacy lurked in her hardened spirit. A good man might redeem her. He sat down, forced his hands onto his lap. Might she say grace?

"Dig in, unless you want to thank the Lord out loud."

"I don't, usually."

"Neither do I," she said, her knife and fork already at work. "If He can't read my thanks in my mind, He's a poor sort."

He kept reminding himself of his mother's lessons in manners, but his hunger rounded the edges of politeness. He watched the diminishing heap on Lindy's plate and tried to keep his at about the same level. He scooped up the final forkful of potatoes just as she did.

Once his stomach stopped demanding more, he sat back with a second cup of coffee, considering how he should pay her for supper, breakfast and a place to spread his bed. Would she be insulted if he offered money?

"I thank you," he began, "for taking me in this way." She waved her hand as if she'd done a negligible thing. *Don't offer money,* the gesture said. "If you've got any little thing I could do around the place—" she stared at him, her eyes narrowed "—before I head on up to Virginia City…"

"I could use some help in the garden. I've harvested most of my turnips and beets, so it's time to seed more, and of course radishes."

Her garden stretched between the house and a patch of corn just above knee-high. A bigger garden than his mother kept on the farm in Indiana for a family of six.

"Why so big?" he blurted. "For just you and—"

"I sell truck to a boardinghouse in Virginia City. Nora Dove's place on A Street. She feeds ten men, sometimes twelve."

She handed him a shovel and a hoe, showed him how she wanted the ridge shaped, so the irrigation water could flow freely on either side. The sandy loam worked easily, not like the heavy, rock-filled clay of his boyhood. A slight breeze cooled his shoulders, the morning sun shone in his face, so he kept his head down and his eyes on his work.

Halfway down the long row he paused, straightened up with his palms pressed in the small of his back. No hoe ever made had a handle long enough for him. When he had his own place…. The straw stuffing of a scarecrow rustled a few feet away. The scarecrow hung on a tall pole, facing away from him. Far down the slope two small fields turned from green to gold. Even at this distance his eye distinguished oats and wheat. Beyond that a meadow, then a line of trees marking the course of a stream, probably the Carson River. On the far bank of the river, through the tall cottonwoods, he saw a range of low hills. Where did she pasture her cattle? On meadows along the river? Downstream, obviously, for upstream a gray, brushy ridge jutted toward the river, narrowing the valley.

He returned to his work. Too bad Saxton hadn't owned the place. Too bad it couldn't be his, although making do with a big, feisty woman like Lindy would try a man. A duty wife, not one he married for love. Lindy would never give her whole heart to a man, never depend upon a man in a way that would make him feel tall as the mountains.

Lindy followed behind now, scratching a shallow trench in the top of the ridge, dropping in seeds and covering them. Once or twice he glanced back under his arm and saw the stretch of the trousers across her rump. Women shouldn't wear trousers. A man couldn't keep his mind on his work, seeing a woman's figure on display.

"You want to see the rest of the garden?" she asked when she caught up with him.

He nodded. "Yes." Be polite, then leave. He shifted his eyes to the trees along the river.

"Here's the snap beans, just coming on. And over there are cucumbers. In another week I'll have cucumbers to take to Virginia. I can dig new potatoes right now—" she pointed to a patch of greenery, the biggest potato plants he'd ever seen "—by lifting them carefully." She tramped between the rows, placing her huge boots carefully. "Kale, and down there's melons. I have to keep them far off, for they spread so. The lettuces I plant under the potatoes, because it's too hot during the summer, unless they're in the shade. That's the last of the spinach, but I plan to try planting some amongst the corn."

The cabbages formed compact stands of green, the round heads just forming. Peas climbed up tall tepees fashioned from poles and twigs, the vines turning brown.

"You can't grow peas here except in the spring, because of the heat. Next week I'll tear them all out and plant more snap beans."

He followed her between rows of evenly spaced carrots, the scarecrow looming overhead. He glanced up so he wouldn't ram into the thing and knock it over.

"Good God Almighty!"

He stumbled backward, trying to dodge carrots, his eyes held by the scarecrow.

"Oh!" she cried. "I forgot to warn you...."

"Where the hell did you get that?" He pointed a wavering finger at the scarecrow, at the grinning skull beneath the tattered straw hat.

"I'm sorry I didn't say something to prepare you, but being here all the time, I get used to it, it's friendly like...."

"But where did it come from?"

"I found it in the garden this spring, when I plowed. The emigrant trail ran through here in '49 and '50. More than one man died in the gold rush."

"And you made a blasted scarecrow out of a man's skull? That's...that's blasphemy!" he exclaimed, knowing as he said it that he used the wrong word. No matter, it served, for she spread her fingers across her open mouth, and her thick brows ceased to be straight, but curved into the shade of her hat.

"You think maybe I should bury him?" she asked weakly.

"It would be more respectful, I believe." My God! What kind of a woman stuck a man's head...

"I considered it, I truly did, but then I thought, if someone found my skull in a field, would I want to be underground, or would I like to be useful. I decided I'd rather be up high, looking out over the countryside, even if I couldn't see."

He stared again at the ragged form on the pole, and only by force of will kept from shuddering at the death's-head.

Barbaric! His father invaded his mind, the orator's voice, reading stories of the Christian martyrs, of heads stuck on pikes above city gates.

"Is the...whole skeleton up there?" he asked, gulping.

"No. I found only the skull. Coyotes probably scattered the rest. You think it's wrong to have it..."

"I don't know," he muttered, to hide his shock. She walked toward the house, he followed, looking beyond the house to the corral, and Buckskin, who would carry him away from the nightmare.

"I can fix you some dinner," she said softly, offering a token to bring peace between them.

"No, I better set out for Virginia City." Eat dinner, he'd be bound to spend the afternoon in her garden, under that grinning skull. He'd ride up the valley, through the pastureland. See the extent of the ranch he'd come so close to owning.

Chapter Three

"How many head of cattle on the ranch?" Lon asked, to take his mind off the scarecrow.

"Four."

"Four hundred or four thousand?"

"No, four, full grown. Those four Jersey cows, right there in the pasture. And their calves."

"I mean, out on the river pastures." Her head tilted to the side, and a crease folded across her eyes, bringing the straight brows to her nose.

"I've got four cows. I'll use the neighbor's bull until I can afford to keep one."

"But isn't this a ranch?"

"That's what Harvey calls it, because he thinks it sounds more elegant that we own a ranch, not a farm. There's eighty acres altogether, but since this is my first year on the place, not much is planted. The wheat, about three acres that Mr. Parker—he owned the place before—put in last fall. And this spring I planted two acres of oats, and five acres in irrigated corn, with pumpkins and squash growing between. And the garden. The thirty or forty acres down by the river is too wet to plow until I hire some levees built, so this year I'm letting it grow up for hay."

Lon looked over the sheds and ramadas with new understanding. No herds grazed on the bottomlands. This was it! A farm! A hardscrabble farm, no better, probably worse, than the one he'd left behind in Indiana.

"Thank God I didn't really win this place!"

"Why? It's a good farm." She flung her head back and squared her shoulders. He had insulted her.

"Saxton said a ranch," he continued, ignoring her glare. "It's nothing but a poverty spread, just like the farm where I grew up in Indiana. We were so poor, I was sixteen before I had underdrawers made of something besides flour sacks." He heard the accusation in his voice, as if his poverty had been her fault, and his chest tightened uneasily.

"This is a good farm," she repeated.

He strode to the corral, shaking his head at his good fortune. A farm with a bit of this and a bit of that, and not enough of anything to make a living. It would wear a man out by the time he turned forty, the hopelessness of it twisting body and mind into cruelty and anger.

Buckskin trotted to the fence, and Lon flung the saddle blanket over his back. He glimpsed Lindy, still standing below the porch. Tall and skinny. Shaped like a gallows. The kind of woman who rode a man and nagged him, would not give him a minute's peace.

Harvey Saxton had not drowned himself in whiskey because of a mistake in an assay report. Less than a year gone by since their wedding, and the poor man jumped into the bottle because Lindy would not give him a moment's rest. She nagged him about that joke with the grinding stone. She fussed and fretted until her poor husband slipped away to the saloon to find quiet.

"Got to get my saddlebags and bedroll," he said on his way into the cabin. His gear lay exactly as he'd left it, stuck under the little table in the corner.

He balanced the bedroll against the corral fence while he slung the saddlebags across, running his fingers down the secret pocket to feel the round edges of the coins. Nothing.

He jerked the bags off, untied the flap. The knot hung loose, not the way he'd tied it. He thrust his fingers into the back of the bag, into the double fold of leather concealed by the seam of the flap. Nothing.

Lindy stood at the porch, staring at him. Filthy, lying, thieving female! He held the bags at arm's length, striding toward her, and the crease appeared once more across her eyes. Dark blue eyes, with highlights from the bright sun. Eyes that reminded him of the blue bottles druggists put poison in. Poison-bottle eyes for a poisoning woman, who decorated scarecrows with skulls and divorced her husband.

"By God! Give me back my money!"

"Money?" she whispered, drawing away from him.

"My five twenty-dollar gold pieces! Like you know nothing about them!" When had she been in the front room of the shack alone? When he'd started work in the garden? No, he'd seen her, walking around the oats and wheat.

"Mr. Anderson, I really *don't* know anything about twenty-dollar gold pieces! Do you take me for a thief?" she challenged.

"I sure do. You and that cheating husband..."

Saxton! Lon replayed the moment when he'd put the coins in the pocket, just outside Rich's place. Saxton had been there, his drunken attention completely taken up with untying his horse and clambering into the saddle. Or so Lon had supposed.

"If I took a hundred dollars out of your saddlebags, would I invite you to stay to dinner?" she cried.

Last night Saxton had left the shack, while he remained behind imagining he owned the farm. In the dark, just before riding away, Saxton had had time to open the flap, find the fold in the leather....

"No," she continued triumphantly, "I'd have wanted you to get on your way quick as possible."

"Where's Saxton gone to?"

"He said he intended to try Carson for a while. You heard him yourself, last night."

"But where did he really go?"

"Carson, I suppose...."

"You don't know?" he asked in surprise. "You don't know where your own husband's likely to be?"

"He...isn't...my...husband," she shouted, each word like a stone aimed at his head. "Or at least, he's not going to be my husband any longer than it takes to file the papers to get rid of him. And the way you're acting, I can see it's unlikely I'll ever want a husband again. All men are the same! Stubborn and unreasonable, and bound to have their own way! Anything that goes wrong, it's the woman's fault!"

Lon stepped back, shocked when he saw he'd stuck the saddlebags nearly in her face. His words repeated themselves in his head—nasty, sarcastic. His father. He dropped his hand and took two steps back.

"I'm sorry, Mrs. Saxton, but it's just the upset at finding one hundred dollars vanished. That's close to enough money to fix a man on a homestead."

"Please don't call me Mrs. Saxton. The name's Lindy. Why do you think Harvey took your money?" Lon explained his movements of the previous night, and felt somewhat mollified when she blanched under her sunburn.

"If he comes back here, he'll hear about it," she said firmly.

"I'm going to the law in Carson," he said. "And I'm looking at all the soused men in the filth of the streets, and if I find Harvey Saxton..." He left the threat incomplete, not wanting to upset a woman. Then he laughed at his hesitation. This woman, who decorated poles with human skulls, likely never got upset. Except to get fiercely angry.

"How often do you go to Virginia City?" he asked.

"Twice a week. Tuesdays and Saturdays."

"If you see your husband there, report him to the sheriff.'' Would it do any good? Could a wife turn in her husband for robbery?

"I'll let you know," she said. "You'll be in Virginia?"

"Yes, unless I decide to stay in Carson," he said evasively. No need to let this woman and her thieving husband know his whereabouts. After all, their estrangement might be a sham, a way to draw in strangers, as they'd pulled him in with the farm Harvey didn't own.

"Wages are better in Virginia," she said. "The best boardinghouse is Dove's, where I sell my truck. Mrs. Dove runs a proper house, and she keeps the bugs under control and the sheets clean. Only forty-five dollars a month for meals and a bed." Lon nodded. "Only two men to a room. Nora's not so greedy that she jams beds in every space."

"I'll look around a bit," he said. "I'll find a job before I contract for room and board."

"Dove's on A Street."

"If I get a job, I'll look her up," said Lon, not meaning a word of it. Giving his hard-earned money to a lady boardinghouse keeper formed no part of his plans.

A hen cackled, the rooster stretched on the ridgepole of the shed, flapped his wings and crowed. Again and again he proclaimed the dawn, even though the sun stood overhead. Lon's anger dissolved at the sight, try as he might to resist. He laughed. Just as well, for to gain Lindy's cooperation, to get his money back, he shouldn't leave with bitter words and unfounded accusations. Honey drew more flies than vinegar, and maybe, if he treated her pleasantly, when Saxton turned up she'd report him to the sheriff.

"I guess you do pretty well for yourself," Lon said, being generous and flattering, while inside he sneered at the miscellany of pens and sheds. "With so many men rushing in with the silver boom, raising vegetables and chickens must provide a fine living."

"I make out," she said.

"It won't be so good in winter, though, I suppose."

She stared at him suspiciously, her poison-bottle eyes narrowed to slits. Her eyes should flash a warning to any man, even one as dazed with drink as Harvey Saxton.

"I'm not telling you how much money I bring in, if that's what you're getting at." She tossed her head, not a very effective gesture with her hair all bound up in a braid. "Let's just say, before winter comes I'm having a real barn built right here. You come down in a month or two, you'll see it. Are you staying in Virginia City?"

"I'll look about," he said cautiously. "This morning I'm going to Carson to find Harvey Saxton. Are you really divorcing him?"

"Sure enough. You want to come courting?" She grinned, his heart quivered and his fingers tingled where the reins touched. He came close to telling her that he would rather jump into a pit of rattlesnakes.

He tramped back to the corral, got his bedroll, tied it behind the saddle without looking at her. He mounted, turned Buckskin's head toward the road.

How often in a lifetime could a man expect to get three queens on the opening deal? Three, perhaps four times, and only if he played poker regularly. He had not, in eight years, seen a hand like that, and now he'd wasted his maybe once-in-a-lifetime chance wagering for this woman. The queens of spades, of clubs, of diamonds. Very appropriate. Because this woman had no heart.

The afternoon sun baked the morning's sweat into his shoulders. If he found Saxton immediately, he might get at least part of his money back, because it was physically impossible for a man to drink up one hundred dollars between ten in the evening and noon. Unless Saxton had found a poker game. All too likely. Lon groaned.

He stuck his head into the first two saloons he passed, glanced at the men hanging around the bar. No Saxton. He inquired at Rich's.

"Too bad," said Rich. "Saxton's a devil of a cheat. I'll not let him play here again."

Lon walked slowly around the square, eyeing the small crowd around an auctioneer trying to rouse interest in a string of bony horses. He investigated the Carson Club without result, then inquired in McCaffrey's store.

"You might ask next door at Pryor's," said McCaffrey.

Lon experienced a moment's excitement when he discovered a body stretched out under a table. He prodded with his toe, and the man crawled out, blond and beardless.

Pryor brushed away the inquiry with a flick of his fingers. He stood on a ladder, hanging a huge painting behind the bar, a portrayal of the ascent to heaven of John Adams and Thomas Jefferson on July 4, 1826. The eagles bearing the two men aloft wore expressions of outrage, perhaps because the horde of female angels displayed bare breasts and naked legs, and fragile wings that wouldn't support the weight of a sparrow.

He considered reporting the theft to the sheriff, but decided against it, because he'd have to confess being horn-swoggled by Saxton. He rode north before sundown, letting Buckskin set the pace up the hill. Even though he knew about Washoe Lake, he gasped in amazement at the top of the ridge. Totally out of place in this desert valley, like a bit of blue sky had tumbled from heaven. But Buckskin knew water when he smelled it; he strained down the hill, and broke into a trot. Lon anticipated cold water on his back, on his legs, washing away the sweat and dust.

The shore turned out to be boggy, and mosquitoes rose in clouds when he walked through the grass. He searched for half an hour before he found a high place that offered a bed site, and a pool suitable for a bath. He stretched out stark naked in the sun and breeze—just enough wind to keep the mosquitoes at bay. He reached for his saddlebags, checked for the third time for the five gold coins, and for the third time found nothing. The little gold heart, engraved

August 13, 1862? He dug deeper. Not there. What difference did it make? He didn't want the woman, so he had no right to the wedding charm. And he was twenty-five dollars to the good, and had stayed out of the zephyr.

Lindy let her mules rest several times on the long pull out of the Carson River valley; the road wound past Silver City and Gold Hill, through the Devil's Gate and Gold Canyon. She paused at the Divide, the ridge that separated the towns of Gold Hill and Virginia City. Traveling slowly had given her time to think about Lon Anderson. Not a bad-looking fellow, but far from bright. Men of Anderson's type swarmed into every new territory, looking for a second chance. Failures at home, they blamed their problems on everyone and everything but themselves. Harvey and Anderson. Two of a kind, except that Harvey was smart enough to avoid work, and Anderson dumb enough to work hard.

She'd made her first and last mistake with Harvey. She counted on her fingers. A little more than ten months since she and Harvey had stood before the preacher in Virginia City, seven months since the trick with the grinding stone tipped Harvey into the solace of whiskey. She should have guessed all along what kind of man he was, but she'd let her heart be fooled, because he flattered her, a handsome, well-to-do man paying court. So different from Ohio, where the only fellow who called was a widower with a filthy house and a passel of kids crying for their mother.

She shook the reins and the mules trotted down the slope, past the outskirts of the town. She slowed them to a walk on the steep grade up to A Street.

She had learned her lesson, and would not make the same mistake twice. When a new barn towered over the sheds and the cabin, when haystacks lined the fields, and oats and wheat lay in bins, in another year, with six or eight milk cows in the pasture, and the garden twice as big, men would ignore her six feet and her plain face. She'd listen to no flattering lies; she'd ignore gifts meant to blind her eye. The next marriage would be a straight business deal. She'd ask each man for proof of dollars in the bank, of wages paid at the end of the month. And she'd make it clear that wildcat stocks weren't investments, but gambling.

Mr. Dove sat in the front window, waiting for her. He swung out on his crutches, pretending to help with the unloading. He managed to loop the handle of the basket of rhubarb over his arm. It bumped awkwardly against his legs as he hobbled in the door.

"Nora's in the kitchen," he explained unnecessarily. Nora furnished a hot breakfast and supper to her boarders, besides filling their dinner buckets, and since the mines worked twenty-four hours a day, the kitchen was her permanent residence.

Lindy heaved the eggs and cheese out of the wagon first, for they'd already sat too long in the sun. She passed Mr. Dove in the front parlor, and dumped her load on the kitchen floor. Two men, their elbows sprawled wide, sat at the table drinking coffee, while Nora turned bacon with one hand and opened the oven door with the other. The men abandoned their coffee and trailed her out to the wagon. By the time they stowed the last basket in the pantry, Nora spread bacon and eggs, beans and biscuits on the table. Mr. Dove collapsed in a rocker by the kitchen window.

"Coffee?" asked Nora, automatically pulling a cup from the shelf.

"Don't mind if I do," Lindy said.

"Set a spell," said one of the miners. "Nora promised to pull out her crystal ball and read our fortune while we eat breakfast."

Nora emptied the coffeepot into Lindy's cup, refilled it from a water bucket and put it back on the cookstove. She pulled a polished wooden box from a high shelf. The men shoved aside the saltcellar, the sugar bowl and the butter dish to make room for the box in the center of the table. Nora lifted the top reverently, exposing a four-inch orb of clear crystal. It glowed warm and rosy, because it rested on a cushion of scarlet velvet. Lindy did not believe for one minute that Nora saw the future in the ball. Nora simply had a very vivid imagination and a knack for inventing stories that gullible people took to be the answers to their questions.

"What we want to know," said one of the miners, his mouth full of biscuit and molasses, "is the Bennett Hill Mine onto something? The owners claim they've hit bonanza, but the ore samples look mighty like rocks from the Yellow Jacket."

"Maybe they're into the same vein as the Yellow Jacket," offered Lindy.

"Can't be. Bennett Hill's on the other side of Gold Canyon."

Nora raised her hands, requesting silence. "Do you have a piece of the ore?" she asked. The miner who had spoken leaned back to expose his pants pockets, fished about, pulled out a bit of yellowish gray rock the size of a man's thumbnail.

"Is that enough? It was all I could break off without they'd notice and suspect I didn't trust them."

"The spirits need very little to reveal the truth," Nora intoned. She placed the fragment in front of the crystal ball.

"Quiet," she ordered as she settled herself to stare into the crystal. Lindy drank her coffee and listened to the sounds of Virginia City. The two miners chewed and slurped, Mr. Dove's rocking chair squeaked, wagons rolled by on A Street, the roar of the stamp mills and steam engines echoed off the mountainside.

"I see a very deep shaft," said Nora. "The miners work in a great chamber, with rank upon rank of timber supports. One shovels rock into ore cars, and—"

"Hell, the Yellow Jacket!" snarled one of the men.

"Bennett Hill's no more than ninety feet deep," said the other. "Rock so hard they haven't bothered to timber yet."

"I think your suspicion is correct," said Nora, fingering the chip of stone. "This came from the Yellow Jacket, or perhaps some other deep mine on the Comstock. The prospectors at the Bennett Hill most likely hauled a bucket of ore to salt the tailings. I suggest you sell your stock, if you bought any."

Lindy called up a mental picture of her cabin wall, trying to read the names on the certificates. Had Harvey taken a chance on the Bennett Hill? The miners sopped the last of the eggs and bacon grease from their plates with biscuits, drained the mugs and took their leave.

"Want me to tell your fortune, Lindy? While I have the ball out."

"Might as well." Nora took so much delight in her fortune-telling abilities, it seemed unfriendly not to give her the pleasure. Between the demands of her crippled husband and her boarders, the poor woman scarcely had a moment to sit down.

Did Nora know she'd kicked Harvey out? Two weeks had passed since he'd staggered through the gate, begging for money. He'd arrived at a bad time, just when she'd come from hoeing the corn, hot and sweaty, with the milking still to be done and the eggs not collected. She had screamed at him, her exasperation and weary muscles forming words she'd never meant to say. By now the news had certainly reached Virginia City.

"Place your hands, palms up, on either side of the ball," said Nora. Lindy leaned across the table and laid out her hands, grimaced at the calluses and the dirt ground into the skin. "Stare into the ball and think of the crystal, nothing else." The clear crystal reminded her of a mountain stream where it settled into a quiet pool. No, she must not think of water, but of the crystal ball.

Nora cleared her throat. "I don't like to give my friends bad news, Lindy, but what I see may mean trouble."

"What sort of trouble?" She looked at Nora instead of the ball.

"With a man. Don't take your eyes from the ball."

"I kicked Harvey out of the house. You must have heard about that since I drove up last Saturday."

"Yes, I'd heard, but this isn't Harvey. The man I see is very tall." Had the tale of Lon Anderson and the poker game already drifted up the hill? "He's crowned with light, which doesn't always mean trouble, you understand, unless it's red, but this aura, one side *is* red. I admit, the other side's blue, but the red dominates at times. Now, the trouble may affect only him, but since you know him, there's always the danger some part of it will touch you."

Lindy placed her hands in her lap and looked at Nora. "I don't know any real tall fellows," she lied.

"You've recently met one," insisted Nora.

"Well, I did meet a tall man a night or two ago, but I really don't know him, and I don't expect to ever see him again."

"You will. Be careful. I believe he's the sort of man women find tempting, and you're in a susceptible frame of mind having separated from Harvey. Do you plan to divorce Harvey?"

"Can't you tell that from your crystal?" Lindy asked.

"Why should I go to all that bother when I can ask you? It takes energy to raise the spirits."

"Yes, I'm divorcing Harvey."

Lindy turned her teams out of town, then down the long grade, stopping frequently for freight wagons and buggies, for uphill traffic had the right of way. She met a long string of wagons loaded with timber, and had to pull far over, to the very edge of the road. Her wheels rested inches from the precipice. On the switchback below a single horse plodded upward. She recognized the horse's golden coat and the rider's long, long body.

"Hello, Mr. Anderson," she hailed, once she had the mules safely back on the road. He lifted his hat briefly, and the lock of hair drooped a little. "You didn't find work in Carson?"

"I didn't look for work. I looked for Harvey Saxton." Lindy gulped. Nora had seen it coming, the trouble this man would bring.

"Did you find him?" she asked, frightened. A man the size of Anderson could pound Harvey into the ground like a tent stake, and he had a right to do exactly that.

He shook his head. "Everybody in Carson thinks he's gone to Virginia. Did you see him there?"

"No. I only go to the Doves' boardinghouse. I don't frequent the places where Harvey's likely to be found."

"I didn't suppose you did, ma'am," he said soberly. He took his hat off completely; the lock of hair fell across his forehead. "I apologize if I insulted you. But if he comes around, you tell him he owes me $135. And I aim to collect, one way or the other."

Trouble! Nora had seen this in her silly ball. If Harvey couldn't make good the money he'd stolen, Anderson would take it out of his hide. She imagined Harvey crippled, bruised and broken in a fight with this giant. Harvey's friends would carry him away to be washed and bandaged and nursed. Who would they think of? His wife! There in plain sight lay the trouble Lon Anderson would bring to her doorstep! Harvey, sick and wounded, would tie her down like Nora Dove, taking care of a crippled man for the rest of her life. A woman couldn't divorce a man in that condition.

"Mr. Anderson, would you please do me a favor?"

"Yes, ma'am, if it's within my power," he said, caution in the words.

"When you meet up with Harvey, and grind him to powder because he stole money from you and can't pay it back, don't leave him alive. Kill him, clean and quick.'' His eyes snapped open; he slammed his hat back on his head, and as an afterthought shoved the lock of hair back up under the crown.

"Kill him?'' he gasped. Shocked again. The way he'd looked when he'd seen the scarecrow. Lon Anderson was without a doubt the most innocent man she'd ever met. She'd pass the remark off as a joke.

"Well, you could save me the expense of the lawyer to get the divorce.'' She shrugged her shoulders and grinned.

A joke, maybe a bit morbid, but a joke. From the way he jerked his reins, from the way his appalled eyes stared at her, she knew he'd heard no jest. He did remember to tip his hat once more, but not enough to release the lock of hair, and his face stretched out stiff and gray as a year-dead tree.

Chapter Four

Lon reined in Buckskin at the top of the ridge and looked down upon Virginia City. All his plans evaporated like drops of water flung on a hot stove. It would not do!

The mining camps he had known in California snuggled in the bottoms of valleys. By riding a mile or so up a creek, a man could find a patch of trees where he might make camp. But Virginia City clung to a mountainside! If trees had ever grown on the slopes, they'd been stripped for firewood. No water flowed in the valley, only a track of light-colored sand, mocking a running stream. Fine alkali dust rose from the feet and wheels of the passing traffic, and drifted here and there on a skittish wind. His golden-brown horse had turned gray. Lon lifted his hat, found it laden a quarter-inch deep.

Shanties climbed the mountain's slope, open to sun, wind and rain. Not one protected spot, where a man might throw his bedroll, or pitch a tent. Forty-five dollars a month for room and board. Nearly half a man's pay! Plus the cost of clothes. Even the sturdiest fabrics disintegrated quickly in the mines. Hopes of saving money wafted into the air with the dust.

He touched his belt with his arm. Almost sixty dollars—the thirty he'd brought over the pass, plus his poker winnings. If he had the hundred Saxton had stolen, he'd turn around and ride back over the Sierra. What an absolute fool he'd been! If he ever found Saxton, he would…

No, he wouldn't. Deep down he felt sorry for Saxton. Not because the man had hit bottom and turned thief, but because the poor fellow had married Lindy. Hitched himself to a nagging, domineering wife. What in the world had possessed Harvey Saxton to ask a woman like Lindy…?

A woman dashed by in a buggy, answering the question. She wore a rose satin dress and a matching hat. Her white breasts bulged over the top of the bodice; she'd hitched her skirt high enough to display a well-turned ankle.

Saxton had been pushed to the altar by the strongest urge of all. Every man eventually got tired of wandering from woman to woman. There came a time when his heart thumped with fear, following a woman who took money. Sooner or later every man wanted a woman of his own, and that meant marriage and settling down.

But Saxton's woman wanted him killed. She'd find an accomplice, of course, in this horde of men. Within a week Lindy would persuade a man to turn murderer so he might possess her.

"By God! I'm not the one!" he exclaimed. He must stop thinking of Lindy, the shape of her hips beneath the clinging trousers, the tight pull of the shirt…he must get settled.

Whistles shrieked, the plumes of steam streaking away from the vents, downhill, where tall head frames straddled shafts, and belching chimneys towered over steam plants, their smoke tailing northward before the wind. That's the way he must go.

He pushed his way into the stream of wagons, horses, mules, burros, carts and buggies. Once off the ridge, he found scarcely room to maneuver Buckskin on the narrow street. The mob carried him toward the center of the town.

Buckskin, unaccustomed to cities and masses of human beings, shied from one unfamiliar sight, then another. Lon struggled, finally got the horse to stand still by wedging him against a post holding up the roof over the boardwalk. He leaned over, patted Buckskin's neck to calm him, and looked for the closest cross street.

Whaa-zing! All four of Buckskin's feet left the ground with the crack of a pistol. He came down closer to the post, jamming Lon's knee into the sharp edge of the timber. A thousand booms echoed from building to building, Buckskin twisted in panic, Lon yelled in pain. He shook his foot out of the stirrup in an effort to dismount, but another shot crashed close to his ear.

Lon twisted in the saddle, searching for the gunman so that he might flee in the opposite direction, but the echoes confused him. Buckskin flung his head up, neighing, his eyes bulging with fright.

A crowd erupted from a saloon directly across the street, right into the path of an overloaded wagon drawn by six straining mules. The first team reared, then bolted, straight across the street. No place to go but onto the boardwalk. Buckskin's front hooves echoed on the planks, the window in front of them disintegrated, turning into a thousand glittering fragments, a silent cascade overwhelmed by reverberating explosions.

Buckskin leapt back toward the center of the street, tangling with the fleeing crowd. Lon glimpsed an empty space beside the saloon. He jerked the reins in that direction. An alley, he prayed. Shelter. More shots, and this time Buckskin dashed for the refuge. Lon made no effort to stop him, for any obstacles in the alley paled in significance before the renewed fusillade.

Buckskin dived through the opening, Lon sprawled on his neck, clinging to the mane, the pommel of the saddle goring his stomach. Hooves clattered in irregular, hollow thuds. A stairway! From the corner of his eye he saw men clamber onto the railing, scrambling to get out of his way. Curses burned his ears.

"This ain't no damned bridle..." someone yelled as he and the horse careened past. The racket must have warned the people on the street below, for when Buckskin made his final leap, Lon found a narrow clearing, space sufficient to get the panicked horse under control.

He slid out of the saddle and leaned against the corner of a building, panting. Buckskin's sides heaved, and his hide twitched with fright. The buildings across the street refused to come into focus, until Lon realized perspiration was running from his forehead into his eyes. He fumbled for his kerchief.

"You're quite a horseman," said a seductive female voice at the level of his elbow. The woman wore the brightest yellow dress he had ever seen. Rouge exaggerated the width of her cheekbones and the fullness of her lips. "I've seen men ride the stairways before, but never at that speed. Come home with me. You could use a drink. I'll furnish that, plus a bit of rest."

"A shooting," he gasped. "In a saloon. Was someone killed?"

"Most likely," she said, shrugging her shoulders, almost shrugging her breasts out of the low-slung bodice. "We'll find out who died tomorrow morning, in the paper."

"The paper?" he croaked. A man, maybe more than one, bled to death a block away and twenty feet up the hill, and this woman would wait to read about it in the paper?

"The *Territorial Enterprise* lets us know who's cut down in the shootings," she explained in a gentle voice. "In plenty of time to go to the funeral. And the trial, if there's to be one. You new in town?" Lon nodded. "Come to my place. Whatever you prefer—whiskey, beer, wine. We'll have a drink and relax." She laid her hand on his arm. "Last night I entertained a man who wouldn't reach your belt buckle with his boots on," she said playfully. She poked him at the spot she mentioned; his belly automatically shrank from her touch. She laughed. "But he's well hung in the male way, no matter being a dwarf. You, taller than a tree, you'll be a nice contrast.'' She aimed her finger at him a second time, lower down.

He slid behind Buckskin, shook his head, jerked on the reins and shoved his way into the crowd of men watching the byplay, all at the same time. He turned left on a cross street so steep the jittery horse planted his front feet and nickered in fright. Lon led him in easy stages from one side of the street to the other, heading for a huge sign at the bottom of the hill: Gould and Curry Mine.

As good a place as any to start his search for work, for he knew nothing of the mines except their names. He tied Buckskin to the hitching rail, took off his spurs and hung them from the saddle.

''Looking for work?'' asked a voice behind him.

The man did not come up to his chin, but his shoulders spread as wide as his own, and the muscles of his arms bulged through both shirt and coat. ''Yes.''

''Ever worked in Virginia before?'' asked the man.

''No.''

''What sort of work you done?'' Did this man hire and fire for one of the mines? A strange place to conduct an interview, in the middle of the street.

''I placer mined in California, then worked at a ranch down south.''

''Can you read and write?'' Lon reared back a little at the insult.

''Of course.''

''How well? Can you write a tolerable sentence?''

''I went through eight sessions at the township school, and read Caesar to about halfway.''

''Read what?'' the miner asked, puzzled.

''I studied Latin with my father, first-year grammar and partway through the second year. Julius Caesar's story of the war in Gaul.''

"Sounds exciting. Why'd you quit halfway?" asked the miner.

"Because Latin's the biggest time-waster on earth. A fool language. Do you know, the Romans didn't have one word for 'and,' but a whole hatful of tricks to confuse you. And they threw sentences together, without rhyme or reason, so you can't get the drift of a remark until all the words are said."

His inquisitor wrinkled his forehead for a moment. "That would slow things down," he agreed.

"And the people who can deal with this aimless nonsense, they swagger about and put on airs and think they're better than a man who speaks plain English."

"I work for the Gould and Curry," said the man, ignoring Lon's further thoughts on Latin. He pointed at the sign over their heads. "I'd like you on my shift. You look strong and capable."

"I try to give full value for my wage."

"I'll take you into the office and see that you get on. Braley's the name. We start work at ten."

"I'll find a place to stay the night," said Lon. He could throw his blankets under a juniper, if he could find one, maybe get dinner and breakfast at Mrs. Dove's on A Street....

"No to need worry about a place to stay until morning. Ten this evening's when we go down. We're the night shift."

Lon contemplated the pictures on the walls of the Old Virginia Saloon. Two paintings of scantily clad women hung on the side wall, and behind the bar a woman, totally naked, reclining on a lounge upholstered in dark red. And he'd been critical of Pryor's loosely robed angels!

He lifted the glass of beer from the table, took a sip unwillingly. He hated the taste of the stuff, but Braley assured him beer cut the film of dust left in a man's throat by a shift in the mine.

"I should bathe in beer," Lon muttered to himself. He imagined the naked woman sinking into a tub of beer, with himself close behind. When the woman turned into Lindy, he jerked back to reality.

He sat on a bench near the window, too tired to join the men at the bar. How many ore cars had he pushed overnight, each loaded with a thousand pounds of rock? He'd gone without a night's sleep many times, but never felt so exhausted as he did right now.

Night-shift miners pressed into the saloon, shouted for beer and whiskey, snagged pickles, crackers and hard-boiled eggs from the bowls on the bar. Lon took a second, larger swig of the beer, hoping it would clear his throat, then another swig to settle his mind. He glanced out the dirty window to assure himself that he sat on the surface of the earth.

He and the other men of the night shift had descended the shaft on a platform hung from a huge windlass. No rails, nothing to hang on to but the cables themselves.

"Payday soon," one of the miners had said joyfully, then added in a solemn voice, "Mustn't forget to put a contribution in for Homer's widow."

"Homer fell two weeks ago," murmured Braley in Lon's ear.

"Fell? Where?"

"Right from this lift. On the way up at the end of the shift, he fainted and fell right over the edge before one of us could grab him. We brought the pieces of his body up in a blanket and powder boxes."

The lift had stopped hundreds of feet below the surface, in a tunnel hotter than any summer's day. Braley had assigned him a rail car, and instructed him to push it from the ore pile to the lift. He did not see the actual mining, for the men dug high above his head, beyond a tangle of gigantic timbers that supported the high ceiling. The only light came from candles on iron spikes stuck into the walls. The heat, the flickering pools of light amidst blackness, reminded him of his father's confident description of hell.

Over dinner, eaten from the buckets they'd carried down, the miners talked about the old-timer who, just a month before, had raced the ore car down the tunnel to get one more load up before the end of the shift. He failed to note that the lift had moved to the drift above. The weight of the car pulled him into the shaft, and he fell hundreds of feet, crashing through the platform covering the sump at the bottom. The miners described in uncomfortable detail how they brought the pieces of his body up in a blanket and powder boxes.

Lon wrapped his hand around the sweaty beer mug. His fingers not only tingled, they absolutely shook if he did not hang on to something. When he lifted the beer, it sloshed about. He wished Braley would join him on the bench, so he'd have someone to talk to. But Braley stood near the bar, chatting with two other men. Lon half rose to join them, but then saw them glance in his direction, and felt they were talking about him. Finally the three men nodded, slapped one another on the shoulder and sauntered to where he sat.

"We're all agreed," said Braley. "Let's go home and fix grub, then catch some sleep."

Lon gladly abandoned his beer on the table, and tagged behind. The two strangers had arms as thick as Braley's, strong men who swung a pick or hammer hour after hour, all night long.

What had they agreed to, there in the bar? He dropped back a few feet. He knew nothing about Braley, except that he bossed a crew for the Gold and Curry. Could Braley and his companions be leading him to some isolated spot, to beat and rob him? He'd have no chance against three men.

He staggered from exhaustion, and the weariness and the effect of half a mug of beer overcame his doubts. He had to find a meal and a bed before he dropped in his tracks, and these men promised to lead him to both. He scarcely noticed the shops they passed—gunsmiths, paper hangers, Chinese laundries, dry goods. An assay office. Had this been Harvey Saxton's office? He recognized the livery stable where he had lodged Buckskin. Maybe he should get the horse and head out of town. Away from Braley and his friends, away from the Gould and Curry and its hellish underground.

Boarding the horse cost fifty cents per day, and that price held just through summer. During the winter he would pay at least one dollar, maybe a dollar and a half. Another fifteen dollars a month out of his wages, double that after the snow flew. If he stayed in Virginia City he'd have to sell Buckskin. Never in his life had he made four dollars a day. Yet in Nevada Territory a man bringing home that princely sum could not afford to keep a horse!

His legs moved only from habit. A man's legs could simply fold up under him. He remembered men on the California trail who collapsed, unable to rise.

Braley climbed up a steep, rocky pitch. On a tiny patch of moderately level ground stood a hut. A night wind had heaped sand against the door. Braley kicked at the dune to make space for the warped door to open.

"Now, let me introduce you," said Braley, pointing at his two companions. "Bill Riddel, works in the Ophir. Art Marron, works in the Chollar. This is Lon Anderson. Welcome to our happy home." His hand swept around, taking in the entirety of the twelve-by-twelve-foot shanty. No two of the planks forming the walls matched in length or breadth; a rusty sheet of iron covered the wall behind the stove. A patched wagon cover flapped on three widely spaced aspen logs that served for rafters.

"Anderson, you start a fire in the stove," said Braley,

pointing to a heap of sagebrush and gnarly roots near the door. Lon obeyed, hoping he managed to stay on his feet long enough to do his job. Marron unwrapped a slab of bacon; Braley flipped a sack of flour off a hook. Riddel knocked flakes of dry batter from a large earthenware bowl.

"Don't need washed," he opined. "Just mixin' more of the same." He dumped in flour and water.

The sage caught the flame quickly, much to Lon's relief. Riddel moved a skillet to the front of the stove, Marron dumped in the bacon. Braley lifted bacon grease from the skillet, spread it over the top of the stove. Twice Riddel flicked a drop of water on the stove top, and twice he grunted his dissatisfaction. The third drop sizzled and vaporized within seconds. He ladled the batter onto the stove top.

In less than half an hour they sat on the floor, eating bacon and flapjacks liberally soused with molasses. Every ear was cocked to the promising hum of the coffeepot as it simmered over what remained of the fire.

"We been living out here this summer," said Braley, "to save our money. We got a mining scheme in the making, and we need a month's wages put by until it pays off. We're looking for another man who ain't afraid to work. I watched you last night. You'll do."

"What kind of project?" asked Lon. He stopped chewing on a strip of half-cooked bacon, knowing suddenly that his question had been a mistake. Exhaustion and beer made him too free with his mouth.

"We have a chance to make thousands of dollars," said Riddel, helping himself to more flapjacks. "But we need one more man, and he's got to be able to read and write, and Braley says you can, and this man, he shouldn't be well-known about Virginia City. Who do you know in town?"

Lon swallowed hard and pretended he had to chew an extra-large bite of flapjack. He knew no one, unless Harvey

Saxton had returned to Virginia. Hunting for a stranger to share a mining scheme didn't make sense; a man who knew no one might be murdered without a soul asking questions. His heart tripped up once or twice. He decided not to answer the question. Braley finally interrupted the long silence by clearing his throat.

"Anderson, you're not afraid to take on something hard, I saw that last night. In my experience, a hardworking man is usually trustworthy. You don't run off at the mouth, which is a good sign, and you don't ask questions unless they're necessary. I figure you can keep a secret. We're planning to open up a prospect not far from here that's laid idle for two years, called the Shirt Tail." He slapped his wrist and grunted with satisfaction as he displayed a dead insect. "Got a big 'un."

"This mine, it's got promise?" asked Lon to keep Braley talking and gain time to think. The Shirt Tail, again. All three men laughed like they'd not heard a good joke in weeks and their funny bones needed tickling. Something bumped on his ankle, distracting his attention from their amusement.

"No promise for mining silver, no," said Riddel between chuckles, "but for mining greenhorns and city men, it's the most promising place about."

"We plan to give up working in the mines for good," said Braley. "No man lasts more than a few years working deep rock. Too much can go wrong with all that machinery. We intend to open a saloon, 'cause Riddel here's a good cook. But opening a saloon takes money. Payday's this week, and we have enough put by to work the Shirt Tail for a month."

"But you said it has no indications," exclaimed Lon, not looking at Braley, but at the large flea perched on his anklebone. He lifted his legs free of the dirt floor. A flea hopped onto the edge of his tin plate, a creature so large he distinctly heard the *plink* when it landed.

"Of course it has no indications! It's almost a certainty that the Shirt Tail isn't within a mile of a silver ledge, but speculators invest in holes with fewer possibilities. The shaft runs horizontal into the mountainside about eighty feet, the rock so hard it needs no timbering. The prospectors who opened the shaft left some equipment, but we'll have to buy powder and fuse, shovels and picks. Best of all, the original company sold only fifteen hundred shares of Shirt Tail stock, and we located seven hundred and fifty of them. Billy Clarr, who's got Clarr's Saloon, he had a hundred, but this spring came a cold snap and he used the certificate to start a fire in his stove. So that's eight hundred and fifty we know of, and we suppose most of the others got burned or lost."

Lon understood the plot. They would do just enough work to start rumors flying, the stock would take a spurt, worth a few dollars a share rather than nothing. They would sell the seven hundred and fifty, and abandon the mine.

"We're not greedy," said Marron. "We'll not hold out for the highest price. If we sell at ten dollars, we'll get seventy-five hundred dollars. We'll give you a part for what you'll do, the three of us divide the rest." Lon let this remark settle as he watched a gaggle of acrobatic fleas jump over his boots.

"And what's that? The part you're expecting of me?" he asked, keeping his voice low. If he refused to join them, would they kill him to keep the swindle a secret?

"You came into town just precisely at the right time, when we got enough cash to let the brake out on the scheme," said Braley. "We'll give out a story that you're a geologist fellow from San Francisco—"

"What the hell am I doing working at the Gould and Curry, if I'm a geologist from San Francisco?" Lon exploded.

"You wouldn't be the first scientific fellow who's got a look at the Comstock Lode by going to work in a mine, before sliding out to do some prospecting on his own," Braley said slyly.

"And my prospect is the Shirt Tail?" asked Lon.

"That's right. We keep our mouths shut until we've all quit our jobs and moved out to the mine. We need a day or two to clean up the place, and turn over the top of the tailings pile so it looks fresh worked. You'll write up a report on the property, full of fancy geologist words, and we give it to the newspaper."

"I can't write a geologic report. I couldn't spot a piece of silver ore if I fell over it, and I don't know any geologist words."

"A friend of mine works in the Gould and Curry offices. He slipped me a copy of a report done for the owners by a high-placed fellow from some university back East. You just copy the sentences, and wherever he says east, you write west. When he says two, you change it to four. Things like that, so no one gets suspicious. There's a reporter at the *Territorial Enterprise* who lives and breathes to give the mines a boost. We'll take him out for dinner, with plenty of brandy, then get a buggy from the livery stable—oh! but don't he love to be taken around in a buggy!—out to the mine, and he'll give us a column the next day in the paper, really put the polish on the old Shirt Tail. The San Francisco papers always pick up his pieces, for those folks hunger like spring bears for any tidbit about the Comstock. In two days Shirt Tail shares will be milling on the exchange, and inside a week men'll be fighting for them."

A hundred things bustled about in Lon's mind, but foremost came the determination to keep his mouth shut and his opinions to himself. These men proposed a scheme just one cut above outright robbery. Now that they had exposed their designs to him, would they let him get away? Or must he pretend to go along with the scheme, then creep out as soon as they fell asleep?

No danger that he might fall asleep, he thought grimly.

The fleas had discovered his legs above his stockings, and in a few minutes would be investigating under his shirt.

How long since he'd been in his blankets? Night before last by the lake, the night before that in Lindy's front room—where she'd tacked up a hundred shares of the Shirt Tail in place of wallpaper.

Don't think about sleep, don't think about stock certificates. Get out of here, ride twenty or thirty miles today, so these renegades can't catch up.

"You ever work underground before, Anderson?" asked Marron.

Lon's tired mind refused to deal with two matters at once. He had to consider the question for several seconds before answering. "No."

"How'd you like it in the Gould and Curry?"

"Darker than I expected. I'm partial to seeing the sky above me, I guess." Sky above, grass below. The scarecrow looking with empty sockets across Lindy's valley had it better than the miners. Grass to keep his cattle fat, his horses fed. Grass. The little meadow at the bottom of the pass, and the ragged man selling mine certificates. He did not want to go back into that section of the bowels of the earth called the Gould and Curry.

"You did just fine for a beginner," said Braley. "You didn't run an ore car down the shaft. You took orders and didn't offer no stupid notions. You'll get used to being in the deep and dark. You're of a size to be a good miner."

Lon shrugged his shoulders, afraid of saying something that might expose his irrational fears. Just the thought of hundreds of feet of rock over his head gave him the willies. He did not care how big the timbers were—every minute through the night he had expected them to fold like a paper fan.

He had to get out of here. Get out before they sucked him into the Shirt Tail scheme. Get out before the fleas carted him off as a special, untasted dessert.

"You'll like the Shirt Tail," said Braley. "Easy to get into, because there's no vertical shaft, and the entrance is visible for the whole length. There's no windlass and lift to bother with. We'll blast just once, to keep out the curious folks, and so we have rock to tote out when it's important they see us working like badgers."

If he had a good reason to leave, maybe he could slip away from these men without rousing their suspicions. "These shares in the mines?" he asked casually. "How do you buy and sell them?"

"Down at the exchange, or find someone with a certificate, pay him his price and have him endorse it."

"I know a man with fifty Shirt Tail shares," he said. The three men simultaneously stopped slapping fleas and mopping up molasses with the tag end of a flapjack. "I want to buy them before I write that report."

"Where?" they asked.

"Two or three days ago I met a fellow selling wildcat shares on the trail. This side of the pass. He offered me fifty shares of Shirt Tail."

"Did you get his name?" whispered Riddel.

"How much did he want?" Marron asked suspiciously. He leaned over and said something in Braley's ear, and Lon supposed he asked if they could really trust this new man.

"You'll miss tonight's shift in the mine," said Braley.

Lon shrugged. "Fifty shares of the Shirt Tail will be worth a lot more than four dollars. And owning them gives me a solid reason to write that report," he added, giving Braley a sidelong smile.

Braley slapped his thigh, whether out of agreement or to kill a flea, Lon couldn't tell. "You go get that fifty shares and all the profit from them's yours. We'll pay you two hundred dollars from our share to write the report. If you want to work the mine with us, we'll pay higher than the

Gould and Curry. Six dollars a day? That okay with you fellows?'' Riddel and Marron nodded their heads.

"How long will it take to get them shares?'' asked Marron, still suspicious.

"Four days, maybe five, I suppose,'' offered Lon, figuring the time he needed to ride to the bottom of the pass, find Moseley, then ride back to Virginia City. Except he wasn't coming back.

"By that time we'll be starting work in the Shirt Tail,'' said Braley.

"If we could just find out who has the last five, six hundred shares,'' mused Riddel, "we could swing a few trades before we start. Coming over the pass, did you meet anyone else who mentioned the Shirt Tail?''

"No,'' Lon said honestly, but he thought of drunken Harvey Saxton. Harvey Saxton would be rich for a few weeks, if the sot recalled he owned shares in the Shirt Tail. But the whole excitement might come and go, with the certificate unnoticed on Lindy's wall. The thought brought his own problem to the fore.

"I'm hunting a fellow named Harvey Saxton,'' he said.

"Saxton. How do you know Saxton? I thought you said you didn't know anyone hereabouts,'' said Braley, rearing back.

"I played poker with Saxton evening before last in Carson. He owes me some money.''

"You took Saxton's IOU?'' Riddel asked, his eyes big.

"Yeah, I suppose you could say that's what I did.'' The true story, of playing for the farm and Lindy, had not made it up the hill yet, judging by the men's reaction. When the tale circulated in Virginia, he'd be a laughingstock. He hoped no one would hear of how he'd put a hundred dollars in his saddlebags, with Saxton looking on.

"Saxton's in debt to so many people he quit the town a week or so ago, after his landlady took all his assay equipment for the back rent. More than one man in Virginia City considered attaching that land his wife has, down by the river, what he calls the ranch. But they found out it's not in Saxton's name at all. Old Will Merryman's too smart for him. I supposed Saxton'd go farther away than Carson, what with half of Virginia after him.''

"I asked after him in Carson, they said he'd come here. I intend to find him."

"Give it up. Won't do you no good," offered Braley. "Just a waste of time. You best be riding off to the pass to find that fellow with the Shirt Tail stock. I'll tell the clerks in the mine office that you had to take care of some personal business in Carson, but that I'm real impressed with your work, so's they'll hold a place for you. Just in case you want to try the Gould and Curry again."

Chapter Five

Lon stared, unbelieving, as the three miners spread their blankets on the floor amidst the fleas. He stamped his feet nervously.

"Thanks for the breakfast," he muttered. He turned on his heel, stretched his legs to full-length and bounded down the hill. At the bottom of the rocky stretch, out of sight of the cabin, he shook himself like a dog, beat his pants with his hands, took off his boots and pounded them on a rock to dislodge any tenacious fleas.

The horizon wavered. How long before he simply fell over from lack of sleep? Buckskin desperately needed a day of rest and decent food. But he and the horse must try to make it to the pass today.

He retraced the route to the Carson Valley. He could trust the horse to stay on the track, so occasionally he allowed his head to droop. Twice he did more than doze, and came close to falling out of the saddle. He paused at the junction with the trail leading to Lindy's place. Should he tell Lindy to hang on to the Shirt Tail certificate?

No, he decided, best not say a word. The quarrel between husband and wife might be a sham. Even if their differences were real, drunken husbands always promised to reform, and their wives let them come home. Lindy would innocently speak of the Shirt Tail, and Saxton would turn up at the mine and demand to be part of the swindle. Braley and his friends would know who had talked out of turn.

Besides, if he went to Lindy's place she might suppose he was interested in her. She might suppose he would murder her husband to get her. He rode on into Carson City to buy enough grub to last until he reached the California settlements.

Lindy raised the wooden gate at the head of her irrigation ditch, turning the water from the river into her cornfield. She frowned, studying where the water lapped against the stained boards. She had not marked the level on the gate, but the water seemed to be lower, as if the river had dropped several inches in just the past few days.

The water gushed down the ditch, a stream of light reflecting the early-morning sky. Lindy followed with her shovel, removing the clods and rocks that had fallen into the channel. Now that she thought about it, the river would naturally drop in the summer, as the snowpack on the mountains melted. Would it fall so low that no water flowed into her irrigation ditch?

She hiked back to the river and searched for some mark that showed the previous level. A slanting crack extended partway across one of the planks. Had the crack been visible five days ago? She didn't remember it, but then, she'd had no reason to notice.

She kicked at the dirt heaped along the ditch. Irrigating crops was more complicated than she'd thought. And not only the problem with the river.

Two weeks ago she'd found a broken stake marking the northern corner of the farm. She'd paced off her eighty acres and discovered the water gate lay at least fifty feet beyond the southern boundary. She had no idea who owned the land. Her upstream neighbors had never mentioned the course of her ditch. If the owner should turn up, demand rent for the trespass...

No sense worrying about who owned the land, because now the real threat was the inevitable drop of the river. The spring near the house watered her vegetable garden, but the corn depended upon the ditch from the river.

She stared down the length of the ditch; hard work, with shovel and pick, to deepen it. Each day the oats ripened, and they must be cut before the grain fell from the heads. The wheat would follow in a week or ten days. The haying must be done in the next month or six weeks. The sooner the better, before the grass had gone to seed. Harvest could not wait. But then, neither could the corn, thirsty under the high summer sun.

She sifted through all possible alternatives and, not for the first time, thought of Lon Anderson. He might be stupid, but it didn't take brains to dig a ditch. She imagined his long arms making the dirt fly.

She'd made a huge mistake, getting mad because Harvey had wagered her in a card game. She'd let her pride get in the way of logic. Anderson would be handy to have about for a few weeks. Let him imagine he owned the farm.

Then she remembered he hated the farm. He wanted a ranch, where he could ride around on his horse, giving orders to his *vaqueros*, like a plantation boss.

She shrugged. If she had taken Anderson in, he would have moved on in a day or two, after he learned the truth about the farm. He wouldn't dig her irrigation ditch, because he couldn't do that from the back of his beautiful horse. She'd be facing the same predicament....

If she had let him stay, would he have expected to come into her bedroom, touch her...? Lindy shivered.

What am I doing, standing about mooning over Lon Anderson?

She strode the length of the irrigation ditch, fishing out a rock here and there. The water rollicked far ahead of her, already spreading in the depressions between the corn stalks and the spreading pumpkin vines. She could not be in two places at the same time, and the demands of the wheat and the hay would collide in two weeks. If the river dropped an inch a day, her ditch would be dry in less than a month. She might cut the corn green for silage, but where was the time, with the hay and the wheat?

What had her grandfather done during harvest, on the farm in Ohio? In her mind she sat beside her grandfather at the dinner table, her grandmother across from her, and down the length of the table one, or three, or five hired men, and at threshing, ten or twelve, such a crowd they ate sitting on the grass beneath the spreading maple tree.

She had to hire a man to make the hay. She would cut the wheat, for rough handling might lose half the crop. But hay took only a strong back. The perfect job for someone like Lon Anderson. Why did she keep thinking of Lon Anderson?

"Because he's perfect," she said aloud. "He has more muscle than brains, and he works hard, and he'll take orders. I'll keep a lookout for Lon Anderson," she announced to a sprawling pumpkin vine.

What if he expects more than just pay and bed and board? asked the cautious part of her.

I'll be stern. I'll let him know, the first day, he's not to set foot in my room. I'll take a butcher knife to bed. Unless, unless...

The field of oats stretched before her, the sun reflecting in a golden sheen. Lindy was always surprised how much she enjoyed swinging a scythe. The hypnotic movement reminded her of a slow dance with a languid partner. Except it would be easier with two people. One person to cut, another to bundle the sheaves and stand them in the shocks. Definitely, she should not have been so eager to get rid of Lon Anderson. But would he be willing to tag behind her, bundling and stacking? She didn't need a picky man who complained about the tasks assigned him. Or a lazy man. The other morning, Anderson had worked steadily, until the job was done. His shirt pulled across his shoulders, and when he swung his arms the tail pulled above his belt. Store-bought shirts didn't fit his gigantic frame. He should order them specially made from a seamstress, or get a wife skilled with a needle.

Oats lay on the ground for twenty feet, unsheaved. Lindy shook herself angrily. Dreaming about Lon Anderson's shirts rather than doing her work properly! She dropped the scythe, gathered the long-stemmed oats together in a bundle that filled her arms, twisted one straw about the sheaf to hold it together, and dropped it on the ground. She would come back later in the day and build the shocks. Why did she keep thinking about a man who wouldn't do farm work?

"You stop! You stop that, Lindy Merryman! Get to work!"

She lifted the scythe into position, but it wobbled in her hands. The blade swung at an odd angle, cutting the stalks right below the sagging heads.

"What...?" she cried, just as the handle split. She stared in disbelief at the truncated piece of wood remaining in her hands. The rest of the handle lay on the ground, the long, curved blade catching the sunlight and reflecting it in her eyes.

"I should not think of Lon Anderson!" she cried. "I saw the crack in the handle. I should have put on a new handle before I ever started." She caught herself, and bit her lips. A bad habit, talking out loud with no one around. The consequences of living alone. The oats half cut, and she must go into Carson for a new handle. The whole day, wasted. If only there were two of her!

She picked up the pieces of the scythe, one in either hand, and set out for the house. She must take the wagon, since carrying a scythe handle on muleback was awkward.

She washed her face and hands at the springhouse, considered changing her broad-brimmed straw hat for a sunbonnet, but decided she'd wasted enough time already.

She let the mules laze along the road, for this should be their day of rest. Twice a week they hauled the loaded wagon up the hill to Virginia, three days a week she hitched them up to do work about the farm, but Wednesdays and Sundays, the days after the Virginia trip, they rested.

A disorganized horse auction spread across the central square of Carson City. "Look, look!" cried a man clinging to a spinning, bucking horse. "See his spirit! A real purebred Mexican Durango!"

"Purebred Mexican horse, spit!" Lindy muttered. The horse bounced sideways across the street, raising clouds of dust. The purebred Mexican Durango twisted and bucked. A terrified yelp and a massive cloud of dust told her the rider hadn't managed to stick aboard. The horse dashed south, careening from one side of the street to the other, heading for the outskirts of town. He reared when he saw Lindy's mules, and avoided a collision by twisting in mid-air and tearing back toward the square. Two mounted men dashed after the renegade. Lindy swung onto a side street and pulled up at the rear of McCaffrey's store.

She lifted a block of wood from the wagon, dropped it in front of the lead mule and set about tying down his bridle.

"You can't leave that wagon here. You're blocking traffic," said an authoritative voice attempting to be a baritone. Deputy Clugg stepped out of the passageway between McCaffrey's store and Pryor's Saloon. "You're blocking McCaffrey's back door."

"Blocking traffic!" she exclaimed. "Horses running wild in the square and tearing off down the main street, and you order my mules out of an alley?"

"The horse auction's important business," he shouted, forgetting to control his voice, and it screeched above the tenor range. He took one step toward her. "Men's business, that's what's going on in the square. And with the auction out front, all the more reason you can't impede traffic to McCaffrey's back—"

"Look, Clugg, you misjudged me when you came out to the house. You're not the first man to think ill of a woman because she's alone, so can't we just forget it and—"

"Forget, hell!" yelled Clugg, now a soprano. "Big, clumsy woman! You didn't throw me down no stairs. You ran into me and I overbalanced. And you did it intentionally!"

"Leave her alone, Clugg," said McCaffrey from the doorway. "She's a good customer and won't stay longer than necessary. I don't mind her wagon at my back door."

"She'll...she'll get talking to your missus. Women always do. She's creating a public nuisance...." Clugg's voice wavered into every tone of the scale.

McCaffrey waved him off. "Get out of here, Deputy. You're costing me a sale." Lindy finished tying the mule and eyed Clugg, who finally took one reluctant step back into the passageway, then another. In town he did not come near her. Lindy figured he kept his distance because the top of his head reached her mouth, and having to look up at her made him feel less deputylike.

"Clugg's still smarting from you throwing him down your stairs?" said McCaffrey, making it only half a question.

"I guess. I need a new scythe handle."

"A scythe handle?" repeated McCaffrey. "Now, I know I've got one about somewheres." He lifted his eyes to the ceiling and the jungle of merchandise suspended there. Lindy joined the search, but found looking straight up for more than a few seconds caused a crick in her neck. She leaned over the counter to touch a bolt of Turkey red broadcloth and left McCaffrey to search for the handle.

She'd have no time to sew until winter. How would Lon look in a shirt of Turkey red broadcloth? The front door opened and closed. Mr. McCaffrey spun slowly, examining the upper reaches of the store.

"How you getting on with your new husband, Lindy?" he asked, his back to her.

She did not look at Mr. McCaffrey, for a boyish face framed by a horse collar claimed all her attention. He would look fine in Turkey red.

"He looks like a right strapping young fellow," continued McCaffrey, "and of a size for you. I don't see it in here. Could be that I put all the big handles in the shed back on the alley." Lon Anderson pushed aside a length of chain, stepped into the restricted open space in front of the counter. He blushed across his cheekbones, in a color that almost matched the broadcloth.

Lindy smiled at the rising color on Anderson's cheeks, frowned when she felt her own cheeks warm. She put a hand to her face and wished she had changed into her sunbonnet, so she might hide in its depths.

"Oh," said McCaffrey, completing his turn, only momentarily discomfited. "So you're here together. Glad to see it's working out. I'll go look in the shed." He trotted out the back door.

"What are you doing here?" Lindy asked, tapping the toe of her boot nervously. He should not have come to Carson, for everyone chuckled at the wager of wife and farm. *Why should I care if he's teased?* "I thought you intended to find work in a mine."

"I did. I got a job at the Gould and Curry." He looked down at the floor, and the russet coloring sank a bit lower, toward his neck. She liked a clean-shaven man. Virginia City miners tended to cultivate elaborate beards.

"The Gould and Curry's in Virginia, not down here," she snapped. Her arm muscles ached because she held her elbows tight against her rib cage, lest she ram into him in the cramped space. She hated being in the same room with him. Maybe she should go help McCaffrey search for the scythe handle.

"I work the night shift. I'm running an errand for a friend, besides hunting for that no-good husband of yours to get my $135."

"He's not in Virginia?" she asked, so surprised she forgot about her warm cheeks, forgot to keep her arms tense. Where had Harvey gone, if not back to Virginia City? She needed him to stick around, for he'd surely have to sign some papers in the matter of the divorce.

"Not that I can find."

"You just didn't look hard enough. Virginia's growing so much this summer, it's getting to be a real city."

"Did he come to the farm?" he asked sternly. He lifted his head, his jaw thrust forward, radiating suspicion. Did he suppose she had Harvey tucked away in the chicken coop? She wasn't accustomed to looking up at men. The crick in her neck returned. She stepped back so she could adjust her head to a more comfortable angle, and ran into the mackintosh.

"He's out there, isn't he?" he accused.

"Harvey knows better than to come around the farm. I'm done with him." His eyes were a color between brown and green. An autumnal color. Or the color of a tree sick with the blight. Trouble, just like Nora Dove warned. *I don't believe in that silly crystal ball.* But here he stood, trouble, right in front of her. Six feet and five or six inches of trouble.

"I hope you're enjoying Virginia City," she said to fill the gap of silence between them.

"Enjoy!" he exclaimed. His eyes blazed around the edges of the pupils, a green flame, the color that sometimes shows right at the base of a hot fire. "Nevada Territory is one hell of a place. The first men I meet try to sell me worthless mining stocks. Next, I'm cheated in a poker game, a woman asks me to kill her husband, I suppose so she can put his head up on a pole. I'm nearly run down on the streets of Virginia by a crowd of folks dodging the bullets of a fellow shooting out windows—"

"That was a joke," she cried. He did not pay any attention to her protest.

"Virginia's full of scarlet women in yellow dresses who'll take a man's pay, and swindlers lurk about, promoting holes in the ground as silver mines...."

"Bennett Hill?" she asked.

"No, I didn't meet a man named Bennett Hill. Is he your choice for a second husband?" he jeered. "A juggler of mining stocks? He'll not have any qualms about murdering Harvey Saxton for you, I don't suppose."

"That was a joke," she said quickly, snatching at the chance to get a word in. "I told you before, but you don't pay any heed. Bennett Hill's a mine, not a man. Nora Dove put a piece of the ore the promoters showed off beside her crystal ball, and she saw in the crystal ball the word of the spirits that the ore didn't come from the Bennett Hill at all, but from the Yellow Jacket, in a bucket, so she warned the miners that the whole promotion's a cheat and told them to sell their shares." She stopped for breath.

"Crystal ball?" She could tell by his quizzical look that she'd lost him somewhere between killing Harvey and the Bennett Hill.

"Nora Dove tells fortunes," she explained, "in a ball of rock clear as glass." He threw back his head and laughed, exposing a mouth full of strong, white teeth. His head bumped a coil of chain, which swung against a string of skillets, which rang against the washbasins, so that his laughter joined in a great cacophony. She stepped backward in the face of this ridicule, and the mackintosh slithered to the floor.

"You believe that nonsense?" he sputtered through his laughter. "An old gypsy, telling fortunes?"

"She's not an old gypsy. I didn't believe it," she snapped, "until she told my future yesterday, and she saw you in that ball, and said you were nothing but trouble for me. So you stand clear, unless you intend to behave properly. And please, if you're going to beat up Harvey because he owes you money, don't leave him crippled, so I have to take care of him for the rest of his life. A woman can't morally divorce a crippled-up man."

Well, that shut him up! Or maybe he didn't say anything because McCaffrey walked in at that moment. "I put the scythe handle in your wagon, Lindy," he said.

"I'd better go look at it," she said, glad for an excuse to get out of range of Lon's eyes. "I don't want one already split and dry, one that'll break the first swing."

McCaffrey followed her out the door, mumbling that no one in Nevada Territory trusted anyone else, which she thought just about summed it up. The scythe handle gleamed in the sun, smooth and well sanded, and she felt a trifle ashamed at mistrusting McCaffrey. But with Anderson in the room she'd had no choice but to run.

"Put it on my account," she said. She untied the mules, climbed to the wagon box and circled back to the main street to head home. As the mules trotted by the front of McCaffrey's, she glimpsed Lon Anderson through the single window. An impressive man. Not handsome, exactly, but a fine-looking man. She imagined those bulging arms swinging a scythe. But then, if she married him, he would insist upon always swinging the scythe, and tell her to follow behind, bundling the sheaves and building the shocks. That was the danger in taking a husband. If a woman married a strong, upright man, he took over her life and left her following around behind. And if she found a husband willing to let her be the boss, he'd probably have a weakness for liquor, or dabble in mine frauds.

Then she remembered—again—that Lon Anderson wanted nothing to do with a farm. Just as well; she didn't need a husband. But then again, being without a man had its drawbacks, mostly at night. She imagined Lon Anderson naked, in her bed. Was he big there, too? Her cheeks warmed and she knew they'd grown very red, but no other man or woman rode along the rutted trail to her farm, so instead of regretting the lack of her sunbonnet, she lifted her face to the sun and grinned.

Lon found McCaffrey staring at him, as if he didn't expect to find him still standing in his store.

"You're not going with her?" he asked, jerking his thumb toward the back door and the spot where Lindy's mules and wagon had stood.

"No, that didn't work out."

"Too bad. Lindy's a nice lady. Everyone in town's got mighty fond of her since she moved onto the farm this spring. She's not divorcing Saxton?"

"She says she is."

"Then you'd better move your tail if you want her. Don't put it off, for there're men about who'll cut you off. Brave lady," he added thoughtfully, "to stay out on the place by herself." Lon considered saying that any woman six feet tall who swung a rifle with Lindy's cool confidence did not have to worry about being alone on a farm. He kept his mouth shut. "What can I do for you?" asked McCaffrey.

Lon rattled off the list of things he needed before he set out for California. Crackers, cheese, a small slab of bacon, some dried apples.

"Sounds as if you're heading out on a trip," said McCaffrey. "Going prospecting?"

"Sort of," murmured Lon. In a few days Braley and Riddel and Marron would stop in Carson, inquiring after their erstwhile partner. McCaffrey could say truthfully that Anderson had bought provisions for several days. He'd have a better chance at getting clean away if McCaffrey could say, "Anderson's gone prospecting in the desert ranges."

He rolled his provisions up in his blankets and set out south, toward the pass. The sun glared hot enough to melt tallow, and the road turned to ankle-deep sand. Lon let Buckskin plod along slowly. Sleep tugged at him in persuasive waves; at times he could barely sit upright. Where the trail turned into the canyon he gave up the struggle and sought out the campsite by the river where he had bedded down just a few days ago. The wind had obliterated the mark his blanket had made in the sand, and a faint yellow tinted the green of the meadow on the other side of the stream.

The green of his optimism had certainly yellowed during the few days he'd spent in Nevada. He had ridden down the pass full of confidence, certain that in this new country he could build a prosperous future. Instead, he'd found the 'regs of America, failures from every state, stranded like :caying fish upon the Comstock Ledge. Cowards from >th North and South who fled the war, gamblers, drunk- :ds, petty thieves—and some not so petty—and the /omen they brought with them. Men willing to commit .ny crime or ponder any villainous transaction that prom- sed quick wealth.

He would ride back to the ranch, confess his failure and ask for his job back. His old comrades and the owner would laugh at him, as they had laughed at his dreams when he set out. Land of his own, cattle, a wife and family. Only people with money dared have such aspirations, not bob- tails like himself. He'd confess they were right, and go back to chasing cattle for someone else. And be satisfied with the women who smiled at him on payday.

He laughed aloud, bitterly, surprising Buckskin, who cropped nubbins of grass along the edge of the river. The horse raised its head, stared at him.

"No, old hoss," he said, "there's no ranch and no wife

for us here, is there? Just a woman with a starvation farm and poison-bottle eyes.'' Except today, in McCaffrey's store, her eyes had shone a different shade of blue, dark, almost black. When she blushed beneath her tan, the skin on her cheeks glowed like a late-ripening apple.

He reared up, shocked at this mellow vision of Lindy. She had, he reminded himself, asked him to murder her husband, and if now she protested she'd said the words in jest, she lied to draw him back for another round of robbery. Even supposing she was honest, that eighty acres would grind her husband into the sand, until he shrank into a dried-up medicine-show mummy. As spindly as a skeleton, and then she'd use him for a scarecrow.

He fell asleep before the sun left Carson Valley, and woke in the dark, leaning against an aspen tree, stiff and cold. He'd dreamed he stood in freezing water. He thrashed about blindly to find his blankets, curled up in them messily and dreamed of slender fingers, slicing bread. The knife disappeared, and the fingers dropped to his thigh.

Chapter Six

Lon broke a thin film of morning ice on a shallow pool at the edge of the river. Late June, he marveled, and at the foot of the mountains the temperature dropped below freezing. What a strange country! Had Lindy's vegetables been nipped by the cold snap? He hated to think of those flourishing potato plants leveled by frost.

He built a small fire, cooked his bacon by twisting it around a green stick, and repacked his gear into the smallest bundle possible. He stretched, yawned and congratulated himself on recovering from the night in the Gould and Curry. Buckskin frisked a bit before the saddle went on. The horse looked better for the grazing and rest. They might make it all the way over the pass today, all the way beyond the camp at Strawberry, past the ragged peddlers and the job seekers toiling to Virginia City.

A mile into Hope Valley a kid came dashing out of a grove of trees.

"Mister?" A subdued, uncertain hail. The boy was maybe eight, no more than ten. Was he out here all alone?

"Mister, could you help us? Please?" He didn't cry, but he looked like he wanted to.

"What's wrong?" The boy shook his head, controlled

his wavering chin and pointed into the tangle of brush, boulders and trees along the stream.

"Does someone need help?" Lon asked.

"Ma, she ain't well, and Pa, he fell. We come over the mountains, there." He pointed toward the towering granite cliff in the distance. Lon slid off the horse and followed the boy down a sandy path. He was the "oldest" child Lon had ever seen. Some great weight of troubles had aged him beyond his years. His cheeks flaunted none of the rosy flush of childhood; his narrow gray eyes appeared weary.

A rickety, dried-out wagon leaned against a huge boulder. The wheels had shrunk until the iron tires barely hung on. A bit toward the stream grazed three of the skinniest oxen Lon had ever seen, the skinniest he had ever seen standing on their feet, anyway. A man heaved himself off a rock. He supported himself with a stick, held a foot bound with rags off the ground.

"Thank God! Someone stopped," he cried. "Ma, we got help here!" A moan came from the wagon. "We stopped a week ago because the wife come down sick, and me and the boy done okay, until I fell off a rock a-tryin' to catch a fish." He pointed to the foaming creek, then to his useless leg.

"We got no cornmeal left," said the boy, more to the point.

"You heading for California or for Nevada Territory?" asked Lon.

"The mines," explained the man. "My brother, he's out on the Reese River?" His voice rose strangely on the final words, making the statement a question. "He said for us to come, he's putting up a store out there, and got work for me. Go get the letter, Billy," he added weakly. The man sank down on the rock and lowered his head. The boy tramped stolidly toward the wagon, and since the man didn't seem in the mood for conversation, Lon fell in behind him.

Billy stopped, spun around suddenly and glared. "My ma's sick," he said. Lon nodded, stepped back a few feet. A strange man shouldn't intrude upon a sick woman. Her illness might be some female thing. Billy climbed up on the splintered tongue, reached into the wagon. "That's okay, Ma," he said soothingly. "We got help now."

The boy held out a crumpled sheet of paper for Lon's perusal. The penciled words were barely legible. Lon saw "Reese River" written at the head of the page, and handed the letter back to the boy.

"I'm bound west," he explained.

"How far to the next camp?" asked the man.

"A mile to Hope Valley, and six or seven to Woodfords on down the canyon," said Lon. "Woodfords would be the best place to get help." He eyed the kid. "Can he make it?"

"Sure can, mister!" said the boy. His eyes lit up, only a subdued spark, but at least he'd not given up completely. Lon admired his spunk.

Lon walked back to Buckskin and pretended to remove something from the bedroll, while his hand actually opened the flap on the back side of his belt. He had fifty-five dollars, and food to last until he got to the Central Valley. He'd return to California with the amount of money he'd brought. No Shirt Tail shares. No ties to Nevada Territory. He caressed the twenty-dollar gold piece between his fingers before he slipped it into his pocket.

"Here, boy," he ordered. The kid came running, nearly stumbled, but recovered himself. He stared at Lon with his old eyes. "Hold out your hand."

The boy had been doing so much hard work he had calluses, and bruises and cuts showed along the sides of his right hand. A little blood streaked across the palm. When the kid saw the coin he began blubbering.

"Stop crying, son. Be brave. You walk down this trail until you see some buildings right along the road, you understand." The boy nodded, excited now, with a flame like a candle showing in his eyes. "You get some food, but not more than you need for a day or two. And don't stuff your belly, or you'll get sick. You ask the men there to come and help your folks down the trail, to a farm in the valley where they can settle for a spell and recruit your oxen."

"Yes, sir! Thank you, sir!"

Lon mounted his horse, rejoined the trail without a backward glance, without acknowledging the chorus of thankyous and God bless yous. But his chest swelled, hearing the repeated cries of gratitude.

He sat a bit straighter in the saddle, the way a man sits who's helped the weak and needy. A man's duty required him to share with those less fortunate, and life was better when a man did his duty. That, he supposed, was the value of a wife and children. With a family, a man concentrated on sharing, on doing his duty.

Since he had run off from the farm in Indiana, his life had lacked a center. He thought about his mother and his sisters and his little brother. He'd left them with no one to provide, except his snarling father or his righteous grandfather. He never should have abandoned them.

"But," he said in justification, "at sixteen a man's not yet a man. Sixteen-year-olds are selfish, and think only of themselves. They let their own desires rule their lives, and overcome duty." Never again! If he ever got land, a house, a herd, if he ever got a wife, he'd care for her.

For some unfathomable reason, the mental picture of his little sister turned into Lindy. Lindy, buying a new handle for a scythe. Where he came from, women didn't swing scythes. Why did she need a scythe? He remembered—two acres of oats. A woman should not do that kind of work. But then, a woman shouldn't wear trousers. Lindy of the dark blue eyes, which in the sunshine had the highlights of a poison bottle. Lindy, who wanted her husband dead to save her the trouble of a divorce. Lindy, apple cheeked and a bit pretty when she smiled.

A sign pointed up a spur road to the lake. Why not? He'd seen the sheet of blue-gem water from the pass. Should he ever travel back East, he'd want to brag about standing on the shore of famous Lake Bigler. No, Tahoe they called it now, since Bigler was no longer governor of California.

He might even stay the night at the lake—camping, of course, not at the fancy hotel built for the rich travelers from San Francisco, and the mine owners from the Comstock. By Jupiter! The Lake House! There he'd spread the word about the exhausted family stranded on the trail. The men at the hotel could put together a purse to help them get to Reese River.

He turned toward Lake Tahoe, virtue swelling his chest and providing a splendid sense of his superiority over the men he'd left behind in Nevada Territory. A virtuous man didn't belong in a place like Nevada.

A stagecoach stood before the largest building at Lake House; hostlers led away six steaming horses; three fresh teams tossed their heads in the corral, ready to take their places before the coach. What an opportunity! The men who could afford stage fare from Sacramento to Virginia City were eating their dinner.

Lon ignored his coat, which he had tied behind the saddle, and dashed up the front steps two at a time, pulling off his gloves. No time to waste, for the stage stopped for only fifteen or twenty minutes. He rushed, spurs ringing, across the broad veranda. Halfway through the lobby—his eyes briefly noted the crystal chandelier and the dark wainscoting—a man in a red jacket blocked his way. The gentleman's striped trousers looked brand-new, and he wore a spotless white shirt beneath a black vest.

"Yes? Is there something I can do for you, sir?" he asked haughtily. His eyes coursed from Lon's hat to his boots, and back up again. Lon self-consciously pulled at the sleeves of his ragged, dusty shirt, trying to make them cover his wrist bones. He flipped his gloves against his thigh to restore his determination. Hardly properly attired for the Lake House, but attire be hanged when people were hungry!

"There's a family needs help," he began firmly, "on the old emigrant trail. The woman's sick, the man's hurt his leg and can hardly walk, and the boy, not more than ten years old, is trying to do a man's job. Someone should go…" The man's eyes narrowed.

"Did you see the sick woman?" he asked.

"No, she's not able to get out of the wagon."

"And the boy? Looked a bit strange, didn't he? A bit old for a boy somehow?"

"Yes." How did he know?

"And the boy's pa claimed he'd fallen while fishing, to get food for his family?"

Where had he learned this? The family hadn't passed by Lake House if they'd traveled over the mountains by the emigrant trail.

"Yes. The poor kid has carried the load…" The red-coated man ceased paying any attention. He walked hurriedly to a door at the rear of the lobby.

"Reg, sounds like the Miller gang's out on the road again," he yelled. "A man here saw them…" He turned back to Lon. "When?"

"This morning. A couple hours ago."

"Better send word to Carson by the stage," Red Coat shouted. A bearded man in a frock coat stepped through the door, presumably Reg. He carried himself with military dignity; Red Coat gave a little bobbing bow of his head, letting Lon know who was boss.

"On the old emigrant route," continued Red Coat. "This man saw them."

"I hope, sir, you did not offer them succor," said Reg.

"I...I gave the boy some money, sir, to buy food for his father and mother," Lon stuttered.

"Your bad judgment," snapped Red Coat. "They're a gang of thieves."

"But I saw them," Lon cried. "The man had hurt his leg falling in the creek—"

"But you didn't see the woman, right?" Reg asked, addressing the question at the ceiling, not at Lon, and leaving no time for an answer. "The woman does not exist. Just another man who hides in the wagon and moans. Three skinny oxen? Am I right?" Lon nodded, misery gripping his bowels. "The 'boy' isn't a boy at all, but a dwarf named Wilson Miller. He's the leader of the gang, the smart one. They stay in one location for only a few hours, for fear of the law. The trick isn't new. They hide out along the river below the canyon. When did you see them?"

"Early. Just after sunrise."

"You gave them money?"

"Twenty dollars," said Lon, managing to make the words something other than a groan. He hoped he sounded like a man who could afford to lose twenty dollars. Like a man who still had five or six gold pieces in his pocket.

"There's little use sending someone to flush them out now. All we'd find is the rickety wagon, and with the trees and grass so dry, we'd dare not burn it," said Reg. "They flit all over the territory. But we'll notify the authorities in Carson, although not much good it will do. Sheriff Tipson had them once and let the dwarf go, because he's so good at pretending to be a little boy! And he's the damned leader!"

"Sorry, sir," said Red Coat, turning to Lon. "It is most unfortunate that you should be so discommoded. Please do not judge our mountain resort by the behavior of ruffians. Did you desire to take dinner?" He waved toward a double door, through which Lon glimpsed white-covered tables and crystal goblets.

"No." Twenty dollars stolen from him! He must squeeze every cent to get home to California. Red Coat lifted a hand to his forehead in an informal salute of dismissal.

The long veranda faced the lake, wooden chairs with woven willow seats scattered here and there. Lon sank into one of the chairs, wondering what organ of his body had been gouged out and thrown away. Empty! What a hell of a place Nevada Territory had proved to be! Living here was like dancing the polka across a floor covered with rattlesnakes.

Children who weren't children, miners who plotted bogus mining schemes to manipulate the stock exchange, women who married and divorced without a thought for next week, let alone next year. Gamblers who put worthless paper on the table, with no intention of standing by their IOUs, whores who gave no thought to men dying within fifty feet...

The whore in the yellow dress! She'd bragged about entertaining a man who would not come up to his belt buckle. Was this Miller dwarf the man who'd lain with her that night? The image of the boy, the boy-man, cavorting with a whore sickened him. What a hell of a place! He groaned out loud.

"Is there some way I may help you, my good man?" said a voice so close to his ear he jumped and fell forward, out of the chair. He scrambled onto his hands and knees.

Directly in front of his eyes stood a pair of brand-new boots. As he raised his head, he saw a ragged suit, a full beard and a sagging leather hat, which the man pulled off politely, thus showing the large bite taken from the rear of the brim.

"I've been of assistance to more strangers than any man in Nevada Territory," he continued. "Name's Moseley. Why, I've been in Washoe so long, I knew Mr. Comstock, and I stood by when one of Mr. Comstock's mules up on Mount Davidson—"

"Kicked aside a clod and thus discovered the Comstock Lode," completed Lon, scrambling to his feet.

"We've met?" asked Moseley, clearly astonished.

"I came over the pass last Sunday," said Lon. "You tried to sell me some worthless mining stock. I didn't buy then, and you needn't try now."

"I have none to offer," Moseley said briskly. "A gentleman riding through on Monday, post meridiem, purchased every certificate I possessed, a bargain at only seventy dollars plus a bit of gold for the lot, making it possible for me to become reshod, and to take my dinner today at Lake House. I have nothing at all to offer you, for stock certificates of promise are more difficult to come by than you might imagine. You're not bound back to California, abandoning our fair territory?" he asked suspiciously.

"Yes. Nevada Territory's hell, the very center of evil on this earth, I do believe."

"Whatever led you to that conclusion?" Moseley burst out. "I should think a man of your youth and obvious good health would find the silver mines the very center of opportunity."

"Opportunity to shine the last dollar from a greenhorn." Lon heard his own voice, a snarl, but didn't make any attempt to soften it. "Opportunity to murder a man because a woman finds him inconvenient, plot a scheme that will impoverish a dozen men, so three may profit? If that's the opportunity in Nevada Territory, I want no part of it."

"Why not? Please sir, let us sit down and discuss this matter rationally." Lon allowed Moseley to lead him to a chair. Moseley pulled up another and straddled it, facing him. "Are these trifling dishonesties not pursued in other states and territories of the Union, friend? Are the older settlements free of chicanery and deceit? Just because you encountered a selection of Nevada's scoundrels, who, I remind you, all came from someplace else..."

Everyone in Nevada came from someplace else. Lon let

Moseley babble on while he considered this remark. Was he the only man who crossed the Sierra seeking honest work? Was Nevada Territory nothing but a gathering of thieves, who stole from one another?

"...and, you must admit, the gathering of miscreants in Washoe and Virginia City contributes to the vitality of the nation, for with Nevada drawing a concentration of the dishonest, it relieves the eastern states of maintaining jails to contain them while their armies wage a costly war against the forces..."

Moseley proposed a novel idea! Ship the criminal class to the frontier, so they caused no bother in the eastern states. Nevada contributed to the war against rebellion by containing the felons.

"It has ever been so upon the frontier," continued Moseley. "In the old days I saw men robbed of the very ground upon which they stood, their claim stakes freshly laid, land that later paid millions. Yes, millions of dollars, taken from a vein that once bore the mark of an old prospector's pick. But has he complained? No, sir, he has gone forth, into the heart of the desert itself..."

If everyone in Nevada was a thief, why shouldn't he become one, as well? Just temporarily, of course. But in the dog-eat-dog atmosphere of Virginia City, he could school himself to be the meanest cur about. Why not take advantage of other men, when the crime only robbed a cheat? Was stealing from a thief a sin?

"You sold the shares in the—" Lon swallowed the words. Inquiring about the Shirt Tail would reveal the forthcoming activity on the exchange. He rephrased the question. "You sold all the certificates you had?"

"Every one, to a single gentleman who longed to invest the money he'd won by the sweat of his brow in the silver future of the great state of Nevada, for mark my words, Washington cannot long ignore the fortune in precious metals, and withhold statehood...."

"Was this gentleman bound east or west?"

"West, sir. He traveled to California, expecting to double and treble his money on the exchange in San Francisco, when the true nature of the Comstock and the Reese River deposits becomes better known in that metropolis. Someday, sir, someday this lake will be surrounded by the pleasure palaces of the wealthy, the men who invest their money and energies in unearthing the glorious treasures beneath Nevada's mountains." Moseley waved his arms about and shook his head, setting his hat to flopping like a slow bat. "If silver shows in such a barren spot as the Reese River, sir, where else in the desert may we not find ledges of pure metal? Someday, here where we stand, gold will flow like..."

The Shirt Tail certificate on Lindy's wall hung either the second or third from the bottom in the second row from the window. A distinctive certificate, easy to identify, with an engraving of a miner holding up a nugget, his mouth open wide as if he shouted in triumph, his shirttail flapping in the wind. He could move the bottom certificate up, and she would not notice right away. Possibly not for several weeks.

A mine certificate has to be endorsed to the buyer by the seller, Lon reminded himself. Would Saxton sign away his shares in the Shirt Tail, assuming he could be found? In Lon's mental picture of Lindy's cabin, the box in the corner shifted into focus. The box with the key in the lock and the marriage certificate inside, the paper where Saxton's signature testified to his vow to "have and to hold, till death us do part."

"Or, if not death, the Nevada territorial court," Lon muttered. He smiled, but not at Moseley.

Lon stopped on his way down the canyon to search out the distressed "family," hoping he might bully the dwarf into returning his twenty dollars. But as the man at Lake

House had foreseen, he found only the rickety wagon where the family had "camped" that morning—the wagon and a pile of warm embers marking the spot where the fire had lain. Lon rekindled the flame and cooked some bacon to add relish to his dry crackers.

By the time he reached the lower end of the canyon, evening spread across the Carson Valley from west to east. Shadows engulfed the foot of the mountains long before the sun vanished from the peaks in the distance. He stopped at Woodfords, bought an overpriced tin of peaches, then rode to the campsite overlooking the yellowing meadow. He pried the tin open with his knife and ate all the peaches as his supper, and as a celebration.

"A man condemned to hell will make bargains with the devil to escape," Lon announced to Buckskin, beginning the logical analysis of his fall from grace. "Nevada Territory resembles hell more than any place I've ever been."

Braley had offered him two hundred dollars to impersonate a mining expert and forge a report. And, if he could shake his aversion to being underground, six dollars a day for working in the Shirt Tail. Now, if, on top of that, he owned one hundred shares of Shirt Tail, and the stock went to ten dollars a share during the excitement, he would have over a thousand dollars! Maybe close to fifteen hundred if he could stand to work in the tunnel.

All that money for a few days of dishonesty!

This very spot would make a fine ranch. He thought of the cattle he would buy in California, and drive over the mountains to the meadow across the river. In the failing light he peered across the stream, searching out a level spot above the threat of flood where he might build his cabin, a spot where the snow...

"First thing," he said aloud, "I dare not show my face around Carson and Virginia." The poker game in Carson had called attention to him already. McCaffrey could identify him, and Lindy, and every man he'd gambled with.

Did Lindy lock her house when she went to Virginia? He could not recall any proper locks on the doors. What if neighbors saw him riding to her house? Other farms lay along that road. What excuse could he give to a suspicious neighbor? Why would he, logically, go to Lindy's place?

Lon rubbed his hands together, the plot unfolding. He would need new clothes. Just down the valley the town of Genoa boasted a store and saloon. Buy a few things early in the morning, so as few people as possible saw his face.

Saturday, when Lindy hauled her produce to Virginia City, he would steal the certificate. That meant two days of hanging out here on the river. But Buckskin could surely use the rest and the grazing. He'd spend the time exploring the river and the meadow, seeing exactly where he'd stake his claim.

He stretched out his legs and wondered how he would feel playing the part of a mendacious thief and swindler for the next week or two. Was it a good feeling, taking advantage of others? Did a man become habituated to crime?

No, he decided, no danger to a man who had a basically moral nature. Two weeks of crime; afterward, Harlon Anderson, respected landowner, on a homestead close enough to the emigrant trail that he could watch out for a family passing by, one with a dainty daughter...well, dainty didn't matter so much, just so she possessed a pleasant manner, and made light bread as good as Lindy's.

Lon stuffed his bedroll and extra gear in a clump of willows near the river—hidden, but in a convenient spot, ready to snatch up and tie onto his saddle when he had the Shirt Tail certificate rolled up under his vest. He hated leaving his gear behind, but a bedroll didn't fit in with his role of a gentleman calling upon a lady.

He cut cross-country to the Carson City road, east toward the river. He rode through Lindy's gate bold as brass, not caring who might see him. He had washed his trousers in the river, beaten the dust from his hat and coat, and cleaned his boots and polished them with a little lard he'd begged of a woman in Genoa. His new shirt of blue-and-white-striped chambray almost fit, the sleeves just a bit too short. A new red kerchief circled his neck. He had only a tiny mirror, the one he used to shave, so he stopped long enough to study his reflection in a calm pool at the edge of the river. Fine enough to make his excuse plausible, if the neighbors happened by. The story should wiggle him through any inquiry, although he rather hoped he'd not have to lie.

Lie all you want, he reminded himself. The next two weeks you're a hell-bent thief, a shameful miscreant. The king of the Washoe bad men!

Lindy's rooster hunched on the roof of the chicken coop; speckled hens pecked around the yard. Far in the distance the reddish brown cows grazed a few feet apart, and beyond them the sheep clustered. He had rounded the corner of the house before he noticed the mules in the pasture. *The mules should not be here!* cried an alarm in his head. *They're pulling the wagon to Virginia City!*

The wagon sat in front of the corral, the tongue propped up on a block of wood.

"Hello," she yelled. "What are you doing down the mountain?"

Chapter Seven

She sat on the back steps, her trousered legs spread apart, a white flour sack draped over them to give her a lap. Every bit of blood in Lon's body turned to ice and his heart quivered, wondering where it had vanished to. His stomach turned several flip-flops before it, too, froze into place, in a very awkward position.

A basket of unshelled peas sat beside her on the stoop. She wore dark gray trousers and a blue shirt and no shoes. He had never seen feet so big on a woman. Lon slid off Buckskin, putting the horse between him and Lindy. He jogged his static mind, searching for something to say, cursing inwardly that he had prepared a speech to explain his presence to the neighbors, but not to Lindy herself.

"I...I wasn't sure I'd find you at home," he finally stammered.

"I went up the hill yesterday. The Fourth of July's not the day to take a wagonload of produce into Virginia City."

The Fourth of July! He had paid absolutely no attention to the calendar. In fact, the last time he remembered seeing a calendar... May, maybe? Was it July already?

"I...I suppose," he quavered, "they have quite a celebration on the Fourth of July."

"Absolutely wonderful! This year there's to be a horse

race, and the fire companies will parade, and Governor Nye's coming from Carson City to read the Declaration of Independence from the balcony of the new International Hotel. And one of the newspaper reporters has written an epic poem that he'll read.''

''A heap of fun,'' Lon agreed unwillingly.

''And after dark they'll shoot off fireworks.''

The abyss yawned before him, he mentally measured its width and depth, and could find no clear detour. He damned himself for digging the trap himself. A man did not come calling on a woman all gussied up in a new shirt and kerchief unless he intended to socialize. He regretted the blue striped shirt. Even more he regretted the red kerchief knotted around his neck, but she had seen it, and taking it off would only call more attention to it. He walked to the steps and pulled off his hat. He gulped and forced the lies out between his teeth. Lies bigger than any he'd intended to tell. His throat closed. Maybe he wasn't cut out to be a mendacious thief.

''I was wondering—'' he choked and coughed ''—would you accompany me to Virginia City to enjoy the holiday? I thought to attend myself, but it's more fun with…a friend along.''

Her face lit up like lightning flashing in the darkest night. She clapped her hands together. The flour sack drooped, sending shelled peas bouncing down the steps. Good Lord! She was going to accept!

She calmed down suddenly, and put on a ladylike front.

''Why, how nice of you to ask me, Mr. Anderson. I so wanted to go, but I didn't think it quite proper for a lady in that crowd alone. The respectable women in Virginia City have husbands, and the ones that don't aren't any better than they should be, you understand, and I wouldn't want anyone to think I'm one of them.''

''Of course not,'' he said, nearly strangled. Why couldn't she be too busy? A multitude of things needed doing around the farm at this very minute. Why, from where he stood he could see that the roof over the porch sagged because it lacked a center post, the pipe on the cookstove should stick one length higher above the ramada roof, the rail fence of the pigpen leaned on one corner, probably because the lower rails had dry rot.

But this irresponsible woman intended to accept his invitation, and go gadding off to Virginia City! He would have this big woman in trousers hanging on his arm all day. Talk about making himself conspicuous! And at exactly the time when he should stay out of sight.

By now the tale of the card game must have coursed along the Virginia City grapevine. Being seen with Lindy announced clearly that he'd been the sucker in the game.

I'll take her to some inconspicuous bar on a back street and buy her a beer. Maybe that woman she spoke of on A Street can give us dinner. Perhaps we can climb Mount Davidson. Great idea! Avoid the town altogether.

"I'd love to go, Mr. Anderson. It's so very nice of you to ask. Think of you riding all the way down the mountain to seek out my company!" Worse and worse! He'd have to lie about working in the mine.

"Please call me Lon. That's what my friends call me."

"I'm flattered that you asked me, Lon." His name rolled around a bit in her mouth before it came out, like she tasted it. He rather liked the sound, and wished she'd say it again.

"Lawn." She gathered the flour sack up by its corners to contain the peas, stood up, and whistled. The four mules raised their heads and trotted to the corral.

"In that shed over there you'll find my saddle. Put it on one of the mules. Any will do, but the biggest one is the best rider. I'll get dressed."

She disappeared into the house, into the room where the Shirt Tail certificate hung on the wall. He thought of following her, but wasn't sure she would stay in the bedroom long enough for him to tear off the certificate and move another one up into its place. He needed a minute or two to study Saxton's signature on the marriage certificate. What if he should walk in on her in a state of undress? His blood, which had commenced to slowly thaw, refroze when she leaned out the open window of the bedroom, smiled happily at him, then pulled the shutters closed. Did the silly woman think he might spy on her? As if he'd want to see the naked body of a woman built like a gallows, with huge feet…and a bosom a little too thrusting.…

He found the saddle in the shed, and stared in surprise, for it was a side saddle, a Mexican one, with a little fence around the side and the rear. Worn blue velvet covered the pommel, and little silver plaques trimmed the edge of the skirt, with big heavy ones on the corners to keep them from curling. The biggest mule came to him when he offered a handful of oats. It took him several minutes to saddle the creature, because the mule kept turning his head, circling to see what this strange man was up to. Finally he led the animal, saddled and bridled, toward the back steps, and stopped short because the doorway framed an apparition.

Her hair was swept back in a bun, the sides soft and drapey. A straw bonnet bearing a wreath of pink flowers perched on top of her head, with one stray flower under the brim, above her right eye, and a pink bow nestled up by her left ear. The neckline of her pink dress dipped modestly, but it spread wide enough that he glimpsed a suggestion of white shoulders. He shivered. A V of brown skin interrupted the expanse of white, pointing downward, advertising the promise of the valley between her breasts. Modest, yet screaming for attention, more than any whore's scanty bodice.

So much for being inconspicuous. And no woman could climb Mount Davidson dressed in that rig. He would be forced to entertain her in town.

She held the skirt bunched up in front, the pink ruffles of the hem cascading from her waist. He clenched his teeth.

Beneath the pink he glimpsed black boots of thin leather and, above them, the lace edgings of long pantaloons. In her left hand dangled a disk of wire and tape. She held it out to him.

"Now, if you'll just tie my hoops onto the back of that saddle, we can be off."

He brought the mule to the bottom of the steps, struggling to free his eyes from her, but hopelessly transfixed. He offered his hand to help her into the saddle. She smiled down at him as she settled herself on the mule. He hadn't remembered the breadth of her face across her eyes; he'd never noticed how it tapered to a pointy little chin with a dimple, like the china kitten his mother kept on a high shelf, beside the real crystal cream pitcher.

He mounted Buckskin, muttering to himself that a woman six feet tall could not possibly look kittenish, but when he took a second glance, he saw the feline sleekness. Her large eyes shone like those of a cat hunting mice at midnight. For one instant he considered petting her, running his hand down her back, from that low-slung bun of light brown hair to...to...

He pulled his horse to the left and put three or four more feet between them.

"How do you like your job?" she asked.

"Don't particularly. It'll do," he added hastily. No real man could admit to the panic he felt when underground. A cat might like it down there in the dark, with nothing but candles and lanterns. He imagined being in the dark with Lindy, her eyes seeing what escaped him. She would love it in the mines, a deep, dark place just fit for a stalking, cruel, murderous woman.

"I went down once with Harvey, when he had an assay job for the Chollar, before we were married," she said. "It's scary. I'll take a hardscrabble farm any day."

A chill ran the length of his legs. The thought that he

and Lindy agreed on something, anything, frightened him more than conflict.

"They've put up the flag!" exclaimed Lindy as her mule paused on the Divide. Lon surveyed the town, but saw nothing until he followed the direction of her outstretched arm to the top of Mount Davidson. Nothing but a dark flutter, so far away he could not distinguish the red, white and blue.

"It's only put up on special occasions," she said. Lon understood why. First, the banner must weigh hundreds of pounds, being gigantic enough to be seen from this distance; and second, to raise it a man faced a hike two thousand feet up the mountain. Not something even the most devoted patriot would do daily.

They rode into town, right into the middle of a parade, a blaring brass band leading a troop of men drawing a fire engine. Buckskin and Lindy's mule danced all over the street in fright, being unaccustomed to trumpets tooting "Yankee Doodle." Lon leaned over, grabbed Lindy's bridle and headed out of town at a trot. The owner of a cabin near the edge of Virginia City agreed that they might tether their animals in his shed for fifty cents. Lindy waited to dismount until he came to help her.

"You turn around," she said, "so I can finish dressing. If I don't put the hoops on, the skirt drags in the dust."

She stood behind the mule, and Lon stationed himself between her and the sharp eyes staring out the cabin window. A godsend! Her skirt would spread out so wide, he'd not be able to get close to her.

"Now you can look."

Her skirt belled out more than two feet in every direction. He had always considered hoops the most ridiculous fashion ever invented; women who wore them looked as if they'd buried themselves waist deep in a haystack. But now—he gulped—now he had to agree, a woman *could* look good in hoops. But she had to be six feet tall. The wide skirt suited Lindy. She walked toward him, a fairy queen if you ignored her height. She should be flourishing a magic wand and offering him three wishes.

The hoops swayed when she walked, the tips of her black boots darting in and out like frightened ground squirrels. Three wishes? He would wish to be anyplace but here, to start with, sacrificing the last two wishes.

She held out her hand, and he realized she expected to take his arm. He eyed the expanse of her skirt, but once she stood beside him he found the whole arrangement moved. His leg pressed against the hoops on one side, and they swung out on the other.

Before they'd walked twenty feet he learned they were to be the center of attention. Or rather, Lindy was. Any woman who walked the streets of Virginia City drew a multitude of glances. Lindy, towering above most of the men, stood out like a rose in a turnip patch.

The heat of embarrassment warmed his cheeks, so he bent his head, hoping his shame wouldn't be noticed. But that posture seemed to suggest that he hovered over her. He jerked his head up just in time to see a drunk stagger across the street, waving a whiskey bottle.

"Betsy," he yelled. His erratic steps carried him in the general direction of Lindy. "Betsy, who...who...sh thish man? You promised me!"

Lon fended off the drunk with too much enthusiasm, and sent him sprawling in the street. "Watch out here!" he shouted. "You almost ran down a lady!"

Oh, God! Now I'm being protective. Everyone in the territory's come to town, and they'll think for sure I'm Lindy's new beau.

Half the people on the street seemed to know her, but not in a pink ruffled dress with hoops taking up most of the sidewalk. Every six feet a wide-eyed man halted his progress, saying, "Why, hello, Lindy! How nice you look

today.'' What was worse, Lindy would then say, ''So nice
to see you. Do you know my friend, Lon Anderson?'' and
he would be introduced.

As they made their way into the center of town, so many
people crowded C Street it seemed impossible that one
more body could squirm in. The parade circled back, the
brass band blaring ''When this Cruel War is Over,'' and
the flags lifting in the southern breeze.

One of the fire companies had a little blond girl done up
like the Goddess of Liberty, with a crown of silver paper.
She perched on the top of their pumper, holding a scroll
with the words The Union Forever. Behind marched six
little boys, all wearing red, white and blue shirts, with red,
white and blue streamers floating from their hats, long
enough to touch their heels, except that the wind picked
them up and floated them out behind.

The sight of the children brought an unexpected flood of
homesickness. Lon found himself searching the boys' faces
for that of his brother, who had been about that age when
he'd fled the farm. Then he remembered; he'd been gone
eight years. That little boy was now as old as he had been
on the terrible day when his father's anger had driven him
away.

''Lindy,'' yelled a fireman, one of two dozen pulling a
cart full of ladders, ''Hop aboard! You're one of us!''
Lindy politely looked to Lon for permission. He nodded,
and breathed a sigh of relief as she dashed into the street.
A dozen hands lifted her onto the cart.

He tagged along in the wake of the parade, keeping his
eyes on the pink roses swaying atop her bonnet. Men who
knew her yelled her name, and those who did not stared in
admiration and awe.

''Anderson!'' exclaimed Braley. ''So it's true. You won
Saxton's grass widow in a card game?''

''Ssh!'' he hissed, hoping the men pressed close about
had not heard the remark.

"No use trying to keep it a secret," said Braley. "It's all over town, although the man's name isn't generally known. Me and the boys, we put two and two together, since you said you'd played cards with Saxton."

"I'm with Lindy just for today," Lon protested. "She needed a companion to bring her into town for the Fourth."

Braley grinned knowingly. "You get the fifty shares?" he asked. Lon shook his head. "Too bad. You gonna help us in the mine?"

"I'll do the report." He almost added that he'd work in the mine, but sweat sprang out on his palms at the prospect, and he postponed the decision.

"We worked three days getting things ready," continued Braley under his breath, standing on his toes and leaning as close as he could to Lon's ear. "First light to dusk, we arranged the tools nice and neat, and turned the tailings, and built a little dam to hold back the stream what flows from the mine, so we thought a day off not amiss. We're luckier than we knew. Last folks who worked the Shirt Tail, they cut a stope only thirty feet from the entrance. We'll put a charge of powder in there, blast the rock for the new operation, and not have to haul it eighty feet from the face of the tunnel."

"When will you set the charge?" asked Lon, keeping his eyes on Lindy and speaking from the corner of his mouth.

"The entrance to the stope caved in at one spot, and none of us can snake through the hole without a lot of shovel work. I'm looking to hire a small man who can crawl in with the charge." Lon briefly thanked God for making him six feet five inches tall, and broad to go with it.

The parade broke up. The little boys ran by, their faces and hands sticky from the red, white and blue candy sticks the firemen handed out. The Goddess of Liberty's white robes dragged in the dirt, and her silver crown sat cock-eyed.

"See you tomorrow," said Braley. "Down Seven Mile Canyon two miles. You can't miss it." Lon followed the hook and ladder cart until it stopped in front of the company's headquarters. He nearly shoved aside the firemen who fought to lift Lindy down, for a fleeting moment wanting to clasp his hands about her waist and feel her long fingers pressing on his shoulders. He regained his good sense at the last moment.

"Three cheers for Lindy!" a man shouted, and the assembled firemen yelled for thirty seconds. "Next year we'll get you a helmet, Lindy!"

How had Lindy come to know the firemen so intimately? He thought of asking, then decided he didn't want to know.

"A few weeks ago," she said, explaining as if he had asked the question, "a fire broke out on A Street while I made my call at Nora's." Had she read his mind? "I helped them unload the ladders. So now I guess I'm a member of the Nevada Hook and Ladder Company."

Two men lounging in front of the newspaper office stared at Lindy. One reached out to touch the pink ruffles of her skirt. Lon stooped and grabbed the man's dirty shirtfront in his fist, lifted him up until he stood on tiptoes. "What do you think you're doing?"

"Why, just admiring," the fellow croaked. "Didn't mean no harm."

"Just stay a bit away, from now on, and keep your hands to yourself." Lon dropped him, and the miner staggered back, his eyes still on Lindy. She leaned against Lon.

"Thank you. It's so nice to be with a man who treats me like a lady. Maybe I should dress up more often."

He knew his red face had turned redder. As red as the bunting on the speaker's stand on the hotel balcony. A cluster of men in black broadcloth and tall hats gathered on the balcony in preparation for the oratory.

Lon pushed into the crowd, searching for a spot on the boardwalk opposite the hotel, where Lindy would be sheltered from the press of the mob.

"Ice-cold lemonade!" yelled a man flourishing a large dipper above a barrel. "Ice-cold lemonade, just two bits!"

"Look, Lon. He's brought ice down from the mountains."

Sure enough, in the barrel full of lemonade floated a pointed chunk of ice. A few slices of lemon rested on the ice, advertising that the lemonade truly contained fresh fruit. Lon put four bits in the vendor's hand; they both drank a dipperful.

On the balcony a gentleman in a black swallowtail coat raised his hand for silence. Lon stopped on the boardwalk and gave up his search for a place in the shade.

"In Congress, July 4, 1776, the Unanimous Declaration of the thirteen United States of America," he declaimed. The crowd roared. Lon gathered the speaker was Governor Nye.

"When in the course of human events..."

Most of the women had lacy parasols to shade their faces. It reflected badly upon him, as her escort, that Lindy did not carry one. The bulk of Virginia's women earned their living in questionable ways; they had pretty trinkets and Lindy did not, and she worked so hard. There was no justice.

The woman he had nearly ridden down on D Street strolled past, clad in a bright yellow dress far more elegant than the one he'd seen before. She stopped no more than ten feet away, twirling her white parasol, flaunting the yellow and pink silk roses that bordered its edge.

"We hold these truths to be self-evident, that all men are created equal."

Not likely, thought Lon. If everyone was created equal, I'd have a ranch of my own, and Lindy would have a parasol. But Lindy's not my lookout. He turned his head slightly to observe Lindy's face, and verify that she didn't need a man caring for her. The new hair rig changed her face from plain to charming, and the pink dress reminded him of wild rose petals floating down Sierra streams.

"...whenever any form of government becomes destructive of these ends, it is the Right of the People to alter or to abolish it, and to institute new Government."

Lon looked with surprise at the man on the balcony. Was that radical statement really in the Declaration? It sounded a bit too much like the philosophy of the Southern States.

If he had stayed in Indiana, he would be in the Union army. He should have gone home and enlisted. On the day the news came of the outbreak of war, he should have ridden east, volunteered with the Indiana militia, for he certainly favored Lincoln and the Union. If he had gone back, he might at this moment be in the army before Vicksburg. He would not be plotting how to steal a stock certificate from a lone woman.

Too late now. Was it?

A boy slipped surreptitiously through the crowd. Probably up to no good, the normal condition of boys of ten or so.

Not a boy! The dwarf from the trail!

Lon watched the slight figure without turning his head. The dwarf eyed a gold watch protruding from the pocket of a vest. The vest in question, of gaudy brocade, stretched to cover a very portly stomach, and every time the gentleman breathed, the watch eased out a fraction of an inch. The owner of the watch and all his neighbors were spellbound by Governor Nye's oratory. In another minute the watch would vanish, and neither the owner nor his friends would discover the loss until the ceremonies ended.

It's no concern of mine. The fat man had probably cheated some greenhorn out of his money, and used the ill-gotten gains to buy a gold watch. Now the little man would steal it, in the chain of continuing thievery.

"He has obstructed the Administration of Justice by refusing his Assent to Laws for establishing Judiciary powers."

"Justice" attached itself to Lon's mind, a burr he could not dislodge. No justice in stealing Lindy's Shirt Tail certificate. A man did not fall into crime as easily as he supposed. The dwarf edged closer to the fat man, not once allowing his eyes to rest on the watch. Anybody would have thought the boy paid close attention to the drama overhead.

"Excuse me for a moment, Lindy," Lon whispered. He scrunched down, eased through the crowd until he could reach out and grab the dwarf's shoulder.

"Come on now, Billy," he whispered sternly. "Don't get into mischief today. Just because you're with your uncle Lon instead of your ma and pa, it doesn't mean you can run wild. Come over here and stand by me." His fingers tightened around the thin shoulder. Billy glared at him, opened his mouth as if he meant to yell for help. His face seemed to melt.

"You!"

Lon wrapped his fingers about the back of Billy's neck, steered him along until he once more took his place by Lindy. He kept his left hand resting easily, but heavily, upon the small shoulder.

"In every stage of these Oppressions We have Petitioned for Redress in the most humble terms." The governor entered into the spirit of the words, and spread out his left arm in a gesture of submission.

"That's what I did," whispered Lindy. "I petitioned humbly. I begged Harvey and begged him to stay away from the bottle, but he wouldn't listen. So it's right I ask for my independence."

"Please," muttered Billy from the other side, twisting both his head and mouth upward. "I'll give you your twenty dollars back. I can make five times that in this crowd."

"No. After the speeches are over, we'll go to the sheriff."

"*...a Tyrant is unfit to be the ruler of a free people.*"

"You're a tyr-rant," said the dwarf, raising his voice enough to sound threatening. "That's what you are, a tyr-rant, just 'cause you're bigger'n most men. Let me go, or I'll start hollerin' and cryin' that you're not my pa, and that you kidnapped me and beat me to turn me to thievin'."

"And I'll fetch that whore over yonder who wears yellow dresses, and she can tell the sheriff that you acted the man with her." The shoulder sagged beneath his hand.

"*We must, therefore, acquiesce in the necessity, which denounces our Separation...*"

Braley needed someone small to take the powder charge into the stope. What in hell was a stope, anyway?

"*That these United Colonies are, and of Right ought to be, Free and Independent States...*"

Lindy bounced up and down beside him, her hands clasped between her breasts, awaiting the ultimate words of challenge to the British tyrant. To Harvey Saxton?

"Stick with me," he muttered to Billy. "I'll introduce you to a fellow who needs the help of a small man like you."

"Honest work?" asked Billy, disappointment washing over his face. "I ain't much for—"

"No. The grandest swindle ever." Billy grinned.

"*We mutually pledge to each other our Lives, our Fortunes and our sacred Honor.*"

The governor's voice boomed, the echoes resounding off the buildings of Virginia City. His fist clenched on his chest. The crowd roared its approval, and the roar fell into three separate cheers for Lincoln and the Union. A quarter of the crowd refused to join in, being supporters of the Confederacy. Lon noticed the dwarf stood glumly silent.

"Cheer," he ordered.

"I'm from Texas," said Billy. Lon tightened his grip on the shoulder.

"Cheer anyway." Billy did so, halfheartedly. Lon looked about for Braley, but didn't spy him in the crowd. "Now, you stay here, and don't pick any pockets. Someone might catch you and put you in jail before you have a chance to get rich in this great fraud we're engineering."

"What is it?" begged Billy.

"I can't tell you. I'll send over the man who can."

The reporter replaced Governor Nye at the center of the balcony, and read his epic to the Union, a poem with a ton of *thy*s and *ere*s, and praise of glorious vistas. Then the brass band reappeared. At first they played patriotic airs, but before long they switched to marches, polkas and schottisches. Lindy's hoops swayed and her black boots flicked in and out beneath the pink flounces. Some of the women folded their lacy parasols and accepted invitations to dance. A gentleman in a black broadcloth suit and a top hat bowed in front of Lindy, pointedly ignoring Lon.

"Might I have this dance, Miss Lindy?"

She looked at Lon, as if he might supply the answer to the question. "Do you mind? You brought me, and it's not polite to abandon one's escort...."

"Go ahead," he said.

He pulled his arm free of her hand, let loose a deep sigh as she twirled away. She could dance with every man in Virginia City if she pleased. Prancing about on enough arms, she'd scotch the rumor that he'd taken over where Saxton had left off.

But he could not ignore her. At every bouncing step of the polka her hoops rose, and the entire population of the Nevada Territory saw her ankles and the white lace on the bottom of her pantaloons. He waited for her at the end of the dance, but another man claimed her before she took one step in his direction. Instead of Lindy, he found Braley at his side.

"You be up tomorrow?"

"Yes." No chance to lift the Shirt Tail certificate before next Tuesday at the earliest. "You need a small man?" he asked.

The band played a waltz, and Lindy spun in the arms of her partner. Her pink skirt swung wide behind her. Whoever the man was, he held her too damn close!

"Yes. Someone slight enough he can crawl into the stope. We hand the charge to him, and he'll string the fuse as he crawls out. No need for him to be around when we blast."

"See the kid behind me?"

"Yes. No, Anderson!" Braley exploded. "A thousand times no! I'll not put a boy in that kind of danger."

"He's not a boy, he's a thieving dwarf."

"You sure?"

"I'm sure. He's been lifting watches and playing dirty tricks for ten or twenty dollars. He'll jump at the chance to make a hundred or two for toting a little powder."

Braley circled so he stood between Lon and the dancers. "How do you know him? You seem to be acquainted with more people in Virginia than you admitted a few days back."

"I met him on the trail, on the way to the pass. He took twenty dollars of my money. You tell him he either carries the charge into the stope, or I go to the sheriff. What's a stope, anyway?" He stepped to the side so he could see Lindy. Her partner had tightened his embrace. Lon bit his lip.

Braley hummed tunelessly between his teeth and seemed not to have heard the question. "Well, if you say he's not a kid," he muttered finally. Lon paid no attention when Braley left, didn't turn around to see if he talked to Billy or not.

Lon let four dances go by before he decided his feet deserved some fun. He edged around the crowd, positioned himself so he stepped in front of Lindy the moment the music stopped.

"Now with me," he said.

"Let's get more lemonade first," she replied.

He paid out two bits, handed her the dipper. She gulped in a most unladylike fashion. Her face was flushed and her breath came hard and fast.

"I haven't danced in ever so long," she said. "It's so much fun."

"I'm not very good. Are you game to try one with me?"

"I'll bet you *are* a good dancer. I bet you're good at everything you put your hand to." She lowered her eyelids so her lashes stood out against her tan skin. She was flattering him, and he knew it, but he let his chest expand a bit, anyway. He put his arms about her. The hoop skirt swung out, and with the first scampering steps of the polka, he knew the men standing on the street ogled her ankles.

Her slender and finely shaped ankles. But if they matched the body he held in his arms, strong ankles. He held her a bit tighter than necessary, and inched his fingers down her back very gradually. Strange. He had never felt quite so close to a dance partner before. It took him a minute or two to figure the reason. Lindy did not wear a corset! His fingers sensed the movement of her body through the layers of cotton—through the pink dress and her underbodice or whatever women wore. Somewhere down there she didn't have anything on!

The dance turned to agony. His body surged, wanting to do things with Lindy no upright man would consider doing with a woman who had a husband. Even if she *had* chased that husband off with a rifle! He tried vainly to control the swelling, but the more he concentrated the worse it got. Lindy swung against him, gazed into his eyes and smiled. He looked away.

Another man waited to claim her when the music stopped. Lon retreated into the shade of the boardwalk. She could take any partner she wanted for the rest of the afternoon. Thank heavens she was not a wallflower! If he had to give her all his attention, they might end up in a hotel room, and his whole life would be ruined!

Lon pulled his hat down on his forehead and turned to face the gusty wind, hoping it might dissipate the heat left by the polka. He squinted his eyes against the dust, and noted a scattering of shingles, gloves and hats tumbling down the street toward him, along with one white silk rose. A black cloud oozed over the mountain, trailing veils of gray. As he watched, one of the streamers engulfed the Divide and obliterated the buildings at the upper end of C Street. A few scattered raindrops splashed saucer-sized depressions in the dust. He dashed into the maze of dancers, spotted Lindy's pink dress, took one last glance at the advancing curtain and grabbed her arm.

"Pardon me, but rain's coming, Lindy. We must find shelter."

"It doesn't rain in Virginia City in the summer," retorted her companion. A flurry of great drops contradicted him; the temperature of the wind dropped twenty degrees in two seconds. Lindy's companion looked up, and Lon took advantage of his momentary astonishment to pull Lindy from his arms.

"We'll go to the International Hotel for our dinner." He would show these men that he knew how to entertain a lady. He started across the street at a sedate stroll, but the rain swooped down faster than he had anticipated. Simultaneously he and Lindy gave up any pretense at propriety, and ran, her hoops clearing the way through the mass of men seeking refuge in the hotel.

Chapter Eight

Lindy studied the polished brass lamps mounted on the walls of the dining room. She pretended a great interest in the design of the carpet. She admired the sculptured pattern of the silver, tracing it with her fingers. Anything to keep her eyes off Lon. The average man would fall before a barrage of fluttered lashes and wistful eyes, but Lon Anderson was not an average man. Judging from his behavior, too romantic a gaze embarrassed him, and too clinging a companion scared him to death. Courting Lon Anderson demanded clear thought and careful action.

Nora would, naturally, warn her against Anderson, but she'd never believed Nora's visions before, so why start now? Nora *had* warned men off worthless prospects with her ball, true, but her spirits once forecasted the demise of the Ophir, and the next week the crews blasted into a bonanza.

She'd form a plan to snare Lon Anderson. Lon must never guess that she smoothed the path to the altar, for men liked to think they did the pursuing, but she'd set out to get him. Not just because he was strong and handsome, but because he was kind and thoughtful. Of all the men in Virginia City, only Lon had noticed the little boy getting himself in trouble. He had not shouted at the child, or spanked him, but talked quietly and led him away from temptation. And in response to his gentleness, the boy had stood like a little soldier through the speeches, and afterward sat quietly on a windowsill.

The most difficult problem was to persuade Lon to become a farmer. Perhaps she could tip Nora off ahead of time, so she could manufacture a fine fortune for the two of them on the farm. Lindy recalled Lon's wild laughter when she had mentioned the crystal ball, and dismissed that idea. Lon wouldn't sit still for Nora's fortune-telling.

Besides, Lon was a man of honesty and integrity, and if he found out he'd been tricked, he'd not want her.

The waiter presented leather-bound menus and, to Lon, a handwritten *Carte des Vins*. He waved it away. Another plus for Lon Anderson: he didn't drink.

Lon snatched the card from the waiter's hand. "I'm sorry. I wasn't thinking. Would you like a bottle of wine with dinner? Champagne?"

The wife of a teetotaler must follow his principles. She'd happily give up drink to keep peace in the house.

"No, thank you." She leaned across the table and risked meeting his eyes. "I'm always pleased to meet a Temperance man who stands by his pledge, even in the wilds of Nevada Territory. So many men make promises back home, then forget once they've passed the Rockies."

"I'm not Temperance. I don't like the stuff."

A practical man. She would demonstrate her own practicality. No feminine foibles and indecisions to upset him. She did not open the menu.

"Whatever you're having, order the same for me."

He ordered Tahoe trout à la Chambord, chicken mayonnaise, Brussels cabbage, and asked the waiter if the hotel had buttermilk.

He must like her a little, since he'd ridden all the way to the river this morning to bring her to town. And when they'd danced... She tried to forget what had happened when they'd danced, for the recollection would certainly cause her to blush. Then again, Lon might find feminine blushes attractive. For a few seconds she concentrated on the dance, until she felt a tad of warmth on her cheeks. Lon didn't respond.

Try conversation.

"You were raised on a farm in Indiana?"

"Yes."

Not much of an answer. "Tell me about it."

"Why?"

"I've never been a farmer before. You can be a big help to me."

"Not much to tell. Just sixty acres, more than half rocks, the rest sticky clay."

"And you didn't like it?"

"I've no inclination to be a farmer. My father didn't want to be a farmer, and I saw what it did to him." Good. Each time he opened his mouth, he said more words.

"What did he want to be?"

"A preacher." She waited, but Lon didn't elaborate. The waiter interfered by arriving with the soup plates.

"Being a preacher's wife isn't easy for a woman," she ventured. "Did your ma stand in his way?" He twisted his mouth, looked at the ceiling, then at the soup.

"No, I did." Three words, and Lindy failed to find any immediate meaning in them. Lon picked up the correct spoon and set about eating his soup. Had he been a wild boy?

"I suppose, you being tall for your age, you kept the whole town upset and sideways. Not very good for a preacher's boy." She giggled, then smiled at him, so he'd understand his scrapes at fourteen mattered not at all.

His eyes responded by glazing over, hard and unseeing. He frowned. Lindy pressed her spine against the back of her chair, knowing she'd said the wrong thing. But what?

His eyes brightened, shone green, and his lips drew back a little, revealing clenched teeth.

"I'm sorry, Lon. You don't need to speak of it. I ask too many questions." The silence lasted through the soup.

The waiter removed the soup plates and returned with platters for the fish course. Lon unerringly selected the fish knife.

"This is a beautiful hotel," Lindy whispered, to renew the conversation on a safe topic. "The owners are spending tens of thousands of dollars building the new addition on B Street—'fourteen thousand on the ironwork alone,'" she added, quoting the advertisements placed in the *Territorial Enterprise*. Lon stared at her for a moment, his eyes softened, his mouth twitched and he leaned across the table.

"My father, he didn't want to be a country preacher, but to go east and study with men who knew the Bible in ancient languages. To raise money for the trip, he preached at a tent revival, even though he was but nineteen. Pa's a powerful man, taller than I am, and when he preached, people got excited. Every night the crowds got bigger. A little girl sixteen years old, whose father owned the general store, she came all alone to the meetings. Pa worried about her with no escort, and to make sure no harm came to her, he walked her home. Then one night they both overflowed with the spirit, with the fervor that good preaching pulls from the soul, and they didn't go directly to her house."

He looked blankly at the fish knife in his hand, as if he didn't know where it had come from. He must take after his father, for the energy and fervor of his words pulled something from her soul. She said nothing, hoping he'd continue, for the passion in his words suggested a passion in other things. Under her skirt, in the level of her pantaloons, muscles flexed, independent of her intentions, more exciting than when they had danced.

"He had his stage money all together, to leave for Boston," Lon muttered, "when that girl's father came to him, and told him he'd put her in the family way. What could he do but marry her?'' He waved the fish knife. "What could any man do, and keep his pride? Her father gave them sixty acres as a wedding present. A baby boy came six months later, no way to say he was early when he weighed nine pounds, and after that no one in the township took Pa very seriously as a preacher. He couldn't very well accuse them of sinning, when his own sin walked and talked beside him.''

"You?''

"Me. He hated me because I made him a farmer. He hated the neighbors because they had no schooling. He hated my grandfather—my mother's father—who had let her go to the meetings alone, and then came gunning for the man who'd wronged her. He kept his books on a high shelf, books in Latin and Greek, and sometimes at night he'd read them, and grumble how he'd sacrificed, living without educated company. He tried to teach me, but I didn't see the use of it. I couldn't do anything right, so I left. Ran off.''

"How old were you?''

"Sixteen. Old enough to see that farming ages a man before his time, makes him bitter and nasty, makes him such a total failure, he has no belief in anything.''

She searched for words to put farming in a better light. "My farm doesn't have many rocks. At least, not real big...'' She stopped, aware she sounded trivial and silly.

"Have you ever plowed a furrow in a rocky field?''

"No.''

"You carry a shovel on the plow, to dig the rocks up, for the frost heaves them to the surface. You think you've got a field finally cleared, and next spring the plow hangs up same as before.''

"So you don't want to be a farmer,'' she said, to avoid a public disagreement. "What do you intend to be? A miner?''

"A ranchero, like the big landowners in southern California. I plan to claim a ranch. That's what your husband said he owned, and what he put on the table for his wager. Your husband's the lowest-bellied snake in the territory." The chicken arrived. He stared at the waiter, then at her, and lowered his eyes in embarrassment. "Why are you so determined to be a farmer?" he asked, his pleasant tone forced.

"I like living on a farm better than living in town."

"How do you know? Have you lived in town?"

"My family owns a dry goods store in Ansonia, Ohio, but Ma's folks live on a farm. I spent the summers with them, and I was never so happy as when I woke up, with the smell of hay and Grandma's preserving kettle. I thought I'd marry a farmer, but when you're as tall as I am... well...not many men come courting."

"I don't believe that!" he exclaimed. "A gal as pretty as you? The fellows flocked around like bees to honey, I wager." He was polite to flatter her, and try to make her feel better.

"Not exactly. Fellows came by, but mostly to gawk. I traveled west with my brother, Will. He meant to open a store in Virginia City, but he saw the men who made big money carried goods over the mountains, so now he's in Sacramento. He supplies stores from the Carson Valley to out in Reese River, and on the Humboldt."

"But you stayed in Virginia?"

"By the time Will decided to leave, Harvey had come courting. I got married." Would that satisfy him, or would he ask why she'd married Harvey?

The windblown rain slanted down the street, drenching the remnants of the crowd that had taken shelter under the roof of the boardwalk. Water ran in young creeks from eaves. Dinner finished with charlotte russe, and to her relief he did not ask about Harvey. The waiter finally came running with a glass of buttermilk.

"Tea, coffee and fruit are served in the ladies' parlor, port and cigars in the gentlemen's lounge," he announced.

"If you wish to smoke..." Lindy began.

"I don't smoke."

Did the man have no vices at all? Did his father's religion forbid any pleasure? When he took a woman, did he mate quickly and furtively?

"I traveled to California with a riverboat gambler," he began. "He didn't smoke or drink, because he said his wits must be sharp for the game. I found it's a good rule." He shrugged his shoulders. "In any work, keep your eyes on your job." Suddenly he smiled, the broadest smile she had seen on his face. His eyes, sparkling tan with green fire in the centers, met hers. For the first time she dared fix her attention on him.

Did he mean that she was his job? He watched over her, standing between her and pawing drunks, pulling her from another man's arms when rain threatened. She shivered happily as the truth washed over her. Lon was courting her! She relaxed her face, opened her mouth slightly, widened her eyes. Would it hurry things along if she looked like a love-struck girl? She watched for his reaction, for a change in his smile....

"The mountain's afire!" a man yelled from the front of the dining room. Lon sprang to his feet, his attention beyond her, focused on the emergency outside. He grasped her arm.

"Stay beside me." No, she realized with a thrill. Danger threatened, and he thought of her, first thing.

"Lightning!" he muttered.

How long did a divorce take? She'd say yes to Lon the moment he asked. She followed him without objection through the front door. *I will get him! And I'll get the passion that plays on his face, and in his voice—when he's willing to talk—and the lust he tries to conceal. I'll show him his father's wrong, that a man and a woman together...*

Lon sniffed the air, so Lindy imitated him, to catch the aroma of burning sage. The town smelled of sodden manure, damp people and wet wood. The rain had stopped.

"Where's it burning?" Lon asked in a loud voice, of no one in particular.

"On the very top," said a stranger. "Mount Davidson's become a volcano, that's what I think."

"It's all that digging around on the insides," said another man. "The miners finally blasted through to the fires of hell."

"A mysterious messenger," intoned a woman who shielded her eyes with her furled parasol. "A warning from Providence that we must mend our evil ways, or Virginia City will fall into perdition."

"As if it's not perdition now," Lon muttered, squinting his eyes, looking at the mountaintop. "It's the flag, you fools," he cried.

Lindy dashed across the street to gain a clear view of the summit. A cloud black as funeral drapes covered the sky in every direction, and wrapped around Mount Davidson. On the peak, against that stark backdrop, danced a tongue of flame. It wavered out of sight, then rose again, flickered for all the world like fire. The flag, lit by a beam of sunlight illuminating that spot alone.

"I believe it's a sign from heaven," someone offered.

"A great portent," announced another man.

"Grant has retreated from Vicksburg," said a Southerner.

"More likely Vicksburg has surrendered," retorted a Northerner. "It's the flag of the Union what's lit up."

"Great news, great news, let us praise God that he has seen fit to reveal to us his power to protect his chosen people." The speaker must be a preacher, for his voice carried over the crowd, and silenced the muttering. "Perhaps it portends the end to this cruel war. Pray! Pray this divine manifesto heralds the end of strife, as the angels heralded the birth of Our Lord.''

The flame billowed, winked out, billowed once more. All the peaks surrounding Virginia City moldered under storm clouds, while the sun limited its glory to the flag, a golden spark in the brooding twilight. Lindy's arms erupted in gooseflesh as she thought of her distrust of Nora's spirits. Had they fashioned this demonstration to convince her? No natural force could create such a display.

Lon stood beside her, his eyes on the flag. She inched closer to him, longing to hear his opinion, yet afraid to ask, for fear he might laugh at a supernatural explanation.

His arm slid about her waist. She leaned against him, drawing comfort from his strength in the face of the inexplicable. *He'll think I'm frightened.* She very nearly drew away, rather than let him suppose she suffered from tremors common to other females. *But some men find timid women attractive.* He *had* defended her against the drunk, and had nearly come to blows with the man who had touched her skirt. *He wants to protect me,* she concluded, and cuddled a bit closer.

Lon strained his eyes to find the path of the sunbeam that fired the flag. No miracle, he was sure, but a coincidence of storm clouds and afternoon sun, slanting at precisely the right angle. He congratulated himself on his analytical mind, on his unwillingness to go off half-cocked and find supernatural explanations for an unusual phenomenon. His self-praise wilted a little when he realized his arm curled about Lindy's waist, and had been there for a quarter of an hour. Her head drooped very close to his shoulder.

He forgot about the flag for a moment, concerned that he and Lindy were making a public spectacle of themselves. To make matters worse, Braley stood nearby, grinning. He considered pushing Lindy onto her own two feet.

On the other hand, Lindy obviously needed a man's comfort in this confusing moment. By nature, women tended to believe superstitions, and accept miraculous explanations of perfectly normal events. He thought the situation through carefully. Lindy had come to Virginia City only because he'd asked her; under the circumstances, duty demanded that he calm her.

"Everyone's saying Vicksburg's fallen to Grant," Braley muttered.

"Has anyone checked at the telegraph office?" Lon asked.

"The operator couldn't say, even if it's true. He's bound by contract to put a check on all news from the East until the San Francisco papers print it. They have a monopoly on the wire."

"Let's go to Nora's," murmured Lindy, her head now very definitely on his shoulder. "She'll gaze into her crystal ball and tell us what happened."

Lon opened his mouth to sneer at fortune-telling gypsies, but shut his mouth when he noticed Braley nodding seriously. "A right smart idea, Lindy. Mrs. Dove can see more in her ball about where bonanzas hide than any ten mining experts standing right in the drift."

"You believe that crystal ball...shows the truth?" asked Lon. How could a sturdy miner like Braley be taken in by such nonsense?

"Mrs. Dove tipped off some friends about the Bennett Hill prospect. A double-barreled billy-cock it turned out. And she saw the truth without going near the shaft. Her spirits looked down through hundreds of feet of solid rock and said 'Yellow Jacket.' If they can do that, they should be able to see what's going on at Vicksburg. Spirits can travel from Vicksburg to Virginia City straight through thin air."

Lon pondered the curvature of the earth, which rather got in the way of the spirits coming from Vicksburg in a straight line. He shrugged and followed Lindy up a stair-step boardwalk beside the Opera House.

Dove's Boardinghouse faced Mount Davidson. A crowd had gathered in front of the house, and two boys sat astride the peaked roof. Some men still gazed at the mountain, although the strange display had faded several minutes before.

Lon tried not to stare at Mr. Dove's lopsided body when Lindy introduced him. His withered, misshapen left leg ended in a stump; his left hand bent into a claw. He leaned against the railing of the front porch, and when he turned to go into the house, hopped along with two sticks.

"What happened to him?" Lon whispered to Lindy before they entered the parlor.

"Mine accident. He was foreman of a gang laying a charge, and the powder went off too soon, and flung him the length of a drift and wrapped him about a mine timber eighteen inches thick."

The Doves' parlor smelled of cinnamon and apples. Mrs. Dove bustled about, laying out painted china plates that spoke of a more prosperous past, a cream pitcher painted with pink roses to match the plates, then a pie, a wisp of steam escaping through the moon-shaped slit in the upper crust. Lindy cut the pie while Mrs. Dove helped her husband lay aside his sticks and settle into a chair.

"Nora, offer the gentlemen a drink," ordered Mr. Dove. "Pie and tea's a lady's repast." He turned to the visitors. "Excuse me for not offering you the whiskey myself, but you can see it's difficult."

Lon's knees quivered. He wondered how it affected a man, to be unable to stand at the sideboard and pour a glass of whiskey. *Lindy feared he'd leave her husband like this!* He recalled the moment she'd asked him to kill Harvey, and now heard the breath of her fear. He might thrash Harvey Saxton, might leave him crippled, with no one to care for him but his wife. He saw Lindy bending over Saxton, wrapping his injured limbs, never mentioning divorce, because to abandon a man in his condition violated her honor. And Saxton begging for drink, keeping the pain at bay with a continual stream of whiskey.

And Lindy would bear it.

"If it's not too much trouble, Mrs. Dove," began Braley, armed with his second glass of whiskey, "we wondered if you might bring out your crystal ball and explain the fire on the mountain. Everyone's saying Vicksburg's fallen."

"I've never attempted to see events at such a distance," Mrs. Dove protested. "I doubt that it's possible." Braley looked crestfallen, and Lindy disappointed. Lindy should not be disappointed, any more than she should be doomed to care for a crippled drunk.

"If the spirit of victory laid its power on the mountain," Lon said sincerely, "why shouldn't those spirits still hover nearby?"

"Why, I hadn't thought of that!" exclaimed Mrs. Dove, "but it's true. The spirits have already manifested themselves." She immediately left the room, and returned in half a minute with a box of highly polished dark wood. Lon had to admit the ball, resting on a red velvet cushion, looked magical. Light from a lantern overhead reflected through the crystal in iridescent colors, a glimmering, intoxicating center of the room.

Mrs. Dove removed a small flag from an engraving of the Union forces at Antietam. She placed it at the base of the ball, laid her hands palm up on either side of the crystal.

"Think of the flag," she ordered.

Lon concentrated, but the small paper flag transformed itself into the flag flying at Council Bluffs, where the wagons gathered for the summer trip to California. He had hung about under that flag, along with hundreds of other men who sought to work their way to California. He'd begged for the miserable job of herding a man's loose cattle, not knowing until they trailed well onto the prairie that he had indentured himself to a Mississippi gambler. He seldom thought of the gambler, except when he played poker. And today. Today, for the first time in eight years, he'd spoken of the man. He'd been overly talkative with Lindy, and did not understand why.

"The vision is very confused," said Mrs. Dove. "Please, concentrate on the flag." Lon dragged his mind away from the gambler and the mystery of Lindy, back to the flag beside the crystal ball. He caught himself counting the stars. Only thirty-four, when it should be thirty-five, for on this very day the free western counties of Virginia became a separate state, West Virginia. Nevada, if admitted soon, would be the thirty-sixth.

"Two flags of the Union fly on separate poles," Mrs. Dove announced. "One flies at the top, but one at half-staff. Both reflect in water."

Braley struck his right fist into his left palm. "Vicksburg. On the Mississippi. Is the water muddy?"

"I cannot see."

A very clever seeress, Lon decided. The flag at half-staff gave her a path of retreat in case tomorrow's newspapers announced a Rebel victory. The water could be a river, a lake, even the Atlantic Ocean.

"Now," Mrs. Dove teased, "you come here, Lindy. I'll tell your fortune, for I sense an imminent change in your life." Lon folded his arms across his chest as Lindy took her place at the table. If Mrs. Dove saw a wedding cake, he'd landed himself in a barrel of brine. Lindy placed her hands beside the ball and stared into the crystal, mimicking Mrs. Dove's intensity. Mrs. Dove looked up, puzzled.

"Lindy, have you taken up gambling?"

"No. It's too much like sitting around doing nothing." Another thing they agreed on. Mining, and now cards. Lon crossed his legs. "Do you see me playing cards or dice in that thing?" asked Lindy.

"I don't see you, but the cards are plain. A good hand, four of a kind. Queens. With the queen of hearts on top."

Lon's hands gripped the arms of the chair. It couldn't be. This fanciful woman couldn't possibly know.... Yes, she could. The story of that poker game had drifted around Virginia City for the past four or five days. Braley had heard, so why not Mrs. Dove? Rich, Price and Saxton had spread the story of Lon Anderson winning Saxton's wife with queens. Gossip never got anything right, and three queens had turned into four.

Lindy pulled her hands off the table and stood, frowning. The crystal ball's message had not pleased her. "It's time we were going. Thank you for the pie."

"We'll see you on Tuesday," said Mr. Dove without rising. "Always so pleasant to have you come. The days string out alike, day after day, except on Tuesdays and Saturdays, when you come, Lindy."

Dear God! A man so destroyed, he looked forward to the days when the vegetables and eggs arrived! Lon imagined himself, trapped in a broken body, unable to leave the house. How easily it happened, how frequently in the mines. He'd never again go down in the Gould and Curry, or any other deep mine. Better to starve.

"It's been such a wonderful day," Lindy said to him as they walked along A Street. The clouds streamed from the mountain, and sunlight touched the peaks around the valley.

"It's not over yet. The fireworks go up at dark."

"I must go home. Four cows and a goat to milk, the eggs not gathered, the cream to skim and the hogs to feed. If I don't get the chickens in by dark, some coyote will sneak in and eat them for sure."

Lon reclaimed the horse and the mule. They rode the steep five miles to the valley, past the mills of Empire City, down the river road.

"I do love the Fourth of July," Lindy said. "Coming at a time when the farm's so busy, it's a wonderful holiday."

"I remember, back in Indiana, hoeing corn, and cutting oats, and weeding the garden, day after day, except for Sunday, when we went to church and read improving books. But on the Fourth, we went to town and heard the speeches."

Sometimes his father had taken them. Sometimes his father had been willing to harness the horses and devote their energy to simple, secular amusement.

"The Methodist ladies made ice cream to raise money to roof the church." His father had stood before the draped table, undecided, clutching the dime in his big hands. As a child he hadn't understood how hard dimes were to come by. He'd only felt the great disappointment when his father had led the children away, unsatisfied.

"I'm glad you invited me," Lindy said. "Thank you." They rode for a quarter mile in silence. "Thank you for not drinking. I have a hard time with drunks."

"Why'd you marry Harvey Saxton?" he asked. The question had surfaced in his mind several times during the day.

She pursed her lips and wrinkled her forehead. She looked even more like a gigantic kitten, for she'd taken off her hat and it hung from the blue velvet pommel. She bit her lower lip.

"Tell me, Lon, do you like to romp?"

"Romp? Well, I polka and waltz, but I've not—"

"No, romp. Like married people do, in bed."

Lon gulped, put his hand to his throat to cover the movement. His face must be as red as the kerchief. Had she noticed what had happened to him when they'd danced? Or did she just assume that every man wanted to shove a woman into bed?

"Do you?" she asked insistently.

"Yes. With the right woman." The words came out husky, smoky with the desire curling from his fingertips, for they recalled the body beneath the lace.

"Well, that's why I married Harvey," she said, looking down, toying with her hat, and he heard and saw and understood her shame. She'd lain with Harvey before they married. "I like to romp, and he seemed the best catch, with his assay office and all."

And maybe Harvey hadn't been the only one, or even the first. He pulled in a deep, noisy breath, and gripped the reins so hard Buckskin dipped his head in protest.

"Was it a good reason?" he finally asked, lamely.

"No. Next man I marry has to prove he can do something besides that, but I won't hitch up with a man who can't be pretty active in the marriage way."

"That stands to reason," he said. Did she expect to sample the talents of every suitor, before tying the knot? Obviously. How else would she know?

By the time he unsaddled her mule, the clouds had vanished, except for those hanging over the very highest western peaks. The brilliance from the vanished sun tinted the clouds and reflected the light into the valley. He turned the mule into the pasture. She stood on the back porch in trousers and a gingham shirt.

"Why's this house built on stilts? And why is it backward?" he asked. "The porch is on the back, not the front."

"The man who settled this farm, Mr. Parker, he came from Louisiana. He feared the river would rise, like the Mississippi. And he said he had an interest in his crops and his animals, but not much in an empty road, so he put the porch on the back, where he could sit of an evening. And I agree with him. It's nice to sit on my porch and look out over everything I own. From here I can see my fat pigs and my cows with their calves, and the mules, and out beyond, the corn growing taller, and the shocks of oats."

Lon gazed over the farm, trying to see it with her eyes. Everything appeared as before, except that the corn had grown, and the oats had been cut. Hardscrabble. Work accumulating faster than a man could possibly get it done. Much faster than a lone woman. The Nevada replication of the life he had fled.

"I think you'd better marry a farmer when you go about picking your next husband," he offered.

"I think so, too. Come on in. After the milking's done, I'll fix us a bite of supper."

"No, I'll ride back to the ri...back to town."

"Lon, do you still mean to look for Harvey?"

"He owes me money," he said flatly. He could not touch Saxton. He might threaten to go to the sheriff, but he could not beat Saxton to a pulp.

"I don't know if this will help you, but the reason we quarreled the last time, I wanted him to go to Steamboat, to the hospital Doc Ellis built by the hot springs. Men who go on a spree and end up seeing two-headed snakes and chopped-up bodies, they live at Steamboat for a week or two and the hot water soaks the whiskey out of them. They come back to town peachy and healthy, like they haven't been in a saloon for a year."

"You think he may have gone to Steamboat?"

"I don't know, but it's possible. Please, Lon, if you find him, don't hurt him. He can't help what he is."

"If he used the money to get the whiskey boiled away, I'll call it a good investment," he said, mounting Buckskin.

He rode up the river, retrieved his gear from the willow clump and turned the horse north. The wide road through Franktown and Washoe City was plain, even in the dark. He passed tempting homesteads with snug cabins, yellow light spilling through glazed windows. He envied the men who possessed such opulence. On the height above Washoe Lake he stopped to gaze at the stars, then at the eastern horizon, toward the heights concealing Virginia City.

To get a ranch he must return to Virginia City and the Shirt Tail. At least Braley would furnish him grub while he wrote the report. After lemonade and dinner, and a contribution to the Sanitary Commission, he had $8.14. Not enough to live more than a day or two in Virginia City.

He could go back to the Gould and Curry. His stomach churned at the thought of the deep shaft and the dark heat. A mine had blasted Mr. Dove to a wreckage. Mrs. Dove cooked meals for miners to support her husband. A degrading position for a man, to be supported by a woman.

He tried to polish the memory of the mine, change the miners' lamps and candles into stars against the distant, black ceiling. But they remained distant fires of hell. One of Nevada's assortment of hells. He would write the report, get Lindy's Shirt Tail certificate, then head west as fast as his horse could carry him.

A red flower blossomed in the sky above the ridge. Green stars puffed outward into graceful, languid lilies against the dark sky. He wished Lindy could see them, but in the little valley where her farm lay...

He didn't have to steal the Shirt Tail certificate!

The realization blossomed warm and welcome in his chest, like the flower in the sky. If he found Saxton at Steamboat, he didn't have to steal the certificate. A newly dried out, newly contrite Saxton would be happy to settle with him by signing over the Shirt Tail shares. No need to mention the sheriff, just a quiet conversation about five twenty-dollar gold pieces, and the little gold charm in the shape of a heart. Saxton should keep that memento of Lindy.

One hundred shares—a thousand dollars, when the Shirt Tail excitement hit its peak. He had never in his life had a thousand dollars all at once. If he decided against homesteading the meadow on the river, with a thousand dollars he could start a business in Sacramento.

He found a level spot a few feet above the stream running from the hot springs. He threw his blanket on the sand, and let Buckskin roam free to find the clumps of grass growing beside the tepid water. If he found Saxton, he had no need to keep the appointment with Braley tomorrow. And if he didn't find Saxton...well, Braley could wait.

Maybe Lindy would take her husband back if he signed a temperance pledge. And quit gambling on cards and wildcat mines. A wisp of sadness drifted through his mind, and he wondered at his melancholy.

Chapter Nine

From the ridge, Lon studied Steamboat. The hot water flowed from a low mound, through dozens of vents, each marked on this cool morning by a column of steam. Even from a distance he heard the rumble of boiling water in the crevices, and smelled the sulphur of the underworld. He walked slowly to the cluster of buildings at the foot of the steaming mound, keeping an eye out for fissures.

A number of men lounged in a stone-lined pool. He examined each head for dark hair and full beard, but didn't see Saxton. In the largest building—identified by a large sign as the hospital—a clerk sat behind a desk. He tilted his head sideways, like a bird, while he listened to Lon's inquiry.

"No, we have no Mr. Saxton here," said the clerk, after examining a large registration book. "Was he to meet you?"

"Not exactly. I mean, we hadn't made definite plans. But I thought he intended to take the hot water cure."

"Tomorrow, perhaps," said the clerk. "Most men will extend their Independence celebrations an extra day, seeing as the Fourth fell on Saturday. Tomorrow the horde will stumble down, to enjoy the springs' restorative qualities following overindulgence. Would you care to try them, sir?''

''No, thanks.'' The clerk tagged behind as Lon walked to the front steps.

''And after a hard week in the mines, the water rejuvenates the muscles, and strengthens the bones. You're a miner, I presume, sir.''

Not willingly, thought Lon. He examined the faces of a dozen uncomfortable-looking men sitting in the morning sun wrapped in wet sheets. He was so intent on finding a dark beard that he almost stepped in front of a horse that galloped to a sudden stop at the foot of the stairs.

''Heard the news?'' shouted the rider. ''Vicksburg's fallen to Grant, and Meade defeated Lee in Pennsylvania, at some place called Gettysburg. July Fourth, the greatest day in the Union's history!'' He took off his hat, twirled it in the air and let out a war whoop.

''The flag!'' exclaimed one of the men on the porch, throwing off his damp sheet. ''The flag told us the Union armies won!''

A cascade of chills ran down Lon's backbone, then climbed back up. He walked stiffly down the creek to his campsite. The flag. The sun and the storm cloud had moved around in the sky, had taken the proper position to inform Virginia City of Union victories.

No, he reminded himself, it had been a perfectly normal, natural phenomenon. Nothing but coincidence that it happened on the Fourth of July, on the day that Vicksburg fell...nothing at all to do with spirits. But how had Mrs. Dove seen queens in her crystal ball? Four queens?

''Four queens proves it was gossip, not spirits,'' he muttered, to convince himself that the world remained right side up. ''Spirits would know the truth. Three queens. Gossip, on the other hand, always twists stories.''

All but the queen of hearts. Lindy had glowered at Mrs. Dove's vision, displeased. Perhaps one of the men she'd slept with before she married Harvey had called her Queen of Hearts, and Mrs. Dove's ball displayed her sin. Many men must desire her. Hell, he wanted her! The chills slithered all the way to his feet, reflected off his boot soles, came wavering upward, now hot and exciting.

Could he romp with Lindy and not end up her farmer husband? He stumbled on a rock and almost went flat on his face. *Pay attention to where you're going,* he snarled to himself. Some hurt troubled his mind. What had happened to the euphoria of the night before? Then he remembered. He had not found Saxton. He had to steal the Shirt Tail shares from Lindy.

"I shore wish I could do that," said Billy. He leaned on the plank balanced between the two flattish rocks Lon had hauled from the mine dump. Not a stable desk, but better than writing on the ground. Billy's slight weight tipped the board away from him.

"Get off my desk," ordered Lon. "You'll jog the pen." Billy stood up straight, making himself nearly as tall as Lon, who sat on the candle box.

Braley, Riddel and Marron had moved out of the shack, bringing their canvas roof with them; they'd set up housekeeping at the tunnel entrance, next to the stream that gurgled from the mine. Lon found the camp a great deal more comfortable than the cabin, for the fleas had failed to pack up and move. The canvas flapped lazily overhead, reminding him he must finish writing the report before the afternoon wind picked up.

"Where'd you learn to do that?" persisted Billy, pointing at the moving pen.

"I went to school."

"Pa wouldn't let me go. He said I'd get beat up and maybe kilt. Besides, he said larnin's a phe-nom-en-ist waste of a man's time." He leaned to within an inch of the plank, but kept his weight precariously balanced on his feet. "Is it true Braley's payin' you hundreds o' dollars just for writin' that paper?''

''I'm getting paid to write lies. There's a big difference between writing a few sentences on a paper, and writing lies so tall they could hold up heaven.''

''Billy, get in here,'' yelled Braley from the tunnel. ''We're ready to put in the next charge.'' Billy scampered off, and Lon returned to the Gould and Curry report.

The Comstock vein strikes twenty-five degrees east of due north. The propylite boundary of the vein is irregular, while the syenite boundary on the west is regular, descending at angles varying from thirty-five to fifty degrees.

What in hell did that mean? Life would be simpler if his father had taught him something practical, like geology, rather than Latin.

In the lower levels the syenite is separated from the vein by a heavy coating of clay, sedimentary in form, implaced after the deposition of the vein. The clay is an indicator of the presence of the vein, even when the mineral-producing quartz is not present.

He copied the sentences, reversing directions as Braley had suggested. He changed the strike angles to something a bit steeper, and added his own description of the clay layer, drawing upon his recollections of the intractable soil in the fields of his childhood. He wrote *in dubio* instead of *not present,* and threw in what he remembered of Caesar's observations on the agriculture of Gaul.

He skipped the paragraphs describing the Gould and Curry's steam hoisting works, since even the newest arrival, a tenderfoot who confused ore with an apple cart, could see the Shirt Tail had no steam engine, and no need for hoisting works. He added two sentences of his own, pointing out the advantage of a horizontal approach to the vein, even though every other productive mine on the Comstock came at it from above. *Exceptis excipiendis.* A proper exception.

Should he add a description of the mine? Probably so. At least in this matter he could behave like a real geologist. He broke a handful of matches off a block, drew a new candle from the box and stuck it on a candleholder. For several feet into the tunnel he had no need for the candle; even thirty feet in, where the men labored, a faint glow of natural light reflected off the walls. The tiny stream had carved a miniature canyon on the floor of the mine, and the water sparkled silver where it caught the failing light. Two frogs hopped away from the threat of his feet.

The stope, he discovered, was a side excavation a little higher than the tunnel. He heard Billy's voice echo in that shrouded vacancy, shouting at Riddel and Marron about how to shove the powder through the hole.

Another ten feet into the tunnel, Lon lit the candle and held it up. The dry, gray walls absorbed the light, except for one spot where a trickle of water fell into the stream. The wet rock glistened, and a streak of green algae stood out like a stripe of paint.

"*Croak!*" He spun about, almost extinguishing the candle flame. Then he remembered the frogs.

He must look for propylite and syenite. How? When he wouldn't know either if he stubbed his toe on a boulder-sized chunk. He took two determined steps into the growing darkness, turned around to reassure himself that the tunnel still existed behind him, that he could run out into the heat and sunshine at any moment.

Two steps forward, a glance back, over and over again, until he reached the end of the tunnel. The flickering candle illuminated an avalanche of crumbling rocks, the result of the last blast of the previous prospectors. Their final charge had failed to uncover the promised bonanza. Hunger had forced them to move out and move on.

A geologist would take rock samples, he reasoned. He jammed the spike of the candleholder into a crack in the wall, picked up a piece of rock the size of his fist, then thought better of it. A geologist would take rocks at the face, the ultimate reach of the mine. He scrambled up the rock pile and pried three pieces from the shattered rock with his knife. He pulled out the tail of his shirt, and carried the samples as a woman carries apples in her apron. The entrance was a tiny arch of light. He jerked the candle from the wall and stretched his legs to their full-length.

Back at his plank desk he wrote his impressions of the tunnel, using every positive adjective that sprang into his mind. He wrote two paragraphs about the supply of fresh water, without mentioning that the stream contained barely enough water to satisfy five men and a horse.

"Looks good!" enthused Braley, examining his fair copy of the finished document. "Now sign it and I'll take it to that reporter fellow. Maybe I can get him down here tomorrow, which'll give him time to write a shine for the Wednesday paper. We'll blast Wednesday—that'll keep the locals at a distance until the San Francisco papers pick up the news. We don't want anyone poking about here for a day or two, sending derogatory telegrams to their friends. Once the stock starts to move on the exchange, men'll flock here, but by then we'll be hauling rock and can tell them to keep their distance."

Lon stared at the paper long and hard. Sign it? He had not considered putting his name on the damn thing. He wrote "Harlon Anderson" at the bottom of the last page in an illegible scrawl.

"Be better if you wasn't around when the newspaper man comes down," Braley was saying. "He might have questions, and it could be awkward if he stumped you. Or caught you in a howler."

Lon nodded eagerly. What a stroke of luck! Tomorrow, Tuesday, the day Lindy's cabin would stand empty. "I've got some business in Carson City," he said with studied casualness.

"Stick around the territory, though," added Braley. "We'll start hauling rock in a few days, and could use your help. And a friend of mine at the Gould and Curry mentioned he might reopen the Comstock Commander. He'd need a report, and you could write it for him. Before long, you'd have a name for yourself as a mine expert who's good to prospectors."

A mine expert. Of the same ilk as Harvey Saxton, Lon thought, and didn't like the implications.

Lon rolled his bed and extra clothes into a tight bundle, tied them and his coat behind the saddle. Daylight still hung behind the horizon. Early, he must be early, lest he meet Lindy on her way up.

Where the Virginia City road met the river he dismounted, tied Buckskin to a tree along the stream and climbed a low rise that gave him a view of the track to Lindy's farm. In less than a quarter hour he saw the dust raised by her wagon and mules, hanging in a long stain in the still morning air. She passed. He decided to wait another hour, not take any chance that she might return. With his luck, she might remember she'd left the butter in the springhouse.

When he rode into the farmyard, the rooster pulled his head out from under his wing, eyed the intruder, flapped to the ground, scratched aggressively and crowed at the hot sky. The hens had already abandoned their morning search for food, and now dug cool depressions in the dust on the shady side of the house. They paid absolutely no attention to either Lon or the rooster.

Lon led Buckskin close to the porch, where he wouldn't be visible from the road, just in case the neighbors rode by.

His boots made a startling thunder on the splintery planks of the porch. The latch string hung out. The foolish woman didn't suspect she had something valuable to lose.

Sunlight poured through the wavering glass of the front windowpanes. The glare reflected upon dancing dust motes, blinding him, obscuring his view of the opposite wall. Lon stepped beyond the glare…and faced bare clapboards. He closed his eyes, opened them again. Nothing but the rough boards forming the wall of the cabin. Had he dreamed the mine certificates hung there?

He leaned closer. A few nails were still in place, and he identified the holes where others had been driven into the wood. Damn the Fourth of July! While she danced, some man had remarked on the activity down at the Shirt Tail. But that didn't explain why she should take down *all* the certificates—the Pine Nut, the Lady Bryant.

Lon cursed himself for not nabbing the certificate on the Fourth, cursed the dancing that had separated him from Lindy. He should have figured some way to get the certificate the evening of the Fourth. If he had stuck around, if he had risked getting involved with Lindy, he might have pulled the thing off the wall in the dark, just as he left.

"Leaving after she taught me her version of romping," he snarled at the bare wall. "And the man who romps with her will end up marrying her, and marrying this damn farm."

He hammered his fist on the wall, pulled back shocked and calmed, because one of the nails had punched into the heel of his hand. No sense wounding himself, and getting lockjaw and dying, just because Lindy had figured out the value of her own property. But they must still be here, in the house! He stepped across the protesting floor, and turned the key in the lock of the chest. A pile of folded papers, the deed on top. A florid proclamation that Melinda Merryman had completed all the requirements in reading, mathematics, geography, history, spelling and penmanship to be graduated from Ansonia Grammar School. Two spoons. Lon turned them over and noted the silver mark. On the very bottom, a length of pink silk fabric, the edges raveled. No marriage certificate, no stock certificates.

The bedroom door opened silently, on well-oiled hinges. A bed covered with a dark comforter. Shelves. Trousers hanging from nails on the wall, along with two sheet-wrapped bundles. He felt them cautiously—lace, the unmistakable shape of long skirts. Her dresses.

He thrust his hand between the mattress and the network of wire supporting it. Nothing. If he had stayed Saturday, he'd have ended up here, unable to resist the seduction of a woman who liked sex and didn't ask for money. What tricks might she use to please a man? He discovered his fingers curling as they gently caressed the comforter.

He shot out of the bedroom, remembering to close the door only after he was halfway to the back door. His frightened energy drove him across the porch and onto Buckskin.

Where to go? If he was very, very careful with money, he might get to one of the foothill towns in California and find work. But jobs in Virginia City paid better. Mining paid the best. Six dollars at the Shirt Tail, but only when the stock shot up and Braley had the money to pay him.

"I'll ask at the livery," he decided, talking to Buckskin. "Maybe they'd let me keep you for free if I work in the stables."

He was near the top of the grade when he spotted Lindy's wagon coming down. He looked for a way to cut off the road and escape her, but she had already spied him.

"Lon!" she cried. "Fancy meeting you here. I thought you'd be asleep this time of day, since you're working the night shift."

"I quit," he said.

"Quit!" she exclaimed. "Why?"

"The foreman—" blame it on Braley "—the foreman who hired me quit to work his own mine, and...the new foreman, he had his own crew and didn't..." He let the explanation die for lack of logic. Fortunately, she interrupted.

"Hang out around the office. They'll want you back soon. What are you doing now?"

"Looking for work."

"I'll need someone to cut the hay in a week or ten days. I can't pay much, but I give room and board, if you call sleeping on the porch room."

"I'll keep that in mind," he lied.

"You know what I did yesterday?" she asked brightly.

"Milked the cows and made butter." The lighthearted tease in his voice startled him, and he realized the corners of his mouth turned up. He forced them down.

"I mean, besides that."

"Can't imagine," he muttered through tight lips.

"I hired a lawyer in Carson City to start my divorce. I was afraid, with Harvey gone, I couldn't do it. But the lawyer said it's better that Harvey left, because I can charge him with abandonment."

"Abandonment?"

"That's right. Harvey's gone away, and failed to support me. I took the marriage certificate, to show how Harvey had tried to sell me off, and all those worthless mining shares, to prove he'd wasted money instead of supporting me."

"I hope you got a good lawyer." Some lawyer in Carson had the Shirt Tail stock. Idle men hung about lawyers' offices. One of them would hear of the Shirt Tail being reopened, and would snag the certificate. How long before the lawyer sent the paper to the court, along with a petition outlining Harvey Saxton's misbehavior? "Which lawyer?"

"Mr. Stone. People claim he's the best in the territory for this sort of thing. He got Sam Randall a divorce because his wife ran off."

"Abandoned him?"

"Yes. After the divorce she married the superintendent of the Yellow Jacket, and lives in one of the biggest houses in Gold Hill."

"Is that what you're planning? A big house on top of a mine?"

"No. I just want to keep the farm, and not be bothered."

"But Harvey isn't bothering you. He's gone. Why worry about a divorce?"

"Because a woman can't be married to two men at the same time, Lon Anderson," she teased. "You know that! One's got to be dead or divorced." Lon contemplated the skyline so as not to give her encouragement.

"I suppose Mr. Stone kept all those documents, for evidence," he offered cautiously.

"Sure did, wrapped them in brown paper with my name on it, and put it on his shelf, the way they do legally. He said when the judge saw that marriage certificate, there'd be no problem. He'd just drop his hammer on the table and say, 'Granted.' A man can't gamble his wife away."

"That's good to know," he said, nodding. "Good thing to know, in case the situation ever arises…"

"Come by for supper," she said. "I had such a good time on the Fourth. And don't forget, if you can't find work, my hay needs cut."

He guided the horse off the road to give her plenty of room to pass, and sat staring after her. *Saxton owes me money,* he repeated to himself. But in a divorce would that certificate belong to Lindy, and the thousand dollars by rights be hers? He thought of Lindy in her pink dress, carrying a pink silk parasol.

I can sell the certificate, take what Saxton owes me and give the rest of the money to her.

He waited for half an hour so there was no risk of catching up with Lindy, then turned around, rode down the long grade and took the turnoff for Carson City.

*   *   *

Stone's law office faced right on the square, occupying the bottom floor of a small frame building. Good! No creaking stairs, or fooling with ladders and climbing through second-story windows. The upper floor of the building was nothing more than an attic under the low-pitched roof, with a single square of glass overlooking the square. He couldn't imagine anyone living in such a narrow, unventilated space. Lon rode past a second time, slowly, then continued out of town until he found a shady place between two boulders. He leaned against one boulder, dozed, woke when the shadows of the western peaks spread across the valley. He dug into his saddlebags for a stub of candle and matches, and put them in his pocket.

Lamplight and raucous music spilled from saloon doors. He tied Buckskin to the crowded hitching rail in front of Pryor's, where the horse's presence would not be noticed. He walked by Stone's front door slowly, studying the lock in the faint light from the saloon two doors down. He rounded the corner of the building into a dark alley, and nearly collided with a flight of steps leading to the second floor. He ran his hand along the back wall until he encountered the frame of a door. He felt both sides of the door with his fingers, and found no lock at all. Just a wooden latch. He lifted the latch, shoved gently. The door opened a finger's width, then stopped. Running his hand up and down the opening, he discovered a wire held the door fast. It wound about two nails, one in the door, the other in the frame.

Patiently he poked at the nail in the door, the only one he could reach. Minutes dragged by before it wobbled in a gradually enlarging hole. He managed to wrap two fingers around it and pull it out, so it did not fall to the floor.

Once inside, he lit the candle stub. Very little furniture in the office—two chairs and a desk with a slanting top, the kind a man stands at to write. Some crude shelves held substantial, leather-bound books and, at the very bottom, what appeared to be parcels. He knelt and moved the candle across the shelves. Lindy had been in only a day ago, so hers should be near the top. Sure enough, the label in black ink: Saxton.

He had no sleeve to shield the candle, so he dared not put it on the desk, where a passerby might spot it. He set it on the floor, knelt, untied the string and opened the brown paper. The top sheet seemed to be nothing more than scribbled notes on Stone's conversation with Lindy. Then came the disfigured marriage certificate, beneath it the mine stocks. Lon opened each carefully. The Monarch of the Mountain. The Pine Nut. The Lady Bryant. The Comstock Commander.

That might have value, if Braley's friend got his scheme going. If he wrote the geologic report... He dropped the paper in horror. He had written one dishonest report, and now contemplated another! It was true! One lawless act made the second easier. Lon shoved the Comstock Commander certificate to the bottom of the pile, telling himself the Shirt Tail would furnish money enough.

The Lady Florence. King of Washoe. Comstock Commander. Somehow, he'd missed the Shirt Tail. He shuffled through the pile a second time and sat back, staring at the scattered papers. The stub of candle sputtered, threatening to die. A thief had already made off with the certificate. Maybe even the lawyer. Mr. Stone had the marriage certificate handy; he could copy Saxton's signature to endorse the Shirt Tail certificate and make it his own. Or sell it to a friend.

He reached out to gather the papers and wrap them back up. The crackle of the brown paper seemed loud as a gunshot, and he sat very still, not daring to breathe.

"Hold it right there."

He squatted behind a chair; the light of the dying candle reflected off the long white nightshirt of a man who, from his angle, looked seven feet tall. The nightshirt billowed to the size of a sail in the breeze from the open back door. For a moment Lon thought he'd met one of Clugg's ghosts, then a revolver slid over the back of the chair, pointing straight at his eyes, the barrel at least six inches in diameter.

"I'm no good at this," he told the man as he raised his hands.

Lindy jostled the tall grass with her booted foot to scare off any rattlesnake that still hung about the drying meadow. She examined the burgeoning flowers of the grass and weeds. The hay must be made before the grass went to seed. She'd put off searching for a man to do the job, just in case Lon came calling, but now she had no alternative.

A week had passed since she'd seen him on the road below the Divide, and he hadn't so much as sent a message—and she'd supposed he liked her, a little. Perhaps he'd gone back to California. Left without so much as a goodbye. The intense blue of the sky dimmed.

So few men would consider a woman six feet tall. Consider marriage, that is. Plenty would dance, and flirt, even buy her dinner. Plenty would look eagerly at her bed. But say "marriage" and they shied like month-old colts. A rattle, the soft sweep of the snake through the grass jerked her back to the meadow.

"Stop mooning about, Melinda," she said. "A woman can ruin her life hankering after a man, not to speak of stepping on a rattlesnake."

She spent the afternoon harvesting vegetables from the garden, turned the water of the spring into the patch while she loaded the wagon in the evening twilight. She gathered the last of the eggs, put the evening's milk in flat pans in the springhouse to let the cream rise. Darkness enveloped the valley before she'd finished feeding the pigs and calves, before she'd shut the chicken coop tight against a fox or coyote.

Only three weeks past midsummer, and already the daylight hours had shortened. July and August brought more work, and less daylight to do it in. She had to find a man to cut the hay. She could not wait for Lon Anderson. After the hay, the irrigation ditch, then the wood.

She washed her face and hands in the tank, and the chilly springwater brought thoughts of winter. Could she make it through the cold months by herself? The woodpile Mr. Parker had left behind was nearly gone. Wood could be hauled free from the mills near Washoe Lake, where great saws cut the timbers for the mines. But time? Time was the problem!

She sighed, and found herself wishing for the hundredth time she had let Lon stay on that first night. If she had not been so stubborn, if she hadn't let herself get mad at Harvey for wagering her at poker, she'd have a big, strong, pleasant man about the house right now. A big, strong, pleasant man, who got excited when he held her in his arms.

"I didn't know him then," she said, explaining away the mistake without much conviction. "I don't know him now. He's so big, he might be awful rough in bed."

She tossed under the coverlet, scolding herself because running after a man wasn't proper. But, then again, she should find out if he'd located Harvey.

The next morning, all the way up the mountain, she debated with herself, and at the Divide decided to swallow her pride and ask around for Lon Anderson.

Chapter Ten

Lindy spoke Lon's name cautiously at Dove's Boarding-house, and learned in a roundabout way that Nora was a bit put out that Lon hadn't come to live in her house, after tasting a sample of her cooking.

The man at the office of the Gould and Curry shook his head. "Ain't about," he said, shifting his cud of tobacco to the other cheek.

Lindy sought out the sheriff.

"You mean that big guy who hung all over you on the Fourth of July? Funny thing, I heard just a day or two ago, he's been arrested in Carson City."

"Arrested ?"

"Yeah. Broke in to a lawyer's office. Lawyer lived above the place and heard somebody riffling through his papers. Caught him dead to rights. He's in jail for thirty days."

"Which lawyer?"

"Stone. The one who got Randall his divorce because his wife ran off. But of course she didn't run off. She just moved on for better money." He smiled at her and winked. Lindy ignored his suggestive leer.

"Why would anyone break in to a lawyer's office? There's nothing of value there," she mused.

"That's what the judge wanted to know, but the guy insisted he needed money, and Stone's office looked easiest. No one believed him, of course. He could have gone after the receipts in McCaffrey's store without even breaking a lock, 'cause Old Man McCaffrey leaves the back door open in case people need groceries when he ain't open."

Lindy nodded and murmured something about Anderson being a strange duck, a big, hulking, stupid sort of man, and that Harvey owed him some money, and that was why she was asking. She hoped that convinced the sheriff she had no personal reasons for hunting him down. She turned the mules toward the Divide and yelled at them to scat.

Lon Anderson had tried to get something out of Stone's office, and it must have to do with her divorce. Why else would he break in to a lawyer's office? Maybe he and Harvey were in cahoots, and Harvey had hired him to destroy the marriage certificate before the lawyer showed it to the judge. Hired him with what? Harvey was broke. No, he had Lon's hundred dollars. Maybe they'd made a bargain—Harvey would give the money back if Anderson did his dirty work.

She jerked the whip, which she hardly ever used, out of its socket and cracked it over the mules' backs. The surprised animals took off, and the empty wagon bounced down the road like a rubber ball on a washboard.

What could Harvey do to keep her from getting a divorce? Even if he hid out close by, say at Lousetown or Woodfords, he had abandoned her. Maybe Harvey meant to show her to be a corrupt women, so he could file, but what difference did it make to Lon whether she or Harvey got the legal paper?

She had quite a head of steam built up by the time she pulled up at the Carson City jail. Lon Anderson was going to tell her why he had interfered with her divorce, if she had to flog it out of him!

Sheriff Tipson wasn't around. Deputy Clugg snored on

the bench along the back wall. Below him the orange jailhouse cat stretched on the floor in imitation of her deputy
master. Lindy tiptoed across the brick floor, slipped the
deputy's gun out of its holster and poked him in the ribs
with the pearl inlaid handle. Clugg sprang up, squealing
like a girl, clutching at his side as if he'd been shot.

"Lindy Saxton," he yelled after he'd drawn a complete
breath. "What're you doing with a gun? Put that thing
down. Women shouldn't ought to touch guns."

She handed him the revolver and he stood up, laid it on
the table in the center of the room, wiggled his hips, found
them too light, grabbed the revolver and dropped it back
in its holster.

"Don't you know that's a crime, taking a lawman's
weapon?"

"Sleeping on the taxpayer's time is okay?" she inquired.
She stepped closer to him, forcing him to look up.

"I wasn't sleeping. Last night a brawl at Jack's Place set
the men fighting until dawn, and one died just an hour or
so ago, so I deserve a bit of rest." Clugg stepped back.

"What's new? There's a fight in a saloon every night. I
want to see Lon Anderson."

"The sheriff ain't here. I don't know he'd want you to
see a prisoner without—"

"What's the sheriff going to say when I tell him I got
your weapon away from you without a struggle?"

"How long you want to see Anderson for?" asked the
deputy with resignation. Lindy stepped away from him.

"Just long enough to cuss him out."

"Go on back." He smirked. "But if I catch you playing
little tricks—"

"Shut up or I'll tell the sheriff," she yelled.

He jerked his thumb over his shoulder. "I got to walk
down to Jack's, see if anyone can identify the perpetrator."

"And get yourself a beer." She completed the statement.
"Take your time. I won't help him escape. He's a desperate

criminal who might come to my place and steal the butter and eggs out of the springhouse.''

The Carson City jail had two cells, only one occupied. Lon lay on a bunk with his heels resting high above his head on a projecting brick. He dropped his legs at the sound of the door, and turned around. His eyebrows shot up.

"What are you doing here?" he asked. He tried to sound gruff and put on a bold front, but his face got red, so she figured it embarrassed him to be found in jail.

"I think I'm the one who should ask that question. What are you doing here, and what's Harvey paying you to keep me from getting my divorce?"

"Your divorce?"

"You went to Stone's office. You were after the marriage certificate. Did you get it?"

"I didn't touch any marriage certificate."

"You didn't look in that parcel with my name on it?" Lying man! She kicked at the bars. He hung his head and shuffled his feet. He rubbed the back of his neck with one of his big hands, and scratched the calf of his right leg with the toe of his left boot.

"That's what I thought," she said. "Harvey got you to break in to Stone's office to steal the papers, so I can't get a divorce."

"Look, Lindy, I don't know your husband, except for playing cards with him that one night."

"Likely story, and I'm not fond of liars."

"I'm not lying."

"Then why in this crumpled world would you rob a lawyer's office? The first time I met you, I thought you were stupid, but on the Fourth I found out that's not true. The back door of McCaffrey's store's always wide open. You could have made off with anything you needed."

He stuck a hand through the bars, palm up, as if presenting her with the truth. He had an unshaven jailhouse grayness about him, and it exaggerated his look of vulnerability. The lock of hair kept falling over his forehead, no matter how often he pushed it up. She stepped back, vowing to stay angry and stern.

"Look, Lindy. I haven't been completely honest."

"So what else is new? Liars, every man I've ever met. It's just that I need the hay made, and winter's coming and no wood is brought from Franktown and..."

She stopped, tightened her cheeks, constricted her throat and widened her eyes so she would not do anything so silly as cry. He looked thin. Maybe the food here didn't agree with him. Maybe Clugg ate part of what the hotel sent over for the prisoners. His eyes had lost the green glow.

"I was after the certificate for the Shirt Tail. The mine's been reopened, just a speculation to jack the stock on the exchange, but the price will probably go to ten dollars a share."

She studied him for a minute, leaning against the bars, then decided to get comfortable. She found a three-legged stool, placed it in front of his cell and sat down.

"How do you know about the Shirt Tail?" she asked.

"Because I met the men who planned the thing. One was foreman at the Gould and Curry when I worked there."

"Did you get the Shirt Tail shares?"

"No. Are you sure you brought it to the office with the other papers, Lindy? It's not there."

"Not there?"

"I went through your parcel twice. If you gave it to Stone, he's put it someplace else, not in the parcel. Maybe he's heard the Shirt Tail's ready to boom."

"I'm paying him to do the divorce. He has no right to take that certificate—whether it's worth money or not. After all, I could still use it for wallpaper."

"It *is* valuable. Or will be. Is that all the shares Harvey owned in the Shirt Tail?"

"I don't know. I never paid any attention. Buying that

paper is gambling, except that you don't know right away that you've lost, like in poker or faro.''

"This time you won.''

"Maybe,'' she said. "I can't believe it, though. Wildcat mines never live up to the brag.'' She looked around the brick walls, and tasted sour dampness. "How long did the judge say you had to stay in here?''

"Thirty days. Thirty days or thirty dollars, and I didn't have thirty dollars.''

"If I pay the bill, will you come out and cut my hay?''

He looked at his boots and flattened his mouth out. He took three deep breaths. Insulting, that he might even *think* jail was better than her company. She tightened her fist, but shoved down the anger that threatened to erupt.

"Yes, Lindy, I'll make your hay. But that's all I'll do. I'll cut the hay, and do any odd jobs you need done before winter, but I'm sleeping on the porch, and when my thirty days are up, I'm leaving, you understand?''

That she could not bear! No matter what she'd confessed in a moment of weakness, a gentleman didn't imply a woman was no better than she should be. She leapt up, drew herself to her full height and grasped the bars.

"Lon Anderson, did I ask you to do anything else? Did I ever mention anything else to you?''

"You mentioned romping, and I'm not romping with you. That's the first step to a big trap called marriage, and marrying you means spending my life between hogs and milk cows. Well, I'm not doing it, Lindy. I'm not wearing out my boots walking behind a plow. I walked all the way to California in the dust of a trail herd to get away from a poor man's farm, and I'm not—''

"Fine,'' she said. "That's fine with me. You leave when the hay's cut. I'll take care of your bail.''

She stomped to the door and flung it open, slammed it loudly to let him know the size of her anger. A man could at least be polite and not show so openly that he couldn't stand the sight of her. She surprised Clugg, who shoved his beer under the bench.

"What'll it cost me to get him out of here?"

"Thirty dollars and costs. The judge put costs at $3.50."

"The sentence was thirty days or thirty dollars. How long's he been in here?"

"With today, seven days."

"So he's served seven dollars' worth, so that's twenty-three dollars left to pay. What'd you plan to do with the other seven?"

She stuck her toe under the bench, and tapped the mug of beer until it went over, sending a rush of liquid toward the sleeping cat.

"What're you doing?" he screamed.

"Why, look at that!" she marveled. "I'm such a big, clumsy woman." She pulled a leather bag from her pocket and sorted through the coins.

"It's $26.50," said the deputy, grabbing the mug to salvage the last spoonful of beer. "Today's not all gone, so I got to charge for today."

"If I take him away now, you don't have to give him his dinner. That saves you a dollar."

"So, $25.50," Clugg said grimly, staring at the empty mug, "and in gold and silver. No greenbacks."

"I don't carry greenbacks," she said. "I like my money to have some weight. I can give you $15.50 right now. You'll have to trust me for the other ten."

"I can't do that, Lindy," said Clugg. She took two steps toward him.

"Yes, you can. I need that man to cut my hay, and it won't wait. Just tell Sheriff Tipson I'll bring ten dollars next week. He won't mind. It must be costing him a pile to feed the prisoner."

"He eats like a horse and then complains he's still hungry."

"See. We both profit."

She dropped the coins on the table. The deputy kicked the cat, who was lapping at the spilled beer. The cat yowled and clawed at his leg. Clugg yowled and the cat went back to the beer. In the confusion, Lindy grabbed the keys from his belt and dashed back to the cells. Clugg yowled at her through the open door. "I'll get you, Lindy Saxton. Just you wait and see if I don't get you yet."

Lon scrambled into the wagon, looking up, not at her. "God, it's good to be out of there! Just look at that blue sky! Look at those mountains!"

Lindy shrugged her shoulders. So much for gratitude. He could at least have shaken her hand and thanked her.

"Lindy," he said hesitantly.

"What now?"

"My horse is at the stable."

"How much is that costing?"

"Fifty cents a day."

"Three dollars, then?"

"I think it'll be $3.50. They want their money in advance."

She handed him her last few coins and waited, the reins hanging listlessly in her hands. She knew she wasn't attractive, and not too many men wanted a big, tall woman, but she'd thought maybe Lon... After all, he was at least four inches taller, and they'd had a good time together in Virginia City. Or had she had a good time, while he'd done his duty?

She heard him coming back, straightened her shoulders and did not so much as glance at him. He tied the horse to the tailgate, threw the saddle among the crates and baskets, then climbed in himself. He dug into his pocket for the change and put it in her hand.

"Three-fifty. Put it on my bill."

She drove in silence for a mile, letting Lon get settled among the baskets and boxes.

"When you went into the lawyer's office looking for the

stock certificate, were you getting it for yourself, or maybe for me?'' He didn't say anything for a long time, and she couldn't turn around to study his face, because one of the mules lagged, letting the other three do the work.

"For myself. I planned to copy Harvey's signature from the marriage certificate to endorse it, then sell it.''

She sighed. "Well, at least you're honest. I like that in a man." On second thought, he was a low-down thief. What right did he have to Harvey's stock certificates?

"Harvey cheated me in a poker game and stole my winnings," he answered as if he'd read her mind. "He owes me $135, and I decided I'd take the only thing of value he had. Shouldn't you talk to Stone, ask where he's put that certificate?"

"If I go into his office alone and face him, he'll just say I'm a complaining woman who has no trust. He might decide he doesn't want to do the divorce, and he's the best lawyer in Carson. I'll bring the matter up when I get my day in court. I'll mention it in front of the judge, so he can ask Stone where the Shirt Tail paper's vanished to. I don't think he'd dare lie in front of the judge."

Lindy sensed Lon's extra weight in the wagon, and thought how nice to have a man around the house. Even if he stayed for just a week or two. Even if he came because he owed her his time.

"Thanks for getting me out of that place, Lindy. I'll give you thirty days, same as the judge said I was to spend in jail."

"Just get the hay in, enough for the winter. That settles things between us."

"What *is* today? The date?" he asked. "I've lost track."

"Tuesday, July 14."

"I'll work for you until August 14. That should pay you back."

"July's got thirty-one days. August 13." Why did the date seem familiar? Her wedding day! Just a year ago she'd sworn to love and obey Harvey until death parted them. And here she was, hauling home another man. Just to cut the hay, she reassured herself, but she knew she lied. She had thirty days to show Lon Anderson where his best interests lay. Thirty days to tempt him from the porch, through her window, so she'd know for sure that she wanted him. Would a month give her enough time?

"Has there been a run on Shirt Tail stock?" he asked.

"Not that I've heard, but I don't pay attention to the exchange."

"Next time you're in Virginia, find out. You may be a rich woman."

"That Shirt Tail certificate belongs to Harvey."

"Claim it in the divorce. It represents the money Harvey didn't spend to take care of you."

While she unloaded the empty baskets and boxes, he carried his gear to the house. He examined the porch, then put his bed, saddle and saddlebags on the end farthest from her bedroom window. Not tonight, or the next. She had her work cut out for her.

He rummaged about in his saddlebags, finally upended one. Three rocks thudded on the planks as she came up the steps. That didn't bode well. Rocks meant he nosed around prospects, and she needed a man to work the farm, not dream about instant wealth from wildcat mines.

"What are those?" she asked.

"Worthless rocks." He pitched them off the porch, then thought better of where they had landed, climbed down the steps and squatted to arrange them as a border in front of a straggling rosebush. Lon had a tendency to neatness. A value in a man, for neat men kept the tools in their place, and didn't stick burning pipes in their pockets.

"Want to see the hay field?" He looked up. A bit of green glistened around the edges of his pupils.

"Sure. Might as well get my work started."

"Not today. But you can see what's to be done."

She led him past the shocked oats, the almost-ripe wheat, around the cornfield. He studied the ditches. Should she mention the problem with the ditch? Not yet. She must not dump all the problems on his shoulders at once. Let him get accustomed to the place. Maybe even fond of it. Then she'd carefully seek his opinion on the ditch.

"I want the haystacks alongside the cornfield. That's the highest part of this field, the last to flood when the river rises."

"Rises!" he exclaimed. "We're a hundred yards from the river, and I don't care that it's called the Carson River, it's nothing but an overgrown creek."

"Wait until spring, when the heat comes all of a sudden, and there're thunderstorms on the snow in the mountains. You'll see a river then. I found trash from floods clear up in the cornfield when I plowed."

"Maybe I should haul the hay closer to the house," he suggested.

"No, stack it here, to save time. After winter sets in, I'll have time to haul hay. There's other more important work now. When I have my new barn…"

"When's that?"

"The carpenter said the middle of August, after they finish a big barn in Washoe Valley." He nodded, and she took it as a nod of approval. Maybe the barn would convince him the farm had possibilities. "It's going to be thirty feet wide and forty feet long, and have a haymow, and separate stalls for the pigs and the sheep and the cows."

He nodded again. Not approval. Was it contempt that darkened his green-brown eyes, dismissing her dream? Or did he feel sorry for her? Getting Lon was going to be harder than she had thought.

"I've got the chores to be done. If you want something to drink, there's buttermilk in the springhouse." He grinned his slow grin.

So that's how to do it! She straightened her shoulders,

which had slumped a bit when he'd reacted so badly to her description of the barn. *Lon Anderson, I'm feeding you better this month than you've ever eaten in your life.*

Her grandmother had told her the way to a man's heart lies directly through his stomach. She'd skimp on the barn if necessary to find the money to feed him. She'd do without glass balls on the lightning rods.

He hung several paces behind her as she walked through the cornfield, around the wheat patch, down the edge of the vegetable garden. Looking back, she saw him sneak a glance at the scarecrow. He didn't pale the way he had before. If he mentioned it, she'd take it down and bury it. She'd even ask him to say a prayer over it, if he thought it proper.

Lon took one look at the laden table and dug his fingernails into his thighs. Fried ham, new potatoes creamed with late peas, radishes. He had to restrain himself or Lindy would think he'd been raised without any manners at all! Turnip greens, a loaf of bread with just the heel sliced off, butter and jam. Green onions fresh from the garden. He anticipated the taste before he put one in his mouth: the mild snap of onion, permeated with the warm, loamy sensation of soil.

She came from the springhouse carrying a pitcher of buttermilk. One of his Latin books had pictured a Roman goddess bearing such a pitcher, her draperies flowing about her. Lindy's draperies didn't flow. In fact, they displayed too much, and the too muchness dampened her appeal. Ended it, actually, he assured himself.

He kept reminding himself to eat slowly, to never fill his fork until he'd chewed the food in his mouth and swallowed, as his mother had taught him. But his stomach growled, and sometimes he yielded to temptation and cut off a bit of ham, or buttered another slice of bread, before the potatoes and peas had quite cleared his gullet.

His stomach signaled its satisfaction long before his mouth had tasted enough. Another slice of bread? He cut it from the loaf—had he really eaten more than half?—as Lindy disappeared out the door. Should he follow her? He slathered the bread with jam. The splash of water. She was preparing to do the dishes. He'd offer to help her with the washing up. Not men's work, of course, but she had worked all day, and all he'd accomplished was to be rescued from the Carson City jail. He shoved back his chair just as Lindy returned with a bowl of stringy, stewed rhubarb, with little pink pillows peeping out here and there.

"Cream?" she asked. The cream poured in a strand that held its shape. It melted on top of the hot rhubarb like spring snow. The pink pillows proved to be sweet dumplings, each no more than a bite, so light they dissolved in his mouth. His stomach protested, but he ate two helpings.

He leaned back, closed his eyes, replete. The taste of rhubarb reminded him of the end of winter, and the rhubarb tonic his mother had forced down the entire family to overcome the winter woes. And rhubarb pie.

His father, at the head of the table, snorted his contempt for so homely a dish, but he wolfed the pie down in quick, spasmodic gulps. His glowering presence dampened everyone's happiness at the first fruit of spring. The man's eternal, smoldering anger turned the air about him to ash, dooming all his family to live under a gray cloud. It suffocated him in his own combustion, and kept the world at arm's length. Even when they pitched in to the after-dinner chores, they did not sing or joke over the tub, for the master of the house stayed seated, his glowering stare criticizing....

Lon opened his eyes at the rasp of Lindy's chair. He sprang up, followed her to the summer kitchen. "Thank you. That's the best meal I've had since—" He tried to think of a dinner so remote it made the praise greater. "Since I ate my mother's cooking."

"Why did you leave?" she asked, whisking the softening soap to foam with a dirty fork.

He fell back upon silence, uncomfortably aware that he resembled the unlovable man who had presided over the dinners of his childhood.

"I told you. I didn't like the farm."

"I mean, what made you take off? Something must have happened for you to run off to California. Like, with me, I didn't intend to come with Will until—" she ducked her head and turned away from him "—a young man I'd expected to call upon me brought a girl to church, and after the sermon she let it out they were betrothed."

"Hurt your feelings?"

"I guess. It shouldn't have, but it did."

"Same with me. My feelings got hurt."

"By a girl?"

"No." He had never told a soul the deep shame of his leaving. Lindy filled a pan with hot water for the rinsing.

"You don't need to help," she said as he took a floursack towel from a nail.

"You cooked, I'll help with the dishes. That's the way it was at home."

She washed, he dried, silently. And for the first time in his life, silence burdened him.

"My father and I'd had a difference during the winter over Latin lessons," he began. He could tell her part of the story. "I wanted to be out with the rest of the boys, cutting wood in the snow, and sleigh riding. I told him I'd never decline another noun or conjugate another verb. After that, nothing I did suited him. Come March, he sent me to plowing a field that had lain fallow for three years. A great pile of rocks can heave up in one year, but three winters! I had to dig every six feet."

Lindy hummed her astonishment.

"Well, he came out to the field that morning, and started ranting on about how the furrow wasn't straight, and he'd

done better when he was ten years old. He shoved me away
from the plow, yelled at the horses, but they didn't get a
rod before the plowshare snagged on a rock, and it must
have been as big as an outhouse, because it didn't budge.
Pa screamed at the horses and they pulled, threw all their
weight into the collars, but that rock hung in there. He
cursed me, said the horses had grown lazy because I didn't
make them work."

"Cursing?" she asked. "I thought he wanted to be a
preacher."

"He didn't curse around other folks, but in the wide
open, he could turn your ears blue when things didn't go
his way. Well, I heard wood shredding, saw the horses
sailing down the field, and I couldn't at first figure what
had happened. Then I saw the plowshare stuck in the
ground, hung up on that boulder. What was left of the plow
bounded along behind the horses, scaring the hide off them,
and the more it bounced, the faster they tore."

Lon remembered the plow, flinging itself across the furrows like a hounded rabbit. He stopped talking because
chuckles bubbled up from his chest. She must have seen
the same vision, because she took her hands out of the
soapy water and smiled. The soapsuds shook on her hands
as she threw back her head and laughed.

"It looked," he choked, "it looked like a big scrawny
rabbit chasing two horses across a field. I tried to stay se-
rious, but one whooping laugh got out, and then another.
Pa turned around, thunder and lightning no more fierce, but
I couldn't stop howling. He hauled off and hit me. So hard
I fell down, right in the furrow I'd plowed."

He had to put down the pitcher he'd been drying, for
fear he'd drop it. The laughter strained his distended stomach.

"Pa ran after the horses, because they'd nearly reached
the neighbor's place. He left me there in the furrow. I
thought hard for about half a minute, decided I wasn't ever

again going to be hit by someone I couldn't hit back. I got up and ran to the house.''

Stop here. No more. Not another word.

"And then?" she asked casually.

He stared at the western mountains harboring the final light. "There was no one there!" The words came in a whisper, as if saying them quietly would keep his secret. "Not Ma, nor Lily, nor Endicott, nor Sally. A paper lay on the table with Pa's name on it. I read it, even though she'd addressed it to him and I knew better than to read someone else's letters. My grandpa'd come that morning, and carried Ma and the children away. She said she couldn't live in hatred any longer, and she and the youngsters would stay with her family in town, and that I should decide for myself where I wanted to live."

He expected Lindy to say something, but she just stared at him, holding a plate above the dishwater.

"That letter scared me more than Pa's fist, because I imagined him coming in and reading it. After the plow breaking, after the horses being so winded by the run, there'd be no more plowing that day. I could hear him screaming and carrying on, and telling me how Ma had run off because of something I'd done. It'd be my fault, for sure, in his way of thinking. But then I thought, I don't want to go to town, and be stuck tending the counter in Grandpa's store. I stuffed everything I owned, which wasn't much, in a bundle, and hiked away."

"For California?"

"I didn't know where. I just turned west, away from town, and when I got to the Missouri, a fellow needed drivers, so I signed on. I got my meals, and fifty dollars when we arrived at Grass Valley. He was a gambler off a riverboat. He opened a fancy gambling hall near a big mine, and he's probably worth a million by now. He gave me grub, fifty dollars and poker lessons for trailing behind his spare oxen from the frontier to California!"

"You at least had an adventure," she said. "Will and I came on the Panama steamer. I got seasick."

Lindy? Seasick? Might as well believe she had consumption.

"I best get the table cleaned up," she said, heading toward the house. "Any crumbs left draw the ants into the house in armies."

"I'll help," he said. Climbing the stairs, he realized how much he'd overeaten. She showed him where to put away the dishes. Two more trips up and down the stairs and his stomach started to settle. He caught himself humming— *Lisa Mary's a river gal.* He cut it off, because the song, one he had learned from the gambler, shouldn't be sung in the presence of a proper woman. But his humming reassured him. Deep down inside, he was not his father.

"Lindy, next time you go to Virginia, find out what's going on at the Shirt Tail. With a speculation like this the price won't stay up forever. You have to sell when it's on the rise."

"I can't sell the shares. They're Harvey's."

"Talk to the lawyer and find out if there's some way to do it. At ten dollars a share, that's a thousand dollars."

"I'll ask," she said. He rewarded himself for his honesty by scraping the last of the rhubarb and dumplings out of the pot before she washed it.

Lindy, he found, did not bother with a lantern or candles. She went to bed at dark. Lon unrolled his blankets, but did not crawl in. He sat on the edge of the porch and traced the constellations, starved for the sight of the night sky.

His sense of peace he ascribed to Lindy's good cooking. The food had loosened his tongue, made him an absolute chatterbox. Never, in eight years, had he told anyone about his last day on the farm, particularly the part about his mother leaving. Even now it smacked of scandal. Good women did not leave their husbands. He remembered the girl in school whose mother ran off with some men who came through town in a wagon, bound for Oregon. The teasing, the ridicule, and it hurt to remember that he had joined in. That, probably more than anything, had pushed him west.

He'd told Lindy, he decided, because she would not condemn his mother. Lindy wasn't a bad woman. Different from any woman he'd ever known, but maybe, out here in the wide desert, women could do a man's work, wear men's clothes, get a divorce, and still remain good women.

But she'd certainly been too free with at least one man before marrying. He measured the distance between his blankets and the open window. He tested several of the boards making up the floor of the porch, and heard satisfying creaks.

Chapter Eleven

Lon swung the scythe, cutting the grass as close as possible to the ground. He'd seen the dust of Lindy's wagon returning from Virginia City, but she did not come to the field. The eastern sky turned to plum. Time to quit. He examined the first haystack, tall as he could make it. The hay for the second lay drying on the ground.

Lindy was hunched against the flanks of one of the red-brown cows, the milk rumbling as it hit the bottom of the empty pail, changing to a hiss as the pail filled. Lon sat on the back steps, carefully sharpened the scythe, ready for morning. Then he searched in all the hens' secret hiding places for the last of the eggs. Lindy had said she'd not hired him to do chores, but he didn't feel right, sitting on the porch, watching her work.

He took off his boots, climbed into the water tank, clothes and all, to rid himself of grass. He picked the burrs from his socks, then draped them over the edge of the porch to dry. He wiggled his bare toes, ran his fingers through his hair to slick it back out of his eyes. His hair needed clipping, especially the blasted cowlick that dropped over his forehead. Occasionally a drift of heat came from the cookstove, and with it fragrant odors.

Lindy took baked steak from the oven, fried potatoes

from a skillet and green beans cooked with bacon from a pan. A dish of cucumbers in vinegar and a sugar cream pie already sat on the table.

He stuffed himself, then ate half the sugar cream pie. He wondered if Lindy had inquired about the Shirt Tail, but felt uneasy about quizzing her, for she might think he still contemplated stealing the certificate.

"Coffee?" she asked.

"Thanks."

"The Shirt Tail deal went bad," she said suddenly, standing so close to him he felt the heat of her body, and smelled her sweat.

"Went bad?"

"Mr. Dove said the reporter from the *Territorial Enterprise* didn't give the mine the kind of notice to encourage anyone to buy."

"But Braley was certain!" cried Lon. "He bought a bottle of brandy…!" Lon snapped his mouth shut, realizing he had nearly betrayed his part in the Shirt Tail scheme. Lindy handed him a folded newspaper.

Reopening Of An Old Prospect

Miners have nailed many a grandiloquent name to claim stakes in the Nevada Territory, most with nothing underground beyond the most wistful hope to support the brag. Monarch of the Mountains and Golden Regina come to mind as glory holes with glory only in nomenclature.

We commend the owners of the Shirt Tail for avoiding so egregious a falsehood, and giving their prospect a name more in keeping with the poverty of both its present and potential. Beware, however, of taking this one act of truthfulness as a guarantee of future honesty. The current operators impressed this writer as no more nor less capable of prevarication than the garden-variety prospector.

The Shirt Tail consists of one horizontal shaft driven into the mountain on the east side of Seven Mile Canyon to a depth of seventy or eighty feet. Such improvements as timbering and tracks for ore cars have not materialized. The dump gives the appearance of having been stirred a bit, but the unpromising nature of the rock therein lies visible to any half-competent observer. The present operators boast that this rock "resembles the Comstock," and so it does, in that both form part of the lithic structure of the earth. The resemblance does not extend to the similarity of brothers, let alone pea-pod twins.

Three men form the company bound to reopen the Shirt Tail. They expect the tunnel, when extended, to strike a rich vein, an extension of the Comstock Lode itself. If their forecast proves right, it will demonstrate the so far unvoiced theory that the Comstock Ledge dives into the bowels of the earth, bounces off the upper reaches of Hades, shoots upward at something approaching a ninety-degree angle, and appears in Seven Mile Canyon without betraying itself in outcrops on the surrounding slopes.

The Shirt Tail operators flourish a "geologic report," and beg us to regard this evidence of their future riches. The author of this report impresses with his knowledge of clay. He discusses clay in agriculture, clay in veins, clay as the matrix for erratic rocks, even quotes Julius Caesar in what purports to be a critique of the clay of Gaul, with an accuracy this reporter cannot judge, having avoided a classical education. The author of the report pontificates on the advantages and disadvantages of clay in every possible circumstance, except as it applies to the Shirt Tail and to the (amazing) reemerging Comstock Ledge.

He boasts of the Shirt Tail's supply of freshwater.

This feature of the mine cannot be denied. We ourselves trod in the stream that gushes from the Shirt Tail, and retreated as water threatened to rise above our boot soles. The flow pours out in amount sufficient for a mining enterprise, so long as the complement of men never exceeds three. Bring in four, and they must augment their liquid refreshment with a plentiful supply of whiskey. The tall tales peddled by the "geologist" suggest he found the substitution necessary.

Lon reared back, nearly cried out his objections to being portrayed as a drunk, then thought better of revealing his intimate association with the report, and went on reading.

The current criers of Shirt Tail possibilities even now prepare to blast their way to its riches. Instead of placing the charge at the face of the tunnel, behind which, their report demonstrates, lies a fabulous deposit of gold and silver, these clever miners plan to concentrate their destructive energies in a barren stope about thirty feet from the entrance. While this facilitates the removal of the rock, how this effort will bring the investors any closer to the fabled ledge this reporter does not pretend to understand. We suspect the investors aim at a speculative mining of customers of the stock exchange, rather than an earnest effort to expand the Shirt Tail.

An experienced miner superintends this operation. We shall not bandy about his name, in consideration of his future need for employment. He exudes sincerity in all discussions of his current endeavor. Yet the skeptic remembers that Attila the Hun had a reputation for sincerity....

"Who is this—" Lon searched for the name "—Mark Twain?"

"A runty reporter for the *Enterprise*. His real name's Clemens."

Why had Braley let a drunken reporter write the article? Because he might be more easily fooled? But this Twain held his brandy well.

"Mr. Dove says Clemens usually boosts the wildcats. In fact, Mr. Dove won't buy shares in any mine Clemens praises, because he's normally so undiscriminating. Every other blue moon his conscience starts to bother him—Mr. Clemens's conscience, that is—and he lets loose a blast at some prospect. The Shirt Tail was unlucky to come around just when guilt overtook him."

"Bad luck." *I'm out my two hundred dollars. And I thought the part about clay particularly well-done.*

He's right, of course, about the water. There's not enough to wet a dry man's whistle more than once. But Braley had thought it important to mention it. Damn Braley! Damn this drunken reporter who used the Shirt Tail as the butt of his joke.

After thinking the matter through for ten seconds, Lon decided the man deserved praise instead of blame. Mr. Clemens, who called himself Mark Twain, might well be the only honest man in Nevada Territory.

Lon propped the scythe between his legs to sharpen the blade. He twisted around to pull the whetstone from his back pocket, paused in that awkward position to look at the three haystacks at the high end of the field. He squinted his eyes, but the growing corn blocked his view. He saw only the peak of the roof of the house, the sun-white hills and the dark mountains to the west.

He made himself concentrate on the sharpening. He wasn't looking at the hay, he knew, or the house, or the mountains. He watched for Lindy. How long since she'd started bringing him his dinner in the field, on those days when she stayed home? He had come to expect it, like a long-established tradition. A warm anticipation spread in his chest, near his heart, and it puzzled him. Hunger came lower down. He caught himself searching the haystacks again.

He tested the blade on his thumb and found it sharp. No excuse remained to stand gazing at the haystacks. He lifted the scythe, made one swing close to the ground; the grass and weeds fell in a precise, straight line. On impulse he turned again, and found Lindy hurrying toward him, a basket over her arm. Had he turned at the right time accidentally, or had some sixth sense told him she was near? *There's no such thing as a sixth sense,* he snorted to himself as he dashed to grab his shirt. He struggled to pull it over his head and down his sweaty chest. He slicked back his hair with his fingers, and by the time she arrived he was presentable. He raked a low pile of grass to sit on.

"You finished another stack yesterday while I was gone," she said. "At this rate, in ten days you'll be done."

"Can't have too much hay. What if the winter lasts till May, or the snow's heavy and the animals can't pasture at all?" He shut his mouth. Each day that passed, he had a harder time keeping still around Lindy. He stared at her, wondering what she did to make him garrulous. With two dozen words he'd committed himself to making more than four or five stacks. Four or five would certainly be enough for her cows and mules and goats and sheep.

She lifted a tablecloth from the top of the basket and spread it on the grass, emptied the basket of boiled eggs, cheese, tiny beets pickled with vinegar and sugar, fresh radishes, and bread still warm from the oven. Plus a covered tin pail of buttermilk.

"I'm late today because the bread was slow rising." She cut off a thick slice, and he covered it with butter from a small crock.

"Ah! Nothing better than fresh bread." He drank the buttermilk straight from the bucket. "You don't need to go to all this trouble, Lindy. I'm accustomed to bacon and beans.''

"It's a pleasure to feed a man who enjoys his food."

She smiled and the bottom of his stomach heaved, sloshing the buttermilk around. Lately he had noticed that spasm when Lindy turned up. Strange, because he'd never before been bothered with a peevish stomach. What was the date? Near the end of July? He had to hold out against her until August 13.

"The carpenter from Washoe came this morning," she announced. "He figures to start my barn in two and a half weeks."

"When will that be? The date?"

"About the middle of August." So he owed her another two and a half weeks! Seventeen or eighteen days, and on five of those she'd be in Virginia City. They'd sit like this with a picnic between them twelve more times. Seventeen or eighteen breakfasts and suppers, when he must keep himself stiff and quiet; seventeen or eighteen evenings when their hands came close during the washing up.

"I keep trying to imagine what the place will look like, with a real barn and a barnyard," she said, looking toward the house.

"Good," he said. "Like a farm back East."

"Like the farm in Indiana you hated?"

"No. Better. Your farm is better than that one."

"I'll fix up some boxes for the hens, so they can lay their eggs away from the skunks and foxes."

Her eyes glowed in anticipation. In the shade of her broad hat they became dark, of no color at all, the blue obscured by a silver glint of reflected sunlight. He cut himself another slice of bread.

You've become a glutton, taking advantage of her good nature, he accused himself, then shifted on the grass uneasily, wondering when he had come to believe that Lindy had a good nature.

"The builder left a book of pictures and plans. I'm to choose which barn I want, so he can haul out the proper timbers. Would you help me?" Lon stopped spreading butter on the bread.

"It's not to be my barn," he said. He'd lain awake for an hour last night, contemplating the barn he'd build, if this were his land.

"But you were raised on a farm, so you can give me good advice."

"The builder knows more than I do. At home we didn't have a fit barn. Not one built all of a piece, from scratch. I'd be no help at all." He felt guilty saying this while he buttered the bread. Eating her food committed him to helping her with the choice of barn. "I'll look at the book, but you make the choice."

"Quit a bit early, before the sun's down," she said, repacking the basket. "So we'll have plenty of time."

He didn't want to get involved with the barn. If he helped her plan the barn, if he helped lay the thing out, he might want to stick around to watch it become reality.

Lon circled the fourth—incomplete—haystack, and looked back on the long swath of cut grass to be stacked tomorrow. The speed with which hay dried in this desert country still amazed him. Back in Indiana he and his father had kept worried eyes cocked at every stray cloud on the horizon, and turned the hay day after day to dry. A thunderstorm, a night of rain, even a heavy dew ruined every bit of grass on the ground. No wonder his father's edgy impatience grew worse in haying season.

Memories carried him far from the Carson Valley, and he walked by the garden and didn't think of the death's-head until it grinned down at him. He was rounding the chicken coop when he noticed the strange horse.

"I'll tell them, Lindy. By God! You're willing to take in that jailbird...." Lon stopped, only partially concealed by the chicken coop and the rail of the hog pen. The voice sounded familiar...that damned deputy from the jail! Had he come to arrest him again? Take him back to jail? He looked back over his shoulder, searching for a hiding place. The shoulder-high corn? The haystacks?

"Lon Anderson is my hired man," Lindy said, unperturbed.

"Hired for what?" asked the deputy with evil suggestion.

"Do you see him about right now? No, because he's out cutting my hay," she sneered.

"I'm not asking much, Lindy. I'll keep my mouth shut about the—"

"Get off my farm, Clugg." An undertone of fear. Arresting Lon Anderson didn't seem to figure largely in Clugg's mind. Lon decided to risk putting in an appearance. He cleared his throat loudly as he approached the porch.

"What if I—" Clugg turned at the sound, his brows rising in alarm. "What if I was to tell the sheriff you're using the place for a bawdy house?"

"Bawdy house?" exclaimed Lindy.

"Everyone in Carson Valley knows Harvey's not here no more, and you got a great big man looking out for you. If I hear of other men skulking about, I'll tell the sheriff and he can go to the judge and charge you—"

"Didn't you hear the lady, Clugg?" Lon said. "She said for you to get off the farm." He hefted the scythe a bit, to put some threat behind his words.

"Now that you mention it," said Clugg. He backed toward his horse. "You think about it, Lindy. It's not a far ride to Genoa, and when that fellow finds out, it's gonna cost you more than I ask." He mounted, turned the horse's head toward the road, but sat twisted in the saddle to keep his eyes on Lindy. Lon moved toward Lindy, then remembered Clugg's charges of improper conduct between them, and stepped back, widening the gap to six feet.

"What did he want?" he asked, once he saw Clugg's horse trotting up the hill. Lindy said nothing, but stared after the deputy. "Lindy, what did Clugg mean, he'd tell them? Tell who?" Lon heard his voice, demanding, dictatorial. Just because he lived with her, it didn't mean her business was his, and he was way out of line asking. "I'm sorry, Lindy. It's none of my business." He turned toward the porch, hauling the whetstone from his pocket to show his intention.

"Clugg went to the trouble of finding out who owns the property next door."

"So?"

"My irrigation ditch, the one to the cornfield, it comes off the river on that property. I didn't put it there. Old Mr. Parker dug it, before Will bought the place, but we didn't know."

"Has the owner complained?"

"No. But Clugg says the man lives in Genoa, and he said he'll go down there and tell him I owe him rent for the trespass of the ditch, unless..." Her voice faded and two red circles sprang out on the points of her cheekbones, accenting her triangular face.

"Unless what?"

"Clugg figures I'll romp with him to keep the secret."

"What?" he exploded. Several seconds passed before Lon sensed the firm muscles of Lindy's shoulders beneath his fingers, and realized he had hold of her. She did not react, but stared beyond him.

"He figures a grass widow is anxious for a man, and he figures that's why I have you here, and he figures to get his share. He knows I don't want to romp with him, so he'd be most pleased to force it. Little fellows are like that."

Lon almost asked her if she *was* anxious for a man, then decided he didn't want to know, because being near her caused the sweat on his chest to spring out again. He dropped his hands and backed away.

"So he'll go to this man who owns the land, and tell him your ditch is on his property?"

"That's what he says."

"A likely story," retorted Lon, gazing upriver to the sage-covered ridge. "Who'd claim a worthless piece of land like that? The little flat down by the river's nothing but marsh until July, and the rest's a hill too steep to plow, too high to get water on. Grows nothing but sagebrush."

"Clugg says the owner lives in Genoa."

"You can check at the recorder's office in Carson City."

"I suppose."

"Next time you go into town, find the name of the man who owns it, then go to him, or write a letter, and tell him about the ditch. That'll put a bar through Clugg's spokes." She nodded. "Once that's settled, you go to the sheriff and tell him what Clugg asked of you, and he'll get fired."

"I doubt that. He's the nephew of someone in the territorial government."

"The damned judge," Lon growled, remembering Clugg's visit during the poker game. "If he can't be fired, I'll teach him to bother you!" Leaping horned toads! What was he saying? He didn't want to fight Deputy Clugg. He'd wasted enough time in Nevada Territory. One swing at a deputy sheriff would land him back in jail. Maybe even in the territorial prison, and for longer than thirty days.

"Thank you, Lon. It's nice to have a man worry about my honor," she said, her eyes wide, the blue so deep the bottom couldn't be reached with a surveyor's rod. "In Virginia City I appreciated it when you stood between me and—" He fled to the water tank, took off his boots, sank completely under the water.

While she bustled about the stove, he crept to the edge of the porch to dry in the evening breeze. That kept sufficient distance between them. But then she went into the house and came out with a large book under her arm.

"Here's the barns," she announced. She sat down on the

porch, placed the open book between them. Lon scooted away.

"Don't want to drip water on the pages," he excused himself, knowing full well that dampness showed only in the crevices of his shirt and trousers.

"Now, the first ones are too large, not the sort of barns for a farm like this." She flipped the pages quickly, dismissing outbuildings with cupolas and turrets, suitable for the country estates of Comstock millionaires. "This one might do." Lon leaned over cautiously. A basic barn, the roof rising in a single pitch to a high gable.

"A barn with a double pitch to the roof gives you more room in the haymow." He drew the profiles in the dust of the porch.

She flipped a few pages, found a picture that answered his description.

"It's nice, but it costs more," she said simply.

"It's easier and cheaper to build right the first time. Go to the bank and borrow a little money."

She laughed. "Do you suppose a banker lends money to a lady farmer?" Lon hadn't thought of that. Of course there must be rules about women taking out loans. And until Lindy had her divorce, her husband had the say-so in the matter of his wife's money. It really didn't seem fair, when Lindy scrimped and saved, and in her husband's hands money flowed like water through a sieve.

Lindy flipped back to the original picture. Lon pretended to squeeze water from his almost dry hair, so he had a reason not to lean over the book and examine the front and rear elevations.

"The carpenter said I must mark on the ground where I want it built." She swung herself down off the porch. "Let's lay it out! I'll get the hoe."

"Do you have string, or twine? The wind will fill a furrow made with a hoe. I'll whittle some stakes, and we'll drive them down deep at the corners."

He memorized the measurements of the floor plan while she brought the twine from the house. Bigger than the barn on the farm in Indiana. And brand-new, not an extension of an old log cabin.

He closed the book partially to turn it toward him; the page fell open to a memory of childhood, a barn beside the road into town. As a child he had supposed the owner of such a barn to be incredibly wealthy. The disparity between that man's riches and his own father's poverty had dampened the joy of a trip into Fort Wayne.

A double-pitched roof, with two cupolas to provide summer ventilation. Broad front doors hanging by rollers on iron tracks. If a man could afford a barn like that, farm life would be rewarding. If a man had the cash to care for his family and animals properly, being a farmer would not drive him to lamentations, and cruelty.

"I can't afford anything like that, Lon!" Lindy laughed above him, and held out a ball of twine.

"Wouldn't it be nice if you could?" he said, and to himself he admitted, *I might stay.*

He had no tape or rule to measure the length and breadth, but Lindy said her feet measured exactly twelve inches with her boots on. Using her feet as a gauge, they estimated his stride, and he paced out the shape of the barn on a level place just beyond the corral. He stomped down the stakes at the corners while she held them, then two more where the double doors would be. The twine glowed faintly in the twilight. Lindy walked through the opening that marked the doors, wide enough to pass a wagon. Lon stepped over the twine, foolishly afraid to be in the barn with her, alone.

"Dinner's ready," she cried. "I forgot all about it, being so excited about the barn. Dinner's in the oven. I've kept you from your dinner." She ran out the door, leaving him alone, to build a fantasy frame of pine, the walls of sturdy planks, the roof of cedar shingles. He would not see the barn, of course. The carpenters would come after he left.

But now it lived in his mind, exactly where he and Lindy had placed it. Next winter, someplace in the gentle climate of California, he would think of Lindy and her stock, snug and warm in the barn.

She had baked some small animal—he supposed a rabbit—with half-grown carrots and onions and potatoes. The gravy combined sweet and spice, so after he cleaned his plate of the first helping, he laid out two thick slices of bread and covered them with gravy.

"What sort of barn did you have on the farm in Indiana?" she asked.

"Not a proper one like yours. An old log cabin built on the place in the days of first settlement." It hurt to say more, for describing that shanty barn told her how truly poverty-stricken they had been. "Pa and I built another bit on the front."

"You know carpentry! If you'd told me that sooner, I wouldn't have asked the builder from Washoe, but would have proposed you take the job!"

He laughed. "We did it when I was six years old, so I don't think you can call me a carpenter. A barn blew down in a spring twister on a place four miles away. They gave us the wood for hauling it off. Evenings, all summer, Pa nailed away, while I held the other end of the boards. It didn't fall down, but only because it had the log cabin to lean against."

And the other farmer had replaced that heap of broken planks with a fine square barn, reddened with linseed oil and ox blood. It sat behind a white rail fence, back of a carriage house and a chicken coop with glass windows finer than those in the house where he lived.

"Lon," she said, her voice dubious in a way he had never heard before. "Next Saturday Mrs. Dove's having a quilting bee, with a dance afterward." He nodded, understanding and agreeing immediately. She wanted to be away for an afternoon and evening, which meant he must do the chores.

"Nothing around here I can't manage. You go ahead."

"Yes, but..."

"I'll do the chores. Don't worry about it. I can see to them for one evening."

"But I want you to come to the dance. If you'd milk the cows and the goat, and get the chickens shut in, I'll see to the rest after we get home."

His chest hurt, and he noticed he'd stopped breathing. The Fourth of July had set tongues wagging, and now, with him living on her farm, everyone probably expected a wedding once the judge granted the divorce. A dance at the Doves' would clinch it.

But a man did grow a bit antsy, living out here on the river, miles from town, seeing no one but Lindy. Not that Lindy was not a fine lady, and interesting to be with, who loosened his tongue amazingly, but a man needed to be with other men occasionally, if only to hear the news.... The damage had been done on the Fourth of July, he rationalized. Another public appearance with Lindy would not trap him any more than he'd trapped himself already.

"What kind of meat did you cook for dinner, Lindy? I'm afraid I ate more than my share."

"You liked it?" she asked cautiously.

"Fine. Just fine."

"Skunk. The jackass rabbits here aren't fit to eat—" Skunk! "—but the skunks from the meadows near the mountains, if you get them young, they're delicious."

Delicious, if you're hungry from a long day's work, and don't ask about the dish until you've already eaten it. He eyed Lindy suspiciously. Was she teasing him, telling another of her "jokes"?

If his father had discovered his mother serving a skunk, even with carrots and potatoes, and gravy that made your mouth ask for more, he would have accused her of feeding the family like poor river squatters. He'd have said there were plenty of provisions, if only she didn't waste so much. Then he would have turned on Lon, and accused him of bringing the stinking thing home. His father would have lain down to keep from getting sick, and would have been bilious for a week.

He leaned back, rubbed his stomach. "Absolutely delicious. And the gravy!" He licked his lips.

"Just a spoonful of currant jelly," she said. "Add currant jelly to plain gravy and it tastes like Christmas."

He contemplated Christmas dinner, but interrupted the fantasy to do the dishes. As he put away the knives, forks and spoons, he remembered he'd not be here come Christmas. He'd be in California. And he'd never see the barn.

Chapter Twelve

Lindy decided to wear the more conservative of her two dresses for the quilting bee, the dark blue cotton with a broad collar of ivory piqué, and a skirt that could be caught up in back to wear without hoops. She spread it carefully on top of the load of eggs, butter and vegetables, wrapped in a sheet she'd made from flour sacks. A brisk breeze stirred the corners of the fabric, and she imagined her dress flying over the precipice, down into Gold Canyon. She started up the stairs to fetch the flatiron to weigh it down, but the three rocks next to the rosebush caught her eye. She arranged them in a row the length of the dress.

Looking back from the road, she could just make out the rhythmic swing of the scythe as Lon worked toward the river. He possessed an unusual combination of strength and precision. He laid his haystacks well; none of her hay would sail away in a Washoe Zephyr this fall. She smiled at the rising sun, optimistic. Since the evening she and Lon had laid out the barn, he'd gone through the plan book twice, describing the features of an ideal barn. Not that she could afford to build that wonderful structure, but if she got a divorce in the fall session of the court, and Lon hung around, maybe the bank... No, she needed the barn before the cold weather came. She dared not wait for Lon to come around to marrying her, after the divorce.

But he'd not turned a hair when he found out she'd cooked skunk. In fact, he praised it so much she'd ask McCaffrey's hunters to bring another one. Lon had a good stomach. She distrusted finicky men who complained about their food, and forever hit on this or that as causing belly-ache. Lon wasn't picky, and that went a long way to convincing her she could trust him. If he weren't busy with the hay, she could trust him to cut the wheat. She could trust him to watch the carpenters, so they didn't skimp on the rafters in the barn. Lon didn't like the farm, but she could trust him to take care of it properly. One question was yet to be answered. Could she trust him with herself? She thought she could, but she'd certainly like to try him out before she agreed to anything permanent.

Three of Nora's boarders helped her unload the wagon. She left it standing in front of the rooming house, but led the teams down the hill to the livery stable, where they might lounge about all day eating hay. She changed into her dress in Nora's back room, and joined the dozen ladies sitting around the quilting frame in the parlor.

On second glance she saw eleven ladies and a woman. What was Sunshine Alice doing here? Even in the morning, Alice wore a bright yellow calico dress, with the neck cut too low for the time of day. The dress clashed with the red, white and blue patchwork. More distressing than Alice's presence, the only empty seat was beside her. Lindy edged around the expanse of the quilting frame.

"Good morning," she said as she sat down.

"Good morning," said a dozen voices. Silence. Every conversation stopped, every needle paused pointing upward. Half the ladies stared at her with cold, hard eyes, and the other half leaned forward with parted lips.

They know I'm divorcing Harvey. They know Lon's living with me.

A few eyes moved from Lindy to Alice, and back again. *They think I'm no better than she is.*

"How are things on the farm, Lindy?" asked Nora.

"Fine. I got a *hired man* to put up my hay. *My* animals won't starve this winter." Not like some did last winter, she nearly added, cows and horses that belonged to people sitting in this room. Poor creatures who roamed the countryside crying for food until they starved to death.

She opened her sewing pocket, pulled out her needles and the tiny scissors she used to cut thread. Sunshine Alice pushed the thread in her direction.

"How do you do it?" asked a sugared voice from across the quilt. "Down there *all alone?*" The last two words were said in a way that told any woman who didn't already know that Lindy's hired man stayed the night.

"Like I said, I got a hired man for the hay."

"Is it true you have retained a lawyer?" asked another. "In the matter of Mr. Saxton, that is."

"Of course she's getting a lawyer," said a loud voice, and Lindy recognized the former Mrs. Randall, now Mrs. Stow, wife of the well-paid superintendent of the Yellow Jacket. "It beats me why you women can't say 'divorce' out loud. When a woman finds herself tied to a no-good, dishonest man, she has the God-given right to rectify the situation by getting a divorce. God never meant for a woman to live in this world with the torments of hell."

Lindy wished she could throw her arms about Mrs. Stow. She smiled as she bent to her work. Alice's needle flashed. Lindy saw why Nora had asked the woman to join in the quilting. Alice made incredibly tiny stitches, so small one might think they'd entered the quilt by magic. Lindy concentrated on matching Alice's skill. After completing one corner of a block, she compared her work to Alice's, and found it wanting. But she stitched better than the lady on her right, whose quilting looked more like basting. The owner of the quilt would rip out everything the woman did. If the owner had any pride, that is.

"The man who's working for you is Anderson?" asked Alice quietly, once the chatter of conversation resumed.

"Yes."

"Too bad Sam Clemens carped so about the mine. Is Anderson planning to try that business again? Maybe find a friendlier reporter."

"Anderson didn't have anything to do with the Shirt Tail speculation. He heard about it when he worked at the Gould and Curry."

Alice reared back, her needle a dagger ready to plunge into the heart of the block she worked on.

"You don't know? Of course Anderson worked at the Shirt Tail. He wrote that geologic report that Clemens poked so much fun at."

"Lon? Anderson?" she repeated, hoping Alice didn't hear her use of his first name. Lindy's heart skipped a single beat, leaving a vague, peevish feeling in her chest. She bent over the quilt, stabbed in her needle and got three stitches on it before she pulled the thread through. The peevish feeling changed to melancholy.

"The man who's living with me, Billy Miller, he worked at the Shirt Tail when Anderson wrote the report," Alice continued remorselessly. "He told me Anderson copied it from some papers from the Gould and Curry. The fellow running the show hired Billy to lay the charges because he's so small. Then they didn't pay him a cent, because he worked contingent on the shares rising on the strength of Clemens's article. Damned reporter! I suppose Anderson's working for you because they couldn't pay him, either."

Lindy nearly blurted out the truth, that Anderson came to work for her because otherwise he'd be languishing in jail. Because he broke in to a lawyer's office to steal Harvey's Shirt Tail stock. The melancholy turned to incoherent anger and she wanted to cry. Lon and Harvey, both schemers in fraudulent wildcat mines! The truth tore her heart.

"I don't believe it," she whispered in Alice's direction, but she knew everything Alice said was true. She worked herself to the bone, cooking fancy meals to please a man who was as dishonest as Harvey! The thread caught on her rough hands. She jerked at it, and cut the side of her palm.

"You work too hard, Lindy," muttered Alice. "You sell that farm and buy a little place on D Street, and you'd have a fortune inside a year. How tall *are* you?"

"Six feet and one-half inch," she muttered.

"Men'll flock from all the mining districts to say they've been with a woman more than six feet tall. The work's really very pleasant, once you get the hang of it, and in a few months you'd have gold and silver enough to retire. You could go to San Francisco and live like a lady. Or buy a saloon, and hire other girls to work, while you sit about in fancy dresses, letting the men admire you."

"No men admire me."

"You're looking in the wrong direction, that's all. When you have a difference about you, it doesn't pay to be an honest woman. Men expect you to be bawdy, and unless you mean to fight all your life, you fit yourself to the expectations of a man's world. Would you let me know if Anderson's thinking of reopening the Shirt Tail?"

"Why should he tell me if he's dealing from the bottom of the deck in a wildcat operation?" snapped Lindy.

He won't tell me, of course. He's a liar, like all men!

She could feel the beat of her heart far down in her belly. Too far down.

"Men eventually tell their women everything, in bed, when they're satisfied and at their ease. That's how I found out about the Shirt Tail scheme three, maybe four months ago. That man Riddel took a fancy to me, and one night he talked too much. I found 450 shares of Shirt Tail down on D Street, got them all in trades for other worthless paper.

Just give Anderson a good feed some evening—'' Alice's whisper turned seductive, and sweat started out all over Lindy's body ''—pleasure him a long time, and make sure he believes you've gone just crazy wild having him. It flatters men terribly when they think a woman's lost all her shame because they're so good in bed. Then whisper in his ear that you're interested in the Shirt Tail. Let me know, and I'll give you a cut of the profits.''

''He doesn't sleep with me,'' whispered Lindy toward the quilt. She had not taken a stitch for several minutes; everyone must notice that her block lagged far behind.

''Doesn't...'' began Alice in a loud voice. She took a dozen of her minuscule stitches. ''You're more a fool than I thought, Lindy Saxton,'' she whispered. ''Why, the first time I saw the man I wanted him in my bed, and so did every other girl on D Street. I hoped to get the details from you today, in a private minute, for all the girls want to know if he's as sizable as he looks.''

Lindy stared at the stitches on her needle with dismay. Some of them stretched as long as her neighbor's, and not regular at all, because her hands shook.

All the whores want him in their bed. And so do I. What does that make me?

''You're not going to tell me?'' asked Alice. Lindy shook her head. ''You're selfish, Lindy Saxton. Before you move to D Street, you'll have to learn to share.''

Lon searched for the rake by the fifth haystack, and only then noticed the horse and buggy and three men standing a hundred yards away, down where Lindy's irrigation ditch branched off from the river. He put the rake down.

''Lindy's problems aren't my concern,'' he muttered to himself. She, or rather her brother, should have settled the matter of the irrigation ditch before they ever agreed to purchase the farm. But being from Ohio, they knew no more about irrigating than he did. Less, in fact. They'd been cheated by the previous owner.

So what else could one expect in Nevada Territory? Except it hurt that Lindy, an honest woman, had been tricked in this, because she'd also been seduced into marriage by a dishonest assayer. Saxton had tempted her, until poor Lindy had no choice but to say yes. Lon hoped she got the divorce and found a better husband.

He walked across the stubble, and paused where he supposed the unmarked boundary lay. One of the men stepped aside. No mistaking the man behind him. Deputy Clugg. Lon took one determined step across the line, then another, remembered he'd left the scythe behind, thought about returning for it, but decided that would look like retreat.

"Howdy, Anderson," said the deputy. "Enjoying your work?"

"Yes. Food's better here than in your establishment." One of Clugg's companions walked with a cane, and as he drew nearer, Lon saw the bent shoulders and tottering gait. The old man seemed only vaguely interested in the ditch Clugg pointed out to him. The other man, short and bulky, had his back turned, studying the route of the ditch from the river.

"I'm just showing the rightful owners of this property how it's being used without their permission or payment," said Clugg. He gestured to the elderly man. "This here's Mr. Miller, who lives in Genoa, and his son." He pointed to the bulky man. "We'll be over shortly to visit Mrs. Saxton, and see how she accounts for the trespass."

"You dig this ditch?" the younger man asked sharply as he turned around.

"This isn't my farm," explained Lon. Thank heavens, he said to himself. "It belongs to a fellow in Sacramento. I'm just hired on to make the hay." He looked at the ground so he didn't stare. The same blunt face with bristles of beard, the dark, bugged-out eyes, the whites so large they suggested a relationship to an owl. Lon tugged his hat a bit farther down on his forehead. Didn't the thief recognize him?

"Fellow in Sacramento!" Clugg exclaimed sarcastically. "The place belongs to Lindy Saxton."

"Check it out!" Lon snorted. "A bit tedious to work through the papers in the recorder's office, but you'd appear less a pathetic ass if you did."

Clugg sputtered, speechless with fury at being challenged. He turned to the man who needed a shave, while flinging a hand toward Lon. "This man...this man don't know nothing. He's a thief who's only out here because Lindy Saxton can't bear a cold bed. There's no owner in Sacramento."

"Merryman," said Lon, hauling back on his urge to land his fist on Clugg's jaw. The name meant nothing to Clugg, for his face did not change, but the bulky man pulled off his hat and eyed Lon with narrowed eyes.

"Merryman?" he asked, turning the hat brim nervously in his hands. "That storekeeper fellow?"

"The one." The man's eyes changed from puzzled to alarmed. "I hope your leg's recovered from that fall you had in the creek," Lon said slowly, so the man heard not only the words, but the threat behind them. "And your little son, he didn't suffer too much on the trip out to the Reese River?" Had the old man been the "wife"? Lon looked directly into the pale eyes, but ascertained nothing from their amiable stare. "And the boy's mother? She's recovered from her fever?"

The young Mr. Miller didn't wait to hear more. He ran, his strides lengthened by panic, through the tangled grass of the flat, toward the buggy. He shrieked, jumped to one side, fell full-length upon the ground. The old man hobbled behind him, calling, "Son! Son!"

Clugg turned his head from the Millers to Lon and back again, wearing out his neck. "What?" he cried.

"Snake!" screamed the young Miller. He didn't bother to get on his feet, but crawled at an amazing speed the final ten feet to the buggy. The white-haired man beat on the ground with his cane. "Come kill it! Billy! Get Billy to kill it! Billy always knows what to do!"

Clugg's cheeks turned the color of dirty snow, and his mouth gaped to show his irregular teeth. "Next time you look for some imposter to play landowner, Clugg, make sure they're not thieves. I'm letting Will Merryman know the Miller gang's in Genoa. Where's the dwarf?"

"I...I don't know what you're talking about."

"Then you're a worse lawman than your reputation has it." Lon hoped his voice did not echo the unnatural speed of his heart, or the sweat on his palms. He started to walk away, but some power drew him back.

"And if you get within so much as a quarter mile of Lindy Saxton—" he stepped close to Clugg to emphasize the ten-inch difference in their heights "—I'll beat your head through the boardwalk next time I'm in Carson City. The first time I'll leave your legs and arms sticking out so you can wave for help, but the second time, so help me God..."

He did not finish, because Clugg staggered toward the buggy, trying to run and avoid rattlesnakes at the same time. The younger Miller pulled his father into the buggy, then flapped the reins and yelled at the horse, with the old man's legs still hanging over the side. Clugg screamed for him to stop, made a flying leap to catch the box behind the seat, and hung on by his fingertips as the buggy bounced through the sagebrush.

The haying went more slowly for the next hour or two. The affair distracted him from his job. Why had he threatened Clugg with such drastic punishment? It wasn't as if Lindy meant *that* much to him.

Lon washed his trousers in the tank and wrapped one of Lindy's flannel towels around his hips while they dried. He carried an armload of freshly cut grass to the chicken coop. The hens came running, trailing their chicks behind. They dived into the mass of grass, scratching and pecking. With their attention distracted, he shut the door. Only after he dropped the bar did he realize he'd locked the rooster in the coop along with the hens. Lon considered the difficulty of releasing him from prison without letting the hens out, then shrugged his shoulders.

"Have fun, old boy," he said to the door of the chicken coop, and for a moment considered the fun of being shut in a room with Lindy.

When he pulled up to the cows with the stool and bucket, they stared at him with their liquid, brown eyes, but proved otherwise docile. The goat, on the other hand, refused to let him near, and he finally abandoned the effort, leaving her bleating with the agony of a full udder. Lindy could take care of it when she got home. He would have to make friends with the goat, so next time.... He reminded himself there would be no next time. In two weeks he'd head over the pass, back to California.

By the time he'd bathed in the tank, shaved and polished his boots with a lump of lard from the springhouse, his trousers had dried sufficiently to put on. He'd hung his blue-and-white shirt out to air that morning, and with the red kerchief he judged he looked fine enough to dance in Virginia City. But he'd not dance with Lindy.

The ride up the mountain took two hours, because the evening ore wagons all headed down at once to beat the darkness, and those that had gone down in the morning now hauled up loads of cut timber. Halfway up the grade he spied a piece of timber, about four inches square and fifteen or sixteen feet long, in the shallow ditch. Lon dismounted, carried the timber away from the road, into the sagebrush.

The confrontation with Clugg and the Millers nagged at the corners of his mind, because he found the permutations of Clugg's scheme obscure. He doubted the Millers owned the property, and they could not be homesteading, for to claim a homestead, a man must live on the land. Extending his thoughts with careful logic, Lon concluded that Clugg did not know the owners of the property, and his threats against Lindy carried no weight.

But if Clugg should go to the trouble of finding the real owner... Lindy should check in the county offices and find out who claimed that marsh and ridge of sand.

Then there was the younger Miller's panic at hearing Merryman's name. The Millers must have tangled with Will Merryman, and had no desire to repeat the experience.

"Hi! Anderson?" Lon didn't recognize the tattered ox driver until he removed his hat.

"Braley? What are you doing driving an ore wagon?" he asked in astonishment.

"I'm a driver because of that damn Sam Clemens! Gotta start all over, and the Gould and Curry's not looking for men at present. But—" he looked around as if there might be eavesdroppers on the road "—we're saving for another try. The Comstock Commander. You write the report, we'll give you four hundred this time, to make up for..."

Lon thought of the stock certificate in Stone's office. Tempted again? "No."

"If you change your mind," called Braley as he rode off, "I'm driving for the Ophir."

Lon tied Buckskin to Lindy's wagon. The ladies were still at their quilting, so he wandered to the kitchen where Mr. Dove entertained the men. The whiskey decanter occupied the center of the kitchen table.

"You're acquainted with Mr. Clemens, of the *Territorial Enterprise?*" inquired Mr. Dove.

Lon greeted the reporter a bit shyly, hoping he hadn't deciphered the scrawled name on the Shirt Tail geologic report. He studied the man surreptitiously, unable to feel very friendly toward the person who had dashed his hopes of quick wealth. Clemens was a young, skinny fellow, of medium height, except that his bush of sandy hair made him appear taller, and made his head look too large for his body.

"And Mr. DeQuille." The second reporter wore a dark beard, and was four inches taller than Clemens.

"Whiskey?" inquired Mr. Dove. Lon shook his head. "Clemens says that General Meade let Lee march his army back to Virginia, without throwing so much as the Ladies' Aid Society out to stop him. What good is it, supporting all those cavalry horses and not putting them to use?"

They talked war, not mines. Good. Lon didn't want Clemens to guess his part in the Shirt Tail.

"The only general the Union's got who's worth a loose cannon is Grant," snorted a man whose dirty boots rested upon the cold fender of the stove. "Now that he's got the Mississippi clear of rebels, Lincoln should order him east to clear out the nest of snakes in Virginia."

"He'll find the snakes under Lee got sharper teeth than those cowards on the Mississippi," retorted another man.

"You could go back to steamboating, Mark," said DeQuille. "The president says, with Vicksburg taken, 'The father of waters rolls unvexed to the sea.' You could certainly thread a steamboat through a few sunken gunboats."

Clemens shook his head. "The river will never be what it was before the war. Railroads everywhere, running straight east. Why ship goods through New Orleans? I'd better find my future in Nevada Territory."

"We've put up the quilt," said Mrs. Dove from the door. "The ladies are spreading the supper table, so stop talking about drifts and ledges and join us."

The parlor wasn't big enough for the crowd Mrs. Dove had invited, particularly since some of the ladies wore hoops. Lon didn't recognize Lindy at first glance, for she was sitting down, and he didn't know the dark blue dress. She and a woman in bright yellow rose from their chairs, walked to the sofa where the quilt lay on display. He kept his eyes on Lindy until she turned around. He smiled across the room. She stared at him coldly, like she'd rather not acknowledge his presence.

The woman in yellow! The whore who had accosted him on D Street! His astonishment doubled when a tiny man joined her. Billy Miller!

A fiddle and guitar struck up a polka, but Lon's stomach growled. Lindy had spoiled him with tasty picnics and filling suppers. He strode across the room to take her arm.

"I'm hungry," he said. "Let's get something to eat."

"You're always hungry," she snapped. Her eyes narrowed to slits, giving him his first solid warning that something had changed since morning. "We'd best go someplace where we can talk." He led her with trepidation into the dining room. Too many people clustered about the sideboard. He went on to the kitchen.

"Why didn't you tell me you were part of the Shirt Tail scheme?" she asked before the door closed behind them.

Why hadn't he? "Because it's not something I'm proud of, Lindy."

"Who else is involved?"

"That man you met at the Fourth celebration, Braley. He was the leader."

"You talked to that little man, that Billy, on the Fourth. He's part of it, too. I thought he was a boy, and when you treated him so patiently and kept him out of trouble, I liked you for being gentle and kind." Her dejected eyes lit with the fire of a woman deceived. "He's twenty-six years old and lives with Sunshine Alice!"

Lon could not think of a thing to say that might mitigate his offense, let alone clear his name. Particularly since such a convincing witness as Billy Miller had testified against him.

"So you came from California to open up a wildcat and cheat the greenhorns," she accused.

"No, I wrote the geologic report for Braley, that's all. I met Braley by accident my first day in Virginia City."

"It's no accident when a man decides to go bad. I thought robbing the lawyer's office was just a fool trick by a man hard up, and I could forgive it, but..." He'd never seen her eyes brimming, the tears threatening to spill over, and he wanted, inexplicably, to sweep her into his arms. Until he recalled the consequences of touching her.

"What kind of man writes a fake report!" she cried. "You're no geologist."

"No. Of course not. Braley pinched a report done for the Gould and Curry. I just copied the sentences, and made changes here and there so no one would suspect, unless they had the two reports side by side. The part about clay deposits, I wrote that, but Twain saw through the fraud."

"Just like Harvey. Just like the assay on the grinding stone! A complete fake!" Her mouth trembled. "So when you came...came...on the Fourth...you already knew about the Shirt Tail...."

"I came to your place on the Fourth to steal the Shirt Tail certificate off the wall. I thought you'd be gone. I didn't know it was the Fourth of July."

From the corner of his eye he saw her hand coming, and dodged. His head collided with the bend in the stovepipe, and he heard the soft whoosh of soot falling into the firebox. Black jets shot up around the stove lids.

He ducked, and her waist twisted right in front of his eyes as she swung for a second try. He grabbed at her, she struggled and got one hand in position to whack him in the side of the head. Nothing to do but pin her arms to her sides and pull her right up against him.

"Please, Lindy. It's not like that now!" he gasped.

"What's new?" she snapped. "A liar, a cheat, and now you show you're a bully."

She held herself stiff as a poker, not fighting him. Her blue eyes, lighter than he'd ever seen them, shone like coals, like a cat's eyes in the dark. A tiger's eyes, and he had the tiger by the tail. If he let go, she would hit him, but embracing her this way sent sparks sliding from the back of his neck down to his toes.

"And you're a snob," she cried. "My farm's not good enough for you! And you! Raised on a place without a decent barn to bed down a cow!"

"Lindy, it's not *your* farm I don't want. It's any farm!"

She glared at him, then relaxed. "I can't get away from you because I'm dizzy," she explained. "I must be hungry. I've worn out my fingers on that blessed quilt. My shoulders ache from leaning over, because they put it too low for someone my height."

"Then let's go to the supper table."

"Don't pay any heed to me this evening," she ordered. "All these women think we're...think that I... They made me sit beside Sunshine Alice."

"I see."

"Alice asked me how big your...poker was." She gave a snort, half giggle, half sob. To his horror, the organ she mentioned surged.

"What did you tell her?"

"I told her we didn't...romp...and she wouldn't believe me, and she got huffy and said I meant to keep a good thing all to myself, and that I wouldn't fit in on D Street, because—"

"D Street!" he yelled.

"Alice said I should give up farming and move to D Street. What do you think?" She relaxed, idly swung her hips, rubbing the folds of her skirt against the misbehaving part of him. Her eyes opened wide, her lips parted just enough so he could see the pink tip of her tongue. If he bent just a little, he could kiss her lips, touch his tongue to the bud of her own, because everything fell in exactly the right place. Never in his life had he held a woman so close to his own height, and she tempted...tempted him to change the hold into an embrace.

She pulled away. "Let me go. I won't hit you."

"Promise?"

"Promise. But you never touch me like that again."

"I didn't touch you!" he protested. "You're the one who swung up against me. I'm just protecting myself."

"Protecting yourself!" she scoffed. "I never heard of a man who protected himself by swelling up that way. What do you do? Swing it about to knock men down?"

Lon dropped his hands, backed away from her, right into the stove.

"You didn't answer my question," she said. "What do you think about me moving to D Street?"

"That's for you to decide," he said gruffly. "There's a name for a man who tempts a woman to that kind of life." She howled with laughter.

"You may dance with me twice," she announced. "A woman doesn't give a man more than two dances unless she's interested in him." Lon turned his back on her, strode across the room to stare at the two flights of steps leading down to B Street. He might escape this way, unseen. But he wasn't finished with the hay. He'd leave the moment he'd given her thirty days. Why did he want to take her upstairs and find a quiet room, when she repulsed him? D Street, indeed! Maybe that's where she belonged, with the other wild women.

"Your backside's all covered with soot," she said. "Here, let me clean you up. I don't want it said I've hired a sloppy man to work on my place."

Lon glanced over his shoulder, to see her coming at him with a broom. He dodged.

"Stand still," she ordered. "You've got to be brushed off."

He clenched his teeth, let her sweep the broom across his rear end. His muscles couldn't have tightened more if she had touched him bare. If he got any bigger in front his trousers would not hold him.

"Better," she concluded. "But don't sit down on Nora's velvet sofa."

Chapter Thirteen

Lon felt more comfortable not dancing at all. Alone with Lindy in the kitchen, he'd been tempted to the brink of the abyss of sex. Best avoid the whole thing. Besides, since the party had attracted only half as many women as men, he found plenty of male companionship. He kept his mouth shut when they talked mines and mining, particularly when Twain joined the group. Whiskey flowed, and the future of the Comstock grew rosier as speech grew more slurred. Lon eyed Billy, hoping to find a chance to speak to him alone, but Sunshine Alice kept him at her skirts, like some pet dog.

Mr. Dove told in grave, horrifying detail of the accident that had crippled him. Lon surreptitiously pulled a kerchief from his pocket to wipe his forehead. Twain got bored and slipped a grasshopper into a man's whiskey while the gentleman danced the polka with Mrs. Dove. The fellow came back thirsty, took a gulp before he noticed the bug, then raised holy hell with Mr. Dove for keeping an unsanitary house. Twain, meanwhile, assumed the innocent mien of an angel, and pontificated on the incompetency of General Meade.

Lon considered going to the wagon and dozing until

Lindy saw fit to go home. The fiddle scraped to a halt. Nora Dove brought out her crystal ball.

"Who wants their fortune told?" she asked, lighting candles to stand on either side of the ball. The heart of the crystal shimmered red.

"Tell us what's happening in the war," someone suggested.

"Everyone sit down and think of the armies in the East," she commanded. Her success with the vision on the Fourth of July must have given her confidence in her long-distance powers. The majority of the men sat on the floor, since chairs were scarce. Lon remembered Lindy's warning about the soot on his pants, and retreated to a corner, nearly hidden behind a wing chair. Twain led Lindy to the wing chair. She towered over him, rather spoiling the reporter's gallantry. Twain leaned against the back of the chair, his mouth not far from Lindy's hair. Lon tried to concentrate on the war, but Twain's breath disturbed the stray hairs on the top of Lindy's head. Must the man stand so close?

What do I care? She compared me to Harvey Saxton, a drunken, dishonest assayer. Writing the Shirt Tail report was not at all like a fake assay. A fake assay report could lead a man to waste months, even years of his life on a worthless prospect.

How is it different?

Well, Saxton was by profession an assayer. A doctor doesn't kill people; a lawyer doesn't turn on his client. Every profession has standards, and a professional man accepted those ethics when he hung out his shingle. Of course, there were always scoundrels, men who used their positions to win ill-gotten wealth, to cheat people.

Cheat people the way the Shirt Tail operation intended to cheat people.

"I see a house," said Mrs. Dove, her voice expressionless in the grip of the spirits. "A white house with columns.

Oh, dear!'' she shrieked. ''It's afire! It's burning!'' She covered her face with her hands.

''Since Grant's taken Vicksburg,'' Lindy said in a low voice to Clemens, ''I suppose it would be only natural that houses round about would be burning.''

''The lady is a skeptic,'' Twain said wryly, directing the remark to Lon. ''What do you think? Are Mrs. Dove's powers real?'' Lon didn't answer, for he no longer held a firm opinion. Nora Dove had seen four queens in the crystal, and that might be gossip, but it could also be a vision. And there was the flag on Mount Davidson and the sun turning it into flame.

''Don't ask me about the war, ever again,'' cried Mrs. Dove. ''I cannot bear it. We must look for a more pleasant topic. Who would like to hear their fortune?'' Twain strutted forward, sat opposite Mrs. Dove, placed his hands on either side of the crystal. Lon scrambled to his feet and claimed Twain's place, leaning on the back of Lindy's chair. He experimented to see if his breath moved her hair, but he was too tall. The light from the overhead lamp reflected on her hair, and the pins holding her bun together shone in little silver crescents.

''Gaze into the ball,'' Mrs. Dove ordered. ''Quiet.'' The silence lasted a full minute. Mrs. Dove's forehead wrinkled. The audience stirred restlessly. Twain sighed with such energy he nearly extinguished one of the candles.

''You have a great future,'' Mrs. Dove said cautiously, ''and it will all begin with a large...frog?''

''A frog!'' exclaimed Twain.

''A frog,'' she said, firmly this time. ''There can be no doubt. The crystal does not lie. At first I refused to believe it, but the vision stays the same. You will rise to fame on a frog.''

''Maybe you'll claim a monopoly on catching frogs down at Washoe Lake, to supply the International Hotel with frog's legs,'' quipped DeQuille.

"No frog's going to determine my future," snorted Twain.

"But, Mr. Clemens, that's what the crystal shows. You stand tall, on the back of a giant frog."

Twain laughed, mocking the vision. DeQuille roared, and soon everyone howled at the image of the strutting reporter in the power of a gigantic frog.

"Maybe it's a she-frog, Mark, and if you kiss her she turns into a giant princess," choked DeQuille. "Something on the order of Lindy here." Lindy slumped a little in her chair. Lon glared at DeQuille. No true gentleman made a slighting remark about a lady in public, so perhaps DeQuille only pretended to be a gentleman. If he wrote about Lindy in the paper... Lon slid his hands across the top of the chair, so the tips of his fingers touched Lindy's shoulders.

He would defend her, even though she despised him.

Twain flushed and shuffled his feet. "I think you left your ball out overnight, and it got damp, and now attracts amphibians." He tramped back across the parlor, tried to reclaim his spot behind Lindy's chair by staring at Lon, but gave up in a few seconds. He leaned in the corner, his face still flaming.

"Anyone else?" Mrs. Dove asked in a strained voice. "Some of you gentlemen must have ore specimens you would like the spirits to judge."

Lindy gasped, twisted around to look into Lon's face, and smiled a wicked little smile. She dashed out the front door without saying a word. Was she leaving? Had his fingers upset her? He'd better follow her. By the time Lon plowed through the crowd to the front door, Lindy had returned, cradling three rocks against her chest. She put them on the table before Mrs. Dove.

"Tell us where these came from. And is there any value there?" She tossed her head and laughed in Lon's direction, her eyes sparkling.

Lon caught the moan as it flowed over his tongue, and he swallowed it. He circled the room, trying to get close to Lindy. Did she really mean to hurt him so much? And Mrs. Dove! Great heavens, what Mrs. Dove might make out of those rocks! She might claim they came from the Yellow Jacket, or the Gould and Curry. She could say they had fallen from heaven, or been carried from California by a giant frog. And then Lindy would announce that they came from the Shirt Tail, and belonged to Lon Anderson. And Twain would know he'd written the geologic report. What fun he'd have with that information!

Mrs. Dove drew the rocks in a circle around the ball, laid her hands on two of them and stared into the crystal. She raised her head and glared at her audience.

"Who has a frog in his pocket? Billy?" The little man shook his head, bewildered. "Alice, check his pockets." The prostitute patted him all over, paying special attention to his hip pockets. Billy snarled, not amused. Alice shook her head.

"Mr. Clemens? I hear you played a joke with a grass-hopper this evening. Where do you have the frog?"

"I don't have a frog," he protested. He turned out his pockets, spilling pipes, tobacco pouches, penknives, pencils, bits of tattered paper, as well as odds and ends of gold and silver coins. He drew back his coat and let DeQuille check for any bulges in his vest and shirt.

"No frog," said DeQuille.

"Not even the giant one that is to bring about my apotheosis," Twain said gaily, a bit mollified at causing his tormentor consternation.

"I should hope not," snapped Mrs. Dove. "Your rise to greatness will come in the future. Does every person here swear there is no living frog in this room?" Twain croaked, overwhelming a chorus of oaths of varying degrees of propriety. Mrs. Dove rewarded him with a withering gaze.

"You may think yourself very clever, Mr. Clemens, but

the crystal does not lie." She settled herself once more before the ball. "I see a tunnel into a hillside, not very deep, but with a stream of water, and in that water are frogs."

Lon, trapped against the back wall in his effort to reach Lindy, stopped dead in his tracks. Who had told Mrs. Dove he'd pried the rocks from the face of the Shirt Tail? He thought back to the moment when Lindy placed them on the table. Had she whispered to Mrs. Dove? No. But they'd had all day, sitting around the quilt, to come up with this trick. But did either Mrs. Dove or Lindy know that frogs lived in the Shirt Tail? If one of them had visited the mine... But he didn't think...

"The frogs carry glittering nuggets in their mouths," Mrs. Dove announced in an awestruck whisper. "I would judge these rocks come from a very rich mine."

As one the crowd rose, women from their chairs, men from the floor, and pressed toward the table. They snatched at the rocks. Lon struggled forward, but was shoved against the dining-room door. Someone clutched at his shirt. He looked down at Sunshine Alice and Billy.

"They're from the Shirt Tail?" asked Alice hoarsely. Lon nodded.

"Let's open it! Let's open it!" Billy whispered excitedly down around his kneecaps. "If we get to Braley yet tonight, he'll sell his shares for next to nothing. Trade them for some Lady Bryant or Smiling Jane."

Comstock Commander, Lon almost said, but instead he squatted down on the floor so he faced the little man.

"They blasted the tunnel shut, Billy," he reminded him. "You put the charges in the stope yourself, and all that rock rolled into the tunnel."

"But it didn't work," he cried. "That blast brought down the ceiling of the stope, with not two bushels coming where they wanted it. Braley said I were in-com-pee-ten, no more use than a six-toed cat."

The rocks passed from hand to hand. Lon got to his feet just in time to intercept one being passed over his shoulder. He looked carefully at the lump of stone, a little bigger than his fist. One side of the rock was dead gray, and the other side green, and in between streaked a thin brown line. The brown stuff flaked under the pressure of his thumbnail, smeared across the back of his hand. Clay. A vein of clay.

The clay is an indicator of the presence of the vein, even when the mineral-producing quartz is not present.

Somewhere beyond the face of that tunnel this thin vein of clay widened out, became quartz, quartz laden with gold and silver. *Bonanza!* The bonanza excavation in the Gould and Curry, with the miners' lights flickering high, high above. An excavation so huge, he had to look up to see the lights of hell. How long had those miners followed a thin line of clay before it widened into a vein the size of a house? How long had they sweltered in the dark, blasting and hauling, before the quartz appeared? How many had fallen, screaming, to have their bodies brought up in blankets and powder boxes?

"No," he said to Billy.

"I'll finance it," said Alice. "I have 450 shares of Shirt Tail."

"Braley wondered who had the rest of the stock."

"Floating around D Street," Alice said gaily. "How much money do you need?"

"I'm not opening any mine," said Lon. "Go talk to Braley and his friends." Some part of his mind wavered beyond his control. *I can't get involved in a wildcat mine, because Lindy wouldn't like it.*

Lindy means nothing to me.

You won't get involved because you don't want to die down in the dark.

"Come into the dining room," said Alice. "We'll talk about it while we eat. I'm hungry."

The fellow who played the fiddle returned. The dancing

did not divert Billy and Alice from the potential riches of
the Shirt Tail, and they stayed in the dining room, cornering
Lon between the wall and the heavy sideboard.

"With Anderson here..." began Billy.

"I'm not in any mining scheme," said Lon with unnecessary vehemence. "Underground work is too damn hard!"
Too frightening.

"You can be our geologist," said Alice. "Your report
said it exactly right. To think Clemens made fun of it!"

"The report's a lie, Alice. I copied it, except for the clay
parts. And what I said about clay shows the caliber of fool
I am."

"Alice," yelled a voice from the door. "There's not
enough ladies as it is, without you hanging back."

"Don't go away," Alice said to Lon. "We've got to
decide when we'll open our mine."

"I don't have a mine," Lon reminded her. "I don't have
one single share in the Shirt Tail." Thank God! What if
he'd managed to get Lindy's certificate? If he had one hundred shares, would he be tempted?

Billy sat cross-legged on Mrs. Dove's sideboard, leaning
against a silver teapot. He put down his glass of whiskey,
bit the end off a cigar and lit it. Lon stared at the shocking
dissolution of the child-man, drinking and smoking. Nothing worse, except perhaps the sight of him with Alice.

"I don't know what you've got against the Shirt Tail,"
Billy began.

"It's not the Shirt Tail specifically," said Lon. "I've got
a reason not to get involved in wildcat mines. A personal
reason." That sounded vague enough.

"You get used to being underground," said Billy. Did
the dwarf suspect he was afraid? "First time I went through
that skinny place in the Shirt Tail, my heart pounded like
a mule team on a downgrade. After that, no problem at
all."

"No mining," said Lon, determined to change the subject and get the information he wanted. "Who's the man who playacted your father up there on the trail? The day you tricked me out of twenty dollars?" Billy didn't stir a hair at this reference to his chicanery; he puffed on the cigar to bring the end to ember brightness.

"My brother. Half brother, really."

"And the old gent?" Billy took the cigar out of his mouth and stared.

"You've met my pa?"

"Today, down near the Carson River."

Billy's brows knit together in what, on his childish face, seemed mock seriousness. "I told Pa and Son to lay low in Genoa."

"Son?"

"My brother. His name's Johnson Miller, 'cause Johnson was his mama's name, just like my name's Wilson Miller, 'cause that was my ma's name. Pa calls him Son. The name's a bit crazy, I guess, when someone other'n Pa says it."

"I met your father and brother standing about a hundred feet from Lindy's property line. They intended to call upon her this afternoon, not knowing she'd tarried at Mrs. Dove's quilting here in Virginia. A deputy sheriff brought them out to survey Lindy's irrigation ditch." Billy's brows became one dark slash across his face. Lon saw an unmistakably adult emotion on the man's face. Fury.

"That rascal Clugg?" he snarled.

"The one."

"What the hell..." he began. His jaw jutted out in a miniature fit of rage. "I thought Pa and Son could stay safe down in Genoa. Clugg hasn't no right to be rutting about there. It's a different county."

"Different county?" Twenty miles apart and Genoa and Carson City were in different counties?

"That's what makes Nevada Territory such a dandy place for my work," explained Billy. "First thing the territorial legislature did was chop up a bunch of little counties, so Carson's in Ormsby County, and Virginia's in Storey County, and Franktown and Washoe City's in Washoe. Genoa, that's the seat of Douglas County." Billy slammed his fist on the polished surface of the sideboard.

"That man Clugg has nerve, botherin' Pa and Son outside his rightful jurs-dec-tion," he continued. "Damn, I deserve a few days' rest, and Alice and me, we got a great thing goin' here. I thought I had them well settled."

"But mightn't the sheriff of Douglas County be looking for them—you—for that thieving on the trail? You held me up in Douglas County, didn't you?"

Billy shrugged. "I figure no one knows, because the state line passes close there, and that part of California's mighty lightly settled."

"No sheriff?"

"Likely no closer than Placerville. I've never seen one about. I best get down to Genoa and roust Pa and Son out, maybe move them to the lake, seeing it's summer. Alice won't like it, because our scheme roars like a river in April."

"What scheme is that?" asked Lon, not expecting an answer.

Billy leaned back and puffed on his cigar, blew a perfect smoke ring. "With so many new men hustlin' into town, we come up with a perfect story. Just perfect! She tells her customers I'm her little brother, that we come west with our old pa. Then she says, real sad like, that Pa's dead, and she doesn't have money enough to send me home to our old mama." He laughed, took another puff on the cigar. "Men don't like seein' a kid in a whorehouse, particularly a boy. Alice asks them to contribute a dollar or two to my home-goin' fund. We make sixty, seventy dollars a night. One night, we divided $120. The only problem is, some men want to 'dopt me. I have to cry that I won't leave my sister dear, and that I'm homesick for Ma. Did Clugg say why he had Pa and Son in tow?''

"He claimed they own the land upriver from Lindy, and that her irrigation ditch trespasses on their property."

Billy laughed so hard the silver teapot slid from behind him, and Lon caught it as it headed over the edge. "Pa, own land!" he choked.

"That's what Clugg claims. Your brother looked mighty serious about his right of ownership, until I let him know I recognized him. Then he ran off in a panic."

"He did what Clugg told him to do. That's how it is with Son, you tell him 'xactly what he's to say, how he's to act, and he can do it. But let one thing go wrong and he stiffens like a corpse, or runs off like a shot antelope. Why, I've seen him freeze in the middle of a little creek, one he's hopped over a hundred times, because someone moved a rock and he doesn't know where to put his foot."

"So your father has nothing to do with that brush ridge next door to Lindy?"

"Pa's spent his life shakin' off anything too big to fit in a pack on his back. Two wives, for starters. He gets antsy if he owns more than he can carry."

"So how do you know Clugg?"

"How do you suppose? When I first got to Nevada Territory, I made the mistake of workin' the road between Carson and Virginia once too often. The sheriff rode up with a posse, and carried us down to Carson jail. I got out, 'cause they supposed I was eight years old, and they didn't want a kid in jail, and they let Pa out to take care of me. Of course, they blamed everything on Son, and he spent thirty days gossipin' with Clugg. Son's often too free with his tongue, because he don't think what he's sayin' from one minute to the next. Anyway, Clugg found out I wasn't eight years old, and Son told him how much money we made. Clugg dreams of fine horses and wild women, same as all men, and a deputy's salary don't go far in Nevada."

"So he wanted in on your schemes?"

"He did. He does. Clugg hampers me in my job, for I can't play the crowds in Ormsby County. Since Carson's the territorial capital, that cuts into my takin's, as you can see, givin' it a minute's thought. I'd like to get shut of Clugg, but murdering a deputy's risky business. There's always someone to notice he's gone."

"I suppose," muttered Lon under his breath, gulping at the casual attitude to murder. "Even in Nevada Territory, I suppose the sheriff would have to investigate if a deputy disappeared."

"Is Clugg onto some scheme what's got to do with Lindy?" asked Billy, his eyes thoughtful.

Lon hesitated. "There's been bad blood between them," he said. Gossiping about Lindy seemed worse than writing the Shirt Tail report.

"I heard some talk that she throwed Clugg down her front steps, right in front of the neighbors. Clugg's vain of his position, and don't care to be made to look foolish. Clugg's just dumb enough to suppose any lone lady must by nature be hankerin' after a man," Billy said dryly. He shook the cigar ashes onto the rug. His voice dropped to a whisper. "Now, I got a great idea. You bein' Lindy's new man, you'll be ready for a partnership on getting rid of Clugg. Protectin' your woman. You don't know how I envy you, bein' big enough to protect your woman. Alice is a fine, lovin' gal, and doesn't throw it in my face that I'm about as much help to her as a three-week kitten, but I know it bothers her. Some men who do business on D Street take advantage of the girls." He looked so sad Lon almost patted him on the head, the way he'd comfort a child, until he realized that Billy meant to enlist him in a murder. Of a lawman.

"I mean to investigate the situation," Lon said lamely.

"In-ves-tee-gate?" snorted Billy. "What's to find out? We already know Clugg's a bastard."

"I can find out who truly owns the land next to Lindy, she can write them a letter and tell them Clugg's trespassing."

"I forgot, you got book larnin' enough to be clever and go to court. You ever read law?"

"No."

"Too bad. I'd like to have you on my side afore a judge. The jury'd be skeered by a man seven feet tall, and they'd find for me every time."

"I'm not seven feet tall, just six feet five inches."

"Close enough."

"Why did Son shy off when I mentioned Will Merryman?"

Billy blew another smoke ring. "You mentioned Merryman?" He laughed when Lon nodded. "We hit one of Merryman's pack trains. Merryman came all the way from Sacramento like a whirlwind, he shoved the sheriff off his rear end, and that's why we got hauled in. Son curses and threatens Merryman regularly, because he didn't like jail, but he's scared of him, scared as a rabbit at night in lantern light."

In the shadows of A Street Lindy slipped Lon some coins, and he went off to fetch the mules.

"I do wish you'd stay the night," said Nora. "Going down that road isn't safe in the dark."

"We'll be fine," Lindy reassured her. "I've got to go, because Mr. Anderson couldn't get close enough to the goat to milk her. She'll be suffering terribly."

"Those animals tie you down, Lindy. A woman in your position should be getting out more into society."

"In what position?"

"Single and all."

Lindy said nothing. She decided not to bother changing out of her dress, since Lon was there to harness the mules.

"You drive," she said to him when he returned, and climbed into the wagon.

The moon had set hours before, but the mules knew the road and would not wander off into the sagebrush or over a precipice. Once they passed the lights of Gold Hill, her eyes adjusted to the starlight. Lon's broad back reared in front of her like a wall.

What was she to do about Lon Anderson?

As a prospective husband he'd washed out. She wanted no man who could be tempted into mining adventures and fake reports. She needed a steady, plodding man. A man interested in bettering the farm. She thought with regret of all the effort she had expended on cooking. All the recipes she had copied from Nora's book so he would eat well.

"Whoa," called Lon.

"Why are you stopping?" she asked, alarmed. She got up on her knees to look ahead, checking that no thieves stood in the middle of the road.

"To pick up something I left in the sagebrush," he said. He climbed down and disappeared into the darkness. She heard the scrape of dry leaves as he collided with a bush. Was he angry with her? Did he intend to abandon her in Gold Canyon?

What are you getting all rattled for? You can get the wagon home in the dark. Just because you've got on a dress, you act like a silly woman.

"What are you looking for?" she called.

"Ouch!" More rustling, a scraping sound. "Here it is," he said. He reappeared, carrying something long and narrow over his shoulder.

"Get down out of the way," he ordered. "I don't want to hit you on the head with this timber." Lindy scrunched against the front of the wagon bed. The mules stirred as the wood thudded into the wagon. Lindy scrambled onto the seat, found the reins looped over the whip socket and pulled so the mules knew they were to stand still. Lon shifted empty baskets and crates, making a place for the timber to settle into a stable position. The starlight glowed on the white stripes of his shirt. Lindy lifted her skirts to climb back into the wagon.

"Stay where you are," he said. "There's room enough for both of us." He swung up beside her and took the reins from her hands.

There was room enough, if she didn't mind sitting right up against him. His heat reflected on her arm, because the sleeves of her dress didn't reach below the elbow. She should have brought a shawl; she should have remembered the cool nights on the mountain. She should have climbed into the wagon bed. She was tempted to snuggle against him.

"What do you want with that big hunk of wood?" she asked.

"It's the right size to make a center post for the porch roof, so it doesn't sag. As it is, a heavy snow'll bring it down."

"Thank you. When the men build the barn, they can put it up for me."

"I can do that, of an evening."

"Your job's haying. You don't have to do other work about the place."

"When I see something to be done, it's my nature to do it."

"Is that why you helped out on the Shirt Tail?" she snapped. "It was something needing to be done?"

"No, Lindy." His exasperation showed in the little snort he made after he said her name.

"But why did you do it?" she cried. It hurt so to think of him as a liar and thief and villain, when she enjoyed baking cream pies for him. When she could hardly wait until one of the young roosters had grown big enough to kill for fried chicken. When all of her got warm when he put his arms about her. When she longed to find out the secret, just like the women on D Street.

"Lindy, I came to the Comstock to work in the mines. On the way over the mountains, every other man tried to sell me worthless mining paper. Your husband cheated me in a poker game, and then had the nerve to steal my money. Every person I've met here has some scheme or other. Why in hell do you look at me like I got two heads, just because I worked on the Shirt Tail?"

"I don't believe goodness and righteousness is figured by what other people do," she said. "Goodness is like a stone mountain. Never changing. I thought you were good, Lon Anderson, truly good, and that you being caught in Stone's office was just some terrible misunderstanding...."

"Listen, Lindy! Nevada Territory is the great humbug capital of the world, so what difference does it make, one humbug more or less."

What difference did it make! It made a difference because she wanted Lon Anderson to marry her! And she could not, dare not, make a second mistake. Her brother lectured her in every letter. It shamed him to write home and tell the relatives in Ohio that Lindy meant to divorce her husband, when no one in the family had ever been divorced before. Every letter from Will begged her to come to Sacramento, bring Harvey, and he listed all the jobs there to fit Harvey's talents.

"Why'd you marry Saxton?" Lon asked. "He was no saint." Lindy swallowed several times.

"Because he was the only man who ever asked me," she admitted. She buried her face in her hands, even though Lon could not possibly see her tears of shame in the darkness.

Chapter Fourteen

Lindy milked the complaining goat while Lon held the lantern. She poured the milk into the cool pans on the shelves of the springhouse. The small, covered bucket of buttermilk reflected the lantern light. What was she to do about Lon? She closed the door without offering him any buttermilk. She washed in the basin in her room, and changed into her nightdress. The wire frame creaked softly when she stretched out on the bed. What was she to do?

He had removed his boots, for she heard only the creaking of the floorboards. He stood outside the open window above her bed, blocking the starlight.

"Lindy, do you want me to leave? If you do, just say so. I'll go." She said nothing. She stiffened so he would not hear the mattress rustle. "I'll find a job and pay you the money you spent to get me out of jail."

The hay made no difference. He'd cut plenty for the winter. But she didn't want him to leave, particularly like this.

"You stay, Lon. Just finish my hay, and then you can go."

"Lindy."

"Yes."

"Lindy, I had a fine time on the Fourth of July. I don't

want you to think I didn't. And this evening, I really wanted to dance with you, but..."

"Why didn't you?" The silence lasted so long she thought he had crept away.

"Because, dancing with you, I feel things I shouldn't. I don't want you to get ideas, because I intend to leave on the thirteenth of August."

She'd freed herself from all that special cooking. No more mixing up sauces for steaks, or rolling out dough for trout pies. She would feed him, but she would not invest her heart in it. Of course, she had the mashed potatoes in the springhouse to make mashed potato doughnuts for breakfast. And the cabbages were of a size now to hollow out and stuff with minced ham and rice, flavored with a bit of Nora's currant jelly. Well, a few nice things here and there made no difference. And he was a pleasure to feed. The woman who fed Lon knew in her heart that he appreciated her hours over a hot stove.

"Lindy." She jumped a little. She had supposed he'd gone to his bedroll.

"Yes."

"Something happened I should tell you. I didn't have a chance at the Doves'." At his first mention of Clugg's name she sat up.

"You're sure those men don't own the place next door?" she asked when he had completed his account.

"They're Billy's brother and father. Billy said they don't own any property."

"Clugg's just whistling in the dark, then. He doesn't know who owns the place."

"That's what I think. But you should find who does."

"It's awkward, a woman going into the county offices. The men hang about, and don't like females bothering their gossip." He said nothing. "I'll see to it next week."

"Lindy?"

"Yes?" What else did he want?

"Lindy, there's something else I lied about. Something besides the Shirt Tail. I didn't work at the Gould and Curry but for one night."

"How long you worked at the Gould and Curry has nothing to do with me."

"But I let you think I worked there, when I didn't. And I've not been honest about why I didn't go back. I was scared. Scared as a fox before the hounds, because I can't stand the thought of hundreds of feet of rock over my head. Even in the Shirt Tail, with daylight behind me, once I had those rocks in my hands, I ran. I nearly stumbled and fell flat. I couldn't help myself. I ran until I saw the sky. I'm a coward, Lindy, and it's best you know the truth."

"You are not a coward!" she cried, the words slipping out before she had time to think.

"Yes, I am. You think badly of me for writing the Shirt Tail report. I'm giving you another reason to think badly of me, and it's for sure true."

Mashed potato doughnuts, Lon decided midway through the fifth one, ranked with sugar cream pie. Especially when he swirled a bit of molasses over the top. For the second morning in a row Lindy had pulled a skillet of lard from the springhouse and fried him doughnuts—better than any his mother had ever made.

"Thanks, Lindy. These doughnuts would take first place in the county fair, if we had one." He rubbed his stomach and took a sixth.

"Lon, would you mind riding into town first thing?" Lindy held up a match block, one lone match standing up like the last tree in a felled forest. "I thought I had another block, but I don't. And I'd rather not hitch up the mules just to get matches. You can ride your horse in."

Buckskin had put on weight. The weeks of grazing in Lindy's pasture had done him good, but he needed exercise. Sunlight blared on the western peaks, promising another hot day. McCaffrey wrapped the match block in paper and string, so Lon could tie it behind his saddle. A wagon piled high with whiskey casks blocked his way on the main street, so he rode around the square.

Ormsby County Offices.

The sign leaned against a building so insignificant that no one would suspect it was the courthouse. A man was unlocking the front door.

"You got the county records in there?" Lon called.

"What you need to see?"

"The plat of the county."

"Up on the wall, here in the front room." Lon slid off Buckskin and flipped the reins around the hitching rail. He needed half a minute to get himself oriented on the map, but once he found the right curve of the river, he saw the eighty-acre plot, the name "Parker" printed across it, then lined out, and "Merryman" written in underneath. He moved his finger along the river, upstream. No boundaries marked the size of the neighboring farm. No name.

"This place, upstream from the Merrymans'?" he asked. "No one owns it?"

"If it's not got a name, it's not got a owner," said the man behind the counter. "Funny, there's nothing there but spring bog and sagebrush, but you're the second person that's asked about it. Last week that boy deputy who hangs about the jail wanted to know who owned it."

"Clugg?"

"That's the fellow."

"If no one owns it," Lon began, thinking as he spoke, "then I suppose a man could put a claim on it."

"I suppose, but the Homestead Act's for farms. No way you can farm that place. You'd starve to death waiting the five years for the deed."

"Where does a man file a claim?" asked Lon.

"Down the street. Land office."

Lon walked, leading the horse, until he found the right plank shanty. He ducked to fit through the door.

"Strange," said the clerk in answer to his question. "That young deputy inquired about that place last week."

"Clugg? Why didn't he put in a claim?"

"Why, he's too young. A man must be of age, twenty-one, to file on a claim, and Clugg's two years too young. Or maybe more. I think he lies about how old he is."

"Nineteen!" exploded Lon. "How can a man be a deputy sheriff when he can't even vote?"

"When his uncle's territorial judge," the clerk said wryly. "I hear he's inquiring about town, trying to find someone to file a claim for him. But filing means you agree to build a house and live on the property, and finding someone willing to live on that piece of waste…" He shook his head, his doubt plain.

Lindy could file on the land, thought Lon. If she claimed the land, her ditch would be on her own property. How far did her house stand from the property line? She could build a shanty on the place. But could a lone woman file a claim? She couldn't get a bank loan, so…. Clugg might have found a partner by hanging about the saloons all day Sunday. He might, at this very moment, be heading for the land office.

"I want to file on that 160 acres," Lon said.

The clerk's eyebrows went up. "Are you crazy as Clugg?"

"No. I know the worth of the land along the river."

"The mill operators look for flat places to build," warned the man. "They won't pay money for that hill."

"I want to file."

The clerk shook his head, pulled on a green eyeshade, uncorked his ink bottle and began filling out the papers in his elegant, round hand. All the while he muttered about people who wasted his time.

Lon stopped for a moment to watch Lindy cutting wheat. Her long body twisted with the swing of the scythe. The sweaty shirt strained against her breasts, outlining their soft curves. She bent, collected the stalks into a sheaf. The spread of her hips showed plain beneath the light canvas of her trousers.

Someone close by beat on a drum. Lon searched for the drummer, then realized the cadence came from blood pounding in his ears. He grasped his scythe, set off for the meadow at a trot. He must not let himself think of Lindy. But a memory of her flexing arms and lithe form moved before him. He jabbed viciously into the heaps of dried grass and weeds, scraped them into a small heap, then the small heaps into a larger pile, and the heaps and piles repeated the curves of her breasts. Of her hips. Of her thighs.

Think of California. Think of riding through Carson River Canyon. Take the road to Sacramento. Get a job at some stable in Sacramento. Lindy's brother lives in Sacramento. All those mule trains to Nevada mining camps, he needs men to tend animals, or drive them. I'll find Will Merryman. Maybe Lindy'd give me a letter. Lindy... And one day Lindy would come. She'd visit her brother.

She walked toward him across the stubble, a basket over her arm, a tin bucket dangling from her other hand. He rushed to find his shirt, raked up a pile of grass to serve as their table. She spread the tablecloth without a word. The first thing, she laid the papers from the land office on the cloth, the papers he'd left on the table in the house.

"What does this mean?" she asked, reaching back into the basket. Pickles, bread, little rolls of thinly sliced ham stuffed with cooked cabbage. The dust of hay filled his throat, so he took a swig of buttermilk.

"It means I own the 160 acres next door. Or will after I've lived there five years."

"But how...I don't understand..." she sputtered.

"No one owns the land. I checked at the county office this morning. Clugg's been hunting for a partner to put a claim on it. He can't because a man must be of age to file a claim, and he's only nineteen years old. Or maybe younger.''

"So you saw your chance?"

"What chance?" Did she think he meant to play Clugg's game? "I saw *your* chance, Lindy," he said earnestly. "I decided we...you had to move fast. Clugg might have found a partner on Sunday, so there wasn't time enough to ride out here, get you and go back to Carson." Lon regretted that accidental "we."

"Are you planning on building a house and settling down?" she asked, smiling, looking across the field.

"No, and my claim's not valid unless I do. The moment I give it up, you file yours. Can women file claims?" Maybe by the time he gave up the claim, Lindy would have a second husband, and he could take care of it. The image of Lindy and that second husband, standing in the land office, changed into a vision of Lindy and that man in a close embrace. And her lithe body. And the places his kisses touched.

"Of course women can file a claim. That's how married people get more than three hundred acres. The husband files for a quarter section, and so does the wife. But I'm not sure what anyone would do with more than three hundred acres. Three acres of wheat's a big lot to cut."

"Use it for pasture until there's a railroad. After that, we'll not be swinging scythes. We'll have reapers and binders to do this work, just like in the eastern states. With machines, one man could plant a hundred acres."

"Would you like that?" she asked shyly.

"I don't know. I've never worked a farm with reapers and binders. Or the big horses to pull them."

"I'll buy your claim from you, as soon as it's legal for you to sell."

"No need. It's worthless, except for your irrigation ditch. Anyway, for now you're safe from Clugg."

"He'll just think of some other way to harass me," she

said, and the sigh in her voice startled him, for he'd always thought of Lindy as strong and certain. "I never should have been so energetic with him the first time he came out. But, you realize, he touched me, and I don't like to be touched unless I say it's okay."

"That's understandable." Had Clugg opened the buttons of her shirt and slid his fingers toward her breasts? If *he* touched her that way, would she tumble into the unfinished haystack?

She would tumble you, romp you, and next thing you know there'd be a baby on the way, and you'd be stuck on these eighty acres.

Lon eyed Lindy as a stranger, just a woman sitting on the grass. He studied her long legs, her sturdy hips. He stopped before he got to the too-tight shirt.

"Anyway, for now Clugg won't bother you about the irrigation ditch," he said to fill the silence.

"All I've got to worry about is the river dropping," she said.

"The river won't bust into your house, and take off your shirt, and shove you down on the bed," he joked.

"No." She sighed again, very deeply. Her deep blue eyes met his, and he knew for a fact that he could walk right into her bedroom, and she would not resist for one second. How long until August 13?

A burro grazed beside the mules in the pasture. Lon stared at the animal while he walked toward the corral. Where had Lindy picked up a burro? And not even a very healthy one, at that. Lindy's trousered rump stuck up in the air next to the corral fence, not ten feet away. He stumbled on a clod.

"Watch yourself!" he muttered to himself. She squatted beside the fence. She must be searching for eggs hidden in the weeds, for her gathering basket hung over her arm. She straightened when she saw him.

"Chickens aren't very smart, but they're smart enough to keep one step ahead of me when it comes to hiding their eggs. You got company," she added, pointing toward the house with the hand holding the egg basket. Lon side-stepped until he had a view of the porch. Billy sat on the top step, amid the baskets and boxes Lindy was preparing for tomorrow's trip into Virginia City. Billy stared at his boots, his head in his hands.

"He says you're the only true friend he has."

"Friend!" exploded Lon.

"He says you're both freaks and belong in a medicine show, because he's so short and you're so tall. I can't make head nor tail of the story he tells, about his pa and son, and Clugg. So I can't say what he might ask of you."

"I can imagine it's not anything legal." He headed for the porch. He would talk to Billy while he sharpened the scythe, then send him on his way. Billy spotted him round-ing the chicken coop, jumped up and dashed down the steps, his short legs churning.

"Anderson! By God, we've got to do something about Clugg."

"I did something about Clugg. I've got no more prob-lems with Clugg, and neither does Lindy. You're on your own."

"Please! I can't do it by myself, and Pa's too old and feeble to be of help in a thing like this, and I daren't bring in Son, 'cause he's so skittish in a mer-gen-see."

Lon sat on the porch with his legs dangling over the edge, pulled the whetstone from his back pocket and set to work on the scythe. His lack of excitement sent Billy into a frenzy of thrashing arms and restless feet.

"Do you know what he's done now?" The little man danced in front of him, his tiny boots pounding on the ground, raising a cloud that nearly enveloped him.

"Clugg or Son?" Lon asked, fanning his hat in front of his face. "Stand still. You raise more dust than a mule."

"Clugg." Billy stood still, his feet together, his hands on his hips. "That fake lawman went to Pa and Son, and made a im-prop-per-cit-tion. He wants they should try the old trick on the trail, but bein' as I'm busy in Virginia, he says they'll use a real kid!" He snorted and shook his head violently to show his outrage, but kept his feet still. "A child! That man will cor-ry-upt a child!"

"A child?" asked Lon.

"Not just any child! A little girl child!" shrieked Billy. "Has he tried it?"

"No. But only because I spent two days carryin' Pa and Son up to camp at Lake Tahoe. They're takin' their meals at Lake House. *That* costs me a penny and a half! I've missed three days at Alice's. A hundred, two hundred dollars dish-olved like bread in a drowned man's pocket. But I slipped Pa and Son out of Clugg's reach for a week or two, long enough for me to take care of him for sure and always. I'm pretty certain they're across the line into California up there, so they're out of the reach of any sheriff who takes a notion to go huntin' for easy prey. We got to do something, to protect Pa and Son from Clugg's next wild notion, and it's got to be soon, for they can't stay there past first snow. I hope you're not a coward, Anderson, 'cause Lindy's your woman, and he's after her in a filthy way— it's your duty as a man. God don't love no coward!"

Lindy stood at the bottom of the stairs, right behind Billy, the basket of eggs hanging over her arm. At first she stared at the top of Billy's head, but at his final words she lifted her eyes and glared at Lon. His tongue froze. Would she accuse him of spreading gossip about her?

"I figure," continued Billy, "the best thing would be for you to write a letter, pretending it's from Lindy. You're smart. You can put in the sort of words a lady says when she's in her heat for a man." Billy leaned forward conspiratorially; Lindy's eyes blazed above him.

"If you need some hints, I hear what the gals on D Street

say when they're anxious. I hear what they say about you,"
he added with a wink. "Anyway, put it in the letter that
she'll meet him somewheres about here, and she'll let him
poke her. I'll set behind a bush, pretendin' to be Lindy.
You slip her shawl outa the house for me to wear. You
skulk about until he's busy takin' his pants down, then
whack him over the head with a axe."

"You'd have blood and guts all over yourself," said
Lindy. "But no brains, of course." Billy jumped a foot in
the air, came down with one boot on the bottom step, out
of balance, and sprawled in the dust.

"You'll do no such thing as write a letter like that,"
Lindy cried. "Clugg would wave it about in every saloon
in Carson City. In two hours half the men would think for
certain I'm a loose woman!"

"It's to protect you," Billy gasped.

"Protect! Ruining my name protects me? What's this all
about, Lon?" Lindy asked, stepping over Billy. "I know
you think I want you to kill Harvey, but what's led you to
suppose I want you to murder Clugg, too?"

"Lindy, I don't think you expect me to murder Harvey.
I haven't thought that since the Fourth of July."

"What changed your mind?"

"I saw what you were afraid of. You thought I'd beat
him flat, that you'd be left like Mrs. Dove, with a crippled
man to take care of. And killing Clugg is Billy's idea, not
mine. It never occurred to me you wanted him dead."

"I'm glad you've formed a better opinion of me," she
snapped.

"Maybe Billy's got a point," Lon teased, knowing he
did it to keep Lindy's eyes on his. They weren't poison-
bottle eyes, but matched the varigated blue of the sky over
the mountains. "You said Clugg wouldn't give up. You
said he'd think of something else, after the irrigation
ditch."

"What Clugg *might* do is no reason to murder the man.

And he's really only a boy. When his uncle's term as judge is up, he'll leave Nevada Territory and we'll both be free.''

Billy leapt to his feet, brushing himself off. "That'll be a year, two years," he objected. "You don't know what's in Clugg's mind. You don't know what he intends for that pretty little girl down in Genoa, with golden curls and red cheeks, like cherries, they are. Why, she's not so tall as me, and Clugg wants to set her feet on the road to D Street," he cried. His voice rose feverishly, and he rambled on about skinny oxen, Son's mental condition, Pa's frailty and the advisability of operating over the state line.

Lindy's face lengthened, her head tilted to the side and she looked like a curious kitten surprised by a creeping wooly worm. Lon half expected her hand to reach out like a soft paw, and give Billy a curious tap. See if he would run. Lon could see she had no idea what Billy jabbered on about. Billy paused for breath.

"Clugg plans to set up a trap for emigrants on the trail, using a little girl from Genoa as the bait," Lon said quickly before Billy got going again. "He tried to get Billy's pa and brother to help him, but Billy spirited them away to the lake."

"Clugg'll think of something else," Billy said glumly. He stamped his feet, then remembered the dust and stood still. "The best thing's to get rid of him. If you don't want Lindy brought into this, then write a letter pretending it's from me." He scratched his head. "I can't recall if Clugg knows I'm not a scholar. Anyway, tell him I'm willin' to go along with his schemes. We can meet down on that sandy stretch of the trail, where it turns into the canyon. While he's jabberin', you sneak up and break his neck. We'll bury him in the sand, where no one'd think to look."

"Why in all your cockeyed plots do I get to kill Clugg?" Lon asked.

"Because you're bigger. I couldn't kill him, except with a gun, and my arm sags with a six-shooter, them being so heavy. Alice's got a pepperbox of a proper weight, but when you pull the trigger you never know what you're gonna hit. Once a man broke in to her place and she shot at him, but the ball hit the lantern over the door, blowed it all over D Street, and the thief got away in the shoutin'.''

"There're ways to handle Clugg without killing him," Lindy said sternly. "Just this morning Lon fixed him good by filing a claim on the land next door."

"He can do things like that," protested Billy, "because he's got book larnin'." He sat down on the bottom step. His shoulders curved inward, he lowered his head into his stubby hands. "You got to help me. You're my last hope. I can't leave Nevada. It's just the best place in the world for shady deals."

"How's your appetite?" Lindy asked as she walked to the summer kitchen. Why did she always feel sorry for men when they'd sunk into despair? Or pretended to be in despair? She flung open the oven, stood back and shielded her face against the heat. Billy clung to her legs, his head almost in the oven.

"Roast venison and onions! I never have nothing like this at Alice's place."

"Seems like food goes a long way to boosting your spirit," she teased. "You help me with the chores, and then we'll have supper."

She found it difficult to treat Billy like an adult. She served dinner on the porch, being uncertain of his table manners, and she didn't want crumbs spread all over the floor attracting ants and mice. And she did not have time to sweep, because tomorrow was Tuesday, and the wagon had yet to be loaded.

Lon fetched a pole from a stack behind the corral and measured the distance between the porch and the sagging roof. He sharpened the old saw from the shed and cut the pole long enough to wedge between the roof beam and the floor; he hammered it into place. His mouth puckered in thought, and his hat moved on his head as his forehead wrinkled.

"Here, Billy. You pack the eggs for me," Lindy said, keeping her eyes on Lon. She showed Billy how to layer the eggs with sawdust, and watched until she was certain his little hands clasped each egg firmly. She loaded the baskets of snap beans, turnips, potatoes, beets and greens, sneaking a glance at Lon every time she raised her head.

Lon whittled small wedges. Kneeling on the porch, he hammered one under the foot of the pole, raising the beam by a fraction of an inch. He hammered another on the opposite side, carefully, so as not to dislodge the first. His big hands knew exactly how to hold the hammer, exactly how much force to put behind each blow. If he came to her bed, his hands would slide over her at first like the wind, and when he'd figured out where she liked to be touched, he'd focus his attention. His force.

The sagging beam creaked with the strain exerted by the wedges. Lon returned to his whittling, his face thoughtful, and when he held up the small wedge he'd just made, he nodded a trifle.

"There's a way to get rid of Clugg without murder, I believe," he said seriously.

"What?" asked Billy, startled while lifting an egg. He juggled it, caught it an inch away from splattering on the porch.

"Clugg's superstitious. He's afraid of ghosts."

"How do you know?" asked Lindy.

"The day I came to Carson, when I played poker with Price and Saxton and Rick, Clugg came into the restaurant because the wind scared him. He'd heard a story from an old Indian, about how the wind carried the ghosts of his people killed by the whites."

"You can dress up like a mighty mean ghost," exclaimed Billy.

"No," said Lon. "You will. Day after tomorrow."

He returned to his whittling, and before darkness came, he'd hammered in two more wedges on each side, raising a squeal of protest from the sagging beam.

Chapter Fifteen

Lindy sat impatiently on the wagon, a quarter mile from Carson City, hidden from the town by a low hill.

"He's forgot us," said Billy behind her. "Left us here to swelter in the sun, while he takes his ease in town, drinkin'...."

Lon's hat appeared on the crest of the hill.

"He's coming right now," she said without glancing over her shoulder. She climbed down from the seat, taking care that she didn't snag her skirt.

Lon stood between her and Billy while she tied on her hoops. He lifted the dummy from the bed of the wagon, and tied the cords that held it upright. The dummy wore a pair of her cast-off trousers and a gingham shirt, and with her sunbonnet, from a distance, no one would know it wasn't her.

"Those knots tight?" Billy asked anxiously. "If this thing should tip over, it'd carry me down, too."

"It's solid," Lon reassured him. He lifted the shirt so Billy could slide through the hole in the back.

"You sure you can drive the mules?" Lon asked as Billy's arms went into the sleeves.

"You've asked me that three times," said Billy, his irritation muffled by the fabric. "You're like everyone else.

Just because I'm not four feet tall you think I got no brains.''

"Both Sheriff Tipson and Clugg are sitting in the front room of the jail, keeping cool, or at least they were five minutes ago when I walked by. Only a few men are on the street, so Clugg will be sure to see you.''

"Billy won't have any trouble,'' Lindy said. "The mules know the way past the jail, around the corner, to the back of McCaffrey's. It's the way I always drive.''

She took off her sunbonnet, and Lon tied it on the skull. Until now the dummy had been just a figure of fun. Seeing it on the wagon, in her clothes, the fun drained away. No ghost, she knew that, for Lon and Billy had spent hours last night and part of this morning constructing the thing, and she had dressed it. But she bit her lower lip, turned away from the grinning death's-head that stared out from her sunbonnet.

"Now, Billy, count to three hundred, slow and easy,'' explained Lon. "That gives me and Lindy time to walk to McCaffrey's and get inside.''

"I know! I know! You told me that before. Get going before I shrivel up like bacon on a griddle. It's hot in here!''

Lon offered his arm and led her up a side street, around the back side of the square. Sweat ran down her midriff and collected around the tight waist. She wished she'd remembered to bring her straw bonnet, for the afternoon sun shone directly in her eyes. Lon wore his blue-and-white-striped shirt, and his red kerchief blazed about his neck.

We look like a courting couple.

They turned onto the boardwalk on the west side of the square, and spotted the mules, the wagon and the ghostly driver heading straight toward them. Lon picked up the pace, shoved McCaffrey's front door open and pushed her inside. Lindy dashed through the tangle of merchandise to the back window.

"Can I help you?" asked McCaffrey, lifting the feed-sack curtain. He must have been eating his dinner, because he wiped his sleeve across his mouth.

"Got to watch for my wagon to come around," said Lindy, not even glancing at McCaffrey. She sensed Lon behind her, looking over her head. The mules rounded the corner.

"Here he comes." She bounced up on her toes, then remembered Lon wanted to see, and she schooled herself to stand still. "Is it going to work?"

"Lindy Saxton!" Clugg wasn't in view, but his baritone bellow rang through the fragile walls. "You can't leave that wagon here behind McCaffrey's." He strode from the passageway between the store and the saloon. "I've told you a hundred times, you're impeding traffic."

"Damn Clugg and his interference," said McCaffrey, his hand on the latch of the back door.

"Don't," said Lon, pulling him back. "Watch." McCaffrey glanced out the window, then back at Lindy, his mouth open and his eyes wide.

"But..."

"Watch!"

Billy twisted the top of the dummy slowly in Clugg's direction just as Clugg took a step forward, only a few feet away from the window.

"The law says... Aaaaaaaaah!" Clugg's hands framed his face like claws, his mouth, his eyes and his nostrils flaring.

"A doomed soul, catching his first sight of the devil," said Lon, and Lindy thought his description most appropriate. Clugg's legs jerked up and down pretending to run, but he stayed in one spot.

"Aaaaaaaaah!" At the second scream his feet moved, but he cut too close to the rear of the wagon, caught his boot on the wheel and sprawled full-length in the dust. He crawled around the corner of the store.

"Come on, Lindy," said Lon, grabbing her shoulders and steering her out the back door. The dummy twisted and writhed like a tortured demon.

"I'm dying," Billy gasped as Lon pulled him free. "It's a hunderd and ten inside that thing. Point me to the saloon so's I can get a beer."

"You'll miss all the fun," said Lindy. Lon slipped the knots in the cords, pushed the dummy backward into Lindy's hands. She grabbed the rake from the bed of the wagon and piled hay over the recumbent figure. At the last minute she remembered her sunbonnet, snatched it off the skull without untying the bow, and slid it over her braids. By the time Sheriff Tipson rounded the corner, she was lifting out the block to tie the lead mule.

"She's dead, she's dead," sobbed Clugg, staggering along behind him. "I saw her, and she's died out at that cabin, and her ghost's driven into town."

"What's going on?" called the sheriff. "You all right, Lindy?"

Lindy paid no heed, but hooked the tie-down rope to the mule's bridle.

"She's dead, nothing but bones inside them clothes of hers," cried Clugg. He covered his face with his hands, and managed to cower standing on his feet. "Somebody must of murdered her, and her spirit can't rest...."

"Shut up, Clugg," the sheriff ordered. "Lindy, are you okay?"

"I'd be fine if that stupid boy-deputy of yours would leave me alone. Every time I come into town, he's here like a shot, ordering me off until McCaffrey tells him to git."

Clugg peeked through his fingers, gaped, squealed like a stuck pig.

"Clugg came rushing in the jail, said you'd driven into town in your wagon, but you were dead," said the sheriff, stifling an unmanly giggle.

"Well, in this heat I suppose I might appear a bit wilted," said Lindy. She patted her skirt. "Even though today I tried to dress real nice, and look ladylike."

"You were dead, Lindy Saxton," yelled Clugg. "I saw under that bonnet, a death's-head, grinning at me, drawing me into the jaws of death!"

"Now, I know I'm skinny—" began Lindy, but Lon interrupted her.

"I think your deputy's been in the sun too long," he offered. "I think he needs a beer and a nap." A small crowd had spilled out the back door of Pryor's Saloon. Billy climbed up on the wagon and lifted a hand, like an orator commanding silence.

"Deputy Clugg here saw Lindy drive into town," he announced, "and he says she was nothing but dry bones, dead for weeks, and picked over by buzzards."

"Lindy looks pretty perky to me," offered the barkeep.

"In a dress, too," offered another man. "I guess that's what comes of her taking a husband bigger than she is."

"Of course I'm perky," Lindy said, ignoring the remark about husbands. "Clugg's just seeing things. That's what happens when a boy's allowed to frequent the saloon like a grown man. He sees snakes and dancing skeletons and giant bugs. Maybe Clugg needs to take the water cure up at Steamboat. Doc Ellis does some wonderful things in his baths. Men who're seeing demons and such—"

"I'm not drunk," yelled Clugg. "I had but two beers today. Doc Ellis is a big fake. I'll not set around in water, for it ain't good for a person, and hot water's the worst, drains a man's power for sure."

"You certain you saw Lindy dead?" asked Billy, taking advantage of Clugg's loquacity to draw him more firmly into the web.

"I tell you, her face inside that bonnet—" he pointed at Lindy's blue sunbonnet "—was a death's-head. A grinning skeleton!" He raised his hands in the clawing gesture of a witch, close to his face. "Her bony hands reached out for me, drawin' me to my grave."

"Me?" asked Lindy, truly astonished. "I just came to town to get ten pounds of sugar and a vanilla bean, so I can make sugar cream pie."

The barkeep shook his head, licked his lips and grinned at Lon. "You sure are one lucky man. Makes me wish I stood tall enough to fancy her." He jerked a thumb at Clugg. "He needs the water cure for sure. Don't you fellows think Doc Ellis could help him?" he inquired of the growing crowd.

Clugg yelled, but his "No" turned into a shriek of terror. His hands shook. For a moment Lindy thought he might quiver so hard he'd drop right down in the street.

"Hi-dro-fo-bee," pronounced Billy, stamping his foot in triumph on the wagon box. "He's got the water scare. You had any mad dogs around here, Sheriff? I bet Clugg's got bit and didn't tell you."

Clugg began crying, the tears plowing furrows through the dust on his face. "She was dead! She was dead and dry!" He put his hands to his face, dashed toward the jail, shoving through the crowd by waving his elbows wildly, pursued by laughter that expanded like a bubble.

"Do I get my beer or not?" asked Billy.

"Later," said Lindy. "I got my shopping to take care of." She turned with all the dignity she could muster, her chest heaving with laughter she dared not let out. She winked at Lon as she passed.

She leaned over the counter, howling, shaking, wishing the waist of her dress had an inch more give in it. Lon grabbed her shoulders and spun her around. She leaned into him to keep from falling over, then wondered if they both might fall down, since he was howling, too.

"What's going on here?" demanded McCaffrey.

"Clugg really thought...he really thought..." Lindy gasped. Billy danced around them, grabbing at her skirts, giggling and whooping. She had to hang on to Lon's shoulders.

"It worked!" Billy cried.

Lon's laughter stopped abruptly. His hands tightened around her waist, but his stiff body provided only cold support. She stared at him, found his face long and wondering. Suddenly he smacked his lips against hers, a kiss of half a second, then pushed her away, grinning like an idiot.

"We did it," he said, but the words came out flat, like his confession to the Shirt Tail scheme.

"The story's spreading like wildfire," cried Billy. "From now on, when Clugg steps into a saloon, everyone'll yell 'She's dead!'"

Something still connected her lips to Lon's.

"It worked, Lindy!" Lon said. The kiss hung between them. Mortar between two bricks.

"It worked," she agreed breathlessly. "It worked." She nodded her head to convince herself, for the kiss overshadowed the clever trick. "We'd better get that wagon out of town before someone sees what's in it."

"Hurry," cried Billy, tugging on her skirt, the beer forgotten. "I want to be first up the hill, so I can tell everyone in Virginia."

She turned to McCaffrey behind the counter, his grin spreading as he figured out the joke.

"You didn't see anything," she said, half begging. His eyes widened with understanding.

"Course not, Lindy. Didn't see anything that might have spooked that crazy deputy!"

She pulled herself upright, straight and tall, pretending everything was normal. Lon must not suspect her reaction to his impulsive kiss. It meant nothing to him, merely a way of showing his happiness that the trick had succeeded. She pressed her fingers on the edge of the counter until they turned white.

"I need ten pounds of sugar," she said stoutly. "And a vanilla bean."

Lindy sat beside him on the wagon seat, her hands clasped in her lap. Lon could not see her face, for she looked at her hands, uncharacteristically sober. The kiss had been a terrible mistake, for it had spoiled her delight. One lighthearted kiss, and everything had changed.

Billy giggled and kicked his boots against the side of the wagon bed. "Wait'll I tell the men in Virginia about Lindy being dead! Free drinks up and down C Street!"

He bounced and cheered behind them, waving a long licorice whip at passersby. Lindy had bought him licorice instead of beer, treating Billy like a child. Billy's twenty-six years old, Lon thought, but the laughter and the licorice whip makes it seem like we have a kid in the back of the wagon.

He shifted on the hard slab seat and gripped the reins a little tighter, because the turnoff lay just ahead. He squinted his eyes in the glare of the sun and wondered at being a bit dizzy and disoriented. His spirit lifted out of his body, and he saw how it would be. He and Lindy, the wagon full of children—five of them, two girls and three boys—and Lindy beside him, looking down at her lap; not at her hands, but at the baby asleep against her bosom.

One of the girls perched on the side of the wagon, putting distance between herself and her boisterous sister and brothers. Thirteen or fourteen, her skirts still short, but the curves of womanhood in potential, and she primed herself for the change.

The mules swung onto the river road, and the image dissolved into heat and dust. The reins threaded through numb fingers, but his hip touching Lindy's vibrated with power. Behind him Billy howled, "She's dead! Clugg says she's dead!" at a pair of men tottering uphill from the river.

"I forgive you," whispered Lindy.

"Forgive me? For what?"

"For writing that report on the Shirt Tail. But you must never do anything like that again. It's not honest. But you don't drink, and that's good, and you don't frequent D Street, else Alice wouldn't have asked me—you know. So I forgive you." She reached over and patted his thigh.

The kiss! A dreadful mistake! He'd meant it as a joke, a snappy prelude to pushing her away. A means to end the closeness, for he couldn't stand it, even when laughter brought them together. And now she sat beside him, and he felt her leg move through her petticoats. Her heat had brought a fever on him, and caused strange visions.

What a pickle he was in! One quick kiss, and Lindy caved in! She'd marry a man who'd been knee-deep in a mining scheme. Did she want him so much she might come out on the porch? The touch of her hand in the right place, while he slept, and he'd sink into her without a thought. He gripped the reins so hard that the edges of the dry leather cut into his hands. Nothing but his own resolution stood between his freedom and Lindy's hardscrabble farm. And six children! But that couldn't be true! A fever!

He turned the wagon through the gate, and to avoid Lindy he helped Billy saddle his burro.

"Now, don't let out the secret. We want everyone to believe that Clugg sees things." Billy nodded. "If people know the trick, men'll be creeping in here to steal Lindy's scarecrow. Not to speak of the revenge Clugg would take if he learned we hornswoggled him." Billy nodded, this time more seriously.

"I won't say a word. Not even to Alice."

"Especially not Alice," Lon said. "She'd spread the gossip all over D Street. Someday, when Clugg and his uncle have gone back East, we can let it out."

"Well, just tellin' about Clugg's eyes poppin' like he's a big bug will get me plenty of drinks," said Billy. "You s'pose they'll take him to Steamboat?"

Lon shrugged. He had other things to worry about besides Clugg's future. His own future, for instance. He still owed Lindy a week. Well, six days. He had to keep his wits about him, or he'd tumble into the deadfall he'd dug with that kiss.

"In a few days you ride to Steamboat," suggested Billy. "They'll tell you if Clugg's got over his fright."

"I'm leaving in a few days, Billy."

"Leavin'?"

"Going back to California."

"But you and Lindy...?"

"There is no 'me and Lindy.' I'm her hired man. I'm not staying on this ragged farm any longer than I agreed to."

He watched Billy head out the gate, kicking and yelling in a vain attempt to force the burro into a trot. Lindy stood on the porch, her blue dress replaced with pants and shirt. When their eyes met she smiled a soft smile, the smile of a woman who lays one trap after another, and is sure the last one has worked. Lon studied the overhead beam to avoid her eyes. Return her smile and he'd be dead as a doornail.

He sat on the edge of the porch and concentrated on his whittling. Lindy bustled about under the ramada, starting a fire in the cookstove, clashing pots and pans. She disappeared in the direction of the garden, carrying a shovel and a hoe. Lon breathed a sigh, dropped his whittling on the porch and his head into his hands. He'd leave in the middle of the night. After dark he'd get all his gear together, and when he heard her slow sleeping breath, he'd saddle Buckskin and ride away. The wedges beside him said he couldn't leave tonight. Another quarter inch gained this evening, another tomorrow morning. Tomorrow evening he'd put in the permanent post. And the ninth haystack still to finish. He'd slip off tomorrow night.

* * *

Lindy made flapjacks for breakfast, two batches, one with cornmeal and dried apples, and the other plain. Lon layered them alternately in a tall stack, lifted them to shove butter in between, and poured molasses over the top. Lindy placed three fried eggs on the side, done just the way he liked them. Lon automatically raised his head to thank her for the food. He got the full blast of her soft smile and glowing eyes. His stomach tensed. But the feeling passed as he shoveled in the flapjacks and eggs. Just dinner to get through, sitting on the grass, eating from the basket, drinking buttermilk. What if she pushed him down and crawled on top of him?

"Thank you, Lindy. I'm so full, I don't think you need bother bringing me any dinner."

She jeered. "A man who works as hard as you, that breakfast will wear off in three hours!" She dismissed his statement with a wave of her hand. "Now, don't take that the wrong way. I enjoy feeding a man who eats his fill, particularly when he says 'Thank you' the way you do. A woman appreciates knowing she's appreciated." The softest of soft smiles, and his heart twisted and turned, like a body on a gallows.

To furnish an excuse for not meeting her eyes Lon picked up the wedges he'd whittled last night. He hammered them beneath the post slowly, carefully, so he did not move the wedges already under the pole. The porch groaned as the beam lifted to the horizontal. He'd like to groan in the same way, but it would be a terrible insult to Lindy. He picked up the scythe and put the whetstone in his pocket just as a buggy rounded the corner of the house.

"There they are! Arrest them, Sheriff!" a man cried.

Lon spun around, astonished, and spied Sheriff Tipson driving a two-horse buggy. His companion leapt out, pointing a bony finger first at Lindy, then at Lon. Lon clattered down the steps, clasping the scythe business end out, and only after he stood, legs apart, confronting the man, did he realize he'd thrown himself in front of Lindy.

"Arrest them!" he cried again, eyeing the blade of the scythe. "He's threatening me." The fellow had the white hair and fiery eyes of an Old Testament prophet.

"Threatening, hell!" yelled Lon. "You're the one threatening."

Sheriff Tipson climbed out of the buggy slowly, as if it pained him to get involved in the dispute.

"What right do you have to come here, onto my place, and shout about arresting?" Lindy asked sensibly.

"As if you don't know," snorted the prophet in a very unprophetlike way.

"I'm sure I don't," snapped Lindy. "And I'll be pleased if you just get back in your buggy—"

"This is Judge Otis," said Tipson, his voice as heavy as his steps. "Clugg's uncle, the territorial judge."

"And you...and you—" the bony finger came up again, pointing at his eyes "—did some dirty business on my nephew, who this morning had to be taken to Dr. Ellis's hospital, sniveling and crying, insisting he saw you—" the finger shifted slightly so it pointed over his shoulder, at Lindy "—dead, long past time to be buried, driving your wagon."

"I can't help it if your nephew sees things," retorted Lindy.

"What he saw...he saw what you two and that undergrown Miller lad, the three of you, cooked up. I'm certain, for Lester's a—"

"Lester!" Lindy and Lon exclaimed together.

"A good boy, not given to drinking until..."

"He thinks the zephyrs carry the ghosts of dead Indians. He's afraid to stay in the jail when the wind blows." Lon looked to Sheriff Tipson, hoping for verification of his statement, but the man stood stolid and unhappy.

"...playing nasty jokes on my own dead sister's son, doing a man's job, even though he's but nineteen..."

"Seventeen," said Lon, taking an awful chance. "Seventeen at the most." This silenced the judge. He reared back and dropped his accusing finger.

"Who's telling tales out of school?"

That roused Tipson. "Seventeen?" he blurted, shocked from his lethargy.

"No razor ever touched *Less-ter's* face," said Lindy behind him, giving the name a derisive drawl. "I know, because he shoved it right up against mine. He fumbles about when he wants a woman, as green as they come. Maybe only fifteen."

"You've tried to seduce...?" began the judge, but the sheriff, seemingly emboldened by the revelation of Clugg's age, touched his shoulder.

"Deputy Clugg came out here and approached Lindy, sir. There are witnesses."

"Approached!" screamed Lindy. "He tried to rip my shirt off!"

"Liars. All liars," the judge said sternly, moving his arm up and down as if he held a gavel. "Now, it's best you confess everything. What horrible trick did you play on my nephew?"

Lon shrugged. "You tell us. A big crowd gathered back of McCaffrey's, so there must be witnesses."

"It's...it's..." Judge Otis stuttered, then shut his mouth and took a deep breath. "It's men such as yourself that bring disrepute upon Nevada Territory," he began, trying a different tack, and using a judge's tone of voice. "A thief who broke into Stone's office." The hand came up once more. "That dwarf and his gang...pretending to be a boy in trouble. And you—" he pointed over Lon's shoulder "—you...you..."

"Lindy's a lady, and she hasn't been in trouble with the law," Lon said stoutly.

"She has tempted my nephew, who is quite an innocent boy." Lindy let out a loud guffaw. "She dresses inappropriately, and her husband wrote false assay reports."

"You try being a farmer in skirts!" cried Lindy.

"I guess under the law a man might be held responsible for the crimes of his wife, but I never heard of a woman being held for the crimes of her husband," reasoned Lon. "It's the woman who says obey in the wedding."

"Playing at lawyer!" sneered the judge. "Territorial prison's the place for the likes of you. The sordid trick you played will come out soon enough, and we'll charge you with assault on an officer of the law, and you'll appear before *me* in the territorial court, not that namby-pamby county judge...."

Territorial prison. Could a year or two in territorial prison be worse than a life sentence on Lindy's farm? Judge Otis offered deliverance! Lon turned his back on the judge and handed the scythe to Lindy.

"Go up on the porch," he ordered. "Put this away." She gave him the soft smile, took the scythe and climbed the steps to the porch. Would she be willing to say "obey"? Her pants stretched over her hips and legs, showing him quite plainly why he had to get away from the farm.

"You're right, Judge. I played a dirty trick on your nephew. But you're wrong in one thing. Lindy and Billy Miller had nothing to do with it. They didn't even know what was going on. They did what I told them to."

"You did something to send Clugg over the edge?" asked Sheriff Tipson, astonished. "I thought Clugg's mind had just gone off on another of his fool—" He broke off when the judge glared at him.

"I'll go quietly, but you must promise to leave Billy and Lindy alone."

"No, Lon!" Lindy gasped. He spun around and sent her a hard look.

"Stay where you are, Lindy. This is a man's business." Lindy's worried expression cleared, the way a woman's face would change if a knight stepped between her and a dragon.

"Don't sacrifice yourself, Lon," she whispered, adoration open. "Not for me."

"Ready to go?" Lon asked the sheriff. Tipson nodded dumbly. Judge Otis strutted toward the buggy.

Where the road topped the river bluffs, Lon looked back for one last glimpse of the farm, behind him forever. He'd never see it again. No! His heart dropped so far, his stomach felt heavy. Lindy was running as fast as she could across the pasture, toward the grazing mules.

Lindy felt an absolute fool, riding a mule with a side-saddle while dressed in pants, but there hadn't been time to change, and it would take even more time to harness both teams to the wagon. And she didn't own a regular saddle. She wrenched a switch from a willow tree and lashed at the mule's hind end. He took the hint and broke from a trot to a gallop. She'd turned onto the Virginia City road before she remembered Buckskin and Lon's saddle, but dared not waste a quarter hour going back.

"Oh, Lon! I'll save you," she cried. "I'll get Billy and he'll think of something, and you won't go to territorial prison."

Heavens, she should have buried the skull! If the sheriff or the judge snooped around, they'd see the scarecrow, and they'd certainly put two and two together.

Devil's Gate, Gold City, the Divide still above her. Ages, aeons passing, and Lon hauled before the court. She'd hire Stone to defend him. She'd spend the barn money. Once on D Street, she realized she hadn't the slightest idea where Sunshine Alice lived. Ask a man or a woman? A woman would think she was looking for a place to work, and a man would think she already worked. She asked a man.

"I'm new in town," he said, pushing back his hat. "But when you find her...if I see you again...she sounds fascinating. I'm partial to sunshine." She asked a woman wearing a pink satin gown.

"Alice works alone," she said, eyeing Lindy's trousers with disapproval.

"We have business," Lindy said, striving to lend an air of mystery to the words.

"Oh. That dumb mine, I suppose. The cabin at the north end of the street with the blue paper shade on the lantern."

Midmorning, and the lantern hung askew, the fuel exhausted. Lindy pounded on the door. Nothing. Another tattoo on the door, the broad-headed nails and the splintery planks denting her hands, but she paid no heed.

"Alice. Billy. It's Lindy. Help."

The door opened, and she didn't recognize Alice at first because she wore a blue dressing gown. She shoved the door open, with Alice offering only the sleepiest of opposition.

"Where's Billy? I need his help. They're putting Lon in prison."

"What for?"

"Attacking an officer of the law. Where's Billy!" she demanded.

"How should I know? He got back yesterday evening raving about Clugg going wild out of his mind and you being dead, and took off to tell the story at some saloon."

"Which saloon?"

Alice tilted her head, her first sign of real consciousness. "Probably here on D Street, because climbing the hill's hard for his short legs."

"Let's go find him. It's dreadfully important, a matter of life and death."

"You go find him," Alice said. "I just got to sleep, and the nights haven't been very profitable, what with my brother Billy missing. I got to rest before the night shift shows up.''

"Which saloons, Alice?'' Alice waved her hand negligently at the entire street, then with surprising strength shoved Lindy out the door and slammed it.

Lindy expected to spot Billy standing on a bar, regaling the miners with the tale of Clugg and the dummy. Instead, at the third saloon, she discovered him curled up in a corner sound asleep. She threw him over her shoulder and tramped back to Alice's, aware of the eyes fixed upon her. *Oh, well,* she thought, *it gives them something to talk about in the saloons.*

Alice snarled at being roused out of bed a second time, but when she saw Billy's limp body, she willingly set about making a pot of coffee. Lindy decided she could use a cup of coffee herself. An hour passed without Billy uttering one sensible word, and Lindy had frightening visions of Lon confessing everything to protect her, and the judge convening court that very afternoon, after the sheriff rode back to the farm and took the skull off the scarecrow as evidence. Was Clugg sane enough to give evidence? *He'll be evidence himself, standing there mad and raving!*

She poured out the story, while Billy hammered his skull as if to empty the whiskey through his ear.

"My head hurts,'' he finally confessed. She had hope.

"Of course it does. You must have the world's biggest hangover, all jammed together in your little body. Lon's in trouble. Judge Otis brought the sheriff out to the farm.'' She repeated everything she'd said before, but this time Billy nodded occasionally. Alice made more coffee.

After a third recital of her story, Billy heaved himself to his feet. "Well, if we're to rescue that big lummox, we'd best get going. Where's my burro, Alice?''

"Wandering around town, eating garbage. He won't hang around D Street unless you feed him regular.''

"You can ride behind me on the mule," said Lindy. "Where're we going?"

"No, you go back to your place, hitch up the mules and bring the wagon into Carson. Meantime, I'm riding down to manage the riot."

"Riot?"

"Won't take long. Clugg's been a thorn, a barbed thorn and a burr, to a whole army of men in Carson. I'll just hit the saloons and tell a jumble of a story. Not hard to do when your head feels like mine. You be there, in front of the jail."

"The judge said Lon'll go to territorial prison, not the jail."

"You don't go to prison till after the jury's said guilty. He'll be in the county jail. Now, go get your wagon so you can pile Anderson out of town fast when we break down the door."

"Break him out?" Lindy asked, her breath coming fast.

"Well, what did you expect, woman! That we talk nice dip-lo-ma-see to the judge?" His eyes lit up. "You say Clugg's at Steamboat?"

"Yes. Judge Otis said he was raving this morning."

"Must be a sight, a man with hy-dro-pho-bee in the water cure," crowed Billy, clapping his hands against his thighs. "Well, best be off to find the burro. You get the wagon."

"Don't bother with the burro," said Alice. "We'll rent a buggy at the livery. If you think I'm going to miss this fracas, you're stupider than a grasshopper at first frost. But I've got to dress first."

Once Alice had disappeared into the back room, Billy leaned toward Lindy. "You know you're not gonna keep him, don't you?" Lindy stared at the floor. "He told me, he's leavin' first chance he gets."

The truth she had known all along. But it still hurt. No lover behind the quick kiss at McCaffrey's. He'd hardly looked at her since yesterday, and when he did catch her eyes by accident, his eyes shifted as if he followed a bumblebee.

"I know, Billy. But we can't leave him in jail, or to go to trial. I couldn't bear the thought of him in the prison. He doesn't like being shut in."

"Get your wagon," he ordered as Alice dashed from the back room in a yellow dress with a neckline far too low for rioting.

Chapter Sixteen

Lon lay back on the too-short bunk with his heels resting on the protruding brick. Rather like coming home, except Clugg wasn't around to provide stupid comments. The door leading to the front room of the jail opened slowly; Temporary Deputy Price backed through, closed it quietly.

"Got but a minute," said Price in a whisper. "Sheriff's out on the street talking to a friend. The judge's working to find a witness against you, but it seems there ain't a man in Pryor's today who drank there yesterday afternoon." He chuckled at the absurdity of it. "Judge doesn't believe them, of course, but short of jailing all of Pryor's customers, he can't do nothing."

"None of them know anything."

"Someone said they thought Billy drove Lindy's wagon, not her," said Price, his eyes shifting uneasily to the door.

"Surely Clugg, even mad, can tell the difference between a man no more than four feet tall and a lady over six feet?"

"I don't doubt Clugg was seeing things," Price agreed quickly. "He's probably been talking to some old witch doctor, like when he told us of the Paiute ghosts. The sheriff's uneasy, 'cause the judge rides him. He says you promised to confess, and now you're not saying anything."

"I'll tell him the whole story when I've settled down a bit. Getting arrested this morning riled my mind. I've got to think it all over calmly to come up with the truth."

"You'd better hope the judge doesn't find a witness."

"He's got the best witness he's likely to get. Lester Clugg."

"And he doesn't want to believe him, for obvious reasons. How would you feel, hearing your nephew's jug's not full."

"Clugg's jug is overfull, if you ask me," Lon said.

A muted explosion rattled the glass in the barred window.

"Shot," said Price in alarm. Another crack. "Gotta go!" He opened the door a crack, peeked out, then slithered through.

"I'm hungry," yelled Lon before the crack disappeared. "When's dinner?"

He resumed his place on the bunk, staring at the dusty sky beyond the barred window. He hoped the shot had nothing to do with Lindy. Probably not, for it sounded more like a pistol than a rifle, and Lindy owned a rifle. His stomach growled. If he hadn't involved himself in Billy's and Lindy's quarrels with Clugg, he'd be sitting in the hayfield right now, eating Lindy's pickles and sliced ham, and maybe cold sliced venison left over from the other night, and her light bread and, if she'd had time that morning, hot corn bread dripping with butter. And a can of buttermilk to wash it all down.

Not much in the food line to look forward to, once Judge Otis found his witness. More likely, paid a witness. The sheriff might find the scarecrow and guess how the trick had been done, but Sheriff Tipson didn't seem like a man to spend time roaming through a woman's truck garden. He'd refuse to tell his story until the "witness" turned up. Then he'd fashion his confession to match the evidence.

At least he'd escaped the farm, and Lindy and her se-

ductive cooking. No more soft smiles to avoid, no more
luscious hips, or even more luscious views down the neck
of her shirt. And he'd managed it without publicly shaming
Lindy. No one in Carson could tease her about not holding
her man, when that man had been sentenced to a term in
territorial prison. And by the time he got out, she'd have
another husband, one who liked slaving day after day on
eighty acres.

Lon regretted the unfinished post for the porch. He hoped
Lindy's new husband understood that at least two more
wedges should be driven underneath, and that the timber
must be cut exactly the measurement between floor and
roof beam. It should have triangular feet butted against it,
to add strength. If the sheriff and Judge Otis had delayed
for a day, he'd have had that job finished.

And he'd not put the final layer on the ninth haystack.
He hoped Lindy's new husband understood about finishing
off a haystack.

Then there was the irrigation ditch…how was he to keep
title to the land? He sat up quickly. He had to get a message
to Lindy, so she could put her own claim on that quarter
section. Damn it all, he'd not told her his idea of last night,
just before he went to sleep, that the ditch from the river
could be cut farther upstream, and run a lot higher up the
hill, and there'd be more acreage downhill from the water.

Price came in carrying a plate covered with a cloth.

"Dinner," he said. He whipped a spoon out of his vest
pocket. "Sheriff says you're not to have a knife, for fear
you'll kill yourself. But I think it's the judge who gave that
order."

"He can't admit it's Clugg, not me, who's crazy?"

Price pulled off the cloth, taking a cascade of peas with
it. With dismay he watched them roll across the floor.
"You want I should pick them up?"

"No. That's more food than Clugg ever brought me. I

always suspected him of high grading the dinners. Boys of that age have gigantic appetites."

"What age?" asked Price.

"Seventeen."

"You're joshing me!"

"No, the judge admitted, the boy's only seventeen. He didn't do his nephew any favor making him a deputy at seventeen."

"But the sheriff must of knowed," mused Price.

"No, Otis told him Clugg was nineteen."

"No wonder old Tipson's out of sorts today," marveled Price. "Wait'll I pass this on to the boys. Seventeen!"

"What was the shooting?"

"Just a bullet through a picture in Pryor's Saloon, but Pryor's hopping mad. The sheriff's seeing to it."

Lon dug in to his dinner, by this time cold. After he cleaned the plate he thought of Lindy's ever-present loaf of bread. He'd grown accustomed to cutting one final slice, spreading the butter thick. His mouth watered. He looked longingly at the peas spread like green marbles across the floor, just out of reach. Shouting and knocking about in the front room distracted his mind from his stomach. The door opened, and Price and the sheriff steered in a man clutching a package to his breast.

"Don't shove! Don't shove!" he cried. "I'll go willing, but I must have my property. You thieving lawmen would abscond, abscond, I say, with such precious possessions as I...um...possess." He laid the package on the hard bunk and, whipped off his hat, which had a great bite missing from the brim. "How soon before my bail is set?"

"Tomorrow morning," said the sheriff. "Pryor says you gotta pay for the damages."

"But I cannot pay anything, stuck in here! It's as ludicrous as jailing a man for debt! Unless this gentleman—" he gestured toward Lon "—should like to purchase these fine Nevada mining investments. I've been so fortunate as to beg a few shares of the Smiling Jane, Reese River's most promising prospect, and—''

''M-Moseley!'' stammered Lon.

''So you know each other,'' said the sheriff. ''Probably cut from the same cloth, two sides of the same shirt.'' He turned to Lon. ''The judge has found a witness as says he saw you and Lindy and Billy Miller, and he thinks another fellow, come out of McCaffrey's store dressed like ghosts, and you hooted and hallooed so as to wake the dead.''

''Then McCaffrey's in on the joke, too,'' said Lon, ''or he wouldn't have given us shelter. I won't confess to anything that hauls McCaffrey into the mess. No one in Carson will appreciate McCaffrey being jailed, him having the biggest store in town, and a wife who churns the best butter. Other than Lindy.''

''I better speak to the judge on this,'' said the sheriff. ''Take those dishes back to the hotel, Deputy.''

''Yes, sir,'' said Price. He lingered, scraping up the peas with the spoon, until the sheriff shut the door. ''The judge's witness is a Frenchman who's been in town the past day or two, and his English doesn't cover much more than drinking, gambling and whoring. Not very convincing on the witness stand.'' He picked up the plate and slipped out.

''Imagine meeting you here,'' said Moseley. ''What brings you to the Palace Hotel of Carson City?''

''I'm accused of playing a dirty trick on the deputy, which sent him into trembling fits and pushed him to the edge of madness. And you?''

''A misunderstanding. Nothing more. But that saloon keeper Pryor hangs a contemptuous painting behind his bar, showing the *great divinity of democracy,* Thomas Jefferson, joined in glory with that *devil of federalism* and *father of rank abolitionism,* John Adams. I put two bullets through John Adams. I'm from South Carolina,'' he added, as if that explained everything. Lon nodded. ''Now, sir, about the Smiling Jane...''

"I've got no money." Moseley groaned, collapsed onto the bunk and dropped his head in his hands, but just for a moment. "The sheriff or the deputy?" he asked.

"I can't say."

"Perhaps the sheriff will accept the shares as collateral for my bail."

"What mines?" asked Lon.

"As I said, the Smiling Jane, the outstanding prospect of the Reese River, the Monarch of the Mountains on the Humboldt, the..." He commenced to unwrap the parcel and ruffle through the certificates. "The Green Gage, the Shirt Tail, the Stars and Bars, the—"

"How much Shirt Tail?"

"Fifty shares."

"You ask Deputy Price to send a message to Virginia City, to a woman down on D Street named Sunshine Alice. She might pay Pryor damages in return for fifty shares of Shirt Tail."

"I presume, from the name, she is a lady of the night?"

"Right."

"Soiled doves quite often have information denied to those of us in more acceptable professions." Lon laughed without meaning to. "The lady has heard of a new endeavor in the Shirt Tail?"

"The lady intends to open the Shirt Tail herself."

"Ah !" exclaimed Moseley. "The lady has a clientele of the higher reaches of mining society. A geologist, perhaps, has spoken into her pillow...."

"She's heard a silly story about frogs jumping around with nuggets in their mouths, from a woman who reads a crystal ball. Where did you get fifty shares of Shirt Tail? Last time I saw you, you had no stock at all."

"At the Lake House, yes, at that time I possessed no supply, but two days ago a gentleman from California passed by, and gladly parted with the paper for twenty dollars."

"From California?" asked Lon, puzzled. "He'd have made better money taking the certificates to the exchange in San Francisco."

"So I told him, but by his behavior, I concluded the gentleman had reason to avoid the legal boundaries of the state of California. I suspect the certificates' titles will not stand a search of their provenance."

"In that note to Alice, you include a few words for me. 'Lon says for Billy to visit Lake House for a spell.'"

Moseley repeated the words, then, lifting his head, stared at the window. "What is that noise? Is today some holiday that requires a parade in Carson City?"

Shouting rose over a growling undertone, so loud it must come from a rather large crowd.

"Nothing but per-see-cu-cit," cried a high voice with a Texas accent. "In-just-ice, with a capital...with a capital..."

"Forget about the message for Billy," Lon said, resigned.

"Deputy...drunken to seein' snakes and critters of hell..." The muttering grew louder. "Only seventeen... who'd put a child of seventeen...?" More muttering, but also shouts of agreement. "Botherin' worthy women in their homes...stand up, Lindy."

Oh, God! Was Lindy out there? Of course. She'd planned it all. Lit a fire under Billy.

"This honest woman...tossed the beast down her front steps...rightfully so...what you'd all expect from your own sweethearts and wives." Cheers of agreement.

"...so small in the poker, no gal would pay heed." Laughs and cheers. "Eatin' from the plates sent to prisoners in jail...." Gala whoops from men who'd obviously sat in the cells.

"Golden-haired children...golden-haired girl children... not so tall as I...feet on the road to D Street."

Billy, like a good rabble-rouser, had saved the best for

last. The crowd's roar rose shrilly, like the scream of a threatened panther.

"Judge Otis's house…" screamed Billy.

"No," cried the sheriff.

"Steamboat…!"

"No. You just settle down and hear what the judge's witness has to say."

"His witness can't speak English!" yelled someone, and Billy's harangue got tangled up in threats shouted from a dozen throats.

"Little golden-haired girl children…! Sheriff, you in on this? Hungry for money, always… Feet on the road to D Street!"

The front door of the jail slammed so hard Lon felt the vibrations through the bricks. The sheriff burst in, carrying a ring of keys.

"You're getting out of here," snapped Tipson. "They're threatening to burn the judge's house, then march to Steamboat and beat up Clugg."

"No," said Lon, backing away from the cell door. "You bring it in writing from the judge that charges are dismissed for lack of evidence. Then I'll leave." The chance of Judge Otis backing down, Lon thought, lay somewhere between faint and nil.

"The judge's hid out over at the land office with that Frenchman. It'll take me a while to fetch him."

"You best get on the road, then," said Lon. He folded his arms across his chest and glared. The sheriff backed toward the open door.

"Me, too," cried Moseley. "Charges dismissed for lack of evidence."

"The evidence is plain," snapped the sheriff from the door. "John Adams is all blowed to hell."

An hour later Lon couldn't believe his ears. Judge Otis, apologizing for believing a false witness…misjudging the wishes of the citizens of the great territory of Nevada…being misled by the white lies of a young man, "rather a boy…the hasty words of youth…the bonds of blood, gentlemen…my own dead sister's son…the impulses of the heart common to both sexes…"

Lon shuddered. Nothing to do now but be honest and cruel with Lindy. The men would taunt her, joke that even a man bigger than she wouldn't have her. At least he could do it in private, with a modicum of politeness. He'd go home with her, tell her the way things were, on her own porch, so she understood he was leaving on Thursday, the thirteenth.

The sheriff, the judge and Price arrived, the judge carrying a paper. He shoved it through the bars.

"All in proper form," he said gruffly. The sheriff already had the key in the lock; the hinges squealed as he folded back the door.

"Me, too," cried Moseley. He clasped his bundle of stock certificates to his breast, and jumped up and down. "No shred of evidence exists for you to detain me in this vile hovel!"

The sheriff and Price grabbed Lon's arms. "Get out of here before that crowd turns ugly again," said Tipson.

"I'll tell Sunshine Alice," cried Lon as they hustled him past Moseley's cell. Half a glimpse, a sparkle dropping from Moseley's bundle. Half a glimpse, but enough to see the golden heart slip into a crack between the bricks.

"Where did you get…?" he began, but Price and Tipson pushed him into the front room and slammed the door against Moseley's cries. The judge stepped into the street, held up his hand for silence, but the crowd roared and surged forward. Billy stood on the seat of a buggy shouting, beside him Alice, clapping her hands and screaming. Lindy perched on the seat of her wagon, the reins already raised in her hands.

"Get out of town," said Tipson. "No visiting and celebrating in the saloons. Town's drunk enough as 'tis."

"I don't drink," protested Lon as they cleared a path through the crowd to Lindy's wagon. He slammed against the tailgate, grabbed the edge of the wagon bed and swung himself over, landing with a thud that shook the running gear.

"Ho!" yelled Lindy at the mules, rolling him against the tailgate with the sudden start. She swung past the buggy.

"Fifty shares of Shirt Tail!" yelled Lon in the two seconds he had Alice and Billy in view. He pointed to the jail.

Several mounted men accompanied them out of town, whooping and hollering at the triumph over Clugg and Judge Otis, and firing their revolvers and rifles into the air. At the top of the rise above the river they turned back, leaving the wagon alone on the rutted, dusty road. The very tips of the mountains caught the last rays of the setting sun. A whole day wasted, and the ninth haystack not done. Lindy slowed the mules to a walk.

"Sorry to be in such a hurry, but the chores aren't done."

She turned around, smiling, but not the soft smile of anticipation. A sad smile.

"You don't want me, do you?"

"It's not you, Lindy. It's your farm."

"I know. Billy told me. It's wrong for a woman to set her cap at a man and try to trap him. I'm sorry."

"It's okay."

"You'll be leaving next Thursday. I'll put up some things for you to carry along, so you won't starve heading over the pass."

"Thank you, Lindy. I'd appreciate that."

"I killed one of the young roosters," Lindy said, shifting on the pile of grass. "Tonight we'll have fried chicken."

"What's the occasion?"

"Nothing. But you should have one last rib-sticking meal before...before you leave. You could have gone days ago, you know." She twisted about to look at the long row of haystacks, and the shirt pulled around her waist, the folds pointing at the peaks of her full breasts.

"I owed the sheriff thirty days. You paid the fine, I give you thirty days. It's been more pleasant to spend it this way, rather than looking at the sky through a square hole with bars."

Lon leaned back against the pile of grass to avoid the sight of her waist, squinted his eyes as he met the brilliance of the sky. "I've never been anyplace where the sky's as blue as it is here," he commented.

"It's the clear air, I guess. Hardly ever any clouds in the summer."

"How much is that new barn of yours costing?" he asked, edging toward an idea he'd had only that morning.

"Three hundred and fifty dollars."

"How much hay do you need for the winter?"

"You've already cut plenty. Don't worry about more."

"The livery stable in Virginia City pays sixty dollars a ton for hay. You make two trips a week with produce. It wouldn't be too much work for those mules of yours to make another trip. I could take up a wagon load of hay tomorrow."

"Tomorrow your time's done. I can't afford to pay you to work for me."

"I'm thinking I'll find a job in Carson or Virginia, the stable maybe, to put some silver in my pockets before I head over the pass."

"If you hang around too long, there'll be snow on the pass."

"Not for a month or six weeks. I might stay to see that barn go up, if it's all the same to you. Maybe the carpenter would hire me. Unless it pains you to have me on the place."

She smiled, not the sad smile of the past two days, not

the soft smile that had followed the kiss. A smile of pleasure.

"No pain. And you could sleep on the porch if you want to."

The quiver started down low, the vibrations hitting his heart in short bursts. He sat up straight and clenched his fists under his legs. What in hell was he doing? If he made one move, if he gave in to that feeling, he'd be trapped. Did he think he could stay in Nevada and not be tempted?

"And I'll still feed you. It's no lie, I enjoy feeding a man who relishes his food." She gathered up the bowls and crocks, and piled them into the basket. He watched her hands, slender, graceful, roughened by work. He stared as she walked away, her hips swaying, the trousers stretched tight against them. He had to leave, without money, with nothing but the leftovers she might pack in his saddlebags. One more day and he rode away free. Not just of the farm, but of her and the temptation of her. One wrong move and he would be stuck for the rest of his days on a farm that would suck him dry. He would become one of those tooth-less old men leaning against the front gate, waiting for a stranger to pass and exchange a few words.

He took off his shirt, picked up the scythe and swung it steadily. The grass fell in neat rows, ready for the rake tomorrow. He wouldn't leave right at sunrise. Tomorrow morning he'd finish the tenth haystack.

The new post held up the center of the porch roof. He'd disposed of Clugg. He'd cut her hay. He'd paid her back for getting him out of jail. But rot still worked at the corner of the pigpen, and the irrigation ditch.... Early this morning he'd walked to the inlet of the ditch, and had seen the river flowing below the sill of the gate. The corn, with ears barely set, would droop and die in the summer heat, of no use except as green fodder, and who had time to cut it? The oats and wheat stood in shocks, ready for threshing, but weeds and prickly sage had overgrown the threshing floor.

She'll get a husband to help her, he reassured himself. As soon as the court gave her the divorce from Harvey… Harvey had stolen the little gold heart from his saddlebag, the heart that had represented Lindy in the poker game. The heart that had tumbled from Moseley's grasp. By rights it belonged to him. But he didn't want Lindy. No, that wasn't true. He'd take Lindy in a minute, except that the farm trailed behind her, like a dirty train.

How had Moseley come by the heart? Moseley and Harvey had met, and Harvey had used the heart to buy something from Moseley.

A gentleman, bound for California, Monday, post meridiem.

Harvey had gone to California! Harvey, with the hundred dollars he'd stolen, had purchased Moseley's worthless stock certificates. Harvey Saxton, still seeking instant wealth, had bought the sheaf of Reese River and Humboldt and Comstock wildcat shares. Seventy dollars and a bit of gold, Moseley had said. The heart.

Lon turned at the end of a row and glanced automatically at the tiny triangle of roof visible above the tall corn. The corn now bound to die of thirst. A thin trickle of smoke rose straight toward the sky. Lindy had started the kindling in the cookstove. Fried chicken. He licked his lips. Maybe she would make thick cream gravy to go over potatoes.

The column of smoke thickened as the fire caught. For a second or two he imagined flames at the base of the black cloud. His imagination worked overtime in Nevada, like seeing Lindy and six children. Crimson tongues flashed upward, unmistakable.

The house! The house on fire!

He dropped the scythe and ran, dodging the low piles of hay he'd raked that morning. The flames leapt higher; the black smoke caught in an eddy of breeze, swooped down and obscured the fragment of roof.

He cut through the thickening corn, forgetting the sprawling pumpkin and squash vines hidden among the stalks. A green pumpkin flattened beneath his boot, his foot skidded forward, and he landed on his rear. He scrambled to his feet, dashed down an open row to get out of the corn patch.

Through the stubble of wheat and oats, dodging about the sinking, untended shocks of grain. A half-buried rock tripped him up; he sprawled next to the pigpens. The hogs came trotting over to observe this curious human activity. Lon plunged forward on hands and knees, rounded the hog pen half crawling.

"Lindy!" he shouted. "Lindy!"

The brush roof over the stove crackled in a sheet of flame. For one instant it was a level shelf of fire, then it folded in the center and crashed. Burning branches covered the cookstove. Pots and pans littered the ground between the fire and the house. Lindy did not look at him. She stared at the ruin of her summer kitchen, her arms wrapped around a large skillet filled with raw chicken. Lon grabbed the skillet from her.

"Are you okay?" She looked at him without a spark of recognition. "Are you all right?" His free hand grasped her shoulder; he shook her. She nodded dumbly, her attention focused on the blaze that raged on her stove.

"Come here and sit down." He led her to the back steps, put the skillet on the porch. She did not sit down. He pushed her backward until she folded onto the top step.

"How did it start?"

"I lit a fire in the stove."

"It's my fault," he said quickly. "The pipe should stand one length higher. I thought of it more than once, but forgot to mention it when you went to town. Sparks from the kindling landed on the roof. We'll rebuild the ramada tomorrow. Buy another section of pipe next time you go to Virginia City.''

He sank onto a lower step. She did not look at him, but he saw her eyes cloud with moisture. Two silent drops spilled over and slid down her cheeks, twisting paths through the dust and soot. Two more, taking slightly different routes, created a tracery on her face.

"You don't understand," she said.

He lifted himself to the top step, sat beside her and put his arm about her shoulders. His hand automatically reached for hers, clasped it tightly, before he remembered he should not be this close.

"Nothing's ruined, Lindy. The stove just needs cleaning up, and I can build a new ramada tomorrow morning."

Her shoulders heaved beneath his arm, and she lowered her head to her knees as the sobs claimed her. He was not prepared for this. The idea that Lindy could weep like any other woman took him by surprise.

"Lindy, I'll make everything right," he begged. She turned her face into his bare chest and clutched at him. The damp warmth of her tears reminded him he'd left his shirt behind in the field.

"Lindy, darling," he protested. "It's not so bad. I'll make it right. I'll do anything, just don't cry."

She shook her head against him; the fragments of hay caught in his chest hair moved roughly against his skin. He held her, puzzled by her overreaction. The fragile ramada was no loss. It would have collapsed with the first heavy snowfall.

She put her hands against his chest and pushed him away. She studied the stair where her bare feet rested. He dropped his arms, relieved at her rejection, and moved a step down to put distance between them.

"There's not going to be anything new," she whispered. "Not a new ramada for the stove, or a new barn...or anything."

"Why not?"

"I got a letter from Will this afternoon. The neighbors brought it out from town."

"So?"

"Will intends to sell the place. He says I must come to Sacramento if I won't take Harvey back. I can't stay here through the winter by myself."

"That's not true. Of course you can. You can do anything you set your mind to."

She shook her head, still staring at the splintered planks of the stairs.

"No, Lon, he's right. I can't do it by myself. There's no wood cut for winter. The house isn't fit for cold weather, for the wind blows right through the walls. The corn's dying because the ditch isn't deep enough. The oats and the wheat aren't threshed, because I'm not sure how to do it. I thought I knew everything, but my grandfather had hired men.... A farm needs more than one person. You know that."

"Yes," he agreed reluctantly. "There's something in what you say." He imagined Lindy in Sacramento, in her pink dress with the skirt five feet wide.

Sacramento! He sat up straight, and the edges of his heart curled with pleasure. He could find a job in Sacramento, and court her. He'd leave tomorrow, at first light, ride straight to Sacramento and hunt up Will Merryman. By the time Lindy came in on the stage, he'd be settled. He imagined the dances, Lindy gliding in the waltzes, bouncing in the polkas, his hands about her waist, pressing against her uncorseted back, the hoops carrying the pink lace up, baring her ankles.

"You'd have fun in Sacramento," he said gently. "There's plenty to keep you occupied, parties and dances. You like dances." Lindy's shoulders sagged.

Men hovering over her, men in swallowtail coats and tall hats, men with carriages and houses with brick chimneys.

And before half the winter had passed, as soon as the divorce... His heart leveled. No guarantee she would pick him. Why should she pick him?

He looked across the farmyard, over the pigpen with the sagging rails, and the makeshift chicken coop, the corral with no proper gate. The fire on top of the cookstove flared briefly, then the half-burned branches collapsed into the glowing ashes.

The place needed a man, no question about that.

"I don't want to live in Sacramento," she said between dry sobs. "I like my farm. I know you don't think much of it, but I like it." She straightened up, swallowed and sniffed, and her smeared face assumed the strength of resignation. "Now you can go," she said. "There's going to be no barn. You can get back to whatever it is you want to do. Take some of the hay to Virginia City and sell it. You deserve the money, and it'll give you a start someplace else."

Chapter Seventeen

Responsibility fell on Lon's shoulders like a stone. He tried to escape by moving away from Lindy, down another step. The weight remained. The mounded tops of the haystacks poked over the corn. His haystacks. He could not see the stakes and strings beyond the corral, where he and Lindy had marked out the foundations of the barn, but he knew where they lay, so often had he imagined the barn, whitewashed, or maybe red, like the barns of his youth. More than once, as he'd drifted into sleep, he'd traced the sequence in which the heavy beams would be raised, then the rafters. The cows munching on his hay in their mangers; Lindy milking in the morning light; the lazy rooster perched on one of the upper rafters.

He had to do something, either walk away or take on the duty he did not want. Or had his mind shifted, when he wasn't paying attention? His hand lay on the stair, only a palm's width from her bare foot. He studied how close they were, and how far apart. If he moved his hand a few inches, he committed himself.

Committed himself to engender that crowd in the wagon, committed himself to being a father to that half-grown girl, and the babe on Lindy's lap, and the four in between.

They'd been so happy, each clasping the little packet of candy McCaffrey had put up for them.

Candy! He was so prosperous that he bought candy for five children! He concentrated on the vision. The wagon, not the old one Lindy used, but one so new the yellow varnish glowed on the sides. And not mules. Four horses, of the color he favored, golden-brown. And sure enough, the kids had candy. And Lindy smiled, that soft smile, and with that she declared they all depended upon him.

It's not true, he told himself. The flag glowing on Mount Davidson had been an accident of nature, and the queens in the crystal ball just a piece of gossip Mrs. Dove had picked up. And the vision of the wagon, and the children, and himself and Lindy... How?

He watched, fascinated, as his fingers slid over her foot.

"I don't think I want to go so quick, Lindy."

She crept down the stairs until she faced him, her eyes ten inches from his. She didn't say a word, just studied him, like a kitten who hears a new sound, and doesn't understand if it should scamper to mama or attack.

"I'm getting sort of attached to the place," he said.

"The place?"

"You. I'm getting attached to you."

Her hands rested on his shoulders. She exerted just enough weight so that he leaned toward her. She smelled of the chicken coop and the garden and wood smoke, with just enough of the smell of healthy woman to rouse him. Down the open placket of her shirt he glimpsed her white cotton undervest, and the curves of her breasts. No sense holding back now. He embraced her, but not closely.

"I'm all dirty from the hay," he whispered.

"That's fine," she replied. She closed the gap, and every springy line of her body met his, from hips to chest. Everything sank in upon him at once, her lips, her hands reaching around his chest, exploring his backbone. He investigated the flare of her hips, dropped his hands lower, and dug with his fingers. He depended upon his fingers to confess his urgency, because he felt shy about asking straight out, *Will you romp with me?* He moved his hand so one thumb swung to her inner thigh. Her lips touched his ear, and he heard her ragged breath.

"After the chores," she murmured. "Once we're down in bed, we're not getting up for hours."

"I'll help."

Lon tucked himself against the brown flank of the cow, his arm wedged on the back leg so she could not kick the bucket. The cow mooed anxiously, and turned her head to stare.

"Are you sure you don't want me to do that?" asked Lindy.

"They'd best get used to me."

Lindy smiled, a dazzling smile lighting up her whole face, and her dark eyes glowed. "They'll get used to you. I'll put the washtub in the house for a bath," she said.

"Can't heat any water," he said. "The stove's still buried. I'll wash off in the watering trough, as usual."

"There's water in the reservoir of the stove, and it should be hot, with a fire burning all around it."

He wondered how she could be thinking straight, when she grinned like a silly schoolgirl. She carried the washtub into the house before she started milking.

He watched her skim the cream off the morning milk without missing a drop, and dump the blue skimmed milk in the pigs' trough. He shouldn't be standing just staring at her. He nosed around for the last few eggs, scattered some corn to tempt the hens into the coop.

"The bath's all ready," she said. "Not hot, but at least warm."

"You go ahead," he said. "Ladies first. I'd just fill the water with hay."

"I'll hurry," she said.

He sat on the porch, listening to the splash of water behind him. He looked across the yard to where the barn would stand, and felt a tinge of uncertainty. That barn, this house, those animals, the woman inside, they bound him, and he would never leave this place. He concentrated on the feelings her hands generated. On his urge to care for her. Children. Five children in the back of a wagon, one on Lindy's lap. He closed his eyes, recalling the vision once more, and for the first time identified his own feelings. Happy. At peace, because other people depended upon him. Someone to care for.

"I'm done," she called out the window. He heard the door between the two rooms close.

A scum of gray soapsuds covered the water, but Lindy had hurried, so some warmth remained. He stripped off his trousers and sank into the tub. She'd left a rag and soap. He scrubbed his face and neck and behind his ears carefully, ducked completely under to get the bits of hay out of his hair. The yellow soap smelled strong and utilitarian. Lindy should have pink soap that smelled of roses. He would buy her some after he sold the first load of hay.

He dried himself on a long strip of flannel she'd left folded on a chair. He wrapped it around his middle, and turned to the bedroom door. The door, a plain wooden door, assumed the strength of a fortress.

If I go in there, he thought, *I never get out.* He thought of cold winter mornings, with chores to be done and fingers frozen in his mittens pitching the hay down from the mow. The sheep, lambing in a February blizzard. Twice he stretched out his hand to push the door open, and twice he pulled away.

The warmth of the sun on his back when he cut the hay, and the smell of it when he tossed it onto the tall stacks. The smell of her sitting on the back steps, and the feel of her strong fingers along his backbone. He pushed the door open.

She sat on the bed, wearing nothing but her hair. He had never seen it down before; it covered her to her hips, like a cape. She leaned over, dropped the hairbrush on the floor and shoved it out of the way with her foot, slender, like her hands. He reached out to her, forgetting his hands held the bit of flannel; it hit the floor as he reached her. She lay back against the quilt; he leaned over, brushing the hair aside so he could see all of what she offered. She smelled faintly of lye soap.

"I'll buy you soap that smells like roses," he said.

"Why?"

"Because you deserve it. And I like a sweet-smelling woman."

She'd made the sheets from flour sacks. He'd work hard, to get her—them—some smooth, silky ones. Women should be soft and plump, and a great deal smaller than he. She offered her lips, he kissed her, and noted with delight that he could keep his lips pressed against hers and at the same time feel her hips against his. He ran his hands down her ribs, and everywhere he touched he felt the muscle beneath the skin.

She giggled, and explored him, the way a woman who really likes to romp studies a man, and figures out what he wants her to do. Her exploration reached his stomach, and he had no regrets at all.

Over the rise of her hips, through the open window, the full slope of the hills across the river lay visible. The hills mimicked her curves, an undulant land, a feminine land, reflecting all the fecundity of a woman. Golden hills, the level sun reflecting on gray sage, and the drying grass of summer.

Grass! He had his hands between her thighs, yet let himself be distracted by the grass on the hills. Something about the angle, looking from the height of the house, over the cottonwoods that blocked his view from the hayfield. Golden grass, like her sexual hair, lighter than the tangled aura on her head. The hillside in the setting sun and Lindy merged; he swung himself over her, aware that he mated with the woman and the grass and the land and the river. And the cattle that might graze across the river, scattered so far that nothing equaled the distance they would cover, except the expanse of his affection. And hers.

"We'll go to Sacramento," she gasped. "I don't care about the farm." She didn't understand, but he found no moment to explain, for all time and eternity folded into that instant. Nothing but completion, plunging his claim into the golden hills that metamorphosed into Lindy. She cried out, answering his own cries, urged him to a delirium with frenzy at its heart. The tempest of orgy, then frantic grinding of hips to snatch one final spasm from the storm, and tumultuous kisses of thanks.

They had the night before them, he reminded himself. No need to snatch all satiation from one connection. So different, to anticipate the hours beside her. So conjugal.

Conjugare, to unite. Once he proposed the sexual meaning to his father, who snarled at him and snatched the Latin dictionary from his hands. "Can you think of nothing but filth? You speak of things you know nothing about." Now he knew. Lindy relaxed beside him, murmuring endearments.

Perhaps his father had considered only the second part of *conjugare. Jugum,* yoke. To yoke together. Unpleasant in concept, implying a burden of dumb beasts. Except, Lon reminded himself, he assumed the burden voluntarily.

He made himself lie still, for Lindy's head nestled in the notch of his shoulder; he resisted the impulse to leap up, to pace the room, to shout this thrilling new concept. Voluntarily! The key to his impatient, unhappy father, thrashing about in his philosophy and theology! His father had never accepted his responsibility in the matter. He had never admitted that the tumble in the bushes that created a child had been a voluntary act.

Lon followed the logic carefully. If all these things were true, then this farm, this wife who lay beside him would never fall into the desolation of his childhood. He volunteered. He would not turn mean and nasty, he would never hate the child he might have started moments ago.

The first, that solemn girl. He'd make sure Lindy didn't think he had his heart set on a boy as firstborn. And that girl, he'd take very good care, so when it came her time to do this, she did not suppose all men were stern brutes. He soothed the tangled hair off Lindy's brow. "I do care for you, Lindy. I care very much. I'll take care of you always. And the children. Forever."

Light flashed in a dream; something heavy weighted her chest. Lindy touched the weight to understand it, to push it away, felt the muscles, the silken hair, and remembered.

Lon's arm lay across her, a protection. Another flash, definitely not a dream, the faintest illumination of Lon's face, the thick lock of hair obscuring his forehead. His breath came slowly. She lay still.

She would give up the farm. She had demanded that he sacrifice his dreams and stay with her, certainly not a woman's prerogative. She had forgotten part of being a woman. She would be quite happy with Lon. Anywhere.

A mutter of thunder. He stirred, lifted his head.

"Oh." In sleep he had forgotten, just as she had. She ran a quieting hand down his back.

"Lightning and thunder, far away." He slipped his arm beneath her shoulders and drew her against him.

"Does it frighten you?"

"Not for me, but for the animals. I've heard of mules and cows being struck by lightning. They should have a nice barn, with lightning rods. With glass balls," she added as an afterthought.

He heaved himself out of bed, leaving her suddenly chilled. She heard the rasp of the hinges and his step on the porch. Another flash of light. By the time the tag end of thunder vibrated through the bedroom, he had climbed in beside her.

"Far away, over the Sierra." Caring. After their passion he'd said he would care for her, and he had. Simply, by walking to the porch and bringing news to calm her.

"We'll have the barn in a week or two, but the glass balls on the lightning rods may have to wait until next year. But I'll get them for you, I promise."

"No," she said, lifting the lock of hair, pushing it back from his forehead. "Will's selling the place. You don't want to be a farmer—we'll be happier in Sacramento. I'm sure Will needs big, strong men for his pack trains, and to care for the animals."

"Your brother meant to sell the farm because you had no man about the place. You've got one now."

"You don't want to be a farmer."

"Can't a man change his mind?" She pushed him onto his back, held him down by straddling him. A breeze redolent of mountain air and storm brushed her naked shoulders.

"Not if he's changed it because he pities a woman who's got herself into an awful fix, because she doesn't know about irrigation ditches, or how many days it takes to harvest oats and wheat, or—"

"Lean down, so I can kiss you."

"It's not your fault that I decided I wanted a farm. I thought, living summers with Grandma and Grandpa, I knew what to do, but I don't. In Sacramento we can have a place big enough for me to grow a vegetable garden."

"Lindy, when you said 'sell,' it cleared my mind. The way a man must feel when the judge says, 'hang by the neck until dead.' I'd be losing…"

"A hardscrabble farm?"

"You. Most of all, you. But I want to see the barn, not

just work on it, see it, fill the mow with hay, and build bins for the oats and corn...."

"There'll be no corn. The ditch. Remember?"

"I've got an idea, Lindy. You know how the ridge on my claim stretches out from the hills, almost to the river." He reached up and used her breast to demonstrate the lay of the land. "Your ditch runs down on the flat." He traced a line with his finger at her waistline. "But if we start a ditch farther upstream, and run it higher on the hill—" his fingers returned to her breast "—practically the whole eighty will be downhill from the ditch." She giggled as his fingers spread under her arm.

"But that's just a claim, Lon. You've got to build a house on it, and live there."

"We'll move the house. Lean down, so I can put a claim on my land."

"Move the house!" she exclaimed, disbelieving. He clasped her breast, guided the nipple to his mouth. "Lon Anderson, do you always get crazy notions when you romp?"

He turned his head slightly. "I get good ideas when I romp with you, Lindy," he said very seriously, his voice somewhat muffled by the curve of her breast. "How far is this house from the property line? Seventy-five feet, a hundred feet? When the builder comes for the barn, he and his men can move the house."

She drew him along with her on an airy ride; they danced in the black sky with the stars, and the zephyr kept them airborne for a long, long time, then let them down gently, drifting over the valley until they once more lay in her bed, holding one another.

"It can't get any better than that," he said.

"We can try," she suggested.

They gentled one another until a hint of dawn touched the western peaks and the eastern horizon. He helped her dress.

"I want to know exactly what's covering every part of you," he whispered.

"Let me help you." She pulled the shirt over his head, buttoned his trousers, knelt before him with his boots.

Hand in hand they walked southward, across the unmarked boundary that had no meaning now, kicked at the sand and sagebrush, then traced the new site of the house—the house to validate his claim—by scuffing a rough square in the soil with the toes of their boots. They walked toward the river, eyeing the hillside for the route the new ditch would take.

"I'll have to make a spirit level..." Lon was saying, but Lindy heard no more, nothing but the lilt of water against rocks. And wood. She dropped Lon's hand and ran to the watergate.

"Lon! The water's up!" Little waves lapped against the wooden panel, almost up to the crack that had first hinted at disaster. "How can it be?" He bent over to examine the miraculous truth. He had made love to her, and the water rose. He would care for her; he'd create miracles for her.

"The thunderstorm, last night over the mountains," he explained prosaically. "It rained over the peaks, maybe even as far down as Carson Canyon. Now the high water's reached us."

"You always have a good explanation for everything," she said. "With you around, I won't have miracles."

"No, I can't explain everything, Lindy. Not nearly everything." The dawn reflected in his eyes. "Let's raise the gate, so the corn gets every bit of water the ditch can hold."

"The corn will set seed now," she said confidently. "Without water, the ears would be nothing but nubbins. Barren."

Barren seed. She turned away from him, pretending to watch the water. She bent to take a rock out of the ditch. She should have told him last night.

"Lon, before you say anything final—about us, I mean—

you'd best know, all the time I lived with Harvey, I never had a sign of being in the family way."

He stood close behind her, his arms clasped about her midriff, right under her breasts. "Don't fret. With me it's going to be different."

"It's already different."

"I know." His voice deepened, became husky. He turned her in his arms. "It's different because I want to be here. Voluntarily. Remember that, and remind me if I forget."

The chores took a long time, because whenever they came close to one another, their hands ignored their work and touched, caressed, embraced. She forgot the sequence of her tasks, leaving the chickens in the coop long past sunrise, skimming the cream from the milk pans without dumping the milk in the pigs' trough, leaving her stool sitting in the field after the first cow, and retracing her steps to find it. And Lon came right behind, his hands on her waist, his lips on her throat, her ears, her mouth. She collapsed on the back steps, expecting him to join her there. Instead Lon picked up the whetstone.

"I left the scythe in the field," he said sheepishly.

"Don't go, Lon."

"Lindy, I'm not contributing any money to this marriage, or land, or equipment, or stock, except for Buckskin. So I'd better get to work. If I cut all the grass on your place, and the little bit on mine, I should have four or five loads of hay to take to Virginia."

"I can't marry you, Lon. Not until the divorce is done."

"That's okay. We'll just say the words to each other now, and have it done legally when the time comes."

"You won't mind?"

"No."

"I'll write Will and tell him I've got a man who's a good farmer, one who'll stick around and do the work. But

I don't think he'll put the farm in my name, so you'll be putting a lot of work into something that's not yours."

"The 160 next door *is* mine, or at least it will be in five years. When your brother sees what we do together, he'll give you the eighty. He's suspicious, naturally, after Harvey, and he needs to see I'll not gamble your land away."

She slid her foot underneath his hand and wiggled her toes against his fingers. He tightened his grip so suggestively she felt a chill, then a flash of warmth. The way she felt about Lon, it must be she loved him.

"Lon and Lindy," she said with studied casualness. "Both our names begin with *L*."

"Not really. Mine begins with *H* and yours with *M*. Harlon and Melinda."

"But what we're called, our nicknames, both start with *L*. There's another word that starts with *L*."

He drew his hand away from her foot and looked so serious she knew she'd made a mistake. Some men don't want to talk about love. Saying the word hurt their pride, or their throat, or something. Lon must be one of those. A word wasn't important, she decided.

"You want to hear me say it?" he asked.

"It would be nice. A woman likes nice words as well as rose-scented soap."

"You didn't say that word last night, either," he said. "Don't you think a man likes to hear it, too?"

"I said it once before and it didn't last. It turned out to be a lie."

"Did he say it?"

"No. Never."

"I'll say it if you will," she added, and heard the words echo back in his voice. He grinned and put his hand back on her foot.

"Ladies first," he said.

"No. That would be immodest and improper. The gentleman declares first."

He stared at her, his mouth curled up on one side in amusement. "Lindy, you're the one who brought up the subject of romping. Can a woman talk about playing in bed, and still be a lady? But if she says 'I love you' first, she's not a lady?" He pushed his hat off his forehead, and the lock of hair fell down.

"That's what the books say."

"The man risks being stabbed in the back, is that what the books say? I say, 'I love you,' and then you say, 'I'm not sure, I think I'll look around a bit more first.'"

"Gentlemen are supposed to take the risk."

"I'm not a gentleman."

He turned away from her, so all she saw was the back of his dark head and the breadth of his shoulders. He gazed over the corrals and sheds, and she remembered that today was August 13. He could leave, and she could do nothing at all to keep him here, except love him.

"I love you, Lon."

He squeezed her foot, then climbed up to her step and took her into his arms.

"I love you, Lindy. I've never ever said that to any woman before."

"I said it to a man, but it wasn't true. I mean," she said hurriedly, "I thought I did love him when I said it, but now I know it wasn't true, and I didn't love him at all. I love you."

His lips found hers and didn't let go. She wondered if anyone had ever passed out from being kissed. He let her take one breath. They had come up for air for the third time when she heard the tinkle of harness and the rattle of buggy wheels. *Judge Otis can't...* She saw the yellow dress.

She expected Lon to drop her and slide away, and pretend nothing had been happening. Instead he stood, pulling her along with him, an arm about her waist, so they stood at the bottom of the steps like lovers.

Chapter Eighteen

Billy jumped from the buggy, held out his hand to Alice and stood in front of the wheel like a gentleman so she didn't dirty her dress. Lindy looked with distress at her hands, filthy with moving rocks in the irrigation ditch and milking cows.

"Come in," she said. "Won't you..." She hadn't cleaned up the stove. She couldn't offer them so much as a cup of coffee.

"So it's finally took, has it?" said Alice. "I wondered how long you two would hold out. Thanks for the tip about the Shirt Tail shares."

"Thank you for convincing Judge Otis that he'd put his money on the wrong horse," said Lon.

"That's nothing," Billy said. "Least a man can do for a friend. I had more fun than a terrier in a rat pit, standing on the buggy seat, looking over every man's head. Maybe I'll go into the pol-ee-ti-cal business."

"We got the Shirt Tail certificate from Moseley, but there's something strange, and I puzzled over it for three or four days, and finally decided you should see it." Alice pulled a paper from her bodice.

"Come in," Lindy said. She pointed to the stove with

the arm that wasn't around Lon, "I can't offer you any coffee. We had an accident."

She had only three chairs, but Lon stood, leaning against the frame of the front door. It reminded her of how he'd looked on the night he'd come out with Harvey, the night she should have seduced him and made him stay. Alice laid the paper on the table.

"Moseley endorsed the shares to me," began Alice, "but yesterday, studying at them…" She pointed to the signatures on the back.

"Abraham Moseley to Harvey Saxton. Harvey Saxton to A. Smith. A. Smith to Abraham Moseley. A lot of passing around up there on the pass."

"That's not Harvey's writing," Lindy said, and the sight took her breath.

"That charm that you gave Harvey when you got married, shaped like a heart," Lon said. "Is it pure gold?"

"I had it made for him, with gold from the Yellow Jacket. He wears it on his watch. But that doesn't have anything to do with this."

"He wore it on his watch until the poker game. He put it on the table to represent you, and I won it—you—and I put it in the saddlebag, along with five twenty-dollar gold pieces. Harvey stole it along with the cash."

"Stole?" exclaimed Billy.

"Stole. Cleaned out the secret pocket of my saddlebag."

"That doesn't explain Harvey buying these things from Moseley," objected Alice.

"Just about the first of July—" Lon spoke slowly, and Lindy knew he thought about each word before he said it "—I met Moseley at Lake House, and I asked him about the Shirt Tail shares he'd had earlier, because by then I knew Braley's plans. Moseley had sold them to a man heading west, for seventy dollars and a 'bit of gold.' The man was Harvey, the seventy dollars part of the hundred he stole from me, and the 'bit of gold' the heart charm."

"And we looked all over Nevada Territory for Harvey, and all the time he'd gone off to California," marveled Lindy. "But how do you know about the heart?"

"When the sheriff and Price hustled me out of the jail, so as to calm the mob before they tore the place down—" Billy grinned and bounced up on his toes "—Moseley screamed he wanted out, too, and he jumped up and down and dropped a little gold charm, shaped like a heart, and it rolled across the floor."

"A little gold charm, shaped like a heart," Lindy repeated. She'd given it to Harvey when she'd said "I love you." A symbol of her lie. She never wanted to see the thing again.

"This isn't Harvey's signature?" Alice asked insistently, tapping the paper with her immaculate finger.

"No. Nothing like it," said Lindy.

"I think we'd better go into Carson City," said Alice. "Maybe Moseley's still in town. There's fifty shares of Shirt Tail here, and I don't want my right to them questioned."

"Something's happened to Harvey," Lindy said, finally able to form the words. Why did a lump rise in her throat? Why, from the moment she'd seen the signature, had shadows crossed the sun?

"Probably someone robbed him on the trail," said Alice.

Lindy looked to Lon for reassurance, but found instead a long, bleak face. *He thinks maybe I still love Harvey!* She forced a cheerful smile.

"You're probably right," she said lightly. "Got drunk on the trail, and someone pawed through his pack. I'll get my sunbonnet on, and hitch a team to the wagon."

"We'll all fit in the buggy," said Alice. "If Lon drives, and Billy sits on my lap."

Lindy looked at Alice's resplendent skirt and perky bonnet. That's how a man expected a woman to look. Going to town in her work clothes shamed Lon, and he'd be the butt of jokes in the saloons.

"Let me wash up and change," she said.

She brought in a pitcher of cold water, stripped to her underclothes, leaned over the washstand and scrubbed her face. *Harvey's dead,* she said to herself. *Even drunk, he'd fight for his mine certificates. Harvey's dead, and I should be glad, but I'm not. I'm sorry. I can't show it, or say it, because I told Lon I love him. And I do.* She jerked up her head at a knock on the door.

"Can I help you, Lindy?" asked Alice.

Help? No woman needed help dressing. Except, with Alice around, she'd not think about Harvey, and Harvey being dead. She opened the door. "Thank you."

Alice brushed out her braids and pinned her hair up. No one had brushed her hair since she was fifteen and started putting it up.

"How big?" whispered Alice as the full blue skirt came down over her petticoats. Lindy couldn't help but giggle.

"Just like a normal man."

"You're lying. I can tell, because you're blushing. How big?"

"Perfect," she said, turning away from Alice to button her bodice. "Just perfect, like a normal man."

"If you won't tell me, every girl on D Street will make it her business to seduce him whenever he comes to Virginia. You don't want that."

Lindy tossed her head and pulled herself to her full six feet one-half inch. "You just go ahead and try," she said. "It's only wives no good in the romping business who lose their husbands to D Street."

"Romping?" asked Alice, puzzled, but Lindy didn't explain. She tamped down the strange, queasy feeling about Harvey being dead, because Lon must not think she loved Harvey, so he would never go looking on D Street.

* * *

Lawyer Stone stood beside Sheriff Tipson at the front door of the jail. He pulled off his tall silk hat when he saw the women in the buggy.

"Imagine this!" he exclaimed. "Lindy, we'd just now thought to ride out to visit *you*."

"If you're thinking of arresting Lon again, forget it. He's got too much to do," Lindy said. Acting as if she hadn't a care in the world cost a great deal of effort. She rolled her hands into the folds of her skirt, so she didn't clasp them on her breast. "Alice and Billy have found something strange we think the sheriff should see."

Lon helped her down, and offered his arm in a most becoming manner. She must wear a dress more often. Lon smiled, soft and beckoning, with a hint of question in his eyes. She smiled back, and hoped her fright didn't show. By the time they entered the jail, Alice had shoved the cat off the table and spread out the Shirt Tail certificate.

"Lindy says it's not Saxton's signature," Alice said.

"Sit down, Lindy," said Stone.

"You'll see it's not Harvey's signature if you go get my papers, Mr. Stone. Compare Harvey's writing on the marriage certificate."

"Sit down, Lindy," Stone repeated.

"You think I'm in a delicate condition, that I should sit before anyone else?"

"It would be best if you seated yourself before I tell you the news. Sheriff Tipson and I..." Why should the sheriff be involved in her business? The divorce? But you can't divorce a dead man.

"Please sit down, Lindy." Lon grabbed her arm and rather forcefully guided her to a chair. He stood behind her and put his hands on her shoulders. She loved the way they felt, heavy, holding her down. The lawyer leaned forward, the way people do when they're delivering bad news, as if they think the words won't hurt so much if they haven't so far to travel.

"Lindy, we just learned…in Placerville, I mean, Saxton was in Placerville…"

"Was?"

"And…he…a dispute arose." Stone seemed lost.

"He's dead, Lindy," said the sheriff.

Dead? Of course Harvey was dead. She'd known it for ever so long. And she'd show Lon she didn't care, because she loved him, not Harvey.

"Shot by a gambler who didn't like the way Saxton played. They had a trial, and the jury acquitted the gambler because Saxton had brought the deck of cards, and it had five aces in it, and the gambler hadn't been known to cheat before."

"Dead," she repeated. Relieved someone had said the word, but relief so dark and foreboding she needed a protector. Sadness approaching grief, but a sadness so thin it came and went like a veil of fog. She reached to her shoulders to touch Lon's hands. Tears rolling down her cheeks. Lon's fingers closed on her shoulders, and she remembered waking up in the dark, and him caring enough to go out and find where the storm raged. And the miracle of the water, coming along with the miracle of him saying he loved her.

"It's all right," he said over and over again. "It's all right. You didn't want it to be like this."

He leaned over her, against her, and she turned her face into Lon's chest, struggling to kill the sobs that strangled her. It wouldn't do to cry, because everyone would think she cried for Harvey. Maybe she did cry for Harvey. Two-faced, that's what she was, two-faced for crying for Harvey after what she and Lon had done last night.

"You sure it's Saxton?" asked Lon over her head.

"The sheriff in Placerville seems certain. And Lindy testifies this isn't his signature, so someone took the opportunity to make off with his property. Whoever A. Smith might be. I'll send a deputy to the pass, try to find Moseley, and inquire what the man looked like.''

Lon pulled her out of the chair and drew her into a corner. "It's all right, Lindy," he whispered. "Just go ahead and cry. It's an awful, awful thing.''

"You don't care?" She hiccuped into his chest. "You don't care that I cry because Harvey—''

"That's the wrong way to say it. I care a whole lot. You've a right to cry. We should always cry and mourn when someone we know dies. Death is so damned permanent. And to be shot by a tinhorn gambler!" His arms tightened.

"Who in town can marry us?" Lon asked over her head. He wanted to marry her. Another miracle, like the water, although he would deny anything miraculous about it.

"Why, there're two preachers, and I suppose the county judge, although he may be out of town today, or Judge Otis has the—''

"Judge Otis. The territorial judge sounds more legal.''

"How soon?" asked Alice.

"As soon as Lindy thinks it appropriate. As soon as her mourning's over," said Lon. Lindy lifted her head, shook it vigorously and widened her eyes to get rid of the tears.

"Mourning? I don't even own a black dress! What's mourning got to do with marrying the man I love?''

"Oh, goody, goody!" exclaimed Alice. "We'll do it right now. You run to the judge's house, Billy, and tell him there's to be a wedding.''

"I think," said the sheriff, "it might be better if I made the request. Judge Otis harbors some bitter feelings toward Billy, I believe.''

"Holds a grudge, does he?" said Billy. "Bad sign in a judge.''

"You got a ring, Lon?" asked Alice. "If not, McCaffrey has a few that might be suitable.''

"I can't afford a ring right now," Lon said gruffly. "And

I'm not charging a wedding ring to Lindy's account.'' He dropped his arms. ''You wait just a minute. Let me back in the cells, Price.''

''Homesick?'' asked Price, unlocking the door.

''Billy,'' called Lon, after entering the back room. ''Come here. I need your little fingers.''

Lindy followed Billy, found Lon kneeling beside the bars.

''See down there, the brightness of gold.'' Billy's child-like fingers slid into the crack. Two tries, but on the third he brought out the small heart, pinched between his fingers.

''How did that get in there?'' she whispered, putting her hands behind her back so no one thought she wanted the thing. ''How'd you know?''

''I saw Moseley drop it. I saw it roll into the crack. It's mine by rights, about the only thing I do own, besides my horse and saddle. I'll give it to you, to show I mean my promise.''

She'd take it, but only because Lon wanted to give it to her.

The wedding lunch took place in Pryor's Saloon, every-body drinking except the bride and the groom. ''If I'd known,'' muttered Pryor, ''I'd have made lemonade.''

''Why'd you want the Shirt Tail stock?'' the sheriff asked Alice. ''I thought Sam Clemens shot down that prospect.''

''Sam Clemens don't know mines,'' Billy said with a new confidence and flair. ''The last blast on the face broke into the clay vein. Moseley didn't know, seeing he spent the summer hanging out on the pass, so we got the fifty shares for just twenty-five dollars.''

Stone arrived, carrying a loosely wrapped parcel, which he handed to Lindy. ''This is unnecessary now.'' The brown paper fell open, revealing an engraving of a miner holding up a nugget, his shirttail flapping.

"You did have it!" exclaimed Lon.

"Was that what you tried to find in my office?"

"Yes. But it wasn't there."

"I put it in my safe. I didn't mention it, because I thought I might use it to bribe Saxton for a quiet divorce. Now that's not necessary."

"What made you think it might be valuable?" Lon asked with studied casualness.

"Well, now…" Stone turned red, took one hasty glance at Alice, and looked away. "I visited a woman in Virginia City last spring, and she expressed a curiosity about shares in the Shirt Tail, so I put two and two together, and decided maybe someone had an interest in the old tunnel."

"As Lindy's husband, you've got a hundred shares," said Alice to Lon. "Now you'll help us open the Shirt Tail."

"He's got a farm to run," Lindy said, hoping Lon wasn't tempted, and breathing easier when he shook his head.

"Not interested in being underground. Scares me to death. How about if Lindy signs over her hundred shares to you and Billy, and in return, Billy and you, and his father and brother, all claim a quarter section of the grazing land across the river from Lindy's place?" Lon turned to Billy. "Don't you think your pa might like a quiet retirement place on the river? I'll lease the ground to run my cattle, and Son could do a little herding."

Billy smiled, his new superior smile. "Be great for Son. The same damn thing, day after day."

"I'll tell Nora Dove you two need your fortune told," yelled Alice as the buggy pulled away from the house. Lindy waved from the front steps until she could no longer distinguish the yellow dress. She found Lon sitting at his ease, looking about, like a man at home and satisfied with what he sees.

"We don't need to bother with Nora and her ball," she

said, to forestall his objections. "I've never believed the things she sees in that crystal."

"Did you believe the flag, that it foretold Vicksburg and Gettysburg?"

"I don't know. It sent chills up my spine, seeing it flicker there on the mountaintop, and when I heard what had happened that day back East, it seemed impossible.... But that's different from Nora's ball. She tells men about their ore samples, and she's been wrong, and that silly tale of the four queens, like I've ever played poker!"

"Did Mrs. Dove mention the hand I drew to win you?" Lon asked quietly.

"Hand? I never heard anyone speak of the cards, specifically. What were you dealt?"

"Three queens. Spades, diamonds, clubs. All but the queen of hearts."

"But Nora's ball showed the queen of hearts on top, at least, that's what she said, the queen of hearts on..." Her face grew warm. And it got worse, because Lon stood up and embraced her, and crushed her breasts against his chest.

"And she *was* on top, my queen of hearts, at least once last night," he whispered. "Do you want a forecast of the future from Mrs. Dove?" He pulled her backward as he resumed his seat, so she came down on his lap.

"Nora might say our future lies with some giant frog, like she did to Clemens. Or some truly disgusting creature, like a worm or a snake." She shifted to give him more room to work at the buttons on her bodice.

"Maybe Mrs. Dove could tell us when I'll be able to afford to buy you glass balls for the lightning rod, and a ring."

"A ring's not necessary. In fact, they get in the way. Next time I'm in Virginia City, I'll take the heart to a jeweler and have the name and year changed, and give it back to you."

"I don't have a watch to hang it on, so don't be in any rush to spend the money."

"Maybe you should buy yourself a watch, after you take the first load of hay to Virginia. All fine gentlemen own a watch."

He drew her face to his. "The important times, I know them without a watch," he said. A soft lowing from the pasture fence claimed her attention.

"And the cows always tell me when it's chore time," she said. "I guess the king of hearts has got to wait."

He squeezed her one more time. "I volunteered."

* * * * *

Author's Note

Many of the small way stations and towns mentioned in this novel still exist, much the same as they were in 1863. Strawberry, Hope Valley and Woodfords may be found on U.S. Highway 50, and California Highway 88. Genoa, the oldest settlement in Nevada, maintains its nineteenth-century character, although no longer the county seat of Douglas County. Lake House, however, lies buried under the glitter of South Lake Tahoe.

Virginia City retains the atmosphere of a silver boomtown, and is still the county seat of Storey County. Carson City is now truly a city, but old buildings still line the main street near the state capital, and east of the town, near the river, open spaces remain where my imagination placed Lindy's farm. Washoe is now a bedroom community of Reno, and Franktown has almost disappeared.

This book was complete when I discovered an 1861 survey map of the Carson Valley. Imagine my surprise when I found a farm near the California-Nevada border belonging to Wilson Miller! My apologies to the descendants of the real Wilson Miller, who was of normal stature and not a highwayman!

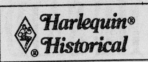

Will the ever-sensible Kate lose her fight against the temptation provided by the handsome Marquis of Wroth?

Find out in Deborah Simmons's
delicious new historical

Coming in June
to your favorite paperback book outlet.

TEMPTING KATE ISBN 28971-5/$4.99

HE SAID

♥

SHE SAID

Explore the mystery of male/female communication in this extraordinary new book from two of your favorite Harlequin authors.

Jasmine Cresswell and Margaret St. George bring you the exciting story of two romantic adversaries—each from their own point of view!

DEV'S STORY. CATHY'S STORY.
As he sees it. As she sees it.
Both sides of the story!

The heat is definitely on, and these two can't stay out of the kitchen!

Don't miss HE SAID, SHE SAID.
Available in July wherever Harlequin books are sold.

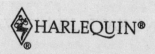

® HARLEQUIN®

Look us up on-line at: http://www.romance.net   HESAID

Harlequin® Historical

Coming this summer from
Award-winning author
Theresa Michaels

The Merry Widows
A heartwarming new Western series

"Michaels at her poignantly moving best."
—*Affaire de Coeur*

"Pure magic!" —*The Literary Times*

"A true gem..." —*Rawhide and Lace*

"Will hold you spellbound." —*Rendezvous*

"Emotionally charged..." —*Romantic Times*

That's what reviewers are saying about
Mary the first book in the Merry Widows trilogy

Coming in June to a store near you.
Keep your eyes peeled!

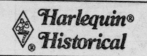

Harlequin® Historical

If your tastes run to
terrific Medieval Romance,
don't miss

The
Bride
Thief

by Susan Spencer Paul

The exciting conclusion to her
Medieval Bride Trilogy

And the Winner Is...
You!

...when you pick up these great titles
from our new promotion at your
favorite retail outlet this June!

Diana Palmer
The Case of the Mesmerizing Boss

Betty Neels
The Convenient Wife

Annette Broadrick
Irresistible

Emma Darcy
A Wedding to Remember

Rachel Lee
Lost Warriors

Marie Ferrarella
Father Goose

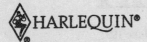 

Look us up on-line at: http://www.romance.net

ATWI397-R

KAREN HARPER

She would risk everything for love....

Brett Benton came to America to claim her inheritance:
one half of Sanborn Shipping. The other half belongs to
Alex Sanborn, a man who awakens the dormant passions
within her—a man committed to a cause that is about to test
his courage, his skill…his very life.

Forced to make a devil's bargain, Brett must betray Alex in
order to protect him. Now, only the hope of love can see them
through to…

DAWN'S EARLY LIGHT

Available in June 1997
at your favorite retail outlet.

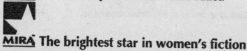

MIRA The brightest star in women's fiction

Look us up on-line at: http://www.romance.net

MKH1

New York Times Bestselling Authors

JENNIFER BLAKE
JANET DAILEY
ELIZABETH GAGE

Three *New York Times* bestselling authors bring you three very sensuous, contemporary love stories—all centered around one magical night!

It is a warm, spring night and masquerading as legendary lovers, the elite of New Orleans society have come to celebrate the twenty-fifth anniversary of the Duchaise masquerade ball. But amidst the beauty, music and revelry, some of the world's most legendary lovers are in trouble....

Come midnight at this year's Duchaise ball, passion and scandal will be...

Unmasked

Revealed at your favorite retail outlet in July 1997.

MIRA The brightest star in women's fiction

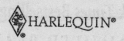

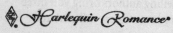

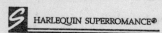